The story is well-balanced. Along with the expected military action and heroics, there is also compassion, humor, and a surprisingly helpful non-human assistant keeping watch over the mission. And, of course, there is a beautiful and brainy girl to lighten the memories of otherwise testosterone-heavy action.

Beneath the arc of the exciting story is an undercurrent of high professionalism, rigid discipline, and raw courage that suffuses the story in a realistic and inspiring way. Readers will learn far more than they could have imagined about the conduct of secret missions in the silent service.

In short, *Operation Vela Redux* is an astounding offering with all the ingredients of a story readers will long remember.

—John Clarke, PhD
Saturation Diving Consultant
Author of the *Jason Parker Trilogy*

Praise for *Operation Vela Redux*

In late 1979, a U.S. Vela satellite detected the characteristic signature of a nuclear test, midway between Africa and Antarctica. Now, in *Operation Vela Redux*, Mac McDowell, newly in command of the *USS Teuthis*, is on his way back to Antarctic waters to investigate reports of an impending second nuclear test. Time is of the essence, and this is Mac's first command, so of course nothing goes quite as planned. In this, the fifth in Robert G. Williscroft's Mac McDowell Cold War submarine series, we're treated to the usual mix of action, allied and enemy submarines, and this time an Israeli commando team, plus a few surprises that hint of more novels to come. I can't wait.

Alastair Mayer
Author of the *T-Space Series*

After reading Robert G. Williscroft's Cold War submarine adventures, I couldn't resist the latest in the Mac McDowell series. After all, I've followed Mac's rise through the ranks and vicariously shared his experiences—professional, romantic, and otherwise. This time, in *Operation Vela Redux*, Mac has achieved a career milestone: for the first time, he has become a Captain and commands his own ship, the *USS Teuthis*. Mac's XO tells him that "the scuttlebutt is when you go to sea with Mac, you're in for a fucking great adventure." Truer word was never said.

We learn the reason why at the novel's very beginning. South Africa intends to test a nuclear weapon on Prince Edward Island, and "No amount of diplomatic activity will prevent" it. Later, Mac is informed of his mission and told they will use Israeli commandos to "prevent the detonation, with no one knowing you were there." It's much easier said than done.

There are many reasons why I enjoyed this novel. First, it's great to see Mac grow into his new role as a skipper. The epic journey across the sea resembles those in other Mac McDowell novels, and as always, I was enthralled by the intricacies and teamwork involved in guiding a submarine to a distant destination. This author really knows how it's done because he's been there! On a personal level, I was glad to see Borysko again, the lovable, amazing Orca from earlier novels. Finally, will Mac succeed in his mission and prevent a nuclear bomb from exploding? The stakes are huge, to say the least. This novel is a page turner, and it kept me prisoner until the end. It should do the same for other readers.

—Professor John B. Rosenman (Retired)
Norfolk State University
Former Chairman of the Board, Horror Writers Association
Author of *A Breath of Fresh Air* and *The Dreamfarer series*

The Cold War was not as "cold" as you might think. Decades before the fall of the Soviet Union, American spy submarine skippers were ordered to place themselves and their crew in harm's way. In some spy subs, Navy saturation divers were a unique crew complement. "Sat divers" were the tip of the spear for intrusion into the secret recesses of worldwide Soviet and Chinese Communist influence.

Robert G. Williscroft is a retired U.S. Navy submarine officer, saturation diving officer, Ph.D. engineer, and an imaginative and prolific author. The latest of his books is *Operation Vela Redux*, the fifth of his *Mac McDowell Missions* novels.

Through compelling first-person narration, Williscroft tells a tale that deserves to be seen on the Big Screen. The heroic McDowell relishes challenging, icy missions: his fictional Navy career mirrors Williscroft's unique operational career. That means Williscroft knows his stuff and writes convincingly about those missions that "never were." Actual missions similar to the ones he describes occurred, no doubt, but you'll never hear about them.

The clandestine undersea mission described in *Operation Vela Redux* began seven years after the Falklands War and two years before the fall of the Soviet Union. McDowell commands the *USS Teuthis* as it transits from Mare Island shipyard in California to the Falklands, thence to ice-covered bays of Antarctica, and eventually to the southernmost islands of South Africa.

Before *Teuthis* returns to the Atlantic-based sub-base in New London, Connecticut, multiple international threats put *Teuthis* and its crew at risk. Also on display is international cooperation, which shows that national interests are highly intertwined. This world is not so big after all.

OPERATION VELA REDUX

A Mac McDowell Mission

USS Teuthis Tracks to Antarctica, Prince Edward Islands, and return to New London

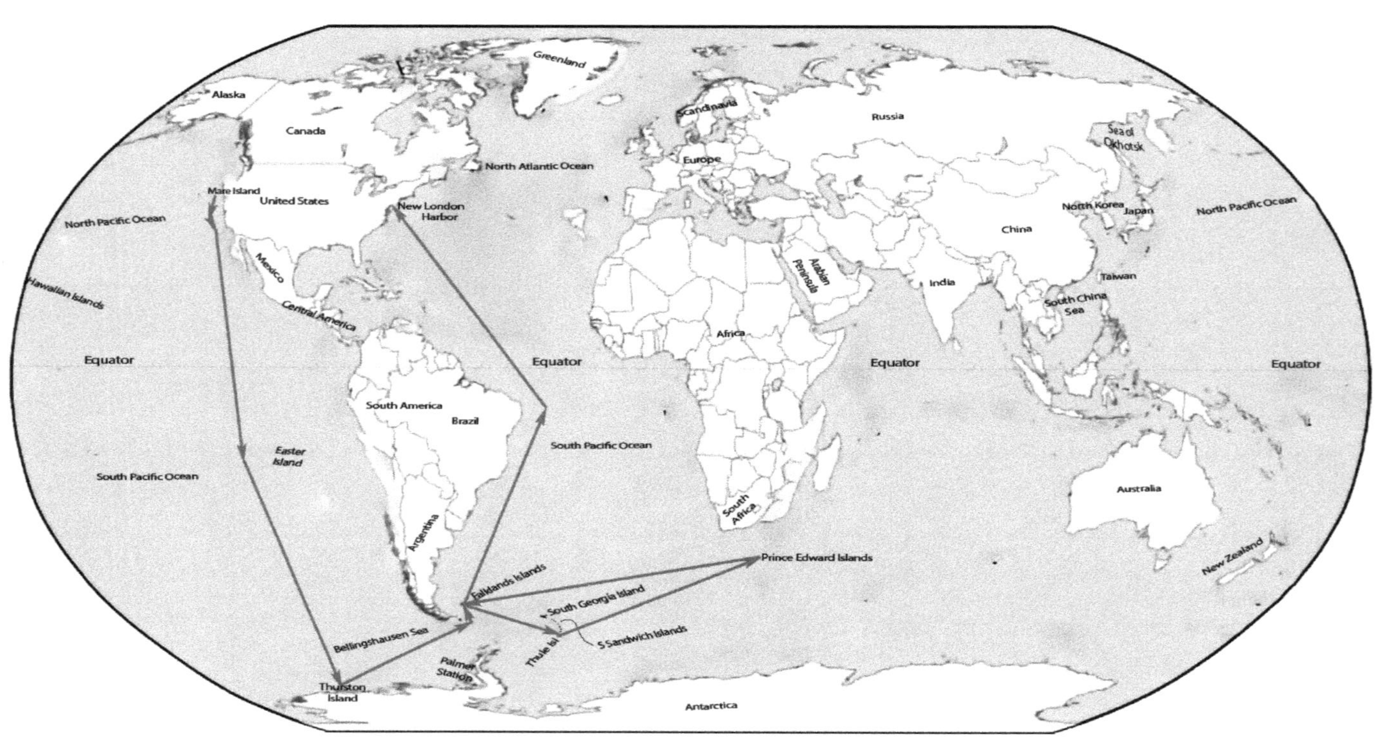

OPERATION VELA REDUX

A MAC McDOWELL MISSION

Robert G. Williscroft

STARMAN
PRESS

Centennial, Colorado

Operation Vela Redux
A Mac McDowell Mission

Starman Press

Email: rgw@RobertWilliscroft.com
Website: RobertWilliscroft.com

Edition 1.0 2024
Edition 2.0 2025

Cover art by Anik
Cover by Stephen Geez
Book design by Robert G. Williscroft

BISAC Subject Headings:
FIC032000 FICTION / War & Military
FIC031050 FICTION / Thrillers / Military
FIC036000 FICTION / Thrillers / Technological

Library of Congress Control Number: 2024913622

ISBN-13: 978-1-968367-39-8 Softcover
ISBN-13: 978-1-968367-38-1 Hardcover
ISBN-13: 978-1-968367-07-7 Ebooks
ISBN-13: 978-1-968367-40-4 Audio

DEDICATION

To Caileigh.

TABLE OF CONTENTS

FOREWORD

by
Captain George W. Jackson USN (Ret.)
aka G. William Weatherly

As l write this in the summer of 2024, the world appears on the edge of more serious wars than the ones raging in Ukraine and Gaza. The President of Russia keeps making threats of the first use of nuclear weapons should the armed forces of Ukraine using western supplied conventional weapons cross unspecified red lines. Iran edges ever closure to weapons grade uranium if they do not already possess it with their thousands of centrifuges spinning continuously. A recent assassination inside Tehran has incensed them with vows of weapon barrages to overwhelm Israeli defenses. The tactician in me would have the last few being nukes. North Korea not only continues building longer range missiles but by supplying their technology to Russia is achieving the one thing they had previously lacked-real world testing under battlefield conditions.

Nothing has changed in China's absolute commitment to reunification with Taiwan by force if necessary. They are building up their IBMs literally as fast as possible. Recent Taiwanese elections have moved the island ever closer to a formal declaration of independence and the similar formal end of the "one China policy" that has ambiguously allowed the United States to avoid an "official" entanglement. Not in my lifetime have the impending U.S. federal elections loomed so importantly over the world at a time when all the listed nations covertly and overtly try to influence the outcome in their favor.

In this background Robert Williscroft has masterfully taken his hero Mac McDowell on another page turning adventure with his dive team and the special operation configured *USS Teuthis*, now under his command. Being the CO opens new challenges and infinitely greater responsibilities that Mac has to meet or fail in his mission to avoid another nation joining the thermo-nuclear weapons club. Unfortunately,

Teuthis is in the wrong ocean and a perilous voyage around the "Horn" is required. Some of the worst weather on earth, not to mention ice cover, Russian and Chinese nuclear submarines bent on destroying the Taiwanese forces of Operation Arctic Sting and the intrepid Americans aboard *Teuthis*. Defections, creative disabling tactics, spies, submarines from five nations, Israeli special forces (Hmmmm), and intrigue; as well as a developing relationship for Mac and his ever-present orca, Borysko—the savior of many a member of *Teuthis's* dive teams.

Robert Williscroft brings an expertise as a saturation diver unique in the world of fiction. That experience shows through in a realism that enlightens his plots with what I suspect is more than accurate. Vela Redux takes the horror of nuclear weapons and adds the one thing that is an absolute requirement for any nation that is committed to developing a thermo-nuclear capability-testing. If the test/demonstration works, another nation joins the nuclear club. If it fails, even if the design is feasible, no national leader would commit to using the weapon against another for the fear of retaliation without the hoped for devastating result.

G. William Weatherly is the pen name Captain Jackson uses to write his alternative history novels of WWII naval thrillers, Sheppard of the Argonne *and* Sheppard and the French Rescue.

ACKNOWLEDGMENTS

I left submarines a long time ago. While I remember a lot, I also forgot much. Capt. George Jackson, retired skipper of three U.S. nuclear subs and author of the Foreword to this book, read my manuscript closely, offering seventeen hand-written pages of suggestions. His input has made this story much better and very much more accurate. Any inconsistencies with actual submarine operations fall on my shoulders, of course.

My engineer wife, Jill Mayer, spent hours poring through these pages, making certain what I wrote could be understood by someone unfamiliar with subs.

Prof. John Rosenman, himself a prolific author, read my story looking for inconsistencies and things that didn't make sense. John Clarke, a PhD researcher who has forgotten more about saturation diving than most experts ever knew, went through my manuscript, making sure I told the saturation diving side of things accurately. Alastair Mayer, the science fiction author who defined T-Space, checked out my story arc and its many subarcs, verifying that I closed them before the story ended.

I must include a heartfelt thanks to Admiral Sir Trevor Soar, former Chief of the British Royal Navy and, earlier in his career, the third Commanding Officer of HMS Talent, *a British nuclear submarine that plays a role in this novel. When, through my research, I was unable to locate the name of* HMS Talent's *first commanding officer, I reached out to Admiral Sir Trevor Soar who told me that British submarine officer was Cmdr. Johnny Harris. Thank you, Sir!*

Without these folks, Operation Vela Redux *could never have come to life. I thank you all.*

Robert G. Williscroft, PhD
Centennial, Colorado
August 2024

DISCLAIMER

Although this is a work of fiction, and the events that take place are fictional, the backdrop against which this story plays out is based upon real events and real people. The *USS Teuthis* and what she accomplishes are fictional, although she represents the kind of missions U.S. submarines routinely undertook during the Cold War and still undertake today. The characteristics of individuals in the saturation dive team are a compilation of actual team members as personally known to the author, but none of the individual divers as depicted in this work are real. The other officers, sailors, and civilians as depicted in this work are compilations of individuals with whom the author served during his twenty-three-year career. Except for several prominent or less prominent individuals, who appear by name doing things they would normally have done, although their recorded actions within this work are fictional, any resemblance to actual persons, living or dead, is entirely coincidental.

AUTHOR'S NOTE

In U.S. Navy submarine operations (and surface ship operations, for that matter), when an order is issued, it is always repeated by the person receiving the order to ensure the order was properly understood. For the most part in this novel, I have omitted nearly all these repeated orders to facilitate the dialogue and make the story move along as it should.

For you diehard military types, just insert the order repetition in your mind as you read this tale of high adventure and derring-do.

USS Teuthis Organizational Chart

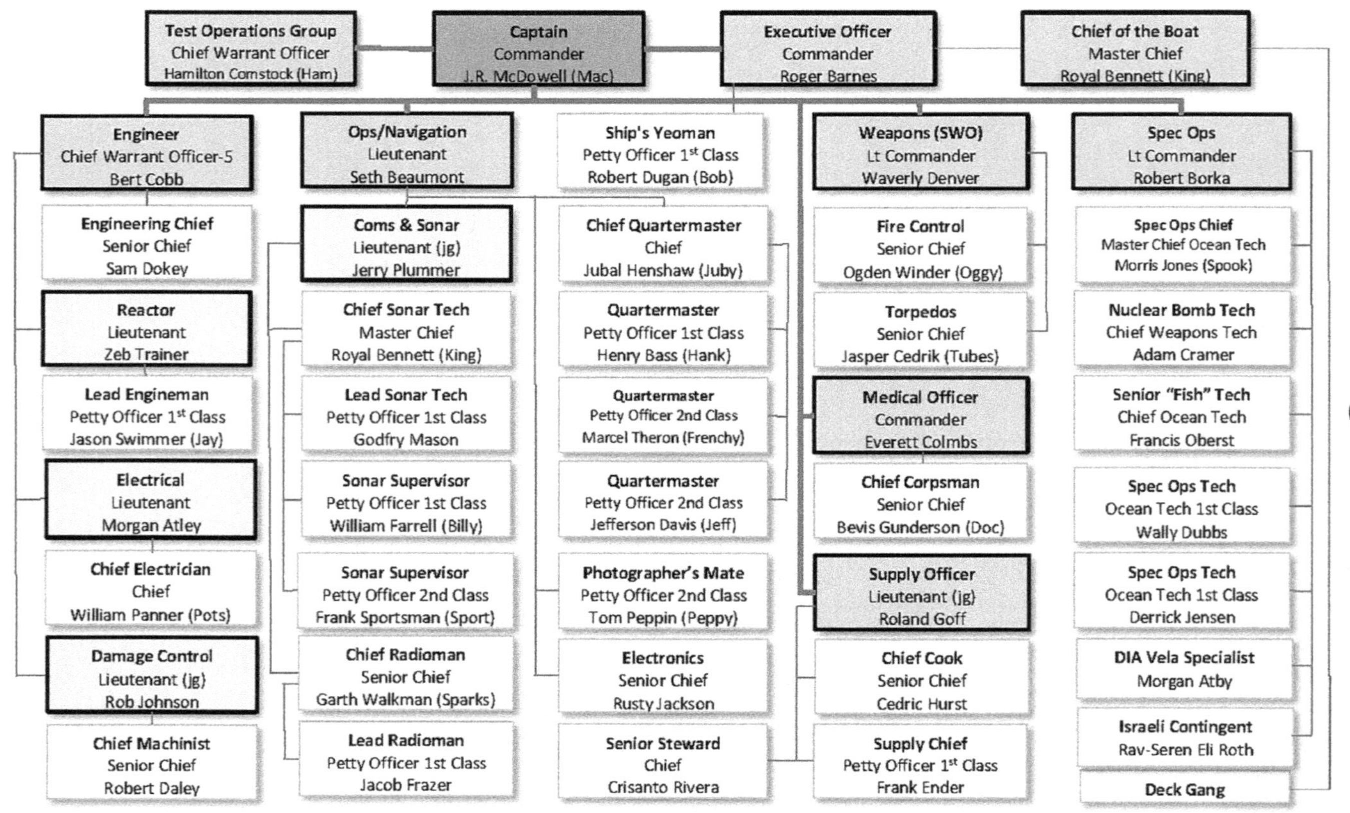

Cast of Characters

USS Teuthis

(See Organizational Chart on previous page)

Test Operations Group (TOG) (the divers)

(Ordered by rank and first name in rank)

Hamilton Comstock (Ham), Chief Warrant Officer—Officer in Charge (OIC) TOG—Master Saturation Diver—Came from Experimental Diving Unit and Man-in-the-Sea Program—Ivy Bells/Ice Breaker/Arctic Sting/White Out

William Fisher (Bill), Chief Petty Officer—Master Saturation Diver—Sonar Tech—Ivy Bells/Ice Breaker/Arctic Sting/ White Out

James Tanner (Jimmy), Petty Officer First-class—Saturation Diver; qualified Dive Console operator Battlefield medic turned saturation diver—Ivy Bells/Ice Breaker/Arctic Sting/White Out

Wlodek Cslauski (Ski), Petty Officer First-class— Saturation Diver; qualified Dive Console operator—Submariner (Engineman) turned saturation diver—Ivy Bells/Ice Breaker/Arctic Sting/White Out

Ezra Batton (Batty), Petty Officer Second-class — Saturation Diver; qualified Dive Console Operator—Submariner (Engineman) turned saturation diver—recent graduate saturation dive class

Gilbert Ross (Gil), Petty Officer Second-class— Saturation Diver; qualified Dive Console Operator—Submariner (Torpedoman) turned saturation diver—White Out

José Romero (José), Petty Officer Second-class— Saturation Diver; qualified Dive Console Operator—Submariner (Electronics Tech) turned saturation diver—White Out

Manfred Boyle (Freddie), Petty Officer Second-class— Saturation Diver; qualified Dive Console Operator—Submariner (Sonar Tech) turned saturation diver—White Out

USS Teuthis **Deck Gang**

(Ordered first name)

Aiken Beverton (Bever). Seaman—Topside Watch, Lookout / Helmsman / Planesman

Basil Walton (Basil), Seaman—Topside Watch, Lookout / Helmsman / Planesman

Clive Orfutt (Clive), Seaman—Topside Watch, Lookout / Helmsman / Planesman

David Ben-Jakob (Jake), Seaman—Topside Watch, Lookout / Planesman

Ezra Ben-Gurion (Ben), Seaman—Topside Watch, Lookout / Helmsman / Planesman

Gus Harvard (Gus), Seaman—Topside Watch, Lookout / Helmsman / Planesman

Herbert Hammer (Dick), Seaman—Topside Watch, Lookout / Planesman

Ivan Tuxin (Tux), Seaman—Topside Watch, Lookout / Helmsman / Planesman

Lloyd Boxer (Boxer), Seaman—Topside Watch, Lookout / Helmsman / Planesman

Peter Gustaffson (Pete), Seaman—Topside Watch, Lookout / Planesman

Pope George (Popeye), Seaman—Topside Watch, Lookout / Helmsman / Planesman

William Chen (Billy, Seaman —Topside Watch, Lookout / Planesman (speaks Mandarin)

Mystic **(DSRV 1)**

(Ordered by rank)

James Deckhart, Lt.—Chief Pilot

Donald Fortue, Lt. —Second Pilot

Warren Gamble, Chief Electronics Tech—*Mystic* technician

Sam Elton, Sonar Tech First-class—*Mystic* technician

Shayetet 13 Contingent

(Ordered by rank and first name in rank)
Hadriel Davidov, Rav Nagad (CWO)—"Ranag"
Bezai Azulay, Rav Samal Mitkadem (Chief Petty Officer)—"Rasam"
Abdiel Mizrahi, Rav Samal Rishon (PO1)—"Rasar"
Chaim Meiyr, Rav Samal Rishon (PO1)—"Rasar"

Submarine Fleet Pacific (ComSubPac)

Michael Colley, Rear Admiral

Submarine Fleet Atlantic (ComSubLant)

Roger F. Bacon, Vice Admiral

USS Pigeon (ASR 21)

(Ordered by rank)
Eric Stanley Glidden, Cmdr.— Commanding Officer
Randal Jeffrey, Lt.—First Lieutenant

USS Pasadena (SSN 752)

Wilson Fritchman, Cmdr.—Commanding Officer

HMS Tireless (S 88)

Timothy P. McClement, Cmdr.—Commanding Officer

HMS Talent (S 92)

Johnny Harris, Cmdr.—Commanding Officer

ARA San Juan (S-42)

Liam Lautaro Romero, Capitán de Fragata (Capt.)—
Commanding Officer

ROCS Hǎi Bào

Zhang Min, Tiong-hāu (Cmdr.)—Commanding Officer

ROCS Hǎi Hǔ Jīng

Chen Zhiwei, Tiong-hāu (Cmdr.)—Commanding Officer

Mare Harbour Garrison—Falkland Islands

(Ordered by rank and first name in rank)
>   Harry Brisbane, Col.—Commanding Officer
>   Ainsley Geoffery, Lt.—Supply Officer
>   Margaret "Maggi" Goss, Lt.—SOSUS Group Commander
>   William Akins, Lt.—Adjutant

Mascot

>   Borysko—(Ukrainian name means fighter/warrior)
>   a 30-foot-long, 12,000-pound Orca.

Incidental Characters

(Ordered first name)
>   Bill Webster—CIA Director
>   George H.W. Bush, President—U.S. President (incoming)
>   George Shultz— U.S. Secretary of State (outgoing)
>   Hsieh Tsung-han, Siōng-hāu (Capt.)—Taiwanese Navy officer.
>   Jim Baker— U.S. Secretary of State (incoming)
>   Jordan Fortnight—U.S. State Dept representative
>   Caileigh Abernathy—U.S. Energy Dept. representative
>   Lonie Franken-Ester, Captain—Commands Submarine Development
>   Group One (former skipper of *USS Teuthis*)
>   Marvin Ramsay—U.S. Assistant Undersecretary of State
>   Moshe Arad—Israeli Ambassador
>   Ronald Reagan, President—U.S. President (outgoing)
>   Shabtai Shavit—Israeli Mossad Director
>   Vladimir Ivanovich Vasnetsov, Captain First Rank—
>   Commanding Officer, Soviet Submarine *Volgograd*

USS Teuthis Underway Watch Sections

Section One—0600 to 1200

    OOD—Lt. Cmdr. Waverly Denver (Weaps)
    JOOD—Chief Warrant Officer Hamilton Comstock (Ham)
    Dive—Chief Torpedoman Jasper Cedrik (Tubes)
    COW—Senior Chief Engineman Sam Dokey
    Nav—Chief Quartermaster Jubal Henhaw (Juby)
    Fairwater/Helm—Seaman Aiken Beverton (Bever)
    Stern/Lookout—Seaman Basil Walton (Basil)
    Stern/Lookout—Seaman Clive Orfutt (Clive)
    Sonar—Senior Chief Sonar Tech Royal Bennett (King)
    Maneuvering—Lt. Zeb Trainer

Section Two—1200 to 1800

    OOD— Lt. Seth Beaumont
    JOOD—
    Dive—Master Chief Ocean Tech Morris Jones (Spook)
    COW—Senior Chief Fire Control Tech Ogden Winder (Oggy)
    Nav—Quartermaster First-class Henry Bass (Hank)
    Fairwater/Helm—Seaman Ezra Ben-Gurion (Ben)
    Stern/Lookout—Seaman Mike Overreach (Mikey)
    Stern/Lookout—Seaman Ivan Tuxin (Tux)
    Sonar—Sonar Tech First-class Godfry Mason
    Maneuvering—Chief Warrant Officer Bert Cobb

Section Three—1800-2400

    OOD—Lt. Cmdr. Robert Borka
    JOOD—Lt. (jg) Roland Goff (Chop)
    Dive—Chief Ocean Tech Francis Oberst
    COW—Chief Electrician William Panner (Pots)
    Nav—Quartermaster Second-class Marcel Theron (Frenchy)
    Fairwater/Helm—Seaman Gus Harvard (Gus)
    Stern/Lookout—Seaman Lloyd Boxer (Boxer)
    Stern/Lookout—Seaman David Ben-Jakob (Jake)
    Sonar—Sonar Tech Second-class William Farrell (Billy)
    Maneuvering—Lt. Morgan Atley

Section Four—2400-0600

OOD—Cmdr. Roger Barnes
JOOD— Lt. (jg) Jerry Plummer
Dive—Senior Chief Electronics Tech Rusty Jackson
COW—Senior Chief Radioman Garth Walkman (Sparks)
Nav—Quartermaster Second-class Jefferson Davis (Jeff)
Fairwater/Helm–Seaman Pope George (Popeye)
Stern/Lookout—Seaman Peter Gustaffson (Pete)
Stern/Lookout—Seaman Herbert Hammer (Dick)
Sonar—Sonar Tech Second-class Frank Sportsman (Sport)
Maneuvering—Lt. (jg) Rob Johnson

List of Ships and Submarines

BAP Angamos (SS 31)—Peruvian submarine built in Germany.

Chángzhēng 35, 4, 4a—ChiCom *Han Class* nuclear submarines.

ROC Hǎi Bào—Taiwanese *Hai Lung Class* submarine with air independent propulsion (AIP) instead of diesels. A modified version of the Dutch Navy's *Zwaardvis Class* which itself is based on the U.S. *Barbel Class*.

ROCS Hǎi Hǔ Jīng—Taiwanese *Hai Lung Class* submarine with AIP instead of diesels. A modified version of the Dutch Navy's *Zwaardvis Class* which itself is based on the U.S. *Barbel Class*.

Kan-Cha 2—ChiCom diving support vessel built it in 1979, with a French Comex saturation diving system good to 300 meters (984 feet).

Mystic (DSRV 1)—One of two U.S. Navy deep submergence rescue vehicles.

USS Pasadena (SSN 752)—U.S. Navy *Los Angeles Class* fast-attack submarine.

USS Pigeon (ASR 21)—One of two U.S. Navy catamaran submarine rescue/saturation diving ships (ASR) designed to carry two DSRVs.

SAS Protea—*Hecla Class* survey vessel built in the United Kingdom for the South African Navy.

SAS President Steyn—*President Class* Type 12 frigate built in the United Kingdom for the South African Navy.

Qiántǐng Yóuchuán Yī & Èr—Taiwanese drone tanker submarines with AIP.

ARA San Juan (S 42)—*TR-1700 Class* diesel-electric submarine built in West Germany for the Argentine Navy.

CS Simpson—Chilean Submarine.

USS Teuthis (SSNR 2)—A specially modified U.S. Navy nuclear submarine outfitted for special operations.

HMS Talent (S 92)—British *Trafalgar Class* nuclear fast-attack submarine.

CS Thomson—Chilean submarine.

HMS Tireless (S 88)—British *Trafalgar Class* nuclear fast-attack
  submarine.
Volgograd—Advanced Soviet *Victor III Class* nuclear fast-attack
  submarine.
Yaroslavl—Advanced Soviet *Sierra I Class* nuclear fast-attack
  submarine.

USS Teuthis—Cross-section

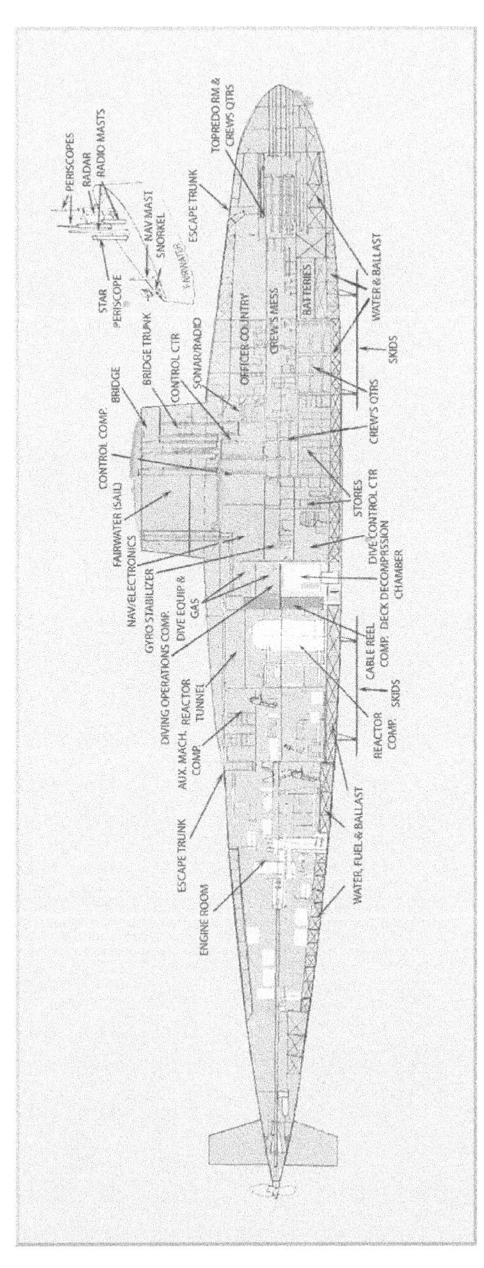

USS Teuthis—Cutaway

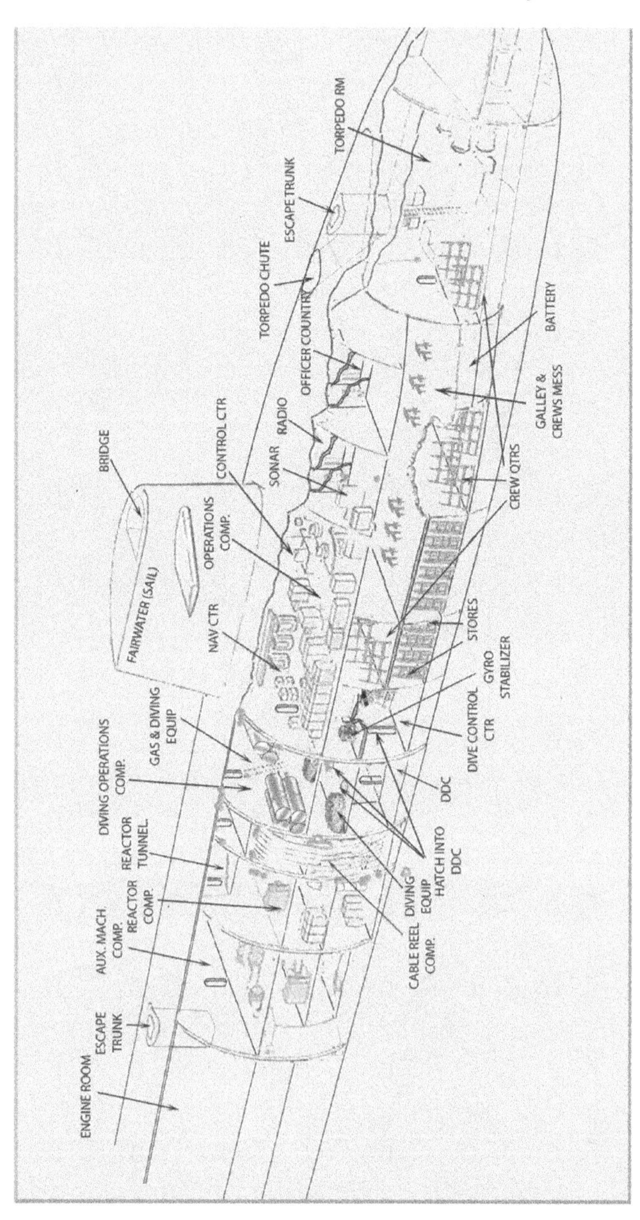

OPERATION VELA REDUX

A MAC McDOWELL MISSION

PROLOG

0353 LOCAL TIME, SATURDAY, SEPTEMBER 22, 1979—PRINCE EDWARD ISLAND, 1,150 NM SE OF CAPE TOWN, SOUTH AFRICA

A blinding double-flash from Prince Edward Island turned the midnight sky bright as day, immediately followed by an ear-shattering explosion and a roiling mushroom cloud that rose several thousand feet above the island. The explosion rousted tens of thousands of seabirds from the jagged cliffs protecting the island—shearwaters, petrels, skuas, gulls, terns, skimmers, sheathbills, and a dozen other species that made this remote subantarctic island their home.

Several warships maintained station on the horizon to the northwest, instruments pointed at the island. When the mushroom cloud dissipated, they cautiously approached, passing through the channel between Prince Edward Island and Marion Island twelve nautical miles to the southwest, turned north and east around Prince Edward, collecting data along the route, and then headed northeast into the Indian Ocean for the 8,300 nautical mile journey home.

High above the Indian Ocean, while following its polar orbit 79,000 miles above the earth, Vela Hotel satellite 5B passed over the Prince Edward Islands. At 12:53 Greenwich time, its sensors detected a double-flash characteristic of a nuclear explosion.

This detection event flashed around the world to Nuclear Test Ban watchdogs in the United States, Australia, New Zealand, and several European nations. Their subsequent investigations arrived at a controversial conclusion that the double-flash was a joint Israeli-South African nuclear test. Not every investigator agreed, and for diplomatic and intelligence reasons, the United States never acknowledged the joint nuclear test. With time, the Vela Incident was mostly forgotten.

0800, TUESDAY, JANUARY 9, 1989—U.S. SECRETARY OF STATE'S OFFICE, FOGGY BOTTOM, WASHINGTON, D.C.

U.S. Secretary of State George Shultz stepped into his wood paneled office on the fifth floor of the Harry S. Truman Building. He pocketed his gloves, shrugged off his drizzle coated overcoat into the waiting hands of his secretary, and handed her his wet umbrella. She hung them in the closet to the right of his expansive dark oak pedestal desk.

"Thanks, Mable," he said with his characteristic grin as he ran his fingers through his damp, sparse hair. "It's nasty out there."

Mable left to get his cup of coffee while Shultz settled into the well-used leather chair behind his desk. He opened his Day-Timer that Mable had laid out before his arrival. A full day, he noted, and an appointment with Jim Baker at two. He smiled to himself. Jim's a good man. He'll do well for President Bush.

Mable returned with his coffee. "That just changed," she said, noting the Day-Timer. "Israeli Ambassador Moshe Arad just arrived unannounced. Mossad Director Shabtai Shavit is with him. They have requested an urgent immediate meeting with you."

Shultz sighed. "Okay, bring them in."

Mable arranged two comfortable chairs facing the coffee table and couch against the wall to the right of the desk and hurried out to get his unexpected guests. Shultz stood and walked around his desk as his guests walked through the door. He held out his hand to the shorter Israeli wearing round wire-rimmed glasses.

"Mr. Ambassador, Moshe, it's an unexpected pleasure." He turned to the second man, shorter and younger than the ambassador, wearing glasses with a thick bar across the bridge of his nose. "Director Shavit, I haven't had the pleasure."

They shook hands as Shultz directed them to the chairs while he took the couch. "Can I offer you coffee, tea…?"

"Tea for us both, thank you," Arad said.

Mable left to prepare the tea. Shultz leaned back against the couch. "You have my undivided attention, Gentlemen."

"I apologize, Mr. Secretary, for the unannounced visit, but…"

"Cut the crap, Moshe. It's just us here." Shultz smiled warmly. "We've seen too many things together."

"Fine, George," Arad said, smiling. "My news has world-class urgency." When Shultz didn't respond, he continued. "You are aware of the Vela Incident in 1979?" Shultz nodded. "I am confirming, and this must remain absolutely confidential, that Israel and South Africa did detonate a nuclear device on Prince Edward Island on September twenty-two." He took a deep breath. "We have since disassociated ourselves from that apartheid regime, but the Mossad," he nodded toward Shavit, "has kept a discrete eye on their nuclear weapons program." He turned to Shavit. "Tell George what you've learned, Shabtai."

Shavit sipped his tea and cleared his throat. "Mr. Secretary…"

"George, please!"

"Ah, George…what I am about to say is factual, and you didn't hear it from me." He smiled. "The world knows that President de Klerk acknowledged the existence of six nuclear devices in South Africa's possession, five deconstructed, and one awaiting deconstruction. We materially assisted in building these six devices—seven, actually. We detonated the seventh in 1979. What de Klerk did not tell the world is that South Africa has built another nuclear bomb, which they intend to detonate atop Prince Edward Island sometime between August three and five, later this year. If the test is successful, they plan on building an arsenal of nuclear bombs."

Shultz stood, waving his visitors to remain in their seats, and went to his desk. He picked up the phone and dialed. "Mr. President, this is George. I need a few minutes of your time, face to face. Yes Sir, I can be there in thirty minutes. Sir, I will be bringing the Israeli Ambassador and the Mossad Director, and I'm asking the Vice President, Jim Baker, and Bill Webster to join us. Yes Sir, thirty minutes." He called Mable on the intercom. "Mable, please call the Vice President, Jim Baker, and Bill Webster. Tell them to meet me in the Oval Office in thirty minutes."

✳

Shultz and the Israelis arrived first. President Reagan greeted them and placed them on the settee to his right. CIA Director Webster and incoming Secretary of State Baker arrived together five minutes later. President-elect George H.W. Bush arrived a bit breathless two minutes after that.

"Sorry," Bush said, floating a rueful smile around the room. "You caught me off guard." He joined Webster and Baker on the settee to Reagan's left.

"Okay, George," Reagan said, looking at Shultz. "It's your dime." He settled into his leather chair behind the Resolute Desk.

Schultz introduced the Israeli Ambassador and the Mossad Director and then asked Arad to explain. Arad spoke briefly, repeating what he had told Shultz, and then turned to Shavit. The Mossad Director briefed the small group as he had Shultz, and then turned to Arad with a question in his eyes. The ambassador nodded slightly.

"My sources inside the de Klerk government tell me that no amount of diplomatic activity will prevent this test. We believe it is essential to stop the South Africans. In Israel, we have a highly skilled commando outfit we call the Shayetet Thirteen unit. In English, this means Flotilla Thirteen. Like your Navy SEALS, Shayetet Thirteen is part of our navy. We believe the best way to stop the South Africans is to deploy a Shayetet Thirteen unit to Prince Edward Island surreptitiously." He stopped talking, letting what he had said sink in. "Israel is officially requesting United States assistance with this operation. You get us there and we will take care of the problem."

Ambassador Arad added, "We understand this is an awkward time to make this request, so I am grateful to see you, Sir, the President-elect, and you, Sir, the incoming Secretary of State at this meeting. Of course, you all understand the sensitive nature of what we have told you this morning." He smiled and adjusted his glasses. "I trust you will be able to give us your assistance. Mossad Director Shavit will be available twenty-four-seven to answer any question and to assist in any way."

0800, SATURDAY, JUNE 10, 1989—MARE ISLAND NAVAL STATION, VALLEJO, CALIFORNIA

As I walked up to the podium set up on the Mare Island pier alongside *USS Teuthis* (SSNR 2), Chief of the Boat Master Chief Jerry Boston called out, "Attention!"

Captain Lonie Franken-Ester stood behind a podium fitted with a microphone. R. Adm. Michael Colley stood to his left and a bit behind. I stepped to the podium and saluted the skipper.

"Attention to orders," the Chief of the Boat (COB) announced.

I turned to the podium and said, "I will now read my orders." I picked up a sheet in large type and commenced reading. "Proceed to the port at which *USS Teuthis* is berthed. Report to the commanding officer as his relief." Turning to Cmdr. Lonnie Franken-Ester, who was standing next to me, I saluted and continued, "I relieve you, Sir."

Cmdr. Franken-Ester responded, "I stand relieved, Sir," and returned my salute.

The crew broke out into wild cheers, completely out of Boston's control. Following a momentary scowl, he, too, joined the cheers. At that moment, I had reached the pinnacle of naval service—command at sea.

The COB let them be for a minute and then held up a hand. When they quieted down, he announced, "Crew, Attention!" as R. Adm. Colley stepped to the mike.

"Commander Lonnie Franken-Ester, front and center!"

The Commander joined Colley at the mike.

"Commander," ComSubPac said, "It is with personal pleasure and great respect that I present you with a Silver Star for your significant accomplishments during your tour as Commanding Officer of *USS Teuthis* (SSNR 2) as detailed in the following citation."

He then read a completely generic citation that only hinted at what Franken-Ester had accomplished as Commanding Officer of *Teuthis*.

Colley stepped back from the mike and the COB took over. He dismissed the crew, sending them to the Enlisted Club for a reception hosted by the outgoing CO. The officers retired to prepare for a reception at the Officers' Club later that afternoon.

✳

Under a bright sun the following morning, the *Teuthis* crew assembled again on the pier, and I stepped to the mike as their Commanding Officer.

"It has been my privilege to serve with most of you for several years, and it is my enduring honor to serve as your commanding officer. I will now read my orders."

The COB came to attention and shouted, "Attention to orders!"

The crew came to attention, anticipation evident on every face. I commenced reading:

DATE: 10 JUNE 1989 1500Z

TO: COMMANDING OFFICER, *USS Teuthis* (SSNR 2)

FROM: COMSUBPAC

SUBJECT: ORDERS

WHEN FULLY PROVISIONED, DEPART WITH DSRV *Mystic* FROM MARE ISLAND NAVAL STATION AND PROCEED SOUTH TO LOCATION 32.549128 N, 120.197040 W, OFF SAN DIEGO. RENDEZVOUS WITH *USS Pigeon* (ASR 21) NLT 1300 LOCAL TIME. CONDUCT DSRV TRAINING OPS FOR THREE DAYS.

STAND BY FOR FURTHER ORDERS.

PART ONE

Southward…Ho!

Mare Island Naval Shipyard. Insert: Path to open Pacific.

CHAPTER ONE—*USS Teuthis* DSRV Mods

0730, MONDAY, JUNE 12, 1989—MARE ISLAND NAVAL SHIPYARD, VALLEJO, CALIFORNIA

I drove my classic Vette across the Mare Island Causeway, turned left down Railroad Avenue, and left again on 14th Street. I crossed Nimitz out onto the tarmac apron, and pulled into a parking slot labeled Commanding Officer. That was me! I had done a lot of things in my life, but this was something totally new. I looked forward to it, but I also knew that I was shouldering an awesome responsibility. I walked toward the brow under a cloudless blue sky. The air was cool with a brisk breeze, but promised to warm to the mid-70s by noon. My crisp summer whites reflected the sun and the gold braid on my cap bill sparkled.

Teuthis was moored starboard side to. Just ahead of her on the pier, a modified semi carrying DSRV *Mystic* on a trailer waited patiently. I guessed *Mystic's* crew was below enjoying one of Cedric's breakfasts.

As I walked toward the brow, Topside Watch Seaman Aiken Beverton announced over the 1MC, "*Teuthis* arriving, *Teuthis* arriving."

A thought crossed my mind, *That's me. I'm* Teuthis*!*

I crossed the brow, didn't salute the fantail because the flag would not be hoisted until 0800, and returned Beverton's salute. "Morning, Bever," I said to the tall, Maine society lad who had run away to sea.

The Assistant Topside Watch, Seaman Clive Orfutt, accompanied me to the open forward hatch. "Nice morning to be topside," I told the Wyoming cowboy.

"Yes, Sir, indeed," he said as I dropped into the Torpedo Room. I headed aft through the Crew's Mess and up a stairwell into Control where my XO, Commander Roger Barnes, met me.

"'Morning, Captain," he said.

We had met two days earlier following the Change of Command ceremony. He was nearly as tall as I, with short, balding brown hair and the physique of a man who regularly worked out. His light brown eyes twinkled as he invited me to join him for a cup of joe. I liked him.

"Let's sit in my cabin," I suggested. "Give me five to change to khakis."

The skipper's cabin, I thought, *my cabin—this is really happening.*

He assented, grabbed two steaming cups from the Wardroom, and joined me just as I buttoned my shirt.

"I walked through the boat this morning before you arrived," he said. "The crew is straining at the leash to get underway. The scuttlebutt is when you go to sea with Mac, you're in for a fucking great adventure." Barnes grinned at me. "You've got to know you're a legend. This crew will follow you through the gates of hell."

"Putting it on a bit thick, don't you think, Roger," I said. "I know what I've done, but without my dive team and the rest of the crew, we probably wouldn't be sitting here now. My legendary status is way overrated."

We sat quietly, sipping our cooling coffee.

"The fairing seems nearly done," I said, picking up the conversation.

"I spoke with Lieutenant Deckhart earlier," Barnes said. "He told me they will load *Mystic* around sixteen hundred. If everything tests out, we can set the sea detail at oh seven hundred."

"Set up Officer's Call right after dinner tonight," I told him. "I want to ensure we're all pulling in the same direction."

After Barnes left, I sat thinking about my new status. I was ready, I had no doubt. At the same time, however, what happened going forward was on me, no one else. Barnes was right; my guys would follow me to Hell, and that put a heavy burden on my shoulders. I had earned their trust. Now, I had to retain it, no matter what.

✳

Teuthis had been limited to ten knots when carrying *Mystic*. Since her role had evolved to one where she nearly always carried the DSRV, Special Projects thought giving *Teuthis* twenty-knot capability while carrying *Mystic* a good thing. Their solution was strengthened latches on both *Mystic* and *Teuthis*, and a fairing aft of the sail that would vector water around *Mystic*.

Mystic's latching mechanisms had been strengthened at her North Island home port in San Diego, and she had been flown to Mare Island yesterday. The *Teuthis* modifications had been underway since before the Change of Command. They were scheduled to be completed sometime today.

I called Eng, CWO-5 Bert Cobb, and Chief Pilot Deckhart to my cabin. Bert, the Engineer, was a tough, grizzled, fifty-something former Master Chief Engineman who had served as the Damage Control Assistant (DCA) on *Teuthis* in her earlier incarnation as a Boomer. He had forgotten more about the inner workings of the boat than anyone else ever knew. Jim Deckhart had been *Mystic*'s Second Pilot since Operation Ice Breaker[1] and just recently fleeted-up to Chief Pilot. He was a lanky, easy-going officer who should be seeing Lt. Cmdr. soon. His blue eyes lit up when he entered my cabin.

"Good to see you, Mac…er, Captain," he said with a broad grin.

"Let's go topside and inspect the progress," I said, grabbing my fore-n-aft cap.

---

1 See *Operation Ice Breaker*, Vol 2 of *The Mac McDowell Missions*.

We were installing two-fold modifications to our after hull around the after escape hatch. The DSRV attaches itself to a latching system comprising two pairs of angled legs that latch to the fore and after locking rings on the DSRV. An X-shaped brace between each leg pair stabilizes them laterally, and a forward jutting brace from each leg gives them longitudinal stability. Each leg also has a hydraulic stabilizer. When the DSRV is latched onto the four legs, the skirt makes a perfect seal against the escape hatch ring.

Our first modification comprised bulking up the four legs and their interconnections and strengthening their hull attachment points. The second modification was a fairing angling back from the deck around the four legs. NavSea[2] designed the fairing to cover the latching legs and generate a laminar flow that would merge with the DSRV laminar flow. It and the legs could be removed when *Teuthis* was not carrying a DSRV.

The strengthened legs had been installed at first light. I examined each, noting how they attached to the deck. We stepped aside as the crane on the DSRV semi moved the fairing in place and sailors bolted it down. It was streamlined steel, shaped to split water flow around the DSRV. I estimated it weighed two tons or more—something we would have to consider when adjusting our ballast.

"Time to load *Mystic*," Deckhart said.

"Make it so," I responded and stepped out of the way with Cobb.

The new COB, the Chief of the Boat, was Master Chief Sonar Tech Royal Bennett—we called him King. King was COB and also headed up the sonar gang. This was a bit unusual, but King wouldn't accept the COB assignment without being able to remain in charge of the sonar gang. He stood on the after deck, his black face glistening in the noon sun, supervising several deck gang members holding guidelines, as Chief Electronics Tech Warren Gamble, senior *Mystic* tech, supervised the entire operation. It took the DSRV fifteen minutes from the trailer bed to resting in the cradle. Petty Officer Sam Elton, First-class Sonar Tech and the second *Mystic* tech, climbed into the DSRV from above and set the latches.

It was time for change of the watch and lunch.

✳

---

2 Naval Sea Systems Command

Senior Chief Cedric Hurst had been with *Teuthis* as senior Commissaryman from the beginning, and he was on *Halibut* before that. Renowned for his bread, rolls, and popovers, he was a slightly corpulent treasure that I, like my predecessors, would not willingly relinquish. Crisanto Rivera had made Chief Steward and petitioned to remain on *Teuthis* one last mission before he retired. He was a proud, handsome Filipino who planned to run a large resort hotel when he left the navy. He was in charge of the Wardroom Mess. Regular meals came from the Crew's Mess, although occasionally, Rivera would prepare something special that he and our Supply Officer, boyish Lt.(jg) Roland Goff, had arranged, like British/Indian curry one Sunday a month.

For the crew, meals were part of their benefits, and submarine food was known throughout the navy as the best there is. Following tradition going back to the British Royal Navy of the seventeenth century, commissioned officers paid for their meals. Traditionally, the navy charged the officers on a rank-based sliding scale. Even so, it could be a hardship for a young officer with a lot of financial obligations, but it was what it was.

I cleaned up and entered the Wardroom. As the officers came to their feet, I waved them back. Traditionally, the skipper is the last officer to come to the meal table, and I stayed with that tradition, but I relaxed the requirement to come to their feet when I appeared. On a small ship like a submarine, it simply made for too much up and down.

Today we had slices of Cedric's fresh-baked bread piled high with tuna salad, served with chips and the ever-present bug juice, as we called the Kool-Aid-like sweet beverage that took the place of beer or wine served on most foreign ships.

Before anyone left, I spoke up. "Remember, we station the maneuvering watch at oh seven hundred. Waverly, show me your watchbill after lunch." I rose, indicating the officers remain seated, and left the Wardroom.

0700, TUESDAY, JUNE 13, 1989—MARE ISLAND NAVAL SHIPYARD, VALLEJO, CALIFORNIA

At 0700, the Chief of the Watch (COW), Senior Chief Engineman Sam Dokey, clicked the 1MC mike. "Now, station the maneuvering watch, station the maneuvering watch."

I took my time going to the bridge. This would be our first time underway with a new skipper and XO, and several new officers and crew. Waverly was the maneuvering watch Officer of the Deck (OOD)—he knew what he was doing. Nevertheless, he would look to me for guidance. I knew this sub's handling characteristics like the back of my hand, but I reminded myself to let Waverly do his job, unless things got out of hand. Trust…my officers and crew needed to know I trusted them. I gave everyone fifteen minutes to get organized before I climbed through the trunk to the bridge.

"Captain on the bridge," Seaman Beverton announced. He was on the starboard fairwater plane wearing a life jacket and was hooked to an eyebolt on the sail top. Seaman Basil Walton was on the port plane, his short-cropped red hair covered by a ball cap. Both planes had lifelines with stanchions at the outside corners.

"Morning, Bever, Basil," I said. "Waverly, how's it proceeding?"

"Internal stations are manned, Sir," he answered, "and we're commencing rig for dive, but it's still unofficial."

King was on deck with his line handlers. They all wore life jackets, had raised both capstans, and had just taken down the last lifeline stanchion. They were stowing the lines and stanchions in deck bins, appropriately cushioned so they would not make noise. Four shipyard sailors stood by our lines on the dock.

The sky was cloudy, and the air was a chilly 54 degrees. I was glad I wore my jacket. Waverly glanced at me, and I nodded. He picked up the bullhorn.

"Single up all lines," he announced to the deck below. On the squawk box, he said, "Chief of the Watch, lower both outboards."

The COW repeated the order while the sailors on the dock dropped the doubling lines so they draped over the single lines. King's deck gang pulled in the excess line and faked it on the deck.

"The wind is from the west, pushing us away from the dock," Waverly said. Over the bullhorn, "Pass the brow to the pier." He checked fore and aft. The quartermaster was manning the fantail colors. "Cast off all lines, shift colors." On the squawk box, "Chief of the Watch, one long blast. Starboard easy, both outboards. Rig the ship for dive."

The quartermaster lowered the fantail colors and Seaman Walton set the underway colors on the bridge. As *Teuthis* moved away from the dock, Waverly toggled the squawk box. "Ahead one-third, left ten degrees rudder."

A minute later, "Rudder amidships, secure the outboards. Set to astern and leave extended."

Teuthis eased into the 160-yard-wide channel. When he neared the center, Waverly ordered on the squawk box, "Right ten degrees rudder, make your course one-four-four."

On deck, King's gang stowed the lines, lowered both capstans, checked each stowage bin for rattles, and dropped below, securing both deck hatches.

"Maintain the maneuvering watch until you pass Mare Island Strait Buoy One," I told Waverly. "I worked with Seth to lay out our track all the way through the Golden Gate. Keep to channel center whenever possible. Stick to ten knots and follow the quartermaster's recommendations unless he's clearly wrong. In that case, get ahold of Seth."

I toggled the squawk box. "Send up five cups of coffee, please."

The wind picked up as the quartermaster got us safely around the southern tip of Mare Island. I could see the navigation periscope turning as he shot landmarks. Waverly ordered up warm jackets for the lookouts and himself, and sent up my parka. It felt good.

Waverly called on the squawk box, "Chief of the Watch, set the underway watch, section one."

Waverly and the lookouts remained on the bridge as section one watchstanders, and Chief Warrant Officer Hamilton Comstock (Ham) joined them as JOOD (Junior Officer of the Deck). Ham now ran the Test Operations Group (TOG), the saturation dive team on *Teuthis*, the job I held what seemed so long ago. I dropped down to Control, checked the Attack Scope, and took my place in the captain's chair. The soft hum of 400 Hz electronics surrounded me like a cocoon. Seth—my Navigator and Ops Officer—and his quartermasters followed our progress on the Plot chart, taking a visual sighting or radar fix every minute or so. They also kept track of the many radar contacts around us. My instructions were to designate any contact that might interfere with our progress. We had about two more hours to go before heading under the Golden Gate and out into the Pacific.

The squawk box sounded. "Chief Warrant Officer Hamilton Comstock has the Conn; Lt. Cmdr. Waverly Denver has the Deck."

Good—Waverly was bringing Ham up to speed. I expected him to qualify quickly as OOD.

Sonar was silent. King had nothing to do on the surface as section sonar supervisor, so he was ensconced with the XO going over crew matters. I had a competent officer topside, and Seth was a fine navigator. I relaxed my attention somewhat and gazed around Control. Chief Torpedoman Jasper Cedrik—everyone called him Tubes—was Diving Officer. He relieved Seaman Clive Orfutt on the helm, so Orfutt could relieve one of the lookouts on the bridge.

The quartermaster recommended the OOD come left to the new course. The bridge issued orders and Tubes complied. The watch section functioned as a well-oiled team. In all my experience thus far, I was part of such a team, contributing my expertise to the overall mission. Now it was my mission. The responsibility for success or failure lay squarely on my shoulders, and yet, without this team and the others aboard *Teuthis*, I would be unable to carry out my mission. A sense of pride swept through me as I looked around Control at the men focused on their individual tasks. The truth was, we were a team—myself included—and by the time we reached our mission op area, I would have honed the crew to the finest possible edge.

✳

At 1015 hours, Waverly had brought us through San Francisco Bay and pointed us to the Golden Gate and the open Pacific. I joined him on the bridge. The sky was still overcast, and the wind was nearly twenty knots from the southwest. Our speed increased the relative wind to nearly thirty. Pacific rollers from the southwest made our transit somewhat uncomfortable.

"Take us to fifteen knots," I told Waverly, "and boost it to twenty once we've passed the Golden Gate."

"Give me a round of contacts," Waverly ordered over the squawk box.

We had a couple of inbound container ships in the south lane several miles out, a dozen or so fishing boats scattered across the water to the horizon, and a large oil tanker four miles behind us, closing at thirty knots.

"He will be on us in about twenty minutes," I told Waverly. "We were in a similar situation when I took the *Halibut* out back in the day. The tanker didn't even see us. We dove prematurely, barely getting below his keel when he passed over us." I checked the waters off our port and starboard bow with my glasses.

"Take a southwestern course, threading through the fishing boats," I told Waverly. "Have the quartermaster keep you away from any big guys and watch out for net draggers. Adjust your heading for the most comfortable ride. We'll head out till change-of-watch. That should be about twenty miles. Maneuver around Southeast Farallon. We can commence surface ops a few miles farther out."

Before dropping down to Control, I added, "Let San Francisco Traffic Control know your intentions. I don't know if they have us on their radar, but let's keep those boys happy." It turned out the traffic controller with whom Waverly spoke was a female Coast Guard petty officer.

✳

Waverly set us on a southwesterly course, passing several miles in front of the incoming container ships with ten minutes to spare before the tanker reached our position. He checked out of San Francisco Traffic Control and pointed us slightly to the right of the incoming rollers. By the time Seth relieved him, we were clear of the fishing vessels, surrounded by nothing but open Pacific.

I met with the *Mystic* crew in the Wardroom. "We will run a race-course on the surface," I said, "varying our speed up to at least twenty-five knots. Our goal is to determine how well the fairing deflects water away from the cradle legs, and how well the DSRV fairs in general." I looked at Jim. "Do you want *Mystic* manned?"

"I do," he said. "Just me and Chief Gamble."

I called Seth on the handset, explaining our intentions. "The fairwater plane lifelines are stowed," he said, "and the lookouts are with me in the bridge well. We're all harnessed to the bridge."

I went to Control and picked up the 1MC mike. "This is the captain. For the next two hours, we will be making high-speed surface runs. The Pacific is throwing ten-to-fifteen-foot waves at us, so this should be an interesting two hours. Take a few minutes to police your watch stations. Let's save the navy a bit of money and avoid broken cups."

It actually took a half hour before we were ready to start our high-speed racetrack run. Quartermaster First-class Henry Bass—Hank, everybody called him—laid out our track on the Plot chart.

Over the squawk box, Seth ordered, "Ahead full." On the 1MC, he announced, "Stand by for a bumpy ride."

And bumpy it was.

We covered the two-mile leg in six minutes. Hank turned us ninety degrees port for a mile of heaving rolling, and then another ninety degrees port, putting the rollers off our port quarter for a relatively comfortable ride. After another six minutes, Hank turned us again ninety degrees port for a mile.

I called Seth on the handset. "Slow us to five knots while we assess. So, how are things up there?"

"Good thing we have our slickers," he answered. "It's totally wet up here."

"How did the fairing do?" I asked.

"Like a charm," he said. "Heavy water didn't get to the cradle legs."

I called Jim. "How did *Mystic* fare?"

"The bumpy ride was interesting, but she's secure and tight."

"We'll do another run at flank. Be prepared to stop us if you see the need."

I walked to Plot. "Flank this time," I told him. "Add a mile to the long legs and a half mile to the short ones."

I called Seth on the handset. "I've lengthened the course by a mile on the longs and a half mile on the shorts. Run it at flank, and have one of your lookouts focus on the fairing and DSRV."

On the squawk box, Seth said, "Radar, a round of contacts."

"Nothing, Sir. Scope is clear."

On the 1MC, Seth announced, "Stand by for an even bumpier ride."

As Seaman Ivan Tuxin—Tux to the crew—cranked our speed to flank, everyone grabbed hold of something. We were approaching thirty knots, and our bow pushed through the oncoming rollers, resulting in a gentler ride than before, although gentle was not a good descriptor.

I called Jim. "Give me an update, please."

"I'm registering some stress on the latches, but it's within tolerance."

We rounded the bend into the cross leg. The rolling effect was less, to the relief of two green crew members in Control. The return leg was nearly smooth, and the second cross leg gave us rolls like the first.

"Jim?" I asked on the DSRV circuit.

"Just fine," Jim answered. "I think we've passed this test, Skipper."

1315, TUESDAY, JUNE 13, 1989—*USS TEUTHIS*, SURFACED, UNDERWAY, 15 NM SW OF SOUTHEAST FARALLON ISLAND

Seth and his lookouts dropped deliberately, without hurry, into Control, Seamen Ezra Ben-Gurion and Mike Overreach first (Ben and Mikey to all), followed by Seth. Overreach pulled the lanyard closing the upper hatch, and Seth cranked it shut. When he dropped to the Control deck, Overreach secured the lower hatch. Tux had the helm and fairwater planes, and Ben took the stern planes. Master Chief Ocean Tech Morris Jones or Spook, as Diving Officer, took his place on the elevated stool between them.

Seth asked Senior Chief Fire Control Tech Ogden Winder (Oggy), the COW, "Rig-for-dive status?"

"Green board, Sir."

"Depth below the keel, Hank?" Seth asked the quartermaster.

"Five-nine-eight-zero feet, Sir."

"Chief of the Watch, sound the diving alarm. Helmsman, ahead one-third. Diving Officer, make your depth six-five feet."

"Dive! Dive!" Oggy announced on the 1MC and sounded the diving alarm twice.

Seth took the Attack Scope checking the forward vent, and I took the Nav Scope, checking the after vent.

"At six-five feet," Spook announced to the Control Room that was silent except for the soft sighing of the plane and rudder hydraulics and the quiet 400 Hz hum that permeated everything forward of the engineering spaces.

I did a 360 turn of the Nav Scope. "Clear," I announced and dropped the scope.

Seth did the same with the Attack Scope. "Clear," he said, slapping the handles up and dropping the mast. "Diving Officer, ten degrees down-bubble—make your depth two-zero-zero feet. Helmsman, left five degrees rudder. Hold that. We're going to cruise in a circle while we set up for our next test."

"Officers Call in ten minutes in the Wardroom," I told Seth. "I'll have the XO relieve you."

Ten minutes later, all the officers joined me in the Wardroom except Bert Cobb in Maneuvering and the XO in Control. We were in excellent hands should anything go wrong.

"We will accomplish two things during the next several hours," I told them. "We'll test the deck and DSRV cradle mods, mostly for speed, but also for angles and dangles. For the latter, of course, we'll also be testing the crew's ability to stow things properly. I want each of you to do your best to produce no crashes on our first angle and dangle." I grinned at them. "So far as I know, this has never happened in the history of the sub fleet. I challenge you to set a new record."

✳

"This is the captain," I said on the 1MC. "We are about to undergo both underwater speed tests and angles and dangles. I told your officers, and now I'm telling you. In the history of the submarine service, no sub has ever done a clean first angle and dangle. This is your chance to make history. We'll commence in fifteen minutes."

Fifteen minutes later, Seth announced on the 1MC, "Commence high-speed runs and angles and dangles." He turned to Plot. "Give me a heading, Hank."

"Two-three-zero, Sir."

"Helmsman, ahead full; make turns for two-zero knots. Come right to new course two-three-zero."

When *Teuthis* was up to speed, Seth triggered the DSRV circuit. "DSRV, what is your status?"

"No stress on the latches."

"Helmsman, make turns for twenty-five knots."

Deckhart reported, "Still no stress on the latches."

"Helmsman, make turns for thirty knots, three-zero knots."

This time, Deckhart reported, "I see some stress on all four latches, but they are within specs. I recommend we do not push it further."

"Helmsman," Seth ordered, "make turns for two-zero knots." Then on the 1MC he said, "Stand by for angles and dangles." Turning to the quartermaster, he asked, "Water under the keel?"

"Six-zero-zero-zero feet, Sir."

"Diving Officer," Seth said, "twenty degree down-bubble, make your depth one-zero-zero-zero feet."

I sat back in my captain's chair and watched as the sub tilted steeply down by the bow. The COW grabbed a cup that was about to slide off the Ballast Control Panel.

"Nice save, Senior Chief," Seth commented as a cup crashed in Sonar, and several crashes floated up from the Crew's Mess.

"At one-zero-zero-zero feet, Sir," Jones, the Diving Officer, announced.

I picked up the 1MC mike. "This is the captain. Well, that didn't go so well." I turned to Seth. "Set General Quarters."

Seth passed the order to the COW, who announced on the 1MC, "General Quarters, General Quarters, all hands man your Battle Stations." He sounded the General Alarm.

I did this to ensure all hands participation, since Watch Section Two had flubbed the "get-it-right-the-first-time test." Waverly, the General Quarters OOD relieved Seth, who placed himself at Plot, his General Quarters station.

It took longer than I expected for the sound-powered phone talker to report, "All stations manned and ready." Something else I would have to work on. I made a mental note. I got on the 1MC.

"This is the captain. You have ten minutes to square away things at your station. Perhaps now that everyone is involved, you can do it right."

Ten minutes later, I told Waverly, "Commence angles and dangles."

He turned to his Diving Officer. "Diving Officer, thirty degree up-bubble. Make your depth two-zero-zero feet. Do not come shallower than two-zero-zero feet."

As the Diving Officer announced, "Passing five zero-zero feet," Waverly ordered, "Helmsman, left full rudder."

Already at a thirty-degree bow-up angle, *Teuthis* rolled hard to port, generating crashes through the sub. I sighed in frustration, but this was inevitable. There was a reason no sub had ever gotten it on the first try.

On the 1MC, I said, "This is the captain—that's right, sailors, the sub rolls from side to side, too. I'll give you ten minutes to find what's not yet broken."

While we waited, I said to Waverly, "Give them twenty- and thirty-degree angles and hard rolls both port and starboard."

I checked with Jim. "How are *Mystic* and cradle handing this?"

"The stress needles barely moved," he answered.

When ten minutes had passed, Waverly glanced at me for confirmation. I nodded.

"Diving Officer, twenty degree down-bubble. Make your depth one-zero-zero-zero feet."

At the 500-foot mark, he ordered, "Thirty degree down-bubble. Right full rudder."

As soon as the sub rolled hard to starboard, he ordered, "Shift your rudder, thirty degree up-bubble. Make your depth two-zero-zero feet. Do not come shallower than two-zero-zero feet."

At 300 feet, he ordered, "Rudder amidships, zero bubble, ease to two-zero-zero feet."

Jim called me on the handset. "Skipper, on both hard left and right rolls I got stress indications near the limit on both forward legs. The rear legs showed no stress."

As we reached 200 feet, I clicked the 1MC mike. "Congratulations! That was the toughest test, and you passed with flying colors. We will head for the barn now. We expect to arrive in time for liberty call."

0700, WEDNESDAY, JUNE 14, 1989—MARE ISLAND NAVAL SHIPYARD, VALLEJO, CALIFORNIA

As soon as we surfaced, I sent NavSea a message detailing the stress problem with the forward cradle legs. We had fair skies for most of our return trip to Mare Island Naval Shipyard. As we reached the southern tip of Mare Island, the maneuvering watch took over and got us tied up in record time.

A NavSea team waited on the dock. When the brow went over at 2040 hours, Jim joined them with details of the problem. They came aboard and set to work. At 0123, Jim called me.

"Repairs are completed," he said. "They found a sub-standard brace in the forward yoke assembly. They replaced it, and things should be fine now. We can test it on our way south. If it fails, we can address it again in San Diego."

With that good news, I put in a wake-up call for 0700. Twenty-four hours after that, I intended to be underway.

※

The day started with fair skies and virtually no breeze. It was perfect for topping off our torpedo load and stores. By midafternoon, *Teuthis* was ready for sea. I stepped topside to get some fresh air. Seaman Ben-Gurion had the topside watch. He saluted, and I returned his salute.

"Pleasant afternoon, Ben-Gurion," I said. "How are you holding up?"

"Fine, Captain. Yesterday was my first time at sea on a submarine. I would have to call it the best day of my life so far."

I chuckled. "We're going to give you a lot more excitement than that," I said. "How are your quals coming?"

"I'm making good progress, Captain. I want to be fully qualified by the end of this deployment."

"Keep it up, Son, and you will," I said as I crossed the brow to stretch my legs along the dock.

While I strolled along the dock, the COW announced liberty call. "Now hear this! Liberty call! Liberty expires at oh one hundred. Don't be late. We will set the maneuvering watch at oh seven hundred. You're gonna want a hearty Cedric breakfast before we get underway."

As if by magic, sailors in civies poured out through both hatches, heading into a waiting bus that would take them into downtown Vallejo—not that Vallejo was all that exciting. The divers emerged with Ham. They stopped to greet me. They were off to the Horse and Cow, Vallejo's one claim to submarine fame. Some of the divers had been there with me when I was the Officer in Charge (OIC) of TOG, so long ago. The joint supplied fond memories.

"Enjoy the Winnie and Moo," I said to them as they climbed into a van that had appeared from somewhere. As the door closed, I heard a whispered chorus. "Yo, Diver Boy!"

Track from Southeast Farallon Island to San Diego.
Insert: Path to open Pacific.

CHAPTER TWO—Transit to San Diego

0700, THURSDAY, JUNE 15, 1989—MARE ISLAND NAVAL SHIPYARD, VALLEJO, CALIFORNIA

This was it, the big day for which we all had been waiting. The COW set the maneuvering watch when the Control Room clock second hand hit 0700. Fifteen minutes later, the duty runner reported to me, "Maneuvering watch manned and ready." Time to go to the bridge and take my ship to sea. It felt different today. I was still in awe of my responsibility, but it had settled on my shoulders like a well-used rucksack. I was coming to grips with what being Captain meant. I called Waverly on the handset.

"How's the weather?" I asked.

"A batch of clouds just passed. Looks like fair skies for the rest of the day. No wind. High fifties."

It was a good day to head for sea. I shrugged on my foul-weather jacket, grabbed my fore-n-aft cap, and headed to the bridge.

Down on the deck, King had the deck gang ready to cast off. Safety lines and stanchions were already stowed, and the capstan wrenches were in place, ready to lower them. Yard sailors stood by on the dock to cast us off. I heard a loud whistle off the port side.

"An Orca!" lookout Beverton said, "A fucking Orca!"

The Orca ducked below the surface, displaying his dorsal fin to advantage.

"There's a chunk missing from the back of his dorsal," Waverly said. "Do you think that's Borysko?"

I climbed atop the sail to give the cetacean a better view of me. The Orca looked directly at me, disappeared beneath the surface, and then shot completely out of the water, whistling loudly as he completed a full flip ending in a bellyflop that splashed most of the sailors on the main deck. It was definitely Borysko, the Orca that had befriended my divers during Operation Arctic Sting[3] and accompanied us throughout our Antarctic activities during Operation White Out.[4] The thirty-ton cetacean had a special affinity for me and my departed Kate. Somehow, he had found us moored to the Naval Shipyard pier in the Napa River.

"Single up all lines," Waverly ordered to the deck below. On the squawk box, he said, "Chief of the Watch, lower both outboards." He followed this with a bullhorn order, "Pass the brow to the pier." And when it was done, "Cast off all lines, shift colors." On the squawk box, "Chief of the Watch, one long blast." And since there was no wind, "Starboard full, both outboards. Rig the ship for dive."

And with that we were underway on a mission for which I had an

---

3 See *Operation Arctic Sting*, vol 3 in *The Mac McDowell Missions*.
4 See *Operation White Out*, vol 4 in *The Mac McDowell Missions*.

overview and a tight timeline, but knew nothing of the specific details. Those awaited in my cabin safe.

I watched King secure topside and move his deck gang belowdecks. As we rounded the southern end of Mare Island at a comfortable ten knots, Borysko moved into our bow wave, letting *Teuthis* take up part of the effort to move his mass through the water.

"You did this yesterday," I said to Waverly. "With no wind this morning, it will be a piece of cake. Set the underway watch when you steady up on your next leg."

I dropped below and asked the XO and Seth to meet me in my cabin.

0800, THURSDAY, JUNE 15, 1989—*USS TEUTHIS*, SURFACED, UNDERWAY, SAN PABLO BAY, CALIFORNIA

I sat at my fold-down desk in my cramped cabin and glanced at the small ivory cylinder hanging from my desk light. It was all I had left of Kate. I was tempted to open it, but the spicy-smelling thong had lost most of its scent—I wanted to retain the remainder for as long as possible. A knock on the door, and Roger, the XO, entered with Seth, each with a cup of joe, Seth with an extra one for me. I indicated the easy chair for the XO and the Naugahyde couch for Seth. I turned to my desk, opened the small safe, and extracted a manilla envelope.

I jotted down the time on a notepad and opened the envelope. Inside were three single-page documents labeled respectively CO, XO, and OPS. All were prominently stamped in red TS/SCI, which meant Top Secret and Sensitive Compartmented Information. I handed each officer his copy. I looked at mine while they looked at theirs.

TOP SECRET/SENSITIVE COMPARTMENTED
INFORMATION

DATE:　14 JUNE 1989 1500Z

TO:　　COMMANDING OFFICER, USS TEUTHIS
　　　　(SSNR 2)

FROM:　COMSUBPAC

SUBJECT: ADDENDUM TO ORDERS ISSUED TO
　　　　　COMMANDING OFFICER, *USS Teuthis*
　　　　　(SSNR 2) 10 JUNE 1989.

1. AT 0500 ON 20 JUNE 1989, MEET COMSUBPAC AT
   USS PIGEON WITH MYSTIC FOR TRANSPORT
   TO USS TEUTHIS.

2. STAND BY FOR FURTHER ORDERS.

TOP SECRET/SENSITIVE COMPARTMENTED
INFORMATION

I turned my copy over—nothing on the reverse. "That seems to be it," I said. "So, Rear Admiral Michael Colley is paying us a visit. I expect he will bring our detailed orders. How mysterious." I looked at each of them. "I know you understand the rules, but I'm going to say it, anyway. Discuss this with nobody." I looked at Seth. "Don't even talk in your sleep about it." I left the XO out of that admonition since he had a private stateroom.

"What do you think?" Seth asked. "You must have some idea."

"I have not been briefed," I said. "Let's leave it at that. We'll know in five days." I turned to the XO. "Roger, I want as many forward drills as possible during our transit. Bert's already working on engineering drills."

1000, THURSDAY, JUNE 15, 1989—*USS TEUTHIS*, SURFACED, UNDERWAY, GOLDEN GATE, CALIFORNIA

Waverly called me on the handset. "It's the OOD, Skipper. We're at the Golden Gate. You wanted to be on the bridge for the transit." "I'll be right up, Waverly."

I slipped on my foul-weather jacket, grabbed my fore-n-aft cap, and headed to the bridge. On the way, I instructed the runner, Seaman Orfutt, to send four cups of coffee to the bridge. I already had mine, two-thirds full, so I wouldn't spill it on the way up.

"Captain's on the bridge," Beverton announced as I passed through the upper hatch.

"Coffee's on the way," I told the watchstanders.

"Ham has the Conn," Waverly told me. "Had it since section one assumed the watch."

"How do you like driving the sub on the surface?" I asked Ham.

"A lot to keep track of," he said.

"That's why you've got Juby and his quartermasters down there looking out for you. What are your main contacts?" I asked.

"I got two container ships running away from me out there." He pointed to the bow. "A tanker approaching in the channel to our port and another one coming up our stern."

"When do you start worrying about him?" I asked.

"I am worrying, but I'll get concerned when he's a mile or so behind us."

"What's his closing rate?" I asked.

"Ten knots. He's doing thirty, we're doing twenty. He's three miles back right now, so I've got twelve minutes before he's just a mile back."

"Does he have us on radar?" I asked.

"Don't know, but I assume not."

"What about Traffic Control?" I asked.

"They may have us on radar, but I told them we were here. I presume they'll tell the tanker about us."

"Likely," I said, "but let's not rely on that. Tell Traffic Control that you're cutting across the inbound lane ahead of the tanker. Then take us south of Southeast Farallon."

I was stepping into Waverly's space somewhat, but I wanted to get a handle on how well Ham was grasping the big picture. Waverly understood and kept his mouth shut.

While Ham contacted Traffic Control, I leaned to Waverly and said quietly, "You've trained him well."

I stayed on the bridge while Waverly and Ham took us through what seemed like a thousand fishing vessels. Finally, we passed Southeast

Farallon and turned south. It was nearly time to change the watch. I looked at Waverly.

"Let Ham dive the sub and get himself and his section organized in Control. Then change the watch. If it takes a bit longer, that's fine. He won't have many opportunities to do this."

I left the bridge with a wave to Borysko, who was riding our bow wave. Being Skipper was beginning to feel normal. The responsibility still held me in awe, but running the day-to-day operations was falling into place. *Teuthis* felt like my ship now.

✳

Over the squawk box, I heard Ham say, "Clear the bridge!"

Beverton dropped into Control and took his place at the stern planes. Walton followed, with Ham right behind him. Walton pulled the lanyard while Ham secured the upper hatch and then secured the lower hatch after Ham dropped through.

"Rig-for-dive status?" Ham asked the COW.

"Green board, Sir."

"Quartermaster, water under the keel?"

"Ten thousand feet, Sir. One-zero-zero-zero-zero feet."

"Diving Officer," Ham said to Cedrik, "dive the ship. Make your depth six-five feet." He turned to the COW. "Chief of the Watch, sound the diving alarm."

On the 1MC, Dokey announced, "Dive! Dive!" and sounded the diving alarm twice.

"Helmsman," Ham said, "ahead one-third."

Ham manned the Nav Scope and Waverly manned the Attack Scope.

"Helmsman," Ham said, "come left to new course one seven six."

"At six-five feet, Sir," the Diving Officer announced.

Ham glanced at Waverly, who nodded.

"Diving Officer, ten degree down-bubble, make your depth three-zero-zero feet." Following the acknowledgment, he said, "Helmsman, ahead two-thirds, make turns for twenty knots."

Ham started to report to me, but I interrupted. "I'm right here, Ham. No need to report." I grinned. "Nice job," I said and went to my cabin while the watch changed.

1100, THURSDAY, JUNE 15, 1989—*USS Teuthis*, SUBMERGED AT 300 FT, 5 NM SOUTH OF SOUTHEAST FARALLON ISLAND

The XO called my handset. "I'm ready to commence drills during the change of watch," he said.

"Let them get settled in for a few minutes," I told him. "This is only our second dive. Let's work up to that."

"Aye, Aye, Sir."

Conducting the first drill during change-of-watch was not a bad idea. I just wanted the guys to settle in before we hit them with something like that.

Ten minutes later, the COW announced on the 1MC, "Flooding in the lower Engine Room! Flooding in the lower Engine Room!" followed by the slow rise and fall of the collision/flooding alarm, sounding ever so much like a 1950s police car siren. I stepped out to Control to monitor the drill.

We got the "flooding" under control in about fifteen minutes— probably ten minutes too long. Bert joined me in Control where we discussed how we could improve the reaction time.

"They did everything right," Bert said. "They were just too slow. I think after several of these drills, we'll see significant improvement."

"I hope so," I said. "Keep up the pressure."

We had a "fire" in Sonar and another in the Galley. We gave the torpedomen a hot-running fish in a tube and the auxilliarymen a smoking oxygen generator. We even let the nukes handle a minor secondary coolant spill. This is not normally a big deal since secondary coolant is not supposed to be radioactive, but we treat it as if it were, anyway.

We drilled until dinnertime and then woke the sleepers up at 0130 for another flooding drill—in the Torpedo Room. This flooding drill went much better than the first.

Off Santa Maria, we turned southeast toward our rendezvous point with *USS Pigeon* ten hours ahead of us.

✳

When drilling a submarine crew, the idea is to get the men to compete against their own times and efficiencies. Handling a problem three seconds faster can mean the difference between saving the ship or losing it and everyone onboard. We filled the entire twenty-four hours of our transit to San Diego with improving our ability to save ourselves from an unexpected emergency. By the time we slowed our passage and cast about for the submarine rescue ship, *USS Pigeon* (ASR 21), we had improved in every category, but we weren't there yet. One thing I knew about submariners, and especially about this crew, is they would rise to the task. By the time we faced whatever lay before us, these guys would be ready to handle anything anyone threw at us.

"Conn, Sonar." Sonar Tech First-class Godfry Mason was Sonar Supervisor. "We have *Pigeon* off the starboard bow, five miles away. She's making five knots, running a two-hundred-yard circle."

"List your other contacts," Seth said.

"None, Sir. All we have is *Pigeon*."

I stepped from my cabin to Control. "Set DSRV ops," I told Seth and took my place in the captain's chair.

On the 1MC, he announced, "Now, commence DSRV ops, commence DSRV ops."

Deckhart and Fortune reported to the after escape hatch and requested permission from Conn to open the lower hatch.

"Open the lower hatch," Seth told them.

"Request permission to open the upper hatch," Deckhart requested.

"Granted," Seth told him.

The two pilots and two technicians entered *Mystic*, and Engine Room personnel shut both hatches. Deckhart and Fortune took several minutes to bring up and test their systems.

"*Mystic* ready to launch," Deckhart reported.

Seth picked up the Secure Gertrude mike. "*Pigeon*, this is *Teuthis*, over."

The response was immediate. "This is *Pigeon*, over." The incoming transmission was crystal clear through the spread-spectrum technology of the Secure Gertrude.

"We are northwest of you at five nautical miles and three hundred feet, over."

"Roger that. We will go DIW station keeping and bring *Mystic* up through the well. *Mystic* should approach our port side at one-zero-zero feet. *Pigeon* will assume operational control when *Mystic* is one-zero-zero yards distant at one-zero-zero feet depth. Over."

"Roger," Seth answered. "*Mystic* will carry only pilots and crew on the first leg. Will you deploy divers? Over."

"We will put two divers in the water to assist, if necessary. They will have comms and will remain well out of the way. Over."

"Roger. *Teuthis* will close to a nautical mile, remaining at three-ze-ro-zero feet. We will call when we reach station. Out."

Seth was aware, of course, that I was sitting in the captain's chair, but he did not once look to me for guidance or approval. He just did what the job required.

"Sonar, Conn, give me *Pigeon*'s bearing and range."

"Two-one-zero at four nautical miles, Sir."

"Helmsman, ahead one-third, come left to new course two-one-zero."

A half hour later, Sonar reported, "*Pigeon* is one mile distant, DIW."

"All stop. Back one-third," Seth ordered. He held it for a minute, then ordered, "All stop. Chief of the Watch, mark your depth."

"One-nine-nine feet, Sir."

"Okay. maintain depth within two feet. Lower the outboards. Coordinate with Sonar and the quartermaster to maintain station on *Pigeon* using the outboards."

"Question, Sir," Seaman Ben-Gurion asked.

"What is it, Ben?"

"Why station keep on *Pigeon*? Wouldn't it be easier to just station keep?"

"Currents, Ben," Seth said, "currents. We don't know what they are, and we don't know what *Pigeon* will do to counter them, if anything. But if we keep station on her, then everything is copesetic."

"That makes a lot of sense," Ben-Gurion said.

I smiled to myself. Seth could have scolded the sailor for questioning his order. Instead, he took it as a matter of curiosity, giving the sailor a better understanding of his own job and an appreciation of Seth's knowledge and skill.

✳

Deckhart unlatched *Mystic* from its cradle, propelled up and starboard several feet, and reported by Secure Gertrude, "*Mystic* is free and clear of *Teuthis*."

"*Pigeon* lies zero-three-two, one nautical mile," Seth responded.

"*Mystic*, aye."

Deckhart turned *Mystic* several degrees to starboard and ran her up to four knots, the DSRV's highest speed. He angled her up two degrees and shortly picked up the catamaran on his forward-looking sonar. Fifteen minutes later, Deckhart leveled off, came to a stop, and called *Pigeon* on the Secure Gertrude.

"*Pigeon*, this is *Mystic*, over."

"This is *Pigeon*, over."

"*Pigeon*, *Mystic*. I am one-zero-zero yards off your port side at one-zero-zero feet. Over."

"This is *Pigeon*. Roger. *Teuthis*, this is *Pigeon*. I have assumed operational control."

"This is *Teuthis*. Roger, *Pigeon* has operational control."

"*Mystic*, it's *Pigeon*. I am station keeping with waves of six to eight feet from my stern. Come to my stern at one-zero-zero yards at one-ze-ro-zero feet. I will lower the cradle through the well to one-zero-zero feet. Divers will be standing by several yards forward of the cradle. My stabilizers should maintain an even cradle, but approach cautiously. Over."

"This is *Mystic*. Roger. This is not my first rodeo, so we should be in good shape. Note we have an Orca escort. He has a relationship with *Teuthis* and the divers. They call him Borysko. He will not harm your divers, but he may approach them, looking for his tongue to be scratched. Over."

"This is *Pigeon*…Say what?…Over."

"This is *Mystic*. Borysko will not harm your divers, He is curious and wants to make friends. That's what the tongue scratching is all about. Over."

"This is *Pigeon*. We just observed Borysko surface. He's a big fellow with a chunk missing from his dorsal fin. Over."

"This is *Mystic* That's Borysko. Over."

While Fortune was having the conversation about Borysko, Deckhart moved *Mystic* around to *Pigeon*'s stern.

"This is *Mystic*. I am one-zero-zero yards off your stern at one-zero-zero feet."

"*Pigeon*. Roger."

The descending cradle was clearly visible on Deckhart's forward-looking sonar.

"This is *Pigeon*. Cradle is at one-zero-zero feet. Surface wave activity is moving me six vertical feet. Approach with caution. The automatic compensator is functioning, but do not rely on it. Approach at eight-zero feet and follow standard procedure for moderate surface wave activity. Over."

Deckhart eased the DSRV beneath the catamaran bobbing on the surface above. On his forward sonar, the cradle appeared fixed and stable. He lifted *Mystic* twenty feet, approaching slowly. At eighty feet, the surface wave motion was not perceptible. His sonar monitor displayed a grid pattern that converged to a point—his destination on the cradle. His television monitor showed the brightly illuminated four cables suspending the cradle in the crystal-clear water. Twenty feet below, the cradle waited patiently, barely moving as the automatic system paid out and retrieved the cables, synchronously countering the surface wave action.

Taggert eased *Mystic* down toward the cradle, a foot at a time. After ten minutes, he settled *Mystic* firmly against the cradle and activated the clamps that securely held the DSRV.

"This is *Mystic*. Locked in the cradle. Over."

Without warning, the forward starboard cable let loose as the automatics for this cable failed. *Mystic* began heaving awkwardly with three cables attempting to compensate for *Pigeon*'s vertical movement, while the fourth just hung there, jerking *Mystic*'s starboard bow up and down as *Pigeon* moved above the DSRV.

Without batting an eye, Taggert released the cradle clamps and raised *Mystic* twenty feet.

"This is *Mystic*. The forward starboard cable mechanism failed. I am at eight-zero feet inside the cables. Over."

"This is *Pigeon*. Roger. We are effecting repairs. Pull forward through the cables and stand off my port side at one-zero-zero feet. Over."

Ten minutes later, *Pigeon* announced, "We will need an hour to restore proper functioning of our compensator system. *Mystic* return to *Teuthis*. We will notify you when we are ready to receive you. Over."

"This is *Pigeon*. I am releasing operational control of *Mystic* to *Teuthis*. Over."

"This is *Teuthis*. Roger. Out."

✳

Ninety minutes later, *Pigeon* informed us she was ready to receive *Mystic*. This time, things went by the book. *Pigeon* assumed operational control, and Deckhart drove *Mystic* into position under the catamaran. The ASR was still bouncing around on the surface—perhaps even more, but as Deckhart eased *Mystic* between the cables at eighty feet, the cradle twenty feet down remained virtually motionless. *Mystic* slowly settled to the cradle, and Deckhart activated the clamps.

"*Mystic* is ready to be hoisted aboard, over," Deckhart reported.

In the clear water with virtually no reference points, *Mystic*'s rise was barely perceptible until she fell under *Pigeon*'s shadow. A minute later, the cradle's rubber rollers—they looked a lot like pneumatic tires for a small wagon—engaged the vertical tracks on the inside of each hull as the cradle rose between the hulls to slightly above *Pigeon*'s deck, where the cradle engaged an overhead girdered clamshell that firmly secured the DSRV to the cradle. Then the overhead gantry moved *Mystic* to port until powered gears on the cradle's underside engaged socketed tracks on the deck and moved the cradle with *Mystic* away from the center well.

Strictly speaking, moving *Mystic* away from the center well was unnecessary, but *Pigeon* was drilling having two DSRVs aboard. The deck gang moved *Mystic* aside to make room for a second DSRV coming up through the center well.

Deckhart and the rest of his crew exited *Mystic* and met with *Pigeon*'s First Lieutenant, Randal Jeffrey, the officer in charge of deck operations.

"We lost the after port compensating mechanism the last time we worked with you guys," he told Deckhart. "This time, we took some extra time and overhauled all four. Hopefully, that's the last of our mechanical problems this time out."

"What's next?" Deckhart asked.

"We're gonna launch you off the port side and then pick you up on the starboard side. If that goes well, we'll launch you starboard and retrieve you port. Then we'll launch center well. That should do it for today."

Just then, a loud whistle sounded from the center well. Several sailors ran to the edge to see what it was. Borysko lunged upward so his head and part of his torso appeared above deck level. He squealed his excitement, possibly remembering the events in the eastern Coral Sea during Operation White Out.[5] He dropped back with a tremendous splash.

"That's Borysko," Deckhart said. "*Teuthis* picked him up in the Arctic three missions ago. He has managed to follow us around ever since. Your divers probably met him during our first retrieval."

"Isn't that dangerous?" Jeffrey asked.

"Naw—he's gentle as a pussy cat."

✳

Pigeon's gantry ran athwartships, running on overhead rails attached to the fore and aft bulkheads of the central open deck of the submarine rescue vessel. It was supported by steel girders running through the deck to the ship's structural elements. The vessel was eighty-six feet wide. At the vessel edges, the rails folded inward ninety degrees, meeting at the middle of the deck opening. When extended, the rails added another twenty-five feet to the beam on each side.

Deckhart and his three-man crew returned to *Mystic* and dogged the hatch. The gantry lifted the DSRV, and the clamshell released its hold. Four sailors steadied the DSRV with lines while the gantry slowly moved it to port until it hung free out over the port side. As the ship pitched up and down with the increasing sea state, *Mystic* remained still in her cradle as the compensator system reeled the cable up and down to counter *Pigeon*'s vertical motion. Jeffrey signaled the gantry operator to lower the DSRV, and she dropped slowly toward the heaving water. Once *Mystic* was below the surface, he increased the rate of descent. At one hundred feet, he stopped and signaled *Mystic*.

---

5 See *Operation White Out*, vol 4 in *The Mac McDowell Missions*.

"*Mystic*, this is *Pigeon*. Release the DSRV and move away from the cradle. Descend to two-zero-zero feet and move to my starboard side, one-zero-zero yards distant. Over."

"This is *Mystic*. Roger."

While *Mystic* moved to *Pigeon*'s starboard side, Jeffrey moved the gantry starboard and dropped the cradle to one hundred feet. *Pigeon* signaled *Mystic*, and the second retrieval got underway. It went without a hitch, and forty-five minutes later, *Mystic* once again rested on deck in the cradle, this time on the starboard track.

"This time, we drop you back down on the starboard side and bring you back up on the port side," Jeffrey told Deckhart when he stuck his head through the DSRV upper hatch.

The seas were increasing, and the compensators worked overtime to hold *Mystic* steady while Deckhart released the clamps. He moved clear and returned to the port side.

"*Mystic*, this is *Pigeon*. We are marginally able to maintain a stable cradle off the port side. Do you wish to proceed? Over"

"This is *Mystic*. Lower the cradle and let me decide then. Over."

"This is *Pigeon*. Roger."

Thirty minutes later, *Pigeon* called. "This is *Pigeon*. Cradle is at one-zero-zero feet. Approach from my stern and evaluate. Over."

Deckhart moved toward the cradle. It was heaving several feet with each passing wave, despite the best efforts of the compensating system.

"*Pigeon*, this is *Mystic*. Retrieval is a no-go. We can try the center well where things are much quieter. Over."

❄

While DSRV ops were underway, I sat in Control eavesdropping on the operation. Since *Pigeon* had operational control, I didn't interfere. When Jim suggested retrieving through the center well, I grabbed the Secure Gertrude mike.

"All parties, this is *Teuthis*. Do not, I repeat, do not retrieve *Mystic* through the center well! *Pigeon*, relinquish operational control of *Mystic*. Over."

"This is *Pigeon*. Roger."

"*Teuthis* has operational control of *Mystic*."

"*Pigeon*. Roger."

"*Mystic*. Roger."

"*Mystic*, this is *Teuthis*. Return home. Report when ready to clamp down. Over."

While the DSRV returned, I called *Pigeon* and asked to speak with her skipper, Cmdr. Eric Glidden.

"This is Glidden."

"Eric," I said, "sorry to stop the operation. *Teuthis* is on a tight schedule and cannot afford any delays to repair possible damage to *Mystic*. I have full faith in your people, but I cannot take the chance. Let's ride out the heavy seas and pick up again tomorrow morning. Over."

"I agree. We'll use the time to take another look at our compensating system. Out."

A half hour later, *Mystic* called. "This is *Mystic*. Request permission to come aboard."

✳

By next morning, the seas had backed off, and it looked like they would continue to calm down. I released *Mystic* to *Pigeon*'s control, and they went to it for the rest of the day. That morning, they exercised every possible configuration—up and down outboard of both hulls and through the well. The *Mystic* crew caught lunch aboard *Pigeon*. After lunch, they ran the entire set again. Throughout, Borysko stayed close when possible and cavorted off whichever side of the catamaran the DSRV was operating. He stayed out of the way while making certain he personally greeted each set of safety divers *Pigeon* put into the water. By day's end, both pilots, Deckhart and Fortune, and their two techs, were exhausted.

We terminated operations while daylight still reigned, so *Pigeon*'s deck crew could get in some maintenance. The DSRV crew crashed right after the evening meal, and I instructed the COW to make sure they were not disturbed.

Day three dawned early, with Second Pilot Donald Fortune designated as Acting Chief Pilot. I wasn't worried, because Deckhart would be with him the entire time, and besides, Fortune was more than ready to assume the mantle of Chief Pilot.

I won't bore you with the details. They did everything as the previous day, except Fortune was driving. This time, after supper, which the DSRV crew took aboard *Pigeon*, we continued for three more hours during twilight and darkness. Time of day made no difference to the *Mystic* crew, but *Pigeon*'s deck gang needed experience retrieving and launching the DSRV in darkness.

We knocked off around 2200, with *Mystic* and crew remaining on *Pigeon* overnight, because *Mystic* would be on call commencing 0500, when we expected Rear Admiral Michael Colley, Commander Submarine Force Pacific (ComSubPac), to arrive from Pearl Harbor. He would have arrived by jet the night before at North Island, San Diego, and ordered the earliest possible morning Sea Dragon flight to our location. I first met Colley at Kaohsiung City when we returned from Operation White Out,[6] and was looking forward to seeing him again. He was an officer who didn't let petty bureaucracy get in his way. I liked him.

Adm. Colley knew our schedule and wouldn't tolerate anything that might delay us. He was bringing our final orders and would want to spend face time with me and the XO. I had Cedric set up a table in my cabin with place settings for four—we needed to include Seth, as ship's Navigator, in our discussion.

Promptly at 0500, *Pigeon* received ComSubLant's Sea Dragon. Fortune and the two techs were already inside *Mystic*. Deckhart was waiting in *Pigeon*'s well for the admiral. Colley spent just two minutes on the helo deck chatting with *Pigeon*'s skipper, Cmdr. Glidden. Then they descended the ladderway to the center well. Deckhart saluted, and the admiral returned his salute.

"Lieutenant Deckhart, good to see you again—as Chief Pilot now. Congratulations!"

"Thank you, Admiral. Please follow me."

Deckhart climbed the ladder, followed by the admiral, and then waited on the upper DSRV deck for him.

"Please precede me into the sphere and make yourself comfortable. I'll follow you and dog the hatch on my way down."

---

6 See *Operation White Out*, vol 4 in *The Mac McDowell Missions*.

Twenty minutes later, Deckhart announced he was free of the cradle, and *Teuthis* assumed operational control. Twenty-five minutes after that, *Mystic* locked into her *Teuthis* cradle, Chief Gamble equalized the skirt, and the engineering watch opened the hatches. I stood below the escape hatch, waiting. I signaled the watch who notified the COW.

"ComSubPac arriving," the 1MC announced. "ComSubPac arriving!"

"Good to see you, Mac," the admiral told me.

"Follow me, Sir," I said, and headed forward.

0600, TUESDAY, JUNE 20, 1989—*USS TEUTHIS*, SUBMERGED AT 300 FT, 150 NM OFF NORTH ISLAND NAVAL AIR STATION, SAN DIEGO, CALIFORNIA

I stepped into my cabin and held the door for the admiral. A small table with white linen set for four occupied most of the open deck space in the cabin. I indicated a chair, and Colley sat. I sat across from him.

"How have the exercises with *Pigeon* gone?" he asked without preamble.

I poured cups of joe and briefed him on our three days. "Borysko added a lot of excitement for the *Pigeon* crew," I added.

"Our adversaries should tag him with a transponder," Colley said with a smile. "You've got more speed this time. Think he can keep up?"

"He can sprint to thirty knots or so," I answered. "We'll just have to see."

A knock on the door, and the XO and Seth joined us, followed by the Chief Steward. There wasn't much room, but Chief Rivera managed to pour their coffees and refresh Colley's and mine.

"I'll take individual orders," Rivera said. "Eggs any style, bacon, sausage patties, and Chief Hurst's signature popovers."

"That's Cedric, with us from the *Halibut* days," I said.

With orders placed, the chief left us alone, saying, "I'll be back in ten minutes with your orders."

"While we wait, let me tell you what's going on, why all this secrecy," Colley said, taking a sip of joe. "On January nine, the Israeli Ambassador and their Mossad Director, along with then Secretary of

State George Shultz, visited President Reagan behind closed doors in the Oval Office. CIA Director Webster, incoming Secretary of State Baker, and President-elect George H.W. Bush were also present.

"Israeli Ambassador Moshe Arad introduced Mossad Director Shabtai Shavit, and asked him to brief their hosts. What Shavit told them created a cloud of secrecy and set in motion what you and *Teuthis* are about to undertake."

A knock on the door announced the arrival of breakfast. Neither Colley nor the XO had ever experienced Cedric's popovers. Judging by their expressions after their first bites, they were hooked.

"Amazing, simply amazing!" Colley said. "Why haven't I ever tasted these before?"

"Which is why," I answered, "I and my predecessors pulled every possible string to keep the chief onboard *Teuthis*." I grinned. "He retires after this run to take over the baking department of New York's largest hotel."

Between bites, Colley said, "In nineteen-seventy-nine, the Israelis and South Africans detonated a nuclear device on Prince Edward Island off South Africa. Since then, the Israelis have disassociated themselves from the South Africans, but have kept close tabs on their nuclear weapons program."

"I'm familiar with the Vela Incident," the XO said.

"It's the first time I've heard of it," Seth acknowledged.

I knew about it and said so.

"Well," Colley continued, "the message brought by the Israelis was that South Africa has been less than entirely honest with the international community, at least as to their nuclear weapon arsenal."

That got my attention. I leaned forward in anticipation.

"President de Klerk acknowledged six nuclear weapons, five deconstructed and one in the process of deconstruction. The Israelis tell us this is true, as far as it goes. They say the South Africans have a seventh device, a much smaller one—you could call it a suitcase nuke, that they intend to detonate on Prince Edward Island between August one and four." Colley paused and looked around the table. "Your job," he said, looking directly at me, "is to interdict their operation and prevent the detonation, with no one knowing you were there." The admiral sat back, quietly contemplating the three of us. He picked up a popover, buttered it, and filled it with jam. As he bit into it, he said, "These are marvelous."

Seth refilled our coffees, and we sat around the table thinking about what we had just heard. The admiral finished his coffee, wiped his mouth with his white linen napkin, and pushed back from the table. Seth called Chief Rivers by phone, and within a minute, the table and its fixings had been removed. Adm. Colley moved to the easy chair, the XO and Seth took the Naugahyde couch, and I turned my desk chair around to face them.

"You will pick up a contingent of Israeli Shayetet Thirteen commandos at Mare Harbour in the Falklands. Your job is to get them to Prince Edward Island in time, surreptitiously. Their job is to solve the problem—permanently." Colley placed his elbows on the easy chair arms and tented his fingers in front of him.

"On your way to the Falklands," he continued, "you will stop at the Taiwanese oil facility in Wagoner Inlet, Thurston Island. We believe the Taiwanese are purchasing enriched uranium from South Africa. My intel says the *Hăi Bào* will be there on or about July seven. Commander Zhang Min is still skipper. I trust him; he will be square with you. Find out what you can. And while you're there, check out the cable you ran to Smith Peak." He sat back, sipping a fresh cup of joe that Chief Rivera slipped in during a pause in our conversation. "When you are done at the Prince Edward Islands, return to Mare Harbour to drop off the Shayetet Thirteen unit, then return to Sub Base New London." He slid an envelope from an inner pocket. "Here are the details. Remember, Gentlemen, not a word of this to anyone. Lieutenant Beaumont, you are personally responsible for ensuring your quartermasters know *Teuthis's* location at all times, but remain unaware of your purpose."

"Are the Soviets aware of this?" I asked.

"Not officially. This has the tightest security trappings of anything I have seen in my career. Unofficially, someone may have leaked the details to Moscow. You've dealt with these bastards before. You may find yourself doing so again."

Colley stood, and we came to our feet in response. "Good luck, Gentlemen! This will be one tough assignment."

❋

"It's time you were on your way," Colley told me as we left my cabin.

On the 1MC, Seth announced, "Now, set DSRV ops, set DSRV ops."

On our way aft, we diverted through Dive Control so Colley could exchange a few words with Ham, who accompanied us from Control where he was JOOD, and his divers. They were, after all, the single most decorated group in the entire submarine force. The divers gathered around him.

"You fellows will have less to do on this mission than on previous ones," Colley told them, "but know that we in submarine command, Pacific and Atlantic, know who you are and what you have accomplished…*Hooyah*!"

Hooyahs! all around.

We went back up a level and continued aft. By the time we reached the after escape trunk, the *Mystic* crew was in place inside the DSRV, just waiting for Adm. Colley to join them.

Adm. Colley shook my hand. "Good luck, Mac. Show 'em how it's done!" He climbed up through the trunk into *Mystic*.

I went forward to Control, arriving just as Deckhart called, "*Teuthis*, this is *Mystic*. Request permission to unlatch."

The OOD, Waverly, responded, "This is *Teuthis*. Permission granted." And then, "*Pigeon*, this is *Teuthis*. When *Mystic* informs she is one-zero-zero yards off your position, assume operational control."

"This is *Pigeon*, Aye."

An hour and fifteen minutes later, *Mystic* latched down in her cradle over the after escape trunk, disgorged her crew, and the engineering watch secured both hatches. Waverly checked the time and glanced at me. I nodded.

"Sonar, Conn, mark your contacts."

"Conn, Sonar, just the *Pigeon*, bearing zero-zero-seven at one mile, Sir."

"Diving Officer, make your depth six-five feet—periscope depth. Quartermaster, prepare to take a SatNav fix when we reach periscope depth. Have the Nav ETs standing by to reset the SINS." The Submarine Inertial Navigation System sensed the motion of the sub and produced an accurate position, but needed updating from time to time.

The moment we reached periscope depth, the Nav ETs raised the SatNav mast while Waverly and I scanned around us with the Nav and Attack scopes.

Lining the Nav Scope on *Pigeon*, I said, "Mark, the *Pigeon*."

"Bearing zero-zero-seven," Ham said, reading the bearing from the scope bezel.

"Mark the *Pigeon*," Waverly said.

"Bearing zero-zero-seven," Ham said.

Five minutes later, Quartermaster Chief Henshaw announced, "Got the fix. It's a solid three-point."

Both Waverly and I dropped our scopes, and he glanced at me again. I nodded.

"Helmsman, ahead full, make turns for twenty knots. Left full rudder; come to new course one-seven-three. Quartermaster, water beneath the keel."

"One-two-zero-zero-zero feet, Sir."

"Diving Officer, make your depth three-zero-zero feet."

At last, we were underway on Mission Vela Redux.

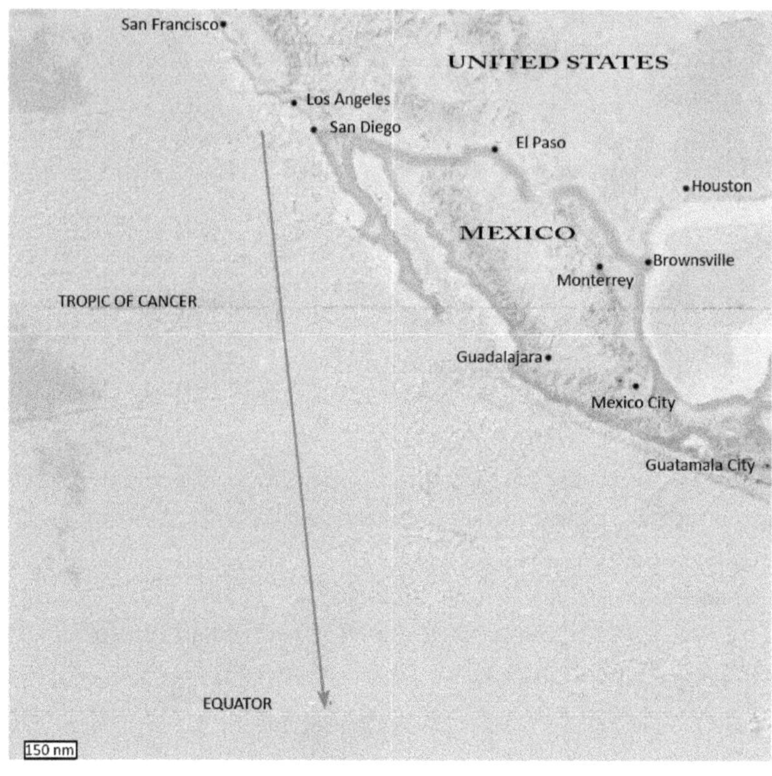

Track from 150 nm off North Island, San Diego, to Equator.

CHAPTER THREE—Transit to the Equator

0800, TUESDAY, JUNE 20, 1989—*USS TEUTHIS*, SUBMERGED AT 300 FT, TRACKING SOUTH 220 NM OFF BAJA CALIFORNIA

To keep the men alert, I had the XO surprise the crew with a flooding drill timed to overlap Waverly's and Seth's watch sections. I observed from the captain's chair in Control. The drill went well. The men were beginning to pull together as a team. That was essential for this mission to succeed. I stepped off the periscope stand over to Plot. Petty Officer Hank Bass was the watch quartermaster.

"Show me the chart," I told him.

48

He rolled back the vinyl-coated cloth cover that kept our position hidden from curious eyes.

"We're a hundred nautical miles down track," he said, and picked up a divider with two sharp steel points. He spanned the distance to the Baja California coast and measured the nautical miles on the latitude scale at the chart edge opposite our position. "Looks like two hundred nine miles off the coast. We passed Ensenada an hour ago." He moved his pencil down the track. "We'll pass two hundred ninety-five nautical miles west of Guadalupe in eleven hours." He pulled out a smaller-scale chart. It already had our track laid out. He followed the track with his pencil from Guadalupe to the equator. "It's seventeen hundred fifty nautical miles from Guadalupe to here." Bass smiled. He did a quick computation. "That's eighty-seven hours."

The kid was sharp, and he was showing off, but that was fine. He and his fellow quartermasters were the guys who would get us to our destination. They had help from some sophisticated equipment like the SINS that sensed direction, speed, and acceleration to maintain a real-time plot of ship's position. It had to be updated from time to time with SatNav fixes, but it was amazingly accurate.

✳

If you have read any of my previous mission accounts, you already know that submarining consists of long stretches of tedious boredom interrupted by moments of sheer panic. When we left *Pigeon* off San Diego, we entered one of those stretches. The Control Room crew always had something to do. Although the helm could be placed in automatic, usually we kept it in manual, so the helmsman kept busy making small course adjustments. In addition, he was responsible for the fairwater planes that he used to maintain ship's depth. The stern planesman was responsible for ship's angle or the bubble, as we call it. So, both planesmen kept busy making small changes in course and angle to keep the sub on the ordered course at the ordered depth. The Diving Officer supervised these activities, so he kept busy, too. The more experienced the planesmen were, the less the Diving Officer had to do.

The Chief of the Watch maintained ship's trim, a skill requiring a lot of finesse. Crew members walked along the sub's length, changing fore and aft ballast. People used water that moved from freshwater tanks to sewage tanks. Other fluids got moved from time to time. The COW kept the sub on an even keel, no matter what was going on. Technically, the Diving Officer supervised the COW, although usually Diving Officers were newer junior officers or newly minted chiefs just getting their feet wet in Control.

COW for this watch section was Senior Chief Fire Control Tech Ogden Winder, a wily older senior chief who had been around the block several times. The Diving Officer was Master Chief Ocean Tech Morris Jones, highly experienced and competent in his area of specialty, but a Diving Officer newbie.

The time was near 1700 and the Control Room watchstanders had settled into their watch routine, looking forward to getting relieved. Jones began to notice *Teuthis* getting a bit heavy by the bow.

"Chief of the Watch," he ordered, "move a thousand pounds of water aft."

"Thousand pounds of water aft, Sir," Winder said with a wide grin and carried out the order.

Still, *Teuthis* was heavy by the bow. "Move another thousand pounds aft, Senior Chief," Jones ordered.

Winder complied.

Instead of settling down to a zero bubble, *Teuthis* continued to nose down. Within five minutes, Jones had Winder move 10,000 pounds of water from the forward tanks to the aftermost available tanks. I stayed in Control in my captain's chair, enjoying the show.

While Jones tried to figure out what had gone wrong with his trimming efforts, the sound of singing floated up from the Crew's Mess. Then a stream of crew members marched up the stairwell in single file, singing "When the Saints go marching in," as they headed aft at a rapid trot.

That's when the light came on for Jones. He started laughing and addressed his COW.

"Hey, Senior Chief Winder, you fucking knew what was happening, didn't you? Move that ten thousand pounds back forward quickly. Try to get ahead of the crew as they move aft."

Winder complied, and the next thing we knew, *Teuthis* had a ten degree down-bubble.

"What happened?" Jones asked. "That water should have compensated for all the crew in the Engine Room."

He was about to move the water aft, when singing erupted from the Crew's Mess once more, and crew members again passed through Control from the Mess, to where they had returned on the deck below us as soon as they passed through Control the last time.

The XO had organized this little charade, arranging for as many crew members as possible to crowd into the Crew's Mess, allow time for Jones to compensate by moving water aft, and then pass through Control. But instead of going aft, they returned to the Crew's Mess again, fooling Jones into moving water the wrong direction.

It was great fun, and Master Chief Jones will likely never forget that incident.

✳

As we headed south of Baja, things got pretty intense for Sonar. Our track took us through the extended fishing grounds of Central America, Ecuador, and Peru. I took *Teuthis* down to 500 feet to avoid single lines and deep trawl nets.

Several hours after leaving Guadalupe behind, King called Control from Sonar. "Conn, Sonar, we are picking up what appear to be hundreds of vessels ahead off our port bow. We can distinguish at least a dozen large, deep draft fishing ships. My preliminary evaluation is they are Chinese factory ships. Beyond them are many smaller fishing vessels—too many to count. We won't designate any of these unless they become a problem."

I stepped into Sonar to see what was going on. King handed me a headset and motioned for a watchstander to scan around.

"Starting at the bow and scanning to the left," King said.

Initially, all I heard was rushing water over our nose, which is pretty intense at twenty knots. Then, through our own noise, I began to hear the unmistakable sound of four-bladed propellors pushing a laden ship along, but not just one set of props, many of them beating in and out of synch. I stuck my head out the door.

"Waverly, when is your next baffle clear?"

"In ten minutes, Captain."

"Do it now," I ordered.

Waverly flipped a coin and then ordered, "Helmsman, slow to one-third, make turns for five knots, right full rudder." He kept his eye on the ship's heading. At the appropriate moment, he ordered, "Shift your rudder to left full." As *Teuthis* rounded the second leg of the figure-eight Waverly had put the sub through, he looked at the section quartermaster, Chief Jubal Henshaw.

"One-seven-two, Sir," Henshaw said.

Waverly ordered, "Ease your rudder, come to course one-seven-two."

Seth had put us on a great circle course to Thurston Island, because it's the closest route. On the Mercator projection charts we used for navigation, great circle tracks are always curved paths except if we are running along the equator or where our destination is directly north or south of us. Steering a great circle course consists of a series of bothersome minor course changes. To make life easier without impacting the time of a journey, the Navigator normally divides the track into a bunch of ten or twenty nautical mile secants—a series of short, straight legs where the course doesn't change.

Our baffle-clearing maneuver allowed Sonar to check the ocean wedge encompassing our screw and engineering spaces. In this case, in addition to giving Sonar a look aft, Sonar got to examine more closely the fishing fleets ahead of us off our port side.

I had remained in Sonar during our baffle clear. King's people identified several more large vessels to the east and singled out the closest smaller vessels beyond them. A watchstander on the machine signaled King.

"I've got something, Senior Chief."

King put a headset earphone to his ear, listened, and asked, "What does it sound like?"

"A submerged diesel sub?"

"He's off the port bow. We have a good broadside view. Let's run an analysis." He picked up the mike. "Conn, Sonar, can you give me ten minutes on this course and speed? Looks like I got a submerged sub off the port bow. Designate Sierra-three-eight."

"You got it, Sonar," Waverly answered.

The signal was strong, and King had a decent analysis within eight minutes. He opened a large format, loose-leaf book, and flipped to a page.

"I got a match," he said.

I leaned over to look. King pointed to the open page.

"That's Peruvian submarine BAP Angamos (SS 31). She's a modern diesel sub built in Germany.

"Can she detect us?" I asked.

"She's a hundred miles out," King said. "Her sonar's not that good. It's a CSU-3 system. It has a twenty degree electronically steered beam good out to thirty miles passive and maybe ten active. At ultra-quiet, he couldn't hear us if we were a hundred yards distant."

"What about those big ships?" I asked. "Can you confirm they're factory vessels?"

"They're not in our catalog, so we'll get several recordings and tell the intel guys what we think."

We listened to the speakers for a minute.

"I think the Angamos is checking out what the factory ships are doing, what they're catching. I suspect they'll try to run through their nets, messing things up for them. Those Chinese factory ships are a huge drain on Peru's offshore resources," King mused.

This was interesting, but I had my schedule to think of. I stuck my head out the door again. "Waverly, get us back on track and speed."

1400, SATURDAY, JUNE 24, 1989—*USS TEUTHIS*, SUBMERGED AT 300 FT, AT THE EQUATOR 2, 140 NM WEST OF ECUADOR

While we were still several hours away from the equator, I got on the 1MC. "This is the captain. The navy has a long tradition of celebrating Crossing the Line—where Slimy Polliwogs become Trusted Shellbacks. The Executive Officer has informed me that nearly three-quarters of the crew are Trusty Shellbacks. *Teuthis* is on a tight schedule, but we have allowed three submerged hours to induct all our Slimy Pollywogs into King Neptune's realm of Trusted Shellbacks.

Commander Barnes will schedule the activities around the watchbill so that everyone can participate in the fun."

With that announcement, I set things in motion for an abbreviated, submerged crossing the line ceremony. To allow the greatest crew participation, I said I would take the Control watch, and I asked Bert to take the Engineering watch. Roger (the XO) and King as COB worked out the details. I overheard them talking in the Wardroom when I went in for a cup of joe.

King was saying, "You are coming up to speed as XO, and I know the crew better than anyone. Will you allow me to take the planning lead on this one?"

"That's fine by me, King," the XO said, "but I have a couple of provisos. One: I don't want anybody hurt or seriously embarrassed—keep a light, humorous touch. Watch out, especially for the divers. They'll take it as far as you let them. Ham will keep herd on them, but they will try to get away from him—especially for diver Pollywogs. Two: Remember that a commissioned Pollywog is still an officer. Have fun with the officer Pollywogs, but keep an element of respect for their commissions."

I left the Wardroom and didn't hear the rest of their conversation.

✳

King set up a two-hour ceremony in the Crew's Mess. Instead of a fully staged Pollywog Revolt the night before the ceremony which was the "official" approach to Crossing the Line, Pollywogs in each watch section before the ceremony conducted an abbreviated controlled chaos event during each watch, setting the stage for their ritual punishment during King Neptune's Court. The Court set up in the Crew's Mess was staged to cover the last hour of Section Two and the first hour of Section Three, so all non-watch-standers could participate.

The shenanigans during the previous watches had set the crew's mood. Shellbacks were eager to avenge their collective "humiliations" from the previous watches. Everyone understood it was in good fun, and everyone closely anticipated the coming two hours.

As Neptune's Court was about to get underway, I entered Control and joined Seth on the periscope stand. He briefed me on the status.

"Captain has the Deck and Conn," I announced.

Down the stairwell in the Crew's Mess, Roger convened his Court, consisting of Ham and King.

Neptune's Pollywog list held twenty-five names, each facing a punishment appropriate to his particular shenanigan. Under Neptune's supervision, Ham and King meted out spectacular punishments. They doused several Pollywogs with a substance that smelled terrible, five Pollywogs lost all their hair to a depilatory mix Doc concocted, and three received reverse mohawks. It was good fun, and nobody took serious offense, although the Mohawk recipients swore vengeance.

✺

The XO dissolved his Court, and shortly thereafter, Lt. Cmdr. Robert Borka, who ran Spec Ops, showed up to relieve me. He had in tow as his JOOD Chop, the Supply Officer, Lt. (jg) Roland Goff. Submarine Supply Officers are traditionally called Chop. I'm told this is because their collar device looks like a porkchop, although I don't put a lot of credence in this.

Chop was not required to qualify, but he wanted to. He showed up with a reverse Mohawk, a legacy of his transition from Slimy Polliwog to Trusted Shellback. He clearly wore his mangled hair as a badge of honor. I liked him—I liked him a lot.

As I stepped down from the periscope stand, Chop announced, "Lieutenant Goff has the Conn."

Borka followed with, "Commander Borka has the Deck."

"Take us up for a SatNav fix," I told Borka.

"Sonar, Conn, mark your contacts."

"Conn, Sonar, nothing, Sir, well at least nothing within a hundred miles."

Borka slowed us to five knots and let Chop take us up. Quartermaster Second-class Marcel Theron (whom everyone called Frenchy) got a solid fix. The SINS needed only a slight adjustment. This was a good sign for the rest of our mission.

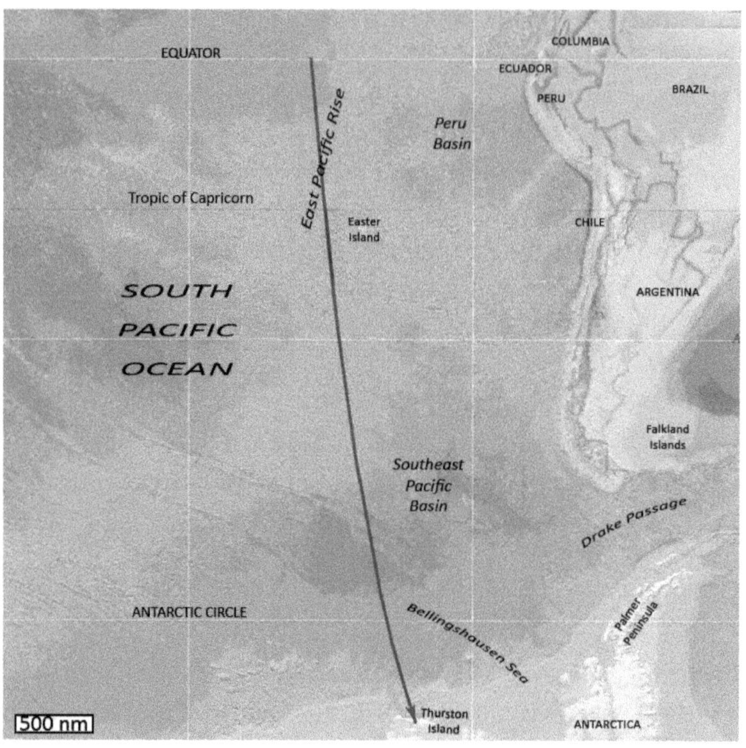

Track from the Equator, 2,140 nm off Ecuador, to Thurston Island.

CHAPTER FOUR—Transit from the Equator to Thurston Island

2000, SATURDAY, JUNE 24, 1989—*USS TEUTHIS*, SUBMERGED AT 300 FT, TRACKING SOUTH 2,140 NM OFF ECUADOR

The fleet of Ecuadoran and Peruvian fishing vessels and the Chinese factory ships that filled the waters off our port bow all the way to the South American coast kept this leg of our journey out of the boring category. King got a dozen excellent recordings of the Chinese vessels and two of Angamos, the Peruvian submarine monitoring the Chinese ships.

King approached his Division Officer, Lt. (jg) Jerry Plummer with a proposal. "If possible," he said, "we need several good, close-up recordings of Angamos. We can do this by diverting our path to the east. I checked with Juby—he says it will only add a day to our trek."

Not having been read into our full mission, Plummer passed the recommendation to his boss, Seth, the Operations Officer. Seth approached me.

"Captain, King wants to divert east to get some good recordings of Angamos. I understand why, but we have a really tight schedule. I don't know how long we will be in Wagoner Inlet, but I've learned that Yogi Berra was right: Everything takes longer than it does. As much as I'd like to get those recordings, I think we need to focus on Thurston right now."

I liked that. Seth brought his Sonar Officer's request to me, but included his own assessment of what that request might involve. And I agreed with him.

"We're going to leave those recordings for another sub to make," I told him. "I agree with your assessment. We need to keep our focus ahead of us without distractions."

King was disappointed, but he was too smart not to understand my reasons. With time as we moved ahead on our mission, he would not only come to understand, but agree wholeheartedly.

✳

The first place of interest beyond the ever-present fishing fleet was Easter Island, four days south of the equator and a mere 180 nautical miles east of our track.

I happened to be in Sonar when Jerry Plummer, the XO's JOOD, announced on the 1MC, "We are passing Easter Island about one hundred eighty nautical miles off our port side. This is the island with nearly a thousand stone heads, some weighing seventy-five tons. If you want to know more, you can check it out in the ship's library."

Second-class Petty Officer Frank Sportsman was the Sonar watch supervisor. He spoke up. "I read about Easter Island last week. It seems that when Polynesians arrived on the island around twelve hundred, there were at least a million trees, some of them a hundred feet tall.

They slashed and burned a lot for farms, and when it was all over, there wasn't a tree on the island. They couldn't even build canoes. It's a text-book example of people destroying their environment."

"There's some recent research from a couple of professors at University of Hawaii that points to a different explanation," I said. "You guys interested in hearing about it?"

Of course, they said, "Yes." I was the captain, after all. But I sensed they were genuinely interested in what I would say.

"Okay, here it goes. When the Polynesians arrived in twelve hundred, they did, indeed, find about a million trees. They cleared some areas for farms, but left most of the forest standing. In their reed canoes, they brought stowaways—Polynesian rats (Rattus exulans, the professors called them). The rodents' favorite food was tree nuts and young tree roots and shoots. The forests died alright, but the Polynesians didn't do it, Rattus exulans did.

"The natives didn't destroy their environment, the rats did. Over time, Rattus exulans became their major food source.

"So, there you have it, a modern spin on an old story." As I left Sonar, the watchstanders were debating whether they would eat rat.

0700, FRIDAY, JUNE 29, 1989—*USS TEUTHIS*, SUBMERGED AT 300 FT, TRACKING SOUTH 1,740 NM OFF CONCEPCIÓN, CHILE

Ham, as Waverly's JOOD, called me at 0700 the following morning, day eighteen since getting underway from Mare Island.

"We have a couple of submarine contacts off our port bow, Captain, Sierra-four-two and four-three."

"Thank you. I'll be in Sonar," I said.

King had the watch. As I stepped into Sonar, he was just looking up something in one of his oversize reference volumes.

"Whaddya have, King?" I asked.

"The entire Chilean submarine fleet, Captain, all two of them." King grinned broadly. "They're CS Simpson and CS Thomson, several miles apart. I think they're trying to herd three Chinese factory ships away from their fishing fleet. They're using active sonar." He paused. "Can we step out to the chart, Sir?"

"Juby," King said as we approached Plot to the right of the periscope stand, "please show the captain what we got."

Chief Henshaw already had rolled the chart cover back. King pointed to three markers on the chart several hundred miles away.

"These are the Chinese factory ships, Sierra-three-nine, four-zero, and four-one, and these," he pointed to two black markers, "are the Chilean subs." He measured their distance from shore with a pair of dividers. "They rarely venture this far out. They're about a thousand miles from home—here at Talcahuano, just west of Concepción."

"You said their entire sub fleet?" I asked.

"Yes, Sir, just the two. The Germans built them at the same ship-yard where they built the Peruvian subs. but I guess the Peruvians had more moolah."

"It's not as if either country has a significant maritime threat," I commented. "They can't detect us," I presume.

"No, Sir. Their range is about a hundred miles."

2200, SUNDAY, JULY 2, 1989—*USS TEUTHIS*, SUBMERGED AT 300 FT, TRACKING SOUTH 1,310 NM WEST OF CAPE HORN

We were about to enter the stormiest waters anywhere on planet Earth. The Antarctic Circumpolar Current forces itself past Thurston Island into Drake Passage's narrow gap, causing water to pile into mountainous waves. The prevailing West Wind Drift gives the water an additional push, but the East Wind Drift just to the south pushes the wave tops back against the current and wind. This results in tumultuous waves rising to a hundred feet or more that have sent many brave but foolhardy square-rig sailing captains to their watery graves over the last four and a half centuries.

A sub cannot survive on the surface in those kinds of seas. Waves that high affect things even to 600 and 700 feet below the surface. We were some 1,300 nautical miles west of Cape Horn, about to enter this realm of extreme watery chaos. Our path took us straight across Bellingshausen Sea that formed a deep basin just west of Drake Passage.

We hadn't updated the SINS since crossing the equator. I wanted everything working in our favor once we dipped below the sea ice off Thurston. I called Seth on the handset.

"Seth, I want you to get the best set of SatNav fixes possible before we enter Bellingshausen Sea, and have the Nav ETs tune the SINS to perfection."

"Already on it, Captain. We need to come to periscope depth in fifteen minutes to take advantage of a three-bird pass."

I called the OOD on the handset. "Robert, I want a SatNav fix before we enter Bellingshausen. I've already informed Seth. Let Roland do the op, since this will be his last chance for a while. Just watch him closely. When you're done, take us down to a thousand feet. I want to avoid the surface mess that almost certainly awaits us out there."

I came out to Control and took my seat in the captain's chair.

"Listen up, everybody," Borka said. "We're going to come to periscope depth to take a final SatNav fix before heading down under the ice." He looked at the Supply Officer. "You ready to take the Conn and get this fix?"

"Yes, Sir!"

"Lieutenant Goff has the Conn," Borka announced.

"I have the Conn," Chop said. "Sonar, Conn, mark your contacts."

"Conn, Sonar," it was Billy Farrell, "I have a clean scope."

"Helmsman, ahead one-third, turns for five knots. Diving Officer, make your depth six-five feet."

As we came to periscope depth, Roland took the Attack Scope, and I took the Nav. We saw nothing, but kept scanning for the few minutes it took Seth and Frenchy to take the fix.

"We got it," Seth announced. "Hardly any SINS adjustment at all."

"Quartermaster, water beneath the keel," Roland said.

"One-seven-zero-zero-zero feet, Sir."

"What's my course, Quartermaster?"

"One-seven-two, Sir."

"Helmsman, come left to new course one-seven-two. Ahead full, make turns for twenty knots. Diving Officer, fifteen degree down-bubble, come to depth one-zero-zero-zero feet smartly."

I had standing orders that whenever we cruised deeper than 500 feet at greater than ten knots, we were to use our forward-looking sonar. In general, this was to avoid uncharted seamounts, but down here, it also served to detect large icebergs.

As we passed 500 feet, Farrell called from Sonar. "Conn, Sonar, I have a new contact bearing two-seven-three. It has suppressed cavitation. It's a submerged sub, Sir. Designate Sierra-four-four."

Borka said quietly to Chop, "Slow to five knots and level off at six hundred feet."

"Diving Officer," Chop said, "Ease your bubble, come to new depth six-zero-zero feet. Helmsman, ahead one-third, turns for five knots."

Borka picked up the mike to Sonar. "Sonar, where is the layer?"

"Five-zero-zero feet, Sir. We picked up Sierra-four-four when we crossed the layer."

"Sonar, estimate her range."

"About a hundred miles, Sir. I've got her broad on the beam. I can get you much more in a few minutes."

I stepped into Sonar. "Can she detect us?" I asked.

"Depends, Captain, on who and what she is. We're getting data now."

Ferrell had called King, and he stepped into Sonar. "Whatcha got, Billy?"

Ferrell showed him.

"I'll be damned," King said quietly. "I'll be double damned."

"Well…" I said.

"Captain, remember that ChiCom four-oh-four that somebody torpedoed before we entered Kaohsiung City harbor? It was tagged *Chángzhēng* Four (Long March Four in English)." He turned to a page in a reference volume. "Here, this one."

"I certainly remember, King. What are you getting at?"

He showed me the waterfall chart of S-44. "They're virtually identical." King leaned back against the table. "This tells me that the ChiComs have another four-oh-four that we don't know about, and that's it, a hundred miles off our starboard beam."

"Do you have her course and speed yet?"

"Working on it, Sir."

King worked up some numbers and went out to Plot, where he laid out a track. I followed him.

"She's headed straight for Wagoner Inlet…or perhaps immediately north of there, where they think they lost *Chángzhēng Thirty-five*. She's doing thirty knots—flank speed. Blind as a bat. She has no idea we're here."

"She'll clear her baffles from time to time, of course," I said.

"No doubt," King said. "I'll have my watchstanders be on the lookout for that."

I went to Control and picked up the 1MC mike. "This is the captain. We have a hostile ChiCom sub off our starboard beam, and our tracks are converging. She seems to be going to the same place we are. She's doing flank, so she cannot detect us, but she will slow down periodically to check her baffles just like we do. When Sonar detects her baffle clear maneuver, well stop our screw and go to condition ultra-quiet. Be prepared to do this instantly. When you hear ultra-quiet, do your part immediately, and then lie down or sit down and stop moving about until the all clear. Turn off all music and keep talking to a whisper. Your lives depend on how well you do this."

The ChiCom sub was far enough off that it was unlikely she could detect us under the best of circumstances, but it never hurt to give the crew a sense of immediate participation. Besides, we knew nothing about this sub. For all I knew, she might have upgraded sonar that matched ours—then she could detect us from her range.

✳

"Conn, Sonar, Crazy Ivan, Crazy Ivan!"

It wasn't, really. Crazy Ivan was a Soviet baffle-clearing maneuver, but there was no harm in applying it to the ChiCom sub. The words got everybody's attention.

The JOOD, Chop, immediately ordered, "Helmsman, all stop. Chief of the Watch, set condition ultra-quiet."

The COW, Chief Panner, announced on the 1MC, "Now set condition ultra-quiet, set condition ultra-quiet."

Almost like magic, sounds throughout the ship stopped—fans, motors, pumps, blowers. People settled in place, maintaining total silence.

Had another sub been lurking a hundred yards from us, listening to our sounds, when we went to ultra-quiet, it would have been as if we had disappeared.

Teuthis drifted ahead as she coasted to a stop. The only sounds in Control were the quiet 400 Hz hum from the electronics and the soft sighing of the planes and rudder hydraulics; these were at a minimum, since the operators knew to minimize hydraulic sounds.

Ten minutes later, Sonar announced, "Sierra-four-four is back to flank."

Chop nodded to Potts. "Secure condition ultra-quiet," he announced on the 1MC.

Chop looked at the quartermaster. "Course still one-seven-two, Frenchy?" he asked.

"Yes, Sir. One-seven-two."

"Helmsman, ahead full, turns for twenty knots, steer one-seven-two." To the Diving Officer, he said, "Chief Oberst, mark your depth."

"One zero-zero-zero feet, Sir."

"Maintain that depth, Diving Officer."

Chop glanced at a display. "Forward sonar shows nothing," he told Borka. "Does it ever," he asked, "show anything, that is?"

"Wait till we're under solid sea ice," Borka answered.

"Or trying to stay inside a narrow canyon near the bottom," Theron added. "We made plenty use of it down here last time."

✳

It took three and a half days to transit Bellingshausen Sea. Our upward-looking ice sonar gave us a good image of the chaotic surface, but at a thousand feet, we did not even feel the effects. I had *Teuthis* on an hourly randomized baffle-clearing schedule, so the Control and Maneuvering watchstanders had something to do every hour. The ChiCom sub, we had decided to name her *Chángzhēng 4a*, seemed to be on a two- to three-hour baffle-clearing schedule. This gave the crew lots of practice going into and out of condition ultra-quiet. Every hour, our tracks converged so that our detection by *Chángzhēng 4a* became increasingly likely. When we reached the sea ice edge, I slowed us to ten knots and put us into a permanent semi ultra-quiet condition.

"Conn, Sonar, I have an intermittent surface contact bearing one-six-zero, range about fifty miles. I think she's at the ice edge. Appears to be DIW with engines running. Designate Sierra-four-five."

0600, THURSDAY, JULY 6, 1989—*USS TEUTHIS*, SUBMERGED AT 200 FT, ICE EDGE NORTH OF THURSTON ISLAND, ANTARCTICA

Once we passed under the ice edge at 200 feet and moved deeper into the ice-protected waters north of Thurston Island, we found ourselves shrouded in silence. Noise from broken shards of ice scraping against one another as the surrounding water moved dissipated as we moved deeper under the solid ice cover that extended out fifty miles or more from Thurston's shores.

As the ice sheet moved up and down with the water, from time to time sharp whip-like sounds resonated through the deep as long, narrow cracks split the surface ice. After this, the ice edges would grind together, shattering the shroud of silence until the edges once more welded together. Leopard Seals and Orca took advantage of these temporary polynyas to grab a breath of air that would last, hopefully, until the next crack opened up.

Our first task was to observe the cable we had laid during Operation White Out,[7] where it exited Potaka Inlet and transited up the glacier to Smith Peak, which meant we had to locate the inlet. During Operation White Out,[8] we placed a small, RTG-powered transponder at the head of Potaka Inlet. It would only respond to a coded signal at a specific frequency. We needed to be sufficiently close for the transponder to hear our signal, and sufficiently far out not to be blocked by the many protruding peninsulas.

The Sonar Officer, Jerry Plummer, worked with his boss, Seth, and with King and Chief Quartermaster Hershaw to position *Teuthis* by dead reckoning, using the SINS for the best chance of activating the transponder.

---

7 See *Operation White Out*, vol 4 in *The Mac McDowell Missions*.
8 See *Operation White Out*, vol 4 in *The Mac McDowell Missions*.

"We know this chart is accurate," Seth said, pointing to the chart on the table. "We corrected it on our last trip. We know the SINS is virtually spot on. We should be able to navigate right between Starr and Kearns Peninsulas."

I stood on one side of Plot, watching and listening. I was about to say something when Seth continued.

"We should be able to, but we won't. Jerry, you and King activate the transponder. Juby, you and I will plot the transponder to verify it shows up right where we put it last time. Then we'll lay out a track into Potaka."

That worked just fine for me. I felt no need to interfere. Seth was on top of it. I turned to King.

"Where is *Chángzhēng Four-alpha*?" I asked.

"Behind us. We lost her in the ice clutter. If she ventures under the ice, we'll pick her up again. Given her original heading, I think she's looking for *Chángzhēng Thirty-five*."

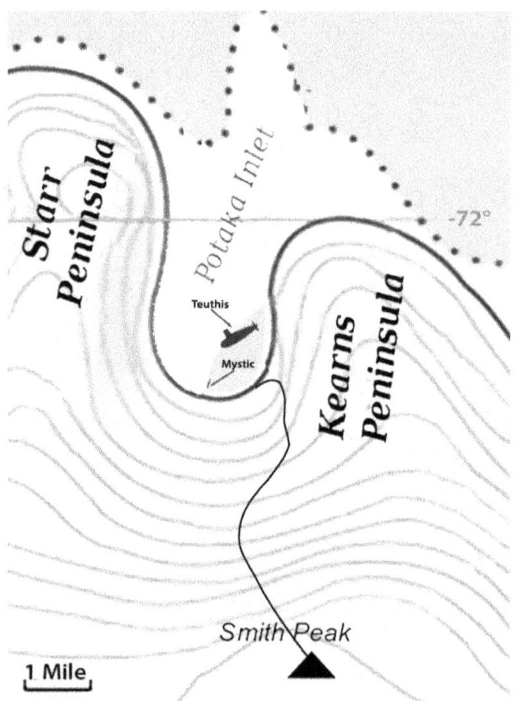

The Polynya in Potaka Inlet, Teuthis *location,* Mystic *mooring spot, and cable run to Smith Peak.*

CHAPTER FIVE—Potaka Inlet, Thurston Island

0200, FRIDAY, JULY 7, 1989—*USS TEUTHIS*, UNDER THE ICE, POTAKA INLET, THURSTON ISLAND, ANTARCTICA

With Plummer, his Sonar Officer, looking over his shoulder, King coded the signal into the sonar transmitter, selected the frequency, checked them twice, and turned to Plummer.

"You want to check them, Sir?"

"I do," Plummer said.

Had he just accepted King's settings without checking them, King would have scolded him privately. There is a reason U.S. Submarines make virtually no mistakes. Every important action is checked and double-checked. With nuclear weapons and reactors, there are even more redundancies. Mistakes are not tolerated.

After checking King's settings, Plummer said, "Let me send the signal. I've never done it before."

"Sure, Lieutenant. Lift this cover and depress the switch. But first we need the skipper's permission."

King called Control. "Conn, Sonar, request permission to transmit the activation signal."

"Stand by, Sonar."

Plummer opened Sonar's door. "I will transmit the signal. Then I'll return to Control," he told the XO, the OOD.

The XO called me, and I went to Sonar.

"Everybody ready?" King asked.

I nodded, and he said to Plummer, "Okay, Sir, send the signal."

On the speakers in Sonar, the transmission sounded like water being poured into a glass, virtually undetectable unless you knew what to listen for.

After several seconds, the sonar operator said, "I've got the transponder bearing one-six-zero." King, Plummer, and I stepped out to Plot where Quartermaster Jefferson Davis plotted the transponder position. "Right where it's supposed to be," he said, his black face grinning from ear to ear, "ten miles ahead of us at the end of the inlet."

"Let's do this slow and easy," I said to Barnes, "and let's hope that polynya is still there."

✳

The XO and Plummer moved *Teuthis* at five knots, 100 feet over the bottom, keeping a close eye on the forward and overhead sonars. The overhead ice sheet was virtually smooth, displaying occasional ridges where cracks had healed. Above the ice, a frigid winter sky harboring temperatures in the minus fifties, cloaked everything in winter darkness. Ahead was only the slowly seafloor. Plummer adjusted his depth to remain a hundred feet above the bottom.

We entered the inlet mouth and continued forward as the water shallowed. At two hours in, about 0500, the water both above and below us was 100 feet.

I took my seat in the captain's chair on the periscope stand. "Roger, launch *Mystic*, and send her ahead to look for the polynya. Last time, we bottomed at the polynya's north end. Let's try for that now."

"Jerry," the XO asked, "have you ever conducted DSRV ops?"

"No, Sir."

"You know what to do, right?"

"I do."

"Okay," Roger said, "you take it, and I'll keep you straight."

"Do you want to hover or bottom?" Plummer asked.

"We'll bottom soon enough anyway, so let's bottom," Roger told him, looking to me for confirmation.

"Good idea," I said.

"Chief of the Watch," Plummer ordered, "lower the skids to full extension, lower the outboards. Helmsman, all stop. Diving Officer, settle to the bottom easy."

The Diving Officer, Senior Chief Electronics Tech Rusty Jackson, guided his COW, Senior Chief Radioman Garth Walkman—Sparks to all, to a soft landing on the muddy bottom, using water brought into the sub's midsection tanks to bring us down.

While *Teuthis* settled, Plummer announced, "Prepare for DSRV ops, prepare for DSRV ops."

"Did you notify the pilots before your announcement?" Roger asked.

"Oops—nope," Plummer said as he got on the hook. "Sorry about that, Jim. We'll launch when you are ready."

I went to my cabin to handle some personal matters while they set up DSRV ops.

The *Mystic* crew had been doing nothing except reading, watching movies, eating, and sleeping for the seventeen days since leaving *Pigeon*. That's not entirely fair, since both Deckhart and Fortune stood several JOOD watches with Seth, but that was out of boredom more than anything else. Deckhart stuck his head in my cabin before heading aft.

"Captain, I can accommodate several off watchstanders if they want to take a ride. We're not in training mode now, and it might give crew members an interesting break."

"I like the idea, Jim," I said. "Please coordinate with the COB, and let the XO know what you're doing."

"Aye, Captain."

That was a good idea. I should have thought of it.

A few minutes later, the XO announced on the 1MC, "We will be conducting DSRV ops on and off for the next several days. Any crew member who wants to take a ride, let your Division Chiefs know. The COB will compile a list of names and missions. *Mystic* will take up to ten people on each mission. We'll try to accommodate everyone who wishes to ride her."

By the time *Mystic* was ready to get underway fifteen minutes later, ten sailors crowded around the after escape hatch, eager to climb into the little submarine. Chief Gamble moved them inside and explained the rules. He kept it simple.

"Find a seat in the Mid or Rescue Sphere and stay in your seat. When you move around, you upset the trim. Once we are underway, one at a time, raise your hand, and I'll take you to the Control Sphere so you can watch how the pilots actually fly this little bird."

"*Teuthis*, this is *Mystic*. Request permission to unlatch, over."

"This is *Teuthis*, stand by while we launch the Basketball, over."

"Dive, Control, launch the Basketball."

Down in Dive Control, which also served as the Spec Ops Center, Ocean Tech First-class Wally Dubbs opened the Basketball house outer door and launched the little tethered ROV. He adjusted the controls for a clear monochrome image and flipped the switch that sent the image to monitors throughout the sub.

As soon as the Basketball image appeared on the Control Room monitor, Plummer ordered, "Dive, move the Basketball so we can watch *Mystic* launch."

The scene on the monitor moved up the sub's starboard side and back to *Mystic*'s cradle.

Plummer called the DSRV. "*Mystic*, this is *Teuthis*, Permission granted to unlatch and launch *Mystic*, over."

Everyone who could locked eyes on a monitor. *Mystic* rose, moved to port, and quickly left the Basketball's field of view.

On the Secure Gertrude, Deckhart reported, "The bottom has shallowed to one hundred feet. I am turning left, looking for the polynya. Water has shallowed to sixty feet. I'm entering the polynya one mile from the end of the inlet. *Teuthis* can approach my position and comfortably bottom under open water at sixty feet."

That was good news. I called *Mystic*. "This is *Teuthis*. Work your way to the end of the polynya. See if you can moor where you did last time."

While *Mystic* made her way to the end of Potaka Inlet, under the XO's watchful eye, Plummer lifted us off the bottom and slowly moved us by outboard until he detected open water above us. He bottomed us in sixty-eight feet of water, pointing west. The bottom sloped down by the bow and starboard side.

"Chief of the Watch," Plummer ordered, "retract the after skids until you have a zero bubble. Then retract the port skids until we are on an even port to starboard plane."

When that was accomplished, Plummer said, "Now pump in five thousand pounds to the port tanks. That'll hold us down and keep the port side anchored."

0700, FRIDAY, JULY 7, 1989—*USS TEUTHIS*, BOTTOMED IN 65 FT, POTAKA INLET POLYNYA, THURSTON ISLAND, ANTARCTICA

Mystic reached the end of the polynya and reported back to *Teuthis* by Secure Gertrude.

"The polynya is skimmed over the entire end with a thin layer of ice. The winter-night sky is overcast and it's snowing. Wind is coming down off the glacier, blowing north over the inlet at least fifty knots. I discovered this by surfacing and opening the upper hatch for a few seconds. If you want to check things out here, you need to send a couple of insulated divers who can brave the water to climb out right at the polynya end."

"Roger that, *Mystic*. Return to *Teuthis*," Waverly responded.

By 1000, *Mystic* was latched down and had disgorged her passengers and crew. The two pilots came to the Wardroom, where Rivera served them steaming cups of hot chocolate. The XO and I joined them.

"It's amazing how cold it gets inside the DSRV when the outside water is twenty-seven degrees," Deckhart said. "I didn't measure the air temperature, but it's well below minus fifty. You wouldn't last five minutes out there without proper protection."

"For the divers," I said, "the warmest place is in the water. With their drysuits and rebreathers, they can spend three hours or more without discomfort. In the air, though, they will cool down rapidly." I checked the wall clock. "Ham is on watch right now. Roger, would you please have him join us?"

The XO called Control on the handset, and Ham joined us in less than a minute.

"Ham," I said, after he got a cup of joe, "we've got a severe weather situation outside, but we want to put eyeballs on the cable leaving the end of the polynya and heading up the glacier. I want a couple of your divers to suit up, ride *Mystic* in the water as far as possible, and then check out where the cable leaves the polynya."

"Shouldn't be a problem, Skipper. We did it last time."

"That was summer. It's the dead of winter now. Jim says it's minus fifty with gale winds coming off the glacier. Your divers will be fine in the water, but will rapidly lose core temperature on the ice." I looked at Ham earnestly. "Whom do you think for this one?"

"That's a no-brainer," Ham answered. "Ski and Jimmy—hands down."

"Why those two?" Roger asked.

I answered. "They have been with Ham and me since Ivy Bells. There are none better, and, speaking for myself, I trust them implicitly."

"Same for me," Ham added.

"Okay, then. Let's get this show on the road," Roger said, coming to his feet.

✳

Ski and Jimmy thought being selected for this op was the cat's meow. I went down to Dive Control to meet with them. They had suited up in their Unisuits with extra-heavy woolly bear undergarments, heavy socks and gloves, and woolen skullcaps.

"I've known you both for a long time," I told them. "We have depended on each other for our very lives on more than one occasion. This time, you are facing danger without me—at least, I won't be out there with you. I would if I could. You know that." They both nodded solemnly. "This is not a snatch and grab like we did in the Arctic. It's a simple look and report. I want no heroics, just good common sense. You know leopard seals prowl these waters. Remember what happened to Sergyi. I want you looking in both directions all the time. Carry your underwater assault weapons—your APSs—at the ready, and don't slack off, guys, not for a second.

"Ride the outside of *Mystic* for as long as possible. Then swim to the end of the Polynya, check out the cable, and return to *Mystic* ASAP. Done right, it's a piece of cake. You won't even have to exit the water."

"We got it, Mac…er, Captain. We won't let you down!" Ski was adamant. Jimmy just smiled and nodded.

"Okay, let's do it," Ham said, as the other divers crowded around. "Give us some room, guys," Ham yelled as we moved toward the ladder.

We headed to the after escape hatch where ten more sailors waited to participate. I could see that Ham was about to intervene, so I whispered to him, "It's okay, Ham. This is a big deal. Let them be part of the op. They'll tell sea stories about it twenty years from now." I grinned at him, and he grinned back.

Ten minutes later, *Mystic* had unlatched and was on her way to the end of the polynya with Ski and Jimmy hitching a ride.

When she reached shallow water at the end, and Deckhart was unwilling to brave pushing forward through the thin ice, he signaled the two divers. Ski and Jimmy each carried a bright helmet torch that shined through the clear water in the direction they looked, and an APS, locked and loaded, ready for instant action.

The water was crystal clear, like really deep water in the middle of the ocean. Their beams were invisible except where they impacted on the bottom or the nearby ice. Ski took the lead, moving forward slowly. Jimmy followed, facing back, APS at the ready.

They took fifteen minutes to reach the end. The glacier surface was four feet above them. It would be difficult to climb out, maybe impossible. They placed themselves against the edge, Ski facing forward and Jimmy facing back. They moved to the left, where Ski's memory said the cable exited the water. After ten minutes of slow progress, Ski found the cable. Comms through the water were not particularly good, so Ski pounded Jimmy's right arm and pointed to the cable. It had worked its way into the glacier edge and was solidly held.

Ski dropped down three feet and spoke slowly. "We need to verify the cable run is clear to the glacier," he said. "And we probably should clear it from this chunk of ice here," pointing to where the cable was ice encased.

Ski grabbed the cable and began using it as a climbing aid out of the water and up the four-foot edge. Jimmy kept his focus toward the polynya. He pointed his headlamp away from the edge.

There…he saw movement. He brought his APS to bear. A shadow slipped in and out of his light. It was big—not like an Orca, but it was big. Then, suddenly, it wasn't just a shadow anymore. It was all mouth and teeth, headed directly for him. He fired three rapid shots directly into the open maw. He saw the darts penetrate the roof of the leopard's mouth above its tongue. Still, it came. He fired several more shots—one struck a large open eye. That stopped the creature, and it thrashed to the surface and stopped moving.

On his belly on the ice, Ski saw the seal rise to the surface. He brought his APS to bear, just in case. Suddenly, without warning, the eleven-hundred-pound creature started thrashing again, emitted a thunderous roar, and dropped beneath the surface. Jimmy fired several more darts as the creature's teeth came within inches of ripping open his torso. Then it stopped moving for good.

Ski jumped into the water from the edge and inspected the leopard seal more closely. "He's dead, alright," Ski said over his suit comms. "The cable's fine topside. The ice anchor is holding it in place. We don't have to do anything."

"Are these things good eating?" Jimmy asked.

"They say the backstrap is especially tasty," Ski answered. "We got enough here for anyone that wants it."

Ski towed the leopard seal to *Mystic*, while Jimmy rode shotgun, looking for any more hungry critters. When they arrived alongside, Deckhart picked them up on his video camera. On the underwater coms, he said "What the hell is that?"

"A fucking big seal," Ski answered. "We're gonna tie this sucker alongside and take him to Cedric."

⁕

"Don't forget to give your camera to the photographer's mate," Ham said.

Ski gave a short, irritated answer, "Shit!"

"What do you mean, Shit!? Ham asked.

"I mean I got so involved with the leopard seal, I forgot to take any photos of the cable."

"Dammit, Ski! That's not like you."

"I don't tangle with an eleven-hundred-pound carnivore every day—but that's not an excuse. I fucked up!"

"You can say that again, sailor. I'll handle it, but be prepared to go out again."

"Let's use three divers this time, two to protect and one to take pretty pictures," Ski said with a wry grin.

Ham approached me, and I could tell by the look on his face that something was wrong. "Captain, in the chaotic milieu the leopard seal caused, nobody took photos of the cable. Ski and Jimmy are ready to go back. If you allow it, I want another diver with them, Petty Officer José Romero. José and Jimmy can protect Ski while he gets the photos."

I wasn't about to scold Ham. His divers were the best the navy had. Sometimes shit just happened. "Make sure all three are armed," I told Ham.

As before, I met the divers in Dive Control before they left. I gave them my pep talk, and then ended up with, "Remember, no heroics. You dealt with the leopard seal just fine, but we don't need any more seal meat. Cedric told me the entire Galley smells like seal. The messcooks hate you guys right now.

"Seriously," I added, "the polynya is too far from open water for a seal to get there on one breath. That means several leopard seals probably make this stretch of water their home. That means you three qualify as a meal—which you already found out. So, be extra vigilant now that we got this figured out." I grinned at them. "*Hooyah!*"

"*Hooyahs!*" back from all the divers.

I turned, climbed the ladder, and returned to Control.

1400, FRIDAY, JULY 7, 1989—MYSTIC, POTAKA INLET POLYNYA, THURSTON ISLAND, ANTARCTICA

The crew was delighted to have another chance to ride *Mystic*. This trip was much more efficient. Deckhart stopped the little DSRV a hundred feet from the four-foot ice wall at the end of the polynya. The three divers headed toward the wall, Ski in the lead, his headlamp piercing all the way to the wall, with Jimmy and José swimming backward, constantly scanning the water behind them for hungry leopard seals.

They reached the wall, and Ski climbed the cable to the ice, pushed from below by José. Ski's camera was a simple Olympus mechanical unit encased in a waterproof plastic shell, with no electronics at all—nothing to fail in the extreme cold. The case was good to about 300 feet.

The camera had thirty-six photos. Ski took several of the cable exiting the water onto the ice. He pointed his headlamp upslope and took several more of the cable run, although weather conditions made their usefulness problematic. He jumped back in the water and finished off the film roll with photos of the cable run to the edge and up the four-foot wall.

They turned to face into the polynya, preparing to return to *Mystic*, when a large black and white form blocked their beams. All three brought their APSs to bear, ready to fire if the creature got any closer.

"Hold your fire!" Ski said over their circuit. "Our darts will just tickle that thing."

It opened its mouth, displaying the remains of a leopard seal before swallowing it. Then it turned sideways, giving the divers a full view of its flank and dorsal fin.

"Look at that chunk missing from the back of the dorsal fin," Ski shouted into his mike. "That's Borysko. Hot damn! That's Borysko!" He swam toward the Orca and scratched its tongue when it opened its mouth. "We're safe as long as he's around," Ski said. "Say Hello! to Borysko."

Jimmy and José approached the thirty-foot long cetacean and cautiously scratched his tongue. Borysko reacted with an underwater squeal of delight.

Borysko accompanied them back to *Mystic* and then stayed with the DSRV back to *Teuthis*.

Ocean Tech Derrick Jensen had taken over the Basketball. When he saw Borysko, he flew the ROV right up to the cetacean's eye, giving the entire crew a sense of getting to know Borysko.

Ski gave his film to the photographer's mate and then met with a bunch of the crew in the Crew's Mess over the evening meal to tell them about their just concluded underwater adventure.

✳

At 1700, I joined the officers in the Wardroom for dinner. They talked almost exclusively about the dive and especially about Borysko's appearance.

"How did he find us?" Plummer wanted to know.

"That's a good question, Jerry," I said. "He was here with us on Operation White Out,[9] so he knew where we were going—at least he thought he did. He's got excellent hearing, and he knows how we sound."

Cobb spoke up. "How did he get from open water to the polynya? An Orca cannot hold its breath that long. Remember during Arctic Sting, after we passed through Fury and Hecla Strait into the Foxe Basin, how we broke holes in the ice every few miles so Borysko wouldn't drown, since he insisted on accompanying us? So, how did he get from open water to here?"

"You may recall," I said, "before that, we transited Victoria Strait and Larsen Sound. They were solid ice. But this was Borysko's home territory. He made his way around the solid ice, sticking to near-shore waters where he could find open water polynyas scattered among the fiords. I'm guessing when he hit the heavy sea ice north of Thurston, he ventured under the ice toward land until he had to turn back. Eventually, he would have stumbled on one of the peninsulas that stick out from Thurston Island, complete with patches of open water. Then he moved along shore until he found us."

"Borysko is one determined Orca," Waverly said. "He seems to be your special friend, Captain."

"Kate and I definitely bonded with him," I said, and then withdrew from the conversation as I thought about the girl I had lost.[10]

---

9 See *Operation White Out*, vol 4 in *The Mac McDowell Missions*.
10 See *Operation Arctic Sting*, vol 3 in *The Mac McDowell Missions*.

1900, FRIDAY, JULY 7, 1989—*USS TEUTHIS*, SUBMERGED AT 100 FT, TRACKING NORTH, POTAKA INLET, THURSTON ISLAND, ANTARCTICA

After dinner, Robert Borka and Roland Goff assumed the watch in Control. Chop had the Conn. He lifted us off the bottom by pumping out the ballast we had taken in to stay bottomed. He retracted the outboards and skids and brought us to periscope depth. Seth took a SatNav fix, and Radio received a dump of the latest traffic.

With the dump was ComSubPac's latest assessment of the Taiwanese oil operation in Wagoner Inlet. *Hǎi Bào* (Sea Leopard in English) was expected to make an appearance within a day. Furthermore, her commanding officer still was Tiong-hāu Zhang Min, the officer I had gotten to know and Adm. Colley's friend. I was looking forward to seeing him again.

Chop put us at seven knots and a hundred feet. Our objective was to round Starr Peninsula into Wagoner Inlet to investigate the Taiwanese oil operation we had discovered during Operation White Out.[11] We were in no particular hurry, but every hour we saved at this end, we could use at Prince Edward Island.

It would take us an hour and then some to round Starr Peninsula, to where we had a clear line of sight, so to speak, to the Taiwanese operation. Chop kept tight control of ship's position as we rounded Starr. He chose to follow the 200-foot contour. Because of the steep drop-off, we stayed relatively close to land. I watched him make sure we had at least a hundred feet of water between our sail and the ice cover while remaining about a hundred feet over the bottom. He didn't anguish over the problem, but seemed to handle it naturally, like a much more seasoned line officer. He was well on his way to earning his gold dolphins. This young officer would go far if he chose to remain in the Navy.

Around 2100, Chop called me on the handset. "Captain, we're clear of Starr Peninsula and have an open track to the Taiwanese oil operation."

---

11 See *Operation White Out*, vol 4 in *The Mac McDowell Missions*.

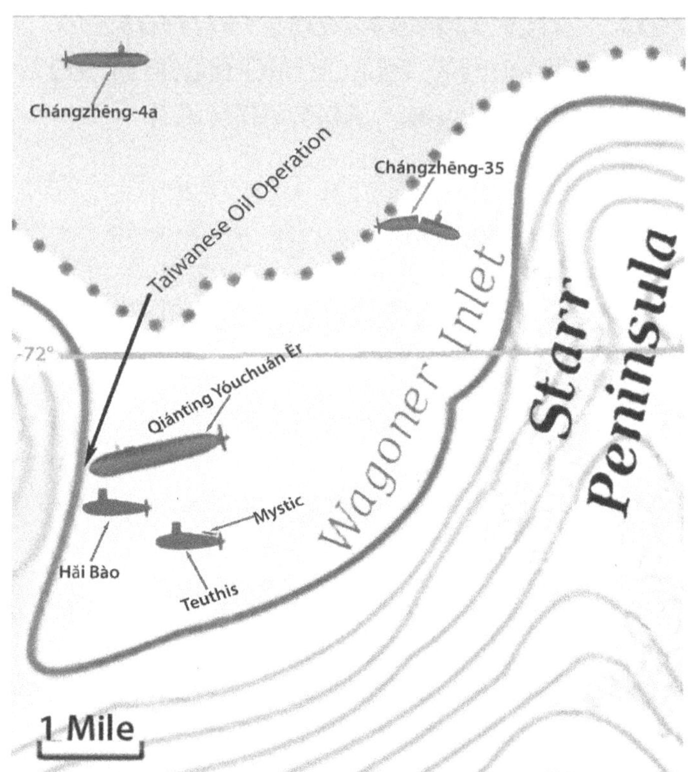

Wagoner Inlet, Teuthis *location with* Mystic,
Hǎi Bào, Chángzhēng 35 *wreck, and* Chángzhēng 4a.

CHAPTER SIX—*Hǎi Bào*

2300, FRIDAY, JULY 7, 1989—*USS TEUTHIS*, UNDER THE ICE, WAGONER INLET, THURSTON ISLAND, ANTARCTICA

Somewhere beyond the ice edge, we thought *Chángzhēng 4a* was searching for the \ wreck. We would worry about her when we detected her again. In the meantime, we crossed Wagoner and approached the oil operation, following the barely audible, rhythmic, low-frequency sound Sonar had acquired when we rounded Starr Peninsula—the oil pump at the oil extraction facility.

The watch changed as we neared the facility. The XO and Plummer took charge in the Control Room. The Sonar Officer assumed the Conn and brought *Teuthis* to a stop.

"Chief of the Watch, lower the outboards and maintain position. Diving Officer, keep us at five-zero feet above the bottom, zero trim, without using hovering." He called Dive Control on the handset. "Chief, launch the Basketball so we can see what we have out there."

As the Basketball moved forward on our starboard side, a girdered structure took shape on the screen, reaching from the top of a low, flat building to within 100 feet of the ice cover 150 feet overhead.

"That's the platform and girder structure for the drill," I said. "Once they had developed a steady crude flow, they no longer needed the drill, but there was no reason to dismantle the support structure." I told Wally, "Maneuver to your right and back off to show the tanker." As the shape emerged from the darkness, I said, "That's *Qiántǐng Yóuchuán Èr*, Submarine Tanker Two. It's the second autonomous drone tanker they built." I told Wally, "Follow *Qiántǐng Yóuchuán Èr* to your right until you reach the stern. Then follow the tubular structure forward until you reach the bow."

The tanker, hovering about fifty feet above the bottom, consisted of an elongated Zeppelin-shaped bladder, with the bottom half encased in a cradle built from hollow metal tubes. The cradle looked like a very large Stokes stretcher without the wire mesh between the rods and ribs. Several clamps along the bladder securely latched to the cradle. At the stern, upper and lower rudders and a pair of horizontal stern planes formed a cross when viewed from behind, with a large five-bladed propellor projecting from the center. An elevated platform level with the bladder upper surface attached to the cradle just forward of the rudder. An enclosed cylindrical structure that looked a lot like a DSRV occupied most of the platform. It held hydraulic pumps, generators, controllers, and a means for pulling air from the surface. The rudder and planes were hydraulically controlled, with the hydraulic control lines running inside the metal tubular structure from the stern planes forward 600 feet to the bow planes. Another cylindrical structure wrapped around the forward end of the propeller shaft. It contained electric motors that drove the shaft. The bladder nose connected to a twenty-foot-hose projecting horizontally from the drilling tower. It appeared very much like the mooring masts for the Zeppelins from the 1930s. An umbrella-like fixture covered a twenty-square-foot area above the junction of the hose and the bladder. It was partially filled with floating crude. As I watched, the crude disappeared down a smaller hose connected to a holding bladder at the base of the large bladder near the bow planes.

I instructed Wally, "Now follow the hose from the tanker bow to the wellhead."

The twenty-foot-long flexible hose had a nozzle controlled by small water jets. As we watched, it pulled out of the socket in the bladder nose and the small amount of released crude rose into the umbrella, where it was sucked into the holding bladder on the tanker.

"Conn Sonar, I have suppressed cavitation bearing three-five-zero. It's very quiet. I estimate it's a mile distant."

I reached for the Secure Gertrude mike. "*Hǎi Bào*, this is *Teuthis*, over."

When we first encountered *Hǎi Bào* during Operation White Out,[12] Captain Franken-Ester made a command decision to install a Secure Gertrude unit on *Hǎi Bào*. His decision was later confirmed by ComSubLant.

"This is *Hǎi Bào*. We did not expect you."

"This is *Teuthis*. We are passing through. Our intelligence said you would be here today, so we adjusted our progress to meet you. Over."

"This is Tiong-hāu Zhang Min. Am I speaking with Mac? Over."

"This is Mac. I am the new commanding officer of *Teuthis*. Over."

"Congratulations, Sir. Are you carrying *Mystic*? Over."

"We are. Over."

"*Qiántǐng Yóuchuán Èr* is about to commence her automated journey to Taiwan. We need to supervise this closely. After she departs, perhaps we can get together for a visit before I need to catch up with the tanker. Over."

"I will clear the area to give you room to maneuver. Call me when you have completed your op. Out."

---

12 See *Operation White Out*, vol 4 in *The Mac McDowell Missions*.

0400, SATURDAY, JULY 8, 1989—*USS TEUTHIS*, UNDER THE ICE, OIL FACILITY, WAGONER INLET, THURSTON ISLAND, ANTARCTICA

Although it's not always obvious, submarines cannot see their surroundings, at least not in the normal sense. Sonar gives one kind of picture—if passive sonar, we know something is out there, and we can gain additional information by using sophisticated analysis equipment, determining bearing, range, heading, and speed. If we have sufficient time, and the signal is sufficiently strong, we can actually identify the specific ship or submarine by comparing waterfall charts with our library of such charts. Detecting depth (for submarines) is always problematic. In active mode, we can get a precise range and bearing, and deduce course and speed, but that's it. In principle, with a high frequency tactical active sonar, we might even get a sense of the object's shape, but *Teuthis* certainly had nothing like that, and to my knowledge, neither did any other U.S. sub.

Teuthis had a distinct advantage over most other subs. We could launch the Basketball, a tethered ROV—remote operating vehicle—with spotlights and video cameras. It was only monochrome, but it could range more than a hundred yards from *Teuthis*, giving us a clear picture of what was actually out there. And then, of course, we had *Mystic*. The DSRV did have high frequency sonar that produced a high resolution image of objects in front of it, and it also had cameras with spotlights looking in all directions. *Mystic* was fully capable of making an up-close, detailed inspection of anything down to 5,000 feet.

Hǎi Bào was preoccupied with getting *Qiántǐng Yóuchuán Èr* underway. What they were doing was no mean undertaking. The tanker carried a million barrels of crude and was capable of driving itself all the way to Taiwan on its air independent propulsion (AIP) system. They had another AIP sub like *Hǎi Bào*, the *Hǎi Hǔ Jīng* (Sea Orca in English), whose job was to ensure the two tankers got there safely. Zhang Min had told me when we met that with two tankers and two subs, they were bringing a million barrels of crude to Taiwan every thirty days.

After two hours, during which I ran a flooding drill, Control received a Secure Gertrude call. "This is *Hǎi Bào*. We are ready to meet with you. Over."

I left my cabin for Control and took the mike. "This is *Teuthis*, Captain McDowell. I request that you bottom *Hǎi Bào* immediately south of the position occupied by your tanker, facing away from shore. When you are bottomed, inform me, and I will come alongside you with my port side to your starboard. Over."

"This is *Hǎi Bào*. That is satisfactory. Out."

✳

About two hours later, *Hǎi Bào* called. "This is *Hǎi Bào*. We are in position. Over."

"This is *Teuthis*. Roger," I answered. "We will bottom one hundred yards off your starboard side. We will notify you when we are in position. Out."

Waverly and Ham had the Control Room watch. Ham had reached the point where Waverly was letting him do virtually everything. This operation differed from what Ham had run before, but Ham had been on the underwater end of similar operations many times.

"Juby," Ham said to the Quartermaster of the Watch, "do you have a good position for the tanker's moored position?"

"I do."

"Okay; generate a track to one-five-zero yards south of that position. Give me a heading and time of arrival at five knots."

"Recommend course two-eight-zero. Time of arrival at five knots is one-eight minutes, Sir."

"Helmsman," Ham ordered, "ahead one-third, turns for five knots. Come to new course two-eight-zero. Diving Officer, set your depth for one-zero-zero feet above the bottom."

Once we were underway, Ham ordered his COW, "Senior Chief Dokey, lower the skids and the outboards. When extended, set the outboards to forward ahead full. Helmsman, as soon as soon as the COW has the outboards pointed in the right direction at full, come to all stop."

"Isn't that a rather complicated set of orders?" Waverly asked Ham.

Ham responded, "Chief of the Watch, repeat my orders to you."

"Lower outboards and skids. Set outboards to forward ahead full, Sir," Dokey answered.

"Helmsman," Ham said, "repeat your orders."

"When the COW says the outboards are forward ahead full, come to all stop, Sir."

Ham grinned at Waverly, but said nothing.

"Juby, how far to position?" Ham asked.

"Five-zero-zero yards, Sir. Recommend all stop on the outboards."

"Senior Chief Dokey, all stop, reverse the outboards."

He called Dive Control on the handset. Jensen answered. "Launch the Basketball," Ham said. On the 1MC, he said, "Prepare for DSRV ops. Prepare for DSRV ops."

"Diving Officer, bring the ship to three-zero feet above bottom. Do it with planes and ballast."

"Two-zero-zero yards to position," the quartermaster said.

"Chief of the Watch," Ham ordered, "ahead full, both outboards."

As *Teuthis* slowed, he said, "Ahead slow, Senior Chief." A minute later, "Stop the after outboard…"

"Two-five yards," the quartermaster reported.

"Stop the forward outboard," Ham said.

The Basketball monitor showed the bottom brightly lit and barely moving. "Diving Officer, bottom the sub."

On the monitor, as the skids settled into the muddy bottom, clouds of silt blocked the Basketball's view. Jensen moved the Basketball out of the cloud.

"Dive Control," Ham said, "bring the Basketball up over *Teuthis* and move off to our port to locate *Hǎi Bào*."

As the Basketball moved away from *Teuthis*, the monitor showed nothing. Then a dull glow appeared. And then a submarine sail appeared, with fairwater planes clearly visible.

I picked up the Secure Gertrude mike. "*Hǎi Bào*, this is *Teuthis*. I am bottomed one hundred yards off your starboard side. I am ready to commence DSRV ops. On your okay, I will send *Mystic* to dock with your after hatch. Over."

"This is *Hǎi Bào*. Roger. Stand by, over."

While we waited, Deckhart got *Mystic* ready to go. Just as he reported his crew was aboard and he was ready to unlatch, *Hǎi Bào* called back.

"This is *Hǎi Bào*. We are ready to receive *Mystic*, over."

"This is *Teuthis*. *Mystic* will be at your after hatch in fifteen minutes. Out."

✳

An hour later, my old friend Tiong-hāu Zhang Min sat in my cabin, sharing a cup of joe and catching up.

"Since their loss of *Chángzhēng Thirty-five*, the ChiComs have pretty much left our oil operation alone," he said.

"Whatever happened to the *Chángzhēng Thirty-five* crew and their commanding officer?" I asked.

"The entire surviving crew opted to remain in Taiwan. Most are serving in our navy. They're happy to be free. Their commander lives in the deepest, darkest hole Taiwan has. Execution is too good for him. He will live out his life in misery and remorse."

We spent more time talking about our lives, he about his family, while I was looking for a way to bring up a subject I needed to address. When Rivera brought a fresh pot of coffee, I took advantage of the break.

"Tell me, my friend, do you know anything about the 1980 secret agreement between Taiwan and South Africa to ship four thousand tons of refined uranium from South Africa to Taiwan?"

"Mac, you stumbled on our oil operation, and we have been most forthcoming with information regarding this program. This is how you knew *Hǎi Bào* would be here now. I would like to share with you what I know about Taiwan's nuclear program, but you know I cannot do that. Just one hundred nautical miles separate Taiwan from one of the world's superpowers—a country that has vowed to take over our country. We are independent, but it seems the world has bowed down to the Chinese Communist Party, withdrawing recognition of our independence. Right now, only South Africa recognizes our independence. When apartheid is abolished—as it should be!—most likely, South Africa will also pull its recognition. We are alone in the world. We need to do whatever is necessary to protect ourselves. Please respect this."

Just then, on the 1MC, "Captain to Control. Set condition ultra-quiet. Set condition ultra-quiet."

1200, SATURDAY, JULY 8, 1989—*USS TEUTHIS*, BOTTOMED, WAGONER INLET SOUTH END, THURSTON ISLAND, ANTARCTICA

Zhang Min and I hurried to Control where Seth, who had assumed the watch, told me, "We just detected *Chángzhēng Four-alpha*, due north at ten miles. Sonar thinks he just slipped beneath the ice edge."

I turned to Zhang Min. "I think you need to return to *Hǎi Bào*. As you heard, we just detected *Chángzhēng Four-alpha* within ten nautical miles. This is a new ChiCom sub, and we are uncertain of her capabilities. We think she is looking for *Chángzhēng Thirty-five*." I turned to the messenger, Seaman Ivan Tuxin. "Tux, get the XO, please."

Roger arrived, rubbing sleep from his eyes. "What's up, Captain?"

"We just reacquired *Chángzhēng Four-alpha*," I said. "Captain Zhang Min needs to return to *Hǎi Bào*. Please escort him aft." I turned to my friend. "Take care and be safe!" We shook hands.

Zhang Min and the XO headed aft. I went into Sonar. Petty Officer Harry Bass was Supervisor. He had called King for backup. I stuck my head out the door and beckoned to Seth.

"Ease us away from here to the middle of the inlet on the outboards and put us on the bottom, starboard side broad to the mouth of the inlet. Do it as quietly as possible."

I turned back to King. "Use this opportunity to get as much tape as possible on this guy."

I asked the messenger to get Waverly. When he entered Sonar, I said, "Confirm your torpedo load and verify current maintenance of the loaded fish. If we have to use one, I don't want a malfunction."

Part of condition ultra-quiet was to communicate by sound-powered phones throughout the ship. As Waverly left, one of the Sonar watchstander who had donned the sound-powered phone headset told me that all stations were manned. I returned to Control but left the Sonar Room door open. For anyone else, King would have closed it, but I guess he assumed I wanted quick access if needed, so he left it open.

Teuthis was eerily quiet as I took my seat on the periscope stand. I know I've described ultra-quiet before, but things were different here. We were in a cul-de-sac, and the only way out was guarded by a hostile modern, fast-attack sub. We were bottomed on our skids with 150 feet of water between the top of the sail and a twenty-foot-thick layer of ice. A friendly sub was somewhere off our starboard bow, trying to evade the hostile sub in her most stealthy manner. And between the friendly sub and the ice edge was an autonomous tanker carrying a million barrels of crude oil with sufficient intelligence to avoid the hostile sub, but with zero capability to defend herself. That was the friendly's job. Quiet hardly describes our situation. Fans and blowers were off; pumps and motors were shut down; all hydraulics were secured. The only sound was a soft 400 Hz hum from our fire-control electronics, and that couldn't penetrate the hull. No one moved anywhere unless it was vital, and then on tiptoe. You could have been a diver in the water five feet from the hull and you would have heard nothing.

I got up and walked quietly into Sonar. "What's *Four-alpha* doing?" I asked King.

"It looks like she is conducting a grid search pattern, Sir. That would be consistent with her being here to locate *Chángzhēng Thirty-five*. She probably is configured with a towed array, giving her a longer baseline for passive ranging. I'm guessing, however, that she's towing a sidescan sonar." He turned to a page in his reference volume. "This says she may or may not have a towed array. It wouldn't be that difficult to give her both."

"Give me your best estimate," I said.

"She's pulling a sidescan at a hundred meters—that's about one hundred nine yards, Sir. She's probably thirty meters above the bottom."

"Can she detect us?"

"I our present condition—no way. Her sidescan is most likely not an ROV—she has to pull it to get results. Her grid seems to be ten klicks long—six miles. It takes her a bit over an hour for each leg plus fifteen minutes to reverse course. She seems to be cutting a fifty-meter swath with each run—about fifty-five yards. She started at the ice edge and is moving in. I calculate it will take her at least a day to find *Chángzhēng Thirty-five*."

A sonar tech at the console raised his hand. "I've reacquired Sierra-four-five, that surface vessel we lost near the edge."

This was a complicated situation. On one hand, I needed to get to the Falklands to pick up the Shayetet 13 unit. I didn't want them spending a lot of time at the pub. On the other hand, a surface vessel hanging out at the ice edge near where *Chángzhēng 35* lay on the bottom, and a ChiCom sub surveying the bottom nearby, took immediate priority. I was beginning to suspect I was looking at a potential salvage situation. Odds on, the surface ship was a ChiCom diving support vessel.

"King, do you have anything on ChiCom diving support vessels?" I asked.

That sent him into the reference library. Several minutes later, he slapped his hand on the table. "Got you, you son of a bitch!" He waved me over. "Look at this, Captain."

He pointed to a page listing a 210 ft vessel with an arched a-frame crane on the stern. "This is the *Kan-Cha 2*, a ChiCom diving support vessel. They built it in seventy-nine, but their domestic saturation diving system had major problems. Eventually, they installed a French Comex system good to three hundred meters—nine hundred eighty-four feet. So basically, it's a thousand-foot system. If you can get *Teuthis* closer, I can verify that Sierra-four-five is this guy."

✳

Moving closer to S-45 also meant moving closer to *Chángzhēng 4a* with her advanced sonar detection systems. But 4a was preoccupied. I had no evidence that she had detected *Teuthis* or *Hǎi Bào*, or even *Qiántǐng Yóuchuán Èr* for that matter. I made a decision.

We were three hours into Borka's watch. *Teuthis* was positioned athwart Wagoner Inlet near the end, pointed west. I waved Borka and Chop to join me at Plot. Petty Officer Theron made room for us. He had marked off the search grid *Chángzhēng 4a* was following, and placed a marker at the presumed position of S-45.

I pointed to a spot three nautical miles from *Chángzhēng 4a*'s current position. "I want to move *Teuthis* here without reducing our level of quiet. Lift us off the bottom twenty feet, and move us horizontally with the outboards."

Borka looked at me quizzically.

"We need to maintain our present aspect so King can continue to get the best possible tracking info on *Four-alpha*." I grinned at Borka.

"What about the outboard noise?" Borka asked.

"Keep them at low power. And stay close to the bottom," I told him. "Work closely with Sonar. If Billy's people detect any change in *Four-alpha*'s behavior, any change at all, stop and settle to the bottom."

"I think it's risky, Captain," Borka said. "What's the pay-off?"

"I agree, it's risky, but not excessively so. I am convinced that Sierra-Forty-five is a saturation diving support vessel. There can be only one reason for her presence. They intend to locate and salvage whatever they can from *Chángzhēng Thirty-five*. If they locate the wreck, they will send divers to investigate. The divers will determine that *Chángzhēng Thirty-five* was torpedoed. That might very well initiate a ChiCom attack on Taiwan, and that could be the start of World War Three." I looked at each of the three men at Plot. "Yes, it's risky, but it's definitely worth the risk."

0000, SUNDAY, JULY 9, 1989—*USS TEUTHIS*, UNDER THE ICE, WAGONER INLET, THURSTON ISLAND, ANTARCTICA

Midnight arrived, bringing in day twenty-eight since leaving Mare Island. *Teuthis* had moved northward nearly two nautical miles, with no indication that *Chángzhēng 4a* was aware of our presence creeping along the bottom just a few nautical miles south of her search grid.

Using his sound-powered phone talker, Sonar Supervisor Frank Sportsman informed the XO, who had assumed the Control Room watch with Jerry Plummer, that they had just detected the incoming submarine tanker *Qiántǐng Yóuchuán Yī*.

I stepped into Sonar. "Keep an eye out for a sub similar to *Hǎi Bào*. She will have detected *Chángzhēng Four-alpha*, and will be on ultra-quiet. She will be unaware of us."

We continued in this mode for another two hours. *Qiántǐng Yóuchuán Yī* arrived at the oil facility and, presumably, was sucking crude. Sonar thought they might have intermittently detected the other Taiwanese sub, *Hǎi Hǔ Jīng*, but they lacked sufficient data to get a track. And we continued inching toward the ChiCom search grid.

I was taking a few minutes of shut-eye in my cabin when the messenger entered and tapped my shoulder. "You are needed in Sonar, Captain."

Frank Sportsman was Watch Supervisor, and King sat quietly against the table at the back.

"Captain," Sportsman said, "I think *Chángzhēng Four-alpha* just located *Chángzhēng* Three-five."

"She's DIW," King added, "right over the wreck. I don't think there's any doubt."

I stepped out to Plot. "How far are we from *Chángzhēng Thirty-five?*" I asked Quartermaster Davis.

"One point eight nautical miles, Sir," he answered without even referring to his chart.

I looked over to the XO. "Get us within a nautical mile of the wreck and then bottom *Teuthis*. Maintain absolute silence."

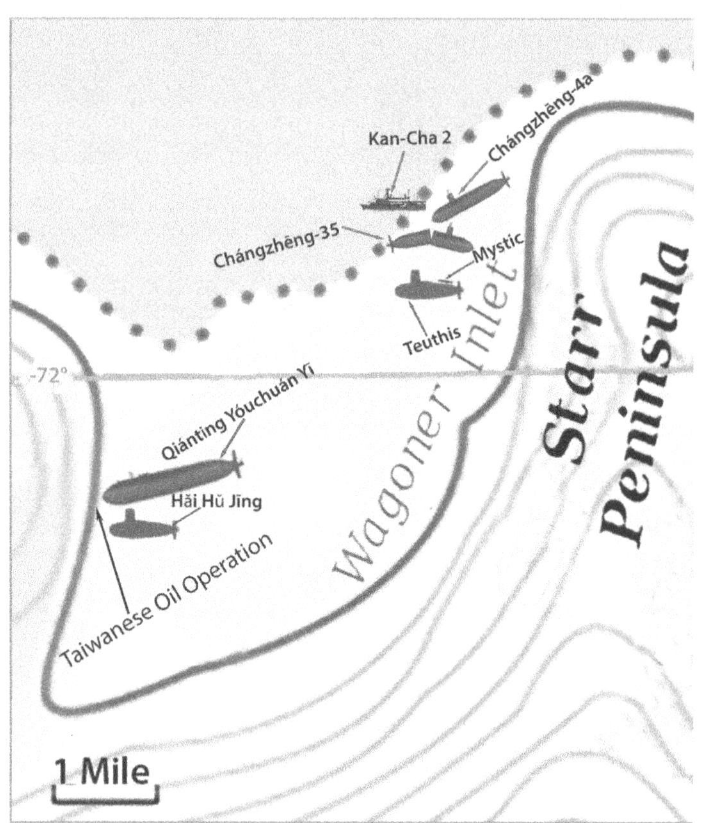

Wagoner Inlet, Teuthis *location with* Mystic, Qiántǐng Yóuchuán Yī, Hǎi Hǔ Jīng, Chángzhēng 35 *wreck*, Chángzhēng 4a, *and* Kan-Cha 2.

CHAPTER SEVEN—*Chángzhēng 35*

0400, SUNDAY, JULY 9, 1989—*USS TEUTHIS*, BOTTOMED IN 720 FT, 0.9 NM SOUTH OF *CHÁNGZHĒNG 35*, WAGONER INLET, THURSTON ISLAND, ANTARCTICA

As we moved into day twenty-eight since leaving Mare Island, *Teuthis* was bottomed on skids in 720 feet of water a scant 1,800 yards south of the *Chángzhēng 35* wreck. *Chángzhēng 4a* hung out near the ice edge, close to what we now knew with certainty was the ChiCom diving support vessel *Kan-Cha 2*.

I called Ham to my cabin. "It looks like ChiCom divers will attempt to check out *Chángzhēng Thirty-five*. We need to try and stop that without revealing our presence." I smiled at him. "What are your thoughts?"

"They have no idea we are here, right?"

"With near certainty," I answered. "As I am sure you remember, back in the Sea of Okhotsk, when the divers were retrieving missile parts from the bottom, they found themselves confronting Soviet divers on the bottom. So far as we know, they left the scene without knowing about our presence."[13]

"But we had to kill all but Sergyi," Ham said. "My guys were not happy about that. They had no problem protecting their lives, but taking out fellow divers didn't sit well with them."

"You know I understand that, Ham. And. I'm alive because of Sergyi." I sighed, knowing a difficult path lay ahead of us.

"Those ChiCom divers will just be doing their jobs," Ham said.

"If they surface knowing about our presence," I said, "they will remain until they have all the answers. We may be forced to sink their support ship and possibly even *Chángzhēng Four-alpha*. That will result in the deaths of both crews and the divers."

"I know you're right, Mac," Ham said, dropping protocol and relying on our close friendship.

I let it go.

"I'll start pressing the guys down. I'd like to be off the watch list for the duration of the dive ops.

"I'll let the XO know," I said.

0700, SUNDAY, JULY 9, 1989—*USS TEUTHIS*, BOTTOMED IN 720 FT, 0.5 NM SOUTH OF *CHÁNGZHĒNG 35*, WAGONER INLET, THURSTON ISLAND, ANTARCTICA

After Ham left, I went out to Control to speak with Waverly. Control was quiet, but the watchstanders were alert. Everyone knew how critical our situation was.

"Waverly," I said, "I want you to move *Teuthis* eight hundred yards closer to *Chángzhēng Thirty-five*. Stay far enough over the bottom so the skids do not scrape. Take your time. Stealth is what we're after."

---

13 See *Operation Ivy Bells*, vol 1 in *The Mac McDowell Missions*.

"Chief of the Watch," Waverly said. "We're gonna test your skills to the limit. Pressurize the Negative Tank very slowly…so slowly that you produce no noise. When Negative is 100 psi over ambient, start blowing water to sea, but very slowly with zero noise. Hold *Teuthis* at five feet over bottom. Then move starboard on the outboards, slowly and noiselessly. Juby will tell you when to stop."

I entered Sonar where King was Supervisor. "King, you need to monitor not only what's out there, but us, too. We are so close to these guys we cannot afford to make any noise." I looked at the sound-powered phone talker. "Tell everyone from the captain to check everything again for anything loose, and remind everybody to remain seated or in their racks. If they must move, do so in absolute silence."

It took Waverly an hour to move *Teuthis* 800 yards. When the quartermaster indicated he had reached the desired location, Senior Chief Dokey stopped the outboards and slowly released pressure from Negative, allowing water to fill the tank. As *Teuthis* settled on her skids, suddenly, the after port side dropped accompanied by a sharp crack!

King stuck his head out of Sonar. "Whatever that was," he said in a loud whisper, "was heard for miles."

I had returned to my cabin during the slow transit, but the loud Crack! brought me out to Control in a hurry. "What do we know?" I asked.

"Nothing yet, Captain. I'm launching the Basketball to investigate."

"King," I asked, "has *Kan-Cha Two* put her PTC, her Personnel Transfer Capsule, in the water yet?"

"I hear deck noises, but there's a lot of brash ice masking. I think they're still setting up on deck."

They're probably pressing down their divers, I thought to myself. *They're in no hurry. That'll take three hours or more.*

I said to the sound-powered phone talker, "Ask Warrant Officer Comstock to come to Control."

"Any reaction to the sound?" I asked King.

"Not that I can tell, Sir. *Chángzhēng Four-alpha* has not moved, same everything. Her sonar people have got to be listening intensely for any repetition. Maybe they thought it was a large table of ice splitting. I think we got lucky."

It showed the after port on the deep side of a five-foot ledge. The hydraulic mechanism appeared to be okay. Derrick moved the Basketball to the after outboard. The propellor and shroud were broken off, lying on the bottom a foot away.

"Senior Chief Dokey, try to raise the after outboard."

It moved, but emitted a squeal. He stopped immediately.

"Let me know if *Chángzhēng Four-alpha* reacts to that," I said to King.

I turned to Waverly. "You've got your work cut out for you," I said. "Come up with a plan for getting us north of that ledge. Brief me as soon as you have one."

I had a good idea what we could do, but this was not only a confirmation of my thinking, but a good test of Waverly's ingenuity. I wanted to see what he came up with.

A few minutes later, Waverly went to Plot and beckoned me to join him. I overlooked the lapse in protocol and went to the chart table. Waverly took a blank paper, sketched the outline of *Teuthis*, and explained his plan. It was close to mine, so I told him to proceed.

✳

Waverly set his plan into motion at 1015.

"Dokey, like you did with Negative, use air to remove water from the starboard after trim tank. Remove only enough water to bring *Teuthis* back on an even keel. Then push water out of Negative until *Teuthis* is afloat by four feet. Let me know when you're there."

Waverly remained on the periscope stand, even though I am certain his every instinct was to look over Senior Chief Dokey's shoulder.

He said to his sound-powered phone talker, "Tell everyone to remain in place, not to move until I give the go-ahead."

In about ten minutes, *Teuthis* lifted off the bottom three feet and hovered. "Senior Chief, using the forward outboard, push the bow to port."

On the Basketball monitor, we all watched the stern move slowly to starboard as *Teuthis* pivoted around her center. When the after port skid was well clear of the ledge, Waverly said, "Okay, Senior Chief, bring water into the after port trim tank until the skid is firmly pressed to the bottom."

That took another five minutes.

"Raise the after starboard skid," Waverly said.

As the COW did, *Teuthis* began to list to the after starboard quarter.

"Remove water from the after starboard trim tank," Waverly ordered.

Once *Teuthis* was balanced on the after port skid, Waverly said, "Senior Chief, with the forward outboard, push the bow to starboard."

Teuthis swung until she was parallel to the ledge and about ten yards north.

"Lower the after starboard skid and flood the forward and after trim tanks," Waverly ordered.

"Nice," I told him. "Now let's put divers in the water to see what we need to do."

1200, SUNDAY, JULY 9, 1989—*USS TEUTHIS*, BOTTOMED IN 720 FT, 990 YDS SOUTH OF *CHÁNGZHĒNG 35*, WAGONER INLET, THURSTON ISLAND, ANTARCTICA

At noon, Seth assumed the watch as diving ops were about to commence. *Teuthis* was still at extreme ultra-quiet. The smoking lamp was out, and the heaters had been shut down for several hours. The air was getting noticeably chilly, and the Atmosphere Tech notified me that atmospheric oxygen level had dropped below 20 percent, and carbon dioxide was rising.

Over the sound-powered phone system, I asked Bert to come to Control. When he arrived, I discussed the situation with him and Seth, the OOD.

"Bleed in oxygen to bring us back to twenty-one percent." I said to Bert. "We can't risk running the scrubber to lower the carbon dioxide level. Can you spread lithium hydroxide in each compartment to give us some relief from carbon dioxide?"

"That's not going to help much," Bert said. "We really need to push air through packed lithium hydroxide pellets to remove carbon dioxide effectively." He gave me a rueful smile. "We're not in trouble yet. I'll put my guys on it. We'll come up with something that will be quiet and give us some relief."

✳

In anticipation of diving ops on the bottom, Ham had already pressed down all six divers, leaving Chief Bill Fisher at the console to run the dive. He put Ski and Jimmy out through the Port Lock on umbilicals to investigate the problem. José tended them from inside the Port Lock. I went to Dive Control to be close to the action. Although both divers were breathing a helium-oxygen mix with a trace of argon that would make their speech nearly unintelligible, their voices came through the descrambler with little distortion. They dropped through the hatch and headed aft.

Before they arrived at the after outboard, Ski shouted, "It's Borysko. Would you believe it? He found us again."

Derrick moved the Basketball close to get a good view. The monitor filled with Orca tongue and teeth as Borysko stuck out his tongue for Ski to scratch. Jimmy got in on the action as well, and then Bill told them, "Focus, guys."

They arrived at the outboard. Ski picked up the shrouded propeller. He held it up to the Basketball. "See, the shaft broke here." He probed into the outboard well with his light. "Looks like the descent shaft is slightly bent." Ski pulled his head from the well. "We need to disconnect the outboard from the shaft and bring it inside. The snipes can decide whether to repair or replace it. I think we can straighten the shaft with a come along. We'll need to weld an eyebolt to the hull to attach the come along." He swam around the damaged outboard. "Jimmy, would you return to the hatch and get a tool roll, two lift bags, and a hundred-pound counterweight?"

Jimmy disappeared from the monitor. Five minutes later, he returned with the tools and bags, with the counterweight suspended beneath a partially inflated bag. Ski grabbed the proper wrench and worked at loosening the first of five bolts holding the outboard to the shaft. After grunting for a minute, Ski said, "Can't loosen it. I need a hammer wrench."

I was wearing a headset with a boom mike to monitor the conversations. "This is the captain," I said, "a hammer wrench is too risky. You need to think of something less noisy."

Ski was silent for a minute. "Ham, we got WD-forty? Not spray—that won't work out here. In a can or bottle?"

"Let me check with the Engineer," Ham answered. "Stand by."

Ham got Bert on the sound-powered circuit. "Do your guys have non-spray WD-forty? In a squirt can?"

"Matter of fact," Bert said. "One of my guys will bring you a couple of cans."

When they arrived, Ham locked them into the port chamber where José Romero was tending the divers in the water.

"Come and get the WD-forty," Ham told Ski.

The can had a nozzle that would emit drops or even a fine stream when the can was squeezed. Ski squeezed himself into the well and applied a generous amount of WD-40 to each bolt.

"Now we wait," Ski said to no one in particular. "We're going to play with Borysko for a few minutes while this stuff does its magic."

✳

After fifteen minutes of carousing with the six-ton cetacean, Ski moved off the monitor and pulled Jimmy with him. "Let's try them now," he said.

He slipped the wrench around the bolt head, braced his fins against the outboard, and pulled. After a few seconds, he broke the tension, and then attacked the next bolt. When all five were loose, he removed them one by one and handed them to Jimmy, who dropped them into a suit pocket. They each picked up a lift bag from the bottom. Ski attached his through a bolt hole where he had just removed the nuts. Jimmy attached his to the broken shaft at the other end. Then they wrapped a piece of line around the center of the outboard and attached it to the counterweight. They each released a bit of gas into the bags until the bags gently lifted the outboard off the bottom. They lifted it sufficiently high, so the counterweight was suspended just above the bottom. Because there wasn't enough room under the keel for the lift-bag-suspended outboard and stabilizing counterweight, they swam the outboard along *Teuthis*'s port side until they reached the hatch.

José had rigged a hoist over the hatch in the Port Lock. He handed Jimmy a length of cable with a loop at each end. Jimmy passed a loop through a bolt hole and then through itself, cinching it tight. Ski passed the other loop around the broken shaft, and then passed the cable over the hoist hook. As José took a strain on the hoist, Ski dropped the counterweight and tipped the outboard so the upper end with the cable through the bolt hole rose into the chamber.

Once the outboard was entirely inside the Port Lock, Ski closed the lower hatch, and the three divers moved into the central lock, the main Deck Decompression Chamber (DDC) and sealed the door into the Port Lock. Bill lowered the pressure in the Port Lock. When it reached one atmosphere, two snipes opened the upper hatch, lowered a hoist, and pulled the outboard out of the lock. They slid it on an overhead rail back to the machinery space, where they would see if it could be repaired.

✳

Bill had the divers open the deck hatch in the Main DDC. As soon as the hatch opened inward, Borysko placed a large eye just below the opening and let out a loud whistle. Ski reached down and pushed. He could not have moved the six-ton cetacean, but Borysko responded to the pressure and moved from the opening.

Ski entered the water, wearing a welding faceplate tipped back over his Kirby-Morgan, He trailed an underwater welding torch and carried several welding rods. José joined him carrying the come along, while Jimmy remained in the DDC tending their umbilicals. As they swam back to the outboard well, Borysko paced them on *Teuthis*'s starboard side before darting to the surface for air. The Basketball followed them down the port side.

When they arrived, José pointed his light at the edge of the well opposite the direction of the bend in the shaft. Ski smeared underwater adhesive on the bolt plate and pressed it against the well edge. He placed a consumable rod in the electrode holder and held it against the junction of the bolt plate and hull. He pulled his faceplate down and pulled the trigger to release the nitrogen flow around the rod and strike the arc.

Underwater welding differs from dry welding. Welding can be considered the melting and fusing of two metal pieces facilitated by a metal rod coated with flux. But this only works in air. Underwater, you have to generate a bubble surrounding the weld area. Since gas bubbles rise in water, you have to supply a continuous stream of an inert gas like nitrogen to maintain a dry bubble. Becoming an efficient underwater welder takes a lot of practice. Even so, an underwater weld typically is not as strong as a dry weld.

Ski had formal underwater welding training and a lot of experience. In ten minutes, he had firmly welded the eyebolt in place. Borysko was a bit put off by the loud rumble and bright light of the arc, and kept his distance during the welding process. Once Ski finished, he came in for a close-up inspection.

I was concerned about the relatively low frequency rumble Ski was producing. I went to Sonar to check, but, surprisingly, the noise seemed to be part of the general background noise.

José handed the come along to Ski, who passed one loop around the shaft and clipped the other to the eyebolt. Slowly, Ski tightened the come along. José kept his light focused on the curved part of the bent shaft. As Ski applied increasing strain, the shaft slowly yielded, returning to a good approximation of a straight shaft.

By this time, Wally was driving the Basketball again. He was careful not to point the camera directly at the welding arc, but I was able to get a good sense in real time of what Ski and José did.

I called Bert in Engineering on the sound-powered phone. "What's the status on the outboard?" I asked.

"We might be able to repair it, but not in a timely manner. I recommend the divers install our spare. We'll keep working on this guy."

I relayed the information to Ham. "The engineers will bring the replacement outboard forward on the rail and lower it to the Port Lock deck. Then your divers can put it in the water and float it to the well." I paused. "Whom will you use?"

"Ski and Jimmy."

"Ski's been working for several hours," I said. "He's tired, I'm sure."

"But Ski and Jimmy removed the outboard and floated it to the DDC. They have the experience. Ski can handle it."

Bert's people hung the replacement outboard from the rail dolly and moved it forward to the Diving Operations Compartment, the DOC. They opened the upper hatch to the Port Lock and lowered the outboard into the lock. Two other snipes in the lock moved it to an overhead hanger. They exited the lock into the Dive Control

Center and sealed the Port lock. Bill pressurized the lock until it equalized with the Main DDC and outside pressure—720 FSW (feet of sea water).

Jimmy, Ski, José, and the remaining three divers waited in the Main Lock for the pressure to equalize. They opened the door between the locks and entered the Port Lock. They opened the deck hatch to sea and then attached the outboard to the overhead hoist while it was still suspended from the overhead hanger. Jimmy and Ski entered the water with lift bags. As José lowered the outboard through the hatch, Ski attached a lift bag through a bolt hole at the end and partially inflated it to keep the end of the outboard off the bottom. Once it was completely through the hatch, suspended horizontally by the lift bag at one end and the hoist at the other, Jimmy attached the second lift bag around the shaft and inflated it to take up the weight. Then he wrapped the line attached to the counterweight around the middle of the outboard. Once the lift bags carried the combined weight of the outboard and counterweight, Jimmy released the hoist.

Now came the critical part: moving the outboard aft. If one of the bags rose a foot, the gas inside would expand, generating more lift, causing it to rise farther. If a bag dropped a foot, its gas would compress, reducing its lift, causing it to drop farther. Borysko watched this process closely, never more than a few feet from the outboard.

Ski and Jimmy were about halfway along their path when a pressure wave, possibly caused by an unseen leopard seal, caused the lift bag carrying the upper end of the outboard to move up about three feet. Immediately, the gas in the bag expanded, generating extra lift, pulling the upper end of the outboard farther up. In just a few seconds, the thousand-pound spare outboard and its hundred-pound counterweight were on their way to the ice, 700 feet overhead. I could see it in my mind's eye, the lift bag expanding until it was entirely full, dragging the thousand-pound outboard behind it, until it slammed into the ice cover, dumping the gas, letting our only spare outboard fall 700 feet to the sea floor. There was no way it could survive such a fall. My heart fell.

Wally pulled the Basketball back to give a wider view. In dismay, I watched the outboard accelerate toward the overhead ice. Suddenly, in a

Wally pulled the Basketball back to give a wider view. In dismay, I watched the outboard accelerate toward the overhead ice. Suddenly, in a flurry of black and white, Borysko raced after it, clamping the expanded lift bag in his massive jaws, thereby dumping the gas and stopping the upward acceleration. With the outboard and attached counterweight, all 1,100 pounds of it, Borysko whistled loudly and swam aft. He gently lowered the outboard to the bottom so that it barely raised a silt cloud. Then he disappeared northward, angling up, probably to get a fresh breath of air.

To say I was astonished by this turn of events would be a total understatement. I made a mental note to describe this event in as much detail as possible when I wrote up my mission report.

Borysko returned as Ski and Jimmy were attaching the replacement outboard to the shaft in the well. When they finished, he approached them with tongue outstretched, wanting to be scratched. He was like an overgrown puppy who brought the lost ball back without damaging it.

＊

The divers had over seven days of decompression ahead of them as I congratulated them and headed to Control. What an amazing team! As it turned out, Bill decided to keep them at pressure, anticipating further possible bottom action.

I arrived in Control at 2300 in the fifth hour of Borka's watch with Chop. They, along with the entire Control watch section, had watched the amazing events of the last five hours.

"I've never seen anything like it," Borka told me. "I don't mean just Borysko, either. Ham's dive team…those guys are the best I ever saw."

"I haven't had the commander's broad experience," Chop said, "but I couldn't agree more. I just can't get over it. At seven hundred feet, those guys removed and replaced a thousand-pound outboard in about seven hours. It would take a shipyard with a drydock two days, at least. I'm impressed!"

"Let's check it out," I said to Borka. "Move *Teuthis* fifty yards closer to *Chángzhēng Thirty-five*."

The outboard raised and lowered flawlessly, and performed perfectly. "Well done, Chop," I said with a smile, because my young supply officer had conducted the move. "Now, I'll try to get a few hours of shut-eye."

0300, MONDAY, JULY 10, 1989—*USS TEUTHIS*, BOTTOMED IN 720 FT, 940 YDS SOUTH OF *CHÁNGZHĒNG 35*, WAGONER INLET, THURSTON ISLAND, ANTARCTICA

Four hours was all the sleep I got. By this twenty-ninth day of my first command, I had already learned this harsh lesson. The messenger awakened me with a gentle touch to my shoulder.

"Captain, you are needed in Sonar, Sir."

I splashed some water on my face, stepped into the Wardroom to grab a cup of joe, and walked aft to Sonar. Second-class Petty Officer William Farrell was the watch supervisor. A few seconds after I entered the quiet, darkened room, King joined us, rubbing sleep from his eyes. He grinned at me and addressed his supervisor.

"Whatcha got, Billy?"

"Something's going on with *Kan-Cha Two*."

"Put it on the speaker, Billy."

King and I listened to a strange, cycling sound that reminded me of electric eggbeaters.

King looked at me. "You know what that is, right?"

I nodded.

"You can figure this out, Billy," King said. "What kind of ship is that?"

"A diving support ship, King."

"Okay, what's she getting ready to do?"

"Put divers over the side?" It was a question.

"The water is over seven hundred feet deep, Billy," King said with a chuckle. "They just gonna dive to the bottom?"

"I guess they're gonna put a bell over the side."

"A PTC—personnel transfer capsule," King corrected.

"Yah, I get it," Ferrell said.

"Billy, what's that water doin' up there?" King winked at me.

"Hey! I got it! Them's station keeping units."

"You got it, Billy. They're getting ready to do what they came here to do."

I said, "King, join me in Plot, please." I set my empty coffee cup down on the table.

*

I had earlier directed Seth to draw a large-scale depiction of what we had out there. Quartermaster Jefferson Davis had the drawing laid out on the chart table. He grinned as we joined him, his white teeth sparkling in his dark face. The drawing showed us, the wreck, *Kan-Cha 2*, and a line indicating the ice edge. The diving support vessel, the wreck, and *Teuthis* were nearly lined up. Kan-Cha hovered at the ice edge, station keeping to maintain position, *Chángzhēng 35* lay on the bottom about a hundred yards south, and we sat on the bottom some 940 yards south of that. He had parked *Chángzhēng 4a* near the northwest corner of the chart. The chart table was three feet wide and two deep. The drawing filled most of the surface.

I picked up a sound-powered handset and called Ham. "Come to Control for a few minutes," I said.

Ham showed up and leaned over the chart table opposite me.

"The ChiCom divers are preparing to investigate *Chángzhēng Thirty-five*," I told him. "They're station keeping right now. I want our divers to intercept them. What do you suggest?"

"When did they start station keeping?" Ham asked.

"They just started," King answered.

"I would have already pressed my divers down," Ham said. "We should assume they already did." He stood silently in thought. "There's no reason for them to slow-walk putting their PTC on the bottom. Give them a half hour to lower it. They'll use three divers for their Comex system, two in-water and one tending. Ten minutes for divers to be in the water on the bottom.

"Their umbilicals are thirty meters long. The wreck is a hundred meters south. If they follow standard practice, they will be able to see *Chángzhēng Thirty-five* in their beams, but won't be able to reach her." Ham looked up at me. "Will they have planned for this?" He placed his hands flat on the table edge. "They are cautious. I don't think they have ever dove to this depth. And, they're doing this out here, at the end of the world." Ham looked at me. "Too many variables, Sir."

I stood there, thinking my way through the problem. I needed to plan for the worst-case scenario. If I assumed they had prepared for a hundred-yard trek, my divers needed to be there before they got there.

"Roger," I said to the XO, who had the Deck, "as quickly as possible, but with maximum stealth, move *Teuthis* to within fifty yards of the wreck. Ham will have divers standing by to enter the water the moment you arrive. Once they are in the water, move back south one hundred fifty yards."

I turned to Ham, but he had already left for Dive Control.

✳

Ham told Bill to shift all the divers to rebreathers so they would not be encumbered by umbilicals. He locked in six APSs with spare dart magazines.

"Listen up!" Bill said over the DDC comm system. "There's a ChiCom fast-attack out there—and she's close. Don't do anything that would catch her attention. I want Gil, Batty, and Freddie in the water," referring to Petty Officers Second-class Gilbert Ross, Ezra Batton, and Manfred Boyle. "Have your APSs locked and loaded, and keep the chatter on low power and to a minimum. Get your butts to the wreck, but remain on this side. Just peak over the top to observe what the two ChiCom divers are doing. ABSOLUTELY, don't let them know you are there. You have to hustle to cover fifty yards.

"Worst case, their umbilicals will let them reach the wreck. If so, let me know immediately. Remember, speed, stealth, and use your goddamn heads for more than a place to park your Kirby-Morgans. *Hooyah!*"

The Dive Control speakers echoed a whispered collective *Hooyah!*

✳

The XO let Plummer handle the move. Jeff, the quartermaster, followed our move on the SINS as it tracked us on the chart table, and let Plummer know when to stop moving. The transit took thirteen long minutes.

"Okay, Mr. Plummer, you're there," Jeff announced quietly.

Plummer set *Teuthis* on the bottom and called Ham. "Divers away!"

The three divers dropped through the hatch and pushed rapidly toward the ChiCom wreck. As they reached the wreck's south side, Borysko joined them with a loud squeal. The divers crept up the submarine side until they could just see over the edge. In the total blackness, they would not be visible to the other divers unless a beam struck them directly.

A hundred yards north, they could clearly see the ChiCom PTC—a ten-foot high, six-foot wide cylinder with a brightly lit port and floodlight beams lighting the bottom around the cylinder. Divers were just emerging; the only reason they were visible was the bright illumination from the floods. The two divers tugged their umbilicals out of the PTC and faked them on the bottom. They pointed their beams at the wreck, but the light barely reached. They wore weighted boots and began tramping toward the wreck. At thirty yards out, the beams illuminated the wreck better, but the divers could not progress farther. They spent several minutes playing their beams along the sub's port side, while the *Teuthis* divers remained well hidden. It looked like they may have been taking photos of the wreck, but the *Teuthis* divers couldn't be sure. Finally, the ChiCom divers turned and trudged back to their PTC. They entered normally through the bottom hatch, and several minutes later, the PTC began rising toward the surface.

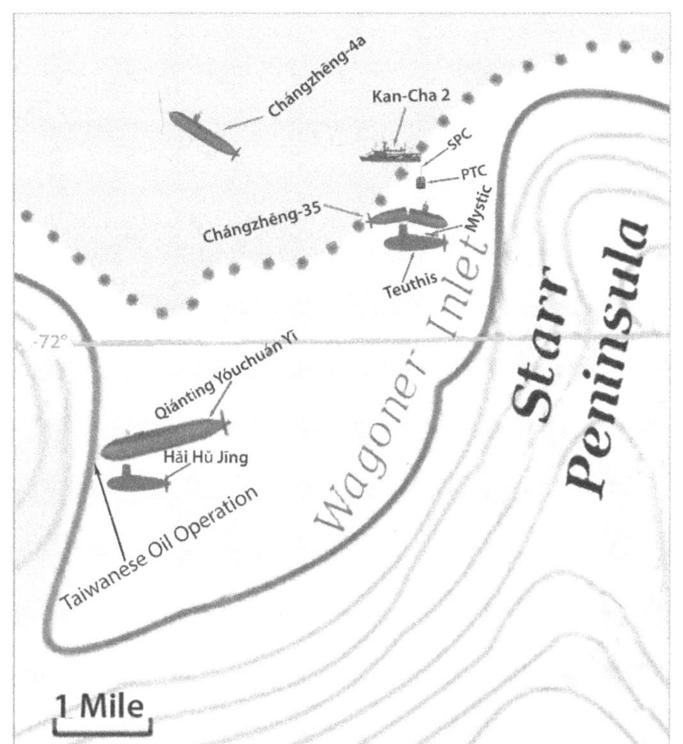

Wagoner Inlet, Teuthis *location with* Mystic, Qiántǐng Yóuchuán Yī, Hǎi Hǔ Jīng, Chángzhēng 35 *wreck*, Kan-Cha 2, *and* Chángzhēng 4a *departing.*

CHAPTER EIGHT—Kan-Cha Diving Ops

0800, MONDAY, JULY 10, 1989—*USS TEUTHIS*, BOTTOMED IN 720 FT, 200 YARDS SOUTH OF *CHÁNGZHĒNG 35*, WAGONER INLET, THURSTON ISLAND, ANTARCTICA

I was in Dive Control talking with Ham and Bill. The divers were back in the DDC, eating a warm meal and catching up on sleep, as every diver will always do when the opportunity presents itself.

"They don't have longer umbilicals," Ham said. "If they had them, they would have employed them the first time."

"I agree," Bill said, "but they are not going away. I predict we see them next in rebreathers."

"They are not in any particular hurry," I added, "but good weather doesn't last very long down here. How long will they take to shift to rebreathers?"

"Three divers," Ham said, "lose the hot water suits, take a pee and dump, grab a snack, and don drysuits—half hour to forty-five minutes."

"Transfer back to the PTC," Bill added, "seal and disconnect it, swing it over the stern and lower—total time I estimate ninety minutes, maybe longer, until they hit the bottom again."

We stood there for a moment, quietly reviewing what we knew. I felt a heavy stone drop around my neck as I constructed a statement internally.

"Here's the situation, Guys. There is no scenario where we let the ChiCom divers discover that *Chángzhēng Thirty-five* was torpedoed and report that info topside. The ChiComs are unaware of our presence, but they damn sure do know about the Taiwanese operation down here. If the ChiCom authorities learn that their sub was torpedoed, they will presume the Taiwanese did it, and strike back. That could very well trigger World War Three. As I see it, you guys are the only thing preventing World War Three.

"So, how do we prevent the divers from communicating their findings topside? I have gone through this a thousand times. The only certain way is to sever their Strength-Power-Communications cable, their SPC cable, before the in-water divers discover why *Chángzhēng Thirty-five* sank."

I quickly walked them through what I wanted the divers to do. I handed Ham three vials and syringes I had received from Dr. Colmbs. "One of these will render a man unconscious for three hours. Capture, if you can. Kill if you must. But they absolutely must not communicate topside."

✳

I returned to Control, where Waverly had the watch. His regular JOOD, Ham, was occupied in Dive Control and would be for the duration of this dive op.

"Waverly, move us one hundred yards closer before the divers enter the water." I trusted Waverly to handle things properly and professionally, but I intended to remain in Control for the entire operation. Too much was at stake for me to be anywhere else.

Waverly moved *Teuthis* quickly. While he did so, Sonar called through their sound-powered phone talker.

"Conn, Sonar. *Chángzhēng Four-alpha* has gotten underway. She's heading three-zero-five at twenty knots."

Waverly looked at me for direction. "Secure condition ultra-quit until the ChiCom divers enter the water," I told him. "Then reset it as rapidly as possible. Keep the sound-powered phone talkers on station."

I had Ham on the sound-powered phone as we moved closer to *Chángzhēng 35*. The moment Waverly reported he was bottomed a hundred yards from *Chángzhēng 35*, I told Ham, "Divers away. Make sure they are armed with APSs, have the Greenlee cutter, the bags, and the vials and syringes."

Ski, Jimmy, José, and Gil entered the water. Ski carried the Greenlee hydraulic cutter suspended from a small lift bag. Jimmy and Gil each carried a rolled-up narrow body-length bag with vents. All four divers swam at thirty feet over the bottom so the ChiCom divers would be less likely to spot them. The Basketball, under Wally's control, followed above them. Wally was poised to extinguish the flood the moment the ChiCom PTC appeared. When they had swum about a hundred yards, they stopped and hung out, waiting. Wally extinguished the Basketball flood. They waited. Five minutes later, Ski clucked his comm unit. Everyone looked up to see the ChiCom PTC descending slowly, downward pointed floods brightly lit.

Ski swam toward the PTC while the other three divers dispersed themselves around the place it would stop. A minute later, the PTC stopped three yards off the bottom, giving the exiting divers sufficient room. Ski swam to the top of the PTC and quietly placed the Greenlee's jaws around the three-inch diameter SPC cable. He placed the hydraulic pump on a horizontal piece of the frame and tied it in place with two zip-ties. He tested the pump, moving the guillotine blade a fraction of an inch toward the SPC cable.

Below the PTC, the hatch opened inward, and moments later, one diver and then a second exited. Ski waited for both ChiCom divers to move away from the PTC, and then he commenced pumping the hydraulic lever as fast as possible.

While Ski pumped, Jimmy dropped down and slid his bag over one of the ChiCom divers. The second ChiCom diver saw what happened, drew his knife, and launched himself toward Jimmy, slashing across his left arm. Gill saw the attack, brought his APS to bear, and fired at the attacker, striking his leg. The injured ChiCom diver dropped to the bottom, grabbing his leg. Then he turned and launched himself toward Gil. Without hesitation, Gill drew a bead on the attacking diver and fired. The APS dart struck him in the chest. He stopped swimming and settled to the bottom. Gil approached the downed diver from behind and ripped his helmet off. After a momentary struggle, the diver stopped moving. Gill pulled the diver's knife from his hand and pinned him to the bottom.

When Ski completed his cut on top of the PTC, it dropped to the ocean floor, remaining upright, and all its lights went dark. Wally pulled the Basketball higher to illuminate a larger area.

"Jimmy, are you injured?" Bill called on the open acoustic circuit.

"My left arm is cut through my suit," Jimmy answered. "I'm returning to *Teuthis*."

"José, accompany Jimmy," Bill ordered.

Ham called me in Control. "Captain, a live diver is still inside the PTC. He can't get out. Do we leave him, or should we attempt to tip over the PTC like we did in the Sea of Okhotsk?"[14]

"We'll tip it, but get your divers back into *Teuthis* so we can move closer."

"What about the bagged diver?"

"That's what your syringe and vial are for. Cut open his suit, jab him and drag him into the DDC. Bind and hood him. If he comes to, don't speak near him."

I turned to Waverly. "Rise to six hundred feet and set down as close as possible to the PTC."

---

14 See *Operation Ivy Bells*, vol 1 in *The Mac McDowell Missions*.

I called Ham. "What's Jimmy's status?"

"A cut in his upper left arm. He treated it himself—stapled it shut. He's ready to participate in tipping the PTC."

1030, MONDAY, JULY 10, 1989—*USS TEUTHIS*, BOTTOMED IN 720 FT, BENEATH *KAN-CHA 2*, WAGONER INLET, THURSTON ISLAND, ANTARCTICA

Ham decided to keep Jimmy inside the DDC, keeping an eye on the unconscious ChiCom divers, tending the other divers, and being available should they need him outside. Jimmy complained, but Ham remained adamant. He assigned Ski and José to attach a hawser to the top of the PTC. He assigned Gil and Batty to man the forward capstan, and Freddie to manhandle the hawser between *Teuthis* and the PTC.

As soon as Waverly put *Teuthis* back on the bottom, the divers exited, this time without being armed. Derrick had assumed the Basketball. He kept close track of the divers in the water. I watched Gill, Batty, and Freddie swim to the forward deck, raise the capstan, and open a hawser locker. Freddie swam one hawser end to Ski and José. Gil placed the capstan wrench into its slot while Batty coiled four wraps of hawser around the capstan.

Derrick moved the Basketball to the PTC, where Ski had just attached the hawser by bowline to a crossbar of the PTC frame. Ski and José swam clear of the PTC, and Ski said over the circuit, "Gil, take up the slack and pull!"

The hawser tightened, and then the PTC tilted toward *Teuthis* and fell on its side. The Basketball moved to the PTC bottom that was pointed away from *Teuthis*. At first, nothing happened. I presumed the diver inside was donning his rebreather and fins. He had no idea what had happened, and may even have presumed that a storm topside had caused everything to go awry.

The PTC hatch swung inward as the occupant released the dogs. Some gas escaped as the sphere partially filled with water. Then a head appeared, wearing a Kirby-Morgan-like helmet. As the diver swam out, Ski and José slipped a bag over his body, confining his movements.

Even so, the ChiCom diver managed to reach his knife and slice open the bag. He certainly was keeping his wits about him.

"Hold him!" Ski said on the circuit. José and Freddie wrapped their arms around his upper and lower body. Ski grabbed his wrist and knocked the knife away. "Tighter," Ski said, "hold him tighter." He was big and strong, and Ski was having trouble holding his wrist.

Gil and Batty joined them, and Gil wrapped his hands around the diver's protruding wrist. Ski cut open the suit, exposing his wrist. Batty produced a vial and filled his syringe, handing it to Ski.

"Hold him—don't let him move," Ski muttered, and jammed the needle into the diver's vein. Within thirty seconds, the ChiCom diver stopped struggling.

Ham came up on the circuit. "Gil and Batty, stuff the dead diver into the PTC and close the hatch. Then grab the unconscious diver and bring him with you. Ski, grab the Greenlee. José and Freddie, release the hawser from the forward capstan and retract the capstan. Close and secure the hawser bin and bring the capstan wrench with you. Leave the hawser on the bottom. Everybody, back to the DDC."

1345, MONDAY, JULY 10, 1989—*USS TEUTHIS,* SUBMERGED AT 500 FT, SOUTH OF *KAN-CHA 2,* WAGONER INLET, THURSTON ISLAND, ANTARCTICA

I picked up the Secure Gertrude mike. "*ROCS Hăi Hŭ Jīng,* this is *USS Teuthis* on the Secure Gertrude, *ROCS Hăi Hŭ Jīng,* this is *USS Teuthis* on the Secure Gertrude, over."

"*USS Teuthis,* this is *ROCS Hăi Hŭ Jīng,* over."

That was what I wanted to hear.

"This is Commander Mac McDowell, commanding *Teuthis.* May I speak with your Commanding Officer, over?"

"Stand by, *Teuthis,* over."

"This is *Hăi Hŭ Jīng,* Tiong-hāu Zhang Zhiwei speaking, over."

"This is Captain McDowell. Can we speak privately, over?"

"Stand by, *Teuthis,* over."

"This is Tiong-hāu Chen Zhiwei speaking privately, over."

"Thank you, Captain. Did Captain Zhang Min brief you on my presence, over?"

"Yes, he did, over."

"The ChiComs were conducting diving ops from their dive support vessel *Kan-Cha Two* on *Chángzhēng Thirty-five*. I stopped them before they could determine that *Chángzhēng Thirty-five* was torpedoed. I have two diver prisoners aboard. I would ask you to take them, but they are still saturated to seven hundred feet. It will take about seven days to bring them to one atmosphere. I am on a tight schedule and must depart. Do you have burst message capability? Over."

"I do, over."

"Would you send a message to your government, asking it to confidentially inform my government of my situation, and request that someone take the prisoners off my hands when I visit Mare Harbour? I will have them ready for transfer at eighteen hundred hours, July 18. Over."

"Roger, I can do that. Do you require any kind of assistance? Over."

"Thank you, no, but my presence here must remain secret. The consequences of Mainland China discovering that *Chángzhēng Thir-ty-five* was torpedoed would be catastrophic, especially for Taiwan. Kam Cha Two will depart for home soon, since she no longer has diving capability. Over."

"This is *Hǎi Hǔ Jīng*. Roger, out."

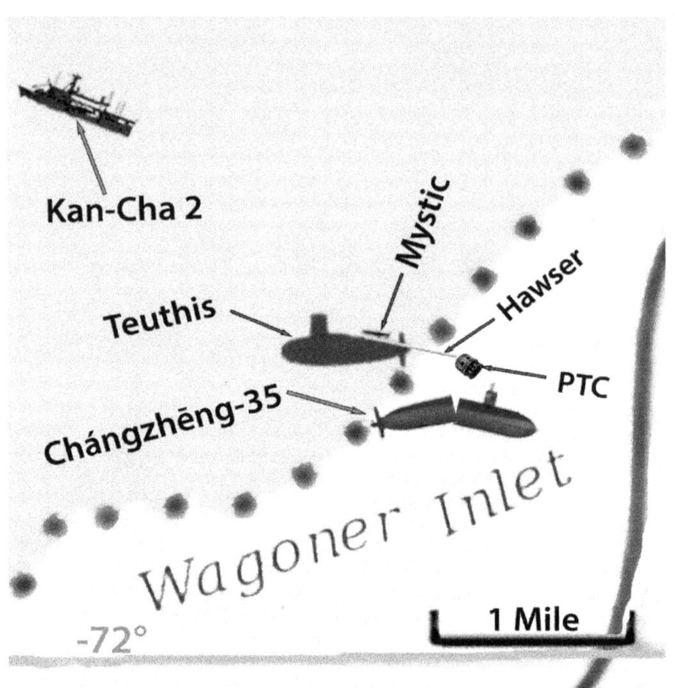

Wagoner Inlet, Teuthis *and* Mystic *towing PTC,*
Chángzhēng 35 *wreck, and* Kan-Cha 2 *departing.*

CHAPTER NINE—The PTC

1600, MONDAY, JULY 10, 1989—*USS TEUTHIS,* SUBMERGED AT 675 FT, TRACKING NORTHWEST TOWARD SHELF BREAK, WAGONER INLET, THURSTON ISLAND, ANTARCTICA

Part of me wondered why I didn't just order my divers to kill the ChiCom divers on contact. The other part understood the reason. Those divers were doing their jobs just like mine were. I presumed they had no animus toward us, especially since they had no idea we were there. Now, of course, they were a problem, one that stretched well beyond *Teuthis* and her mission.

I might have been able to send the burst transmission myself in Drake Passage, but weather being what it was, the odds were against me, at least for sending the message in the next twenty-four hours. I couldn't risk surfacing in a high sea state with *Mystic* on my stern. *Hǎi Hǔ Jīng* was a much better choice. Even so, State would have little time to arrange whatever they would decide. I was sure to get some flak for the short notice, especially from SubLant.

I sighed. Cross that bridge when I get there. I called Ham.

"Ham, you know we're stuck with these divers until Mare Harbour. Seaman Billy Chen speaks Mandarin. Odds are, so do those divers. I'm assigning Billy to you until we offload our prisoners. Be sure to brief him on the importance of not revealing anything to these guys. Treat them humanely, but don't allow any possibility that they can gain the upper hand in the DDC."

※

Chen reported to Ham in Dive Control, not really certain why he was there. This was only his second time there. The first was when he checked Dive Control out for his submarine quals. Ham sat him down and explained things to him.

"We captured two ChiCom divers. They are tied to two bunks in the DDC—the chamber." Ham pointed. "I realize you don't know much about saturation diving, but it will take the guys in the DDC about seven days to decompress so they can leave the chamber. While people are in the chamber under pressure, it is difficult for us out here to understand what people inside are saying. We pass their voices through an electronic descrambler. Even when they speak to each other, it has to pass through the descrambler into their earwigs. It's not perfect, but it makes their speech more intelligible." Ham smiled at him. "You got that, Billy?"

"I guess so. I'm down here because I speak Mandarin, right?"

"You got it. Hopefully, so do they." Ham looked at him earnestly. "Now this is important, Billy, very important. They're going to have a thousand questions. You must not give them any information, not even your name." Ham paused. "You need to understand this. Nothing at all." Ham handed him a sheet of paper. "When we're ready, I want you to tell them this, in Mandarin, of course. It doesn't have to be an exact translation. Just communicate the essence to them. Are you okay with that?"

Chen looked the paper over. "Not a problem, Chief Warrant Officer."

A messcook showed up with a pot of rice, pork, and vegetables and two bowls with chopsticks.

"How are our Chinese friends doing?" Ham asked over the circuit.

"Awake and pissed as hell," Ski answered, his voice still a bit squeaky despite the descrambler. "I let each up to take a leak."

"Can they hear us?"

"Yep."

Ham handed the mike to Chen. "Do the sheet," he said.

"You live because we value life. You are inside a pressure chamber where you must remain for at least eight days. We will conduct another dive, and then we will decompress. You are saturation divers. You understand the process. We do not wish to keep you bound for the entire decompression. If you give me your promise to behave, we will release your bonds so you can move about the chamber. One lapse by either of you, and you both will spend the rest of the decompression bound. We will now send in food. You may sit to eat with hands free, but your feet will remain bound until you finish eating and the utensils have been removed. If you need to urinate, hold up one finger. If you need to defecate, hold up two fingers."

"Ask them for their promise," Ham said.

"I need you to promise good behavior now," Chen said over the circuit in Mandarin.

Two voices answered.

"They promise, and they say, 'Thank you for life'," Chen said.

"Ski," Ham said over the circuit, "let them sit with hands free, but keep their feet bound. Food is coming through the medical lock."

The DDC monitor showed both Chinese divers eating their meals with gusto. Clearly, they were hungry. When they finished, both held out their bowls for more, showing broad smiles. Between them, they cleaned out the rice pot.

Freddie picked up a handset to speak privately with Ham. The conversation from his side still went through the descrambler. "Ham, can you send someone to get my Go board? It's a rolled-up pad under my bedpan. Bring the two stone bags and bowls, too. It will help pass the time and maybe generate some goodwill. Oh, the combination is five–twenty-nine–ten."

"You play Go?"

"I've been known to win a game or two."

✳

The Chinese divers' eyes lit up when they saw the Go board. In no time, Freddie rolled out the board on their table and explained the rules for his fellow divers.

"It's a simple game to understand. Black places the first stone on an intersection. After that, you alternate turns placing stones on intersections. The idea is to completely surround territory, thereby removing anything inside. Whoever has the most territory when you cannot place any more stones is the winner. Simple rules—complex strategy." He pointed at one of the Chinese divers, then at himself, and then the game. The diver smiled, sat at the table, took a black and white stone in his hands, shook them together, separated his hands, and offered them to Freddie. Freddie chose his right—it contained a black stone. The Chinese diver slid the bowl containing the black stones to Freddie and slid the other toward his place. Freddie placed a black stone on the board, and the game was on.

The other *Teuthis* divers didn't understand game strategy, but they could follow the action. When it became clear that Freddie was winning, the Chinese player looked perplexed. He spoke aloud.

"He plays very good for a non-Chinese."

Chen translated the comment. Ham instructed him to say, "Freddie has a special *talent*."

When the game ended after a couple of hours, the Chinese diver pointed to his companion and then to Freddie. Freddie grinned and held up two thumbs. When he won that game as well, both Chinese divers shook his hand and clapped him on his back. A bond was growing, much to Ham's relief. Having to restrain two hostiles would not have been his favorite pastime. This was much preferable.

Ham reported the matter to me. "Nicely handled," I told him. "We're getting ready to dispose of the PTC. We'll need divers in the water twice, once to hook things up, and the second to retrieve the hawser and put things away. Use two divers and a tender so you keep three with the captives."

✳

Borka had the watch, but Chop was running things. At my direction, he was moving *Teuthis* northwesterly at five knots, carefully scanning the bottom. It dropped off slowly, and after we passed from under the ice edge, the water column measured a thousand feet from the ice to the mud below. We were looking for the shelf break, where the slowly descending continental shelf dropped rapidly down the continental slope to the abyssal deep. Our charts lacked definition and resolution down here. What we charted would become part of the next Antarctic chart issue.

Quartermaster Marcel Theron kept an eye on our progress. He was especially keen because he knew his charting would become part of the next chart issue. After we had traveled approximately ten nautical miles beyond the ice edge, he announced the bottom was dropping rapidly.

"I've marked the shelf break," he said. And he made a log entry recording the event.

0000, TUESDAY, JULY 11, 1989—*USS TEUTHIS*, BOTTOMED IN 720 FT, NEAR THE STRANDED PTC, WAGONER INLET, THURSTON ISLAND, ANTARCTICA

The XO and Jerry Plummer brought *Teuthis* back to the stranded PTC on the bottom about a hundred yards inside the ice edge. A storm raged topside that completely disrupted the coherence of the ice along the edge, spreading it northward for several miles. Had the *Kan-Cha 2* remained on station, the storm would have forced her departure, and possibly even endangered the vessel itself.

I was certain the crew didn't know what had happened to their PTC and divers 720 feet below them. The only evidence they had was the sheer cut of their SPC cable just above where it attached to the PTC. A jagged break would have raised fewer questions, but there would have been no way to accomplish that while simultaneously cutting off comms. It would remain an unexplained mystery for their conspiracy theorists.

Ham gave the dive task to his three junior divers, Gil, Batty, and Freddie, with Freddie tending. Once *Teuthis* was firmly pressed to the bottom, Gil and Batty dropped through the Port Lock hatch wearing rebreathers, where they found Borysko waiting. They took a couple of minutes romping with the cetacean before Bill ordered them to their task.

They followed the hawser that they found on the bottom where Ski had left it. It took them to the top of the PTC. They opened the bowline and retied it as a highwayman's hitch with a twenty-foot working end.

They swam back to *Teuthis*, where they flipped a cleat just aft of the sail. Together, they swam the hawser to the cleat, tied a loop at the end, and draped it over the cleat.

I called Ham. "Have the divers hang out by the sail. I'll lower the after outboard and put a strain on the hawser. Once it's taut, have them signal."

In Control, Jerry lifted the stern, lowered the after outboard, and pushed the stern to starboard. After a few seconds, Ham said, "Halt!"

The divers inspected both ends of the hawser. They both had held. We were ready to go as soon as the divers returned to the DDC.

✳

Wally was on the Basketball as Jerry got the show on the road. He eased the sub forward and to the right. As *Teuthis* moved forward in a right-turn circle, the hawser snapped against the DSRV fairing we had installed at Mare Island. After ten minutes, we were pointed north, and the PTC dragged slowly behind us on the bottom, throwing up clouds of silt. Wally pulled back to give a larger view.

The plan was working.

I stepped over to Plot. "How far to the break?" I asked Theron.

"Almost exactly ten nautical miles," he answered, pointing a pencil at the spot he had marked on the chart.

1000, TUESDAY, JULY 11, 1989—*USS TEUTHIS*, SUBMERGED AT 950 FT, TRACKING NORTHWEST NEAR THE SHELF BREAK, WAGONER INLET, THURSTON ISLAND, ANTARCTICA

We dragged the PTC across the continental shelf north of Thurston Island. Derrick had taken over the Basketball from Wally and was following our progress, moving along the hawser, from the sub to the PTC and back. It was tightly stretched, and the PTC threw up billowing clouds of silt behind it.

Waverly and Ham had the watch. For most of it, Ham was in charge. Waverly was there because he had the legal responsibility. Dragging the PTC across the bottom at one knot was not difficult, but it required paying close attention to the depth.

Borysko made himself part of the operation. At first, he hovered near the Basketball, much to the delight of the crew members watching on monitors around the sub. Then his interest turned to the hawser and its tow. First, he inspected the PTC, even nudging it a bit with his snout. Then he checked out the hawser. He seemed particularly interested in the twenty-foot working end that trailed from the highwayman's hitch. While we watched on the monitors, Borysko took the working end in his mouth and swam away. In a moment, the hitch slipped from the PTC that rocked a bit, and stopped moving.

"All stop!" Ham ordered. Since the skids were still lowered, he told the COW to put *Teuthis* on the bottom. He called down to Dive Control and explained the situation.

"Waverly," he said to his OOD, "I need to be in Dive Control while we solve this problem."

"Lieutenant Commander Denver has the deck and conn," Waverly announced to the Control Room.

Down in Dive Control, Ham once again assigned his three junior divers, Gil, Batty, and Freddie, with Freddie tending, to fix things outside.

"Take a four-by-four with you, Ham said. "Try to entice Borysko away from the hawser."

Borysko appeared delighted to see the divers. He cavorted and played, chasing the 4x4 to the surface and back, while Gil and Batty retied the hawser to the PTC with a highwayman's hitch. Borysko saw their actions and approached the working end, eager to pull it again. Both Gil and Batty placed themselves between the hitch and the Orca, pushing their arms away, signaling to Borysko not to approach the hawser. When they swam a few feet away, Borysko again approached the working end. The two divers immediately placed themselves between again, actually pushing on Borysko's snout. This time, when they left, Borysko ignored the hawser and continued playing with his 4x4.

Waverly lifted off the bottom and put a strain on the hawser with the after outboard. When the divers signaled the hawser was holding, he ordered the divers inside and built our speed to one knot.

As the divers returned to the DDC, Borysko followed them closely. They scratched his tongue and then closed the hatch. To everyone's delight, Borysko continued to ignore the hawser for the remainder of our trek.

By the time we reached the shelf break where the bottom dropped off more rapidly, the water was a thousand feet deep. We left a deep scar in the silt, but it would disappear entirely in the next few months.

Once we passed over the break, Ham announced on the 1MC, "Now, prepare for DSRV ops, prepare for DSRV ops."

Fifteen minutes later, Deckhart requested permission to open the after escape hatch and enter *Mystic*. I was in Control and told Ham to grant permission. Before entering *Mystic*, Deckhart called Control on the handset.

I'm taking all four crew members with me. I would be happy to give fifteen *Teuthis* crew members a ride.

On the 1MC, Ham announced, "Anyone wanting to take an hour DSRV ride, report to the after escape hatch. We can accommodate fifteen people. *Mystic* will depart in fifteen minutes."

Eighteen crew members showed up. Three received a signed chit, giving them head-of-the-line privilege for the next joy ride.

✳

Mystic got underway, with the Basketball driven by Derrick standing off to one side, and Borysko monitoring the operation.. Deckhart followed the hawser down to the PTC. It lay on its side with its top pointed downslope. He moved the manipulator arm out of its storage tray and then grabbed the working end of the highwayman's hitch and backed away. In five seconds, the hawser hung free from *Teuthis*, and Borysko immediately approached the end to examine it closely.

"Now comes the interesting part," Deckhart said.

He moved to the left side of the bottom frame of the PTC and gently pushed against the frame. At first, the PTC tried to roll in the direction of his push, but then one of the vertical tubular frames dug into the silt, and the PTC pivoted so the top faced upslope at 45 Degrees.

"Shit!" he muttered and moved *Mystic* to the downslope side to push the PTC parallel with the slope. After a bit of jockeying, it was done.

Deckhart moved *Mystic* upslope of the PTC, approached the center, and placed the end of the manipulator under a vertical frame tube. He lifted carefully, trying to get the PTC to roll. It moved a bit but didn't roll. He placed the manipulator under the next vertical tube. This time, he set the forward thruster to full up. The PTC rolled forward while the manipulator arm slipped out from under the tube, and *Mystic* took a sudden steep up angle. Deckhart corrected the up angle as the forward camera recorded the PTC accelerating down the slope on its two-mile trip to the abyssal deep. For a minute, Borysko chased the PTC down the slope, but gave up when he reached his depth limit. He headed for the surface and a breath of fresh air.

Deckhart brought *Mystic* around and pointed up toward *Teuthis*. The hawser hung from the port cleat just aft of the sail. Using the manipulator jaws, Deckhart removed the eye from the cleat and drove out past the break a hundred yards, where he dropped the hawser. Borysko tried to catch it, but it dropped too quickly. Deckhart returned to the cleat, attached an appropriate wrench to the arm, and loosened the cleat. Then he flipped the cleat over so the deck was flush, and tightened the cleat so it wouldn't rattle.

A full hour had passed by the time Deckhart and his passengers were back inside *Teuthis*. Except for a long scar on the bottom that would disappear with time, nothing remained to tell that *Teuthis* had ever visited Potaka or Wagoner Inlets.

1400, TUESDAY, JULY 11, 1989—*MYSTIC*, DSRV OPS AT *CHÁNGZHĒNG 35*, WAGONER INLET, THURSTON ISLAND, ANTARCTICA

Seth was OOD and set *Teuthis* on the bottom fifty yards south of *Chángzhēng 35*. This would likely be our last opportunity to extract any intelligence from the torpedoed ChiCom submarine. I would have loved to visit *Chángzhēng 35* myself, but U.S. ship commanders do not normally leave their vessel while it is underway. There are exceptions, but this did not qualify as one.

I put Roger in charge of the away team, with King, my leading Sonar Tech and COB, backing him up. I included an electronics tech, an engineer, an electrician, and an atmosphere tech, the latter to ensure the atmosphere was still breathable. They carried a Scott Air Pack for each of them along with sufficient spare air bottles to give each a full spare. My instructions were simple: Bring back as many documents as you can find and take several rolls of photos.

I asked Roger into my cabin before he left. "When we last visited *Chángzhēng Thirty-five*," I said, "we killed two Chinese crew members who had been left on the disabled sub. Their job seems to have been to kill us and scuttle the sub. It didn't turn out that way—fortunately for us." I produced a rueful smile. "Their bodies will have been decomposing since then. You have Scott Air Packs. You'll probably need them." I shifted position and continued. "We grabbed all the documents we saw, but I'm sure there are plenty more in cabinets and drawers." I stood. "Stay safe, my friend."

Deckhart brought the away team in *Mystic* to the same forward hatch we had used in our previous infiltration of *Chángzhēng 35*.[15] He placed the Atmosphere Tech in the Mid Sphere on a Scott Air Pack, and sealed the rest of the team in the Rescue Sphere with his technicians. He sealed himself in the Control Sphere with his co-pilot, Don Fortune.

The Atmosphere Tech drained the skirt, equalized the pressure, and opened the DSRV hatch. Before opening the sub hatch, he checked his Scott Air Pack to ensure he was breathing good air. Then he pushed a

---

15 See *Operation White Out*, vol 4 in *The Mac McDowell Missions*.

wrench into the socket at the top of the hatch and rotated clockwise. The hatch opened with a slight whoosh because of a positive pressure inside the sub. He dropped a sensor through the opening and closed the hatch. The air tested somewhat high in carbon dioxide, but otherwise good. He started to remove his facemask, but recoiled at a strong, putrid smell in the Mid Sphere, and that with the hatch being open for only a few seconds.

He spoke up, the overhead mike picking up his words. "Mr. Deckhart, XO, the air is breathable, but has an overwhelming putrid smell. You gotta wear air packs to go in there."

"Don and I will remain sealed in the Control Sphere," Deckhart said over the circuit. "Away team, don your air packs and open the Mid Sphere hatch. Last man into the sub, close the sub hatch. Warren and Sam remain in *Mystic*, but shut the hatch. Be prepared to lower spare air tanks when the away team requests them."

✳

The XO entered *Chángzhēng 35* first, followed by the rest of his team, King entering last, closing the hatch behind him. Each carried an oversize duffle bag. As they stood in the Torpedo Room well away from the putrefied body of the man who had nearly killed me, the ET suddenly exclaimed, "What the fuck!" He pointed at a mouse running away from the team along the walkway.

While they watched, several more appeared, curious at first, but scampering in fear when anyone made a noise.

"Can you believe it?" King said. "Some of the smell has to be mouse urine."

"It looks like they feasted on the corpse," the XO observed. "Let's get on with it." He assigned each team member an area to cover. He kept the camera and moved from compartment to compartment, taking photos.

At the end of the first hour, the team met in the Torpedo Room to get fresh air tanks. The *Mystic* crew lowered their fresh tanks and retrieved their old ones before sealing the *Mystic* hatch again. The away team took another full hour scavenging everything they could find, stuffing their duffel bags. What nobody saw was one curious mouse that climbed up the side of the engineer's duffel bag, burrowed to the bottom where it made a nest of paper and went to sleep.

＊

A half hour later, *Mystic* was latched into its cradle, but nobody had left. Bert and the XO were in discussion.

"Bert, we're sitting here breathing through Scott Air Packs, because we managed to fill *Mystic* with the putrid odor from *Chángzhēng Thirty-five*. We really don't want this smell in *Teuthis*."

After a short pause while he consulted with his people, Bert responded, "We'll take two people at a time into the escape hatch with their Scott Air Packs. We'll flush the escape trunk with fresh air and then let them out."

Deckhart jumped into the conversation. "I'll keep Petty Officer Elton in *Mystic*. He will draw down our internal pressure and then open the escape trunk hatch. Submarine air will enter *Mystic*. We'll do this several times until the smell is tolerable. The CO-H2 burner[16] can handle the rest."

＊

No one saw the mouse slip out of the engineer's duffel bag, hop over the threshold of the Engine Room hatch, and run into Maneuvering where it settled in a tangle of wires behind the Reactor Control Panel.

---

16 An atmospheric auxiliary machine through which all ship's air passes. It burns CO from smoking and cooking to CO2, H2 from oxygen production to water, and all other hydrocarbons to CO2 and water.

PART TWO

Southern Transit

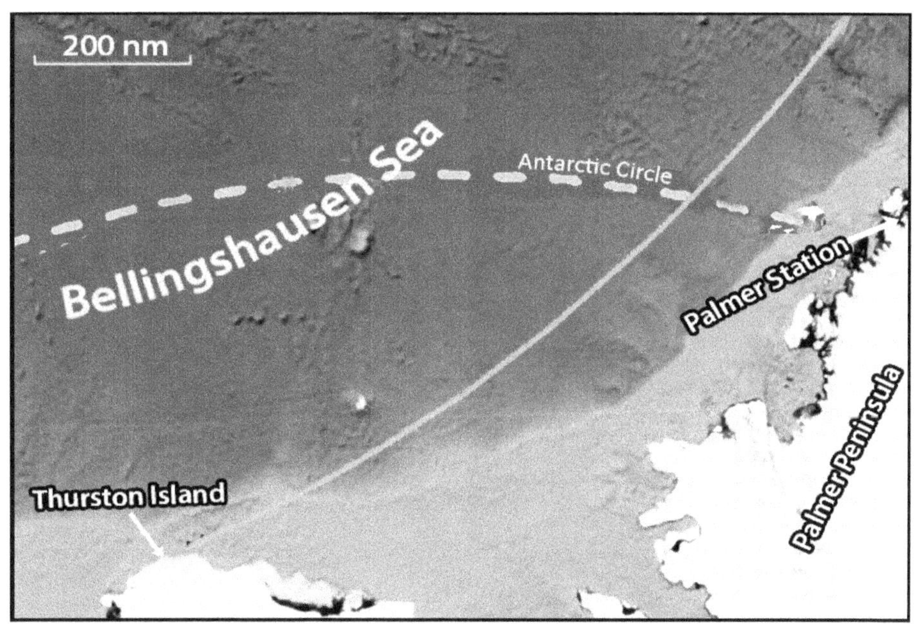

Transit through Bellingshausen Sea and across
Antarctic Circle.

CHAPTER TEN—Bellingshausen Sea

2100, TUESDAY, JULY 11, 1989—*USS TEUTHIS*, SUBMERGED AT 700 FT, DEPARTING THURSTON ISLAND FOR BELLINGSHAUSEN SEA

We were thirty days out from Mare Island. Rob and Chop had the watch under a turbulent sea boasting sixty-foot waves as measured by our upward-looking ice sonar. I told Rob to drop us to 700 feet and keep our speed at ten knots until we crossed the shelf break.

Plot put us on a great circle route directly to the Falklands. We were looking at four days plus at twenty knots.

"Do you know where the layer is?" I asked Chop. Knowing the thermocline or layer depth is important, because its depth impacts sonar transmission both ways.

"Topside action is complicating things down here," he answered. "Sonar says the layer was at six hundred feet, but they had a hard time finding it as we passed through. Can surface waves really do that, Captain?"

"Generally, no," I said. "But things are different down here. Wind and current are generally west to east. The Drake Passage funnels the current, and even to some extent the wind, speeding it up dramatically. A prevailing counter wind just to the south mixes things up pretty good. You end up with what you see above. That's why sailing ships back in the day had so much trouble sailing west around the Horn. Today, big tankers do it regularly. Not so much container ships, though. In waters like above, they tend to lose containers overboard." I grinned at him. "Don't let Sonar relax. Soviet and ChiCom fast-attacks travel this route routinely. They'll be down here with us."

As if to emphasize my words, Sonar called. "Conn, Sonar, I have a suppressed cavitating contact, dead ahead, fading in and out, designate Sierra-four-eight."

I stepped into Sonar, where Bill Farrell had the watch. He was an experienced Second-class Sonar Tech who knew what he was doing. He spoke to me.

"Sierra-forty-eight is probably closing, since we just picked her up for the first time. Once we're closer together, I'll ask for a broadside aspect so we can identify her."

"Any sense of her distance?"

"A hundred miles or so, Sir. We're doing twenty. If she's doing thirty, that gives us two hours before we knock on each other's doors."

Chop called me on the handset a half hour later. "Captain, Sierra-four-eight is still dead ahead. I want to slow, bring her broad to starboard, and run an analysis."

"Permission granted," I said and left my cabin for Sonar.

As we slowed and turned to port, S-48 began sounding loud and clear in Sonar. Farrell ran the analysis.

"It's the *Volgograd*, Sir. She's bearing zero-four-four at five-three miles on a course of one-nine-zero at three-zero knots."

What is a Soviet fast-attack doing down here? I wondered. The Soviets and ChiComs have been warming to each other, but at arm's length. Is *Volgograd* looking for *Chángzhēng Four-alpha*? Did she detect a piece of *Teuthis* and think we were Chinese? I cannot have either Soviet or ChiCom subs track me to Prince Edward.

I stepped out to Control. "Chop, I want the ship ready to set condition ultra-quiet on a moment's notice."

Back in Sonar, I told Farrell, "Watch for Crazy Ivans. Her skipper is one of their best. We need to keep up our speed, but we don't want to get caught flatfooted." I stood around for a couple of minutes. "Do you have any sense of her depth?" I asked Ferrell.

"She's gonna avoid the storm like we are," Farrell answered. "We're at seven hundred feet. They use meters, and that's two hundred thirteen meters, and change. They're gonna do even meters like we normally do even feet. Two hundred meters makes sense for her depth."

Just then, the console watchstander announced, "Conn, Sonar, Crazy Ivan! Crazy Ivan!"

"All stop," Chop ordered. On the 1MC, "Set condition ultra-quiet, set condition ultra-quiet."

Because we were still investigating and analyzing S-48, *Teuthis* was doing only five knots, so setting condition ultra-quiet mostly affected fans, blowers, and equipment.

Volgograd took fifteen minutes to clear her baffles. Then she returned to course 190 and thirty-five knots. The implication was that Captain First Rank Vladimir Ivanovich Vasnetsov was unaware of our presence.

So, what are you doing, Captain First Rank Vladimir Ivanovich Vasnetsov? Do you know about *Chángzhēng Four-alpha*? If so, how? Are you helping the Taiwanese bring their oil north? Too many variables, and insufficient time for me to follow him.

0100, WEDNESDAY, JULY 12, 1989—*USS TEUTHIS*, SUBMERGED AT 700 FT, TRANSITING NORTHEAST AT 20 KTS 400 NM WEST OF PALMER PENINSULA, ANTARCTICA

Palmer Station lies 107 miles north of the Antarctic Circle, and we would pass about 400 nautical miles west of the station. All other U.S. Antarctic stations lie south of the circle. This would be our second time crossing the Antarctic Circle this mission. I did not anticipate any further crossings. The XO had prepared Red Nose certificates for our new crew members, but we did nothing formal for the crossing except announce it on the 1MC. I did see several sailors running around with their noses painted red after our first crossing.

The divers, including our ChiCom prisoners, were slowly decompressing. Every time I checked on them, they were occupied with a Go game. Ham told me his divers and the Chinese divers were developing friendships. The Chinese divers were learning some English words, and our divers were learning some Chinese.

"Do you think it makes sense for this camaraderie to grow?" I asked Ham.

"It can't do any harm, and besides, I don't see any way to stop it."

"How's Chen holding up?"

"He's having a ball. He even played a Go game with one of the captives through the comm system. I think he wants to put in for dive school when we return."

✳

Roughly every two hours, *Volgograd* undertook a Crazy Ivan. She passed us heading southwest and then turned west, well north of Thurston Island. Her track gave no indication she had any interest in the island. The mysterious Captain First Rank's intentions would have to await another day on another mission. Sonar lost him completely the next day.

Sonar's main function was to act as the eyes and ears of the sub. Sonar had another task as well. A junior sonar tech with a sound-short meter visited all the equipment that might conceivably transmit sound to sea. He would measure the sound level on the equipment side of the sound mount and compare it to the sound on the hull side. The hull side should normally be much quieter than the equipment side. If it isn't, the engineers have a problem to repair. *Teuthis* was a very, very quiet sub. A primary reason was the diligence both Sonar and the engineers applied to minimizing these sound shorts.

During our last baffle clear, Sonar picked up a rhythmic rubbing sound that seemed to emanate from somewhere forward of the sail.

"It's low frequency," King told me after analyzing it. "It can be heard a long distance away."

"Define 'long distance'," I said.

"A hundred, two hundred miles, depending on water conditions."

That decided it for me. I called Ham. "Where are your divers, now?" I asked.

"About six hundred feet," he answered.

"Stop the decompression," I told him. "We have to isolate a sound outside the hull. I'll hover the sub at your current decompression depth, and you can send two men out to investigate."

The ability to do this was not normally part of a submarine's toolbox, but it fell squarely inside TOG's designated mission. Ham assigned his two most experienced divers, Ski and Jimmy, to the task.

Jerry, Roger's JOOD, brought *Teuthis* DIW, hovering at 600 feet. Wally met the divers with the Basketball as they ascended up the starboard side. To everyone's surprise, Borysko appeared, loudly whistling his excitement at seeing his diver friends in the water.

At 600 feet, Ski and Jimmy were surrounded by pitch black. The only illumination came from their built-in helmet lights. They started at the sail and moved forward. They reached the bow without finding anything. All that remained were the hawser lockers. The starboard one contained a hawser that was properly secured. Nothing to be the source of the rubbing. They opened the empty port locker. In the bottom, wedged between the locker wall and the hull, was a chewed piece of 4x4. Borysko, who was looking over their shoulders, pushed his snout into the locker, and retrieved his lost toy.

With the 4x4 piece in his jaws, he swam the 600 feet to the surface, took a deep breath, and swam down, offering the wood to Ski. Ski accepted it, held it behind his back, and let go. As it rose, Borysko swam after it, caught it in his mouth, and brought it back. Wally captured the whole thing with the Basketball.

Inside the DDC, the divers whooped and hollered with delight, and once the captive divers figured out what was happening, they whooped along with their captors.

0600, WEDNESDAY, JULY 12, 1989—*USS TEUTHIS*, SUBMERGED AT 700 FT, TRANSITING NORTHEAST 400 NM WEST OF PALMER STATION, ANTARCTICA

Nuclear submarines are designed to run dependably for long periods with nothing more than routine maintenance. In addition to the parts they share with non-nuclear ships, they carry a nuclear reactor that is subject to all the forces the rest of the ship has to endure—unlike nuclear reactors used for civilian power production. *Teuthis* was no different.

We were passing Palmer Station, 400 miles out, when the fateful words sounded throughout the sub, "Reactor scram! Reactor scram!"

The XO with Jerry Plummer had just been relieved in the Control Room by Waverly and Ham. The Reactor Assistant, Lt. Zeb Trainer, had the Maneuvering Watch. While Ham reduced speed, Zeb decreased the ship's power draw to the minimum necessary to sustain operations, powered by the battery bank.

The Engineer, Chief Warrant Officer-5 Bert Cobb, met with me in my cabin. "What happened, Bert?" I asked. He and I had been friends for a long time.

"Captain, right now we don't know. The reactor seems to have spontaneously scrammed—but you know they don't do that. There's always a reason. We'll find it, I promise…soon."

He left to supervise his people.

An hour later, Bert returned, carrying a small plastic bag holding a cloth. He opened the bag, drew out the cloth, and carefully unwrapped it on my desk. It contained a small, carbonized something. Bert looked at me expectantly, but I was baffled.

"If you expect me to figure this out Bert, you are wasting your time. I have no idea what that is."

Bert grinned at me. "Captain, can you spell m-o-u-s-e?"

"What are you talking about, Bert?"

"Once upon a time, this was a live mouse. He—if that's what it was, can't tell now—seems to have built a nest in the wiring behind the Reactor Control Panel. Apparently, he decided he needed more raw material for his nest, so he started gnawing on the insulation of the panel main power feed. Once he hit copper, everything came to an abrupt halt, including him and the reactor.

"We're replacing the feed wire now. We'll be back up in about thirty minutes."

Transit through Drake Passage to the Falkland Islands.

CHAPTER ELEVEN—Drake Passage

1100, WEDNESDAY, JULY 12, 1989—*USS TEUTHIS*, SUBMERGED AT 700 FT, TRANSITING DRAKE PASSAGE TOWARD THE FALKLAND ISLANDS

While we solved the problem of the mouse that roared, we slipped into day thirty-one of our mission. Waverly and Ham were in the Control Room, and Zeb was back in Maneuvering. Palmer Station was due south about 500 nautical miles, and Cape Horn lay 300 nautical miles due north. We were not in the remotest spot on Earth, but we were smack in the middle of the stormiest part.

I've already described how the turbulent waters above us came to be, but what I didn't say is that what we saw on our ice sonar beat anything I had ever seen. As we slipped into the main easterly flow of Drake Passage, the water above us heaped a hundred feet into the air. Eighty-knot winds ripped the tops of the piles of water to shreds, throwing water drops with such force that they would pierce two-by-fours. A sailing ship could have no more survived a passage in either direction than we could survive setting *Teuthis* on the bottom, 10,000 feet below us.

At 700 feet, we still felt the motion of the waves overhead, moving us several feet up and down as they rolled past us toward the east. By this time, most of the crew had their sea legs, but Roger mentioned that two messcooks got a little green around the gills.

King was Sonar Supervisor, but with the racket overhead, and our moving at twenty knots, Sonar was virtually deaf and blind. I was surprised, therefore, when King announced from Sonar, "Conn, Sonar, I have a surface contact dead ahead, range fifty miles or so, designate Sierra-four-nine."

"What's his bearing drift?" Ham asked.

"It's somewhat difficult to determine, but I think she's drifting left," King answered. Then he added, "This girl's on the surface…that surface. This is one very large ship, or there is no possibility she could survive these seas."

1200, THURSDAY, JULY 13, 1989—*USS TEUTHIS*, SUBMERGED AT 700 FT, TRANSITING DRAKE PASSAGE 300 NAUTICAL MILES SOUTH OF CAPE HORN

Although S-49 was no threat to *Teuthis*, I wanted to know what kind of vessel would brave the seas above us—or even could brave them. I had Waverly slow and present a port aspect to S-49.

Despite the turbulent surface, King got a good chart on the vessel and paged through his oversized volumes describing supertankers. I stood behind him, watching. After several minutes, he stopped turning pages.

"I'll be damned!" he muttered. "Look at this, Captain."

He showed me a page with a photo that looked like an ordinary supertanker. The name was Seawise Giant. What he showed me on the next page made it unusual. This tanker was over 1,500 feet long, 255 feet wide, with an 81-foot draft.

"By comparison," King said, "a typical supertanker is about a thousand feet long and one hundred eighty feet wide."

"It must be an exciting ride up there," I said.

"If fully laden," King said, "even a hundred-foot wave is unlikely to move it about much."

"You might be surprised," I said as I worked out a trigonometric problem in my head. "Typical storm waves in Drake are fifteen to thirty feet with a wavelength about the same number in yards. A tanker Seawise Giant's size will sail through those with very little motion. But we've got the mother of all storms up there, with some waves reaching a hundred feet. Wavelength doesn't have much meaning under these circumstances. Seawise Giant is longer than three football fields. She's going to press right through the face of those big ones, ride down the trailing face and push through the next before the first has passed her bridge."

"How's that?" King asked.

"For a hundred-foot wave with a twenty-five-degree slope, the face will be about two hundred fifty feet. It gets shorter as it gets steeper. That's just one-sixth the length of that sucker, and her draft is close to the wave height."

"Okay, I get it, Captain." King shook his head in amazement. "She's gonna move up and down by the bow and stern. She sure doesn't want to take one of those sideways."

"It would take a lot to capsize something that big, but I sure wouldn't want to try it."

✳

As the watch changed, the oncoming Sonar Supervisor, Mason, worked out Seawise Giant's track. She was headed west, probably somewhere in the Orient. Why she chose to round the Horn instead of sailing east around the less hazardous Cape of Good Hope was anybody's guess. Perhaps because she could.

1400, FRIDAY, JULY 14, 1989—*USS TEUTHIS,* SUBMERGED AT 500 FT, PASSING 150 NAUTICAL MILES WEST OF ISLA DE LAS ESTADOS

We made it through Drake Passage without further incident. If there were other contacts out there, we didn't detect them. One hundred fifty nautical miles off our port bow lay Isla de las Estados, marking the edge of South America's continental shelf. Water depth shallowed rapidly to an average of about 4,000 feet. It was day thirty-three, and we were one and a half days out of Mare Harbour.

Expanding on the information I requested the *Hǎi Hǔ Jīng* to relay four days earlier, I prepared a message to ComSubLant detailing the situation with *Kan-Cha 2*. I described the one diver death, capture of two others, and scuttling of the PTC. I confirmed captive delivery at 1800 on July 18 and explained that the two captives had not requested asylum, but I recommended against returning them to the ChiComs, since that would reveal our activities off Thurston Island, including the possibility we had been involved in the loss of *Chángzhēng 35*. I suggested they probably would be pleased to be picked up by the Taiwanese.

I called Jerry to my cabin and gave him the message. "Make this top secret and encrypt it. Send it as soon as we hit periscope depth."

Seth had the watch in Control. Hank Bass was quartermaster at Plot.

"Quartermaster, how long since we set the SINS?" I asked.

"Last one was a week ago, July 7, in Potaka Inlet," Bass answered.

I glanced at the ice sonar indicator. Seas were moderating. I guessed that when we crossed the Isla de las Estados latitude, the heavy seas would disappear.

"What's the latitude of Isla de las Estados?" I asked Bass.

"Fifty-four degrees, forty-five minutes, and seven point seven-nine seconds," he answered.

"When is the next satellite pass?"

"We've got two birds in fifty minutes, Sir."

"When do we cross that latitude?"

"A few minutes before, Sir."

"Seth, bring *Teuthis* to two hundred feet. When you cross the latitude the quartermaster just gave me, slow to five knots, come to periscope depth for a fix. Make sure we get a good one."

I went to my cabin but returned to Control as Seth was preparing to come to periscope depth. I grabbed the Nav Scope, letting him take the Attack Scope. My scope pushed through the surface, the optics continuously washed by three- to five-foot waves. I could see no land, of course. The sky was overcast, and it might have been raining, but I couldn't tell with waves washing over the scope.

"Conn, Sonar, I have four small contacts to our north about ten miles. They're fishing vessels, probably fishing the Burdwood Bank. Designate Sierra-five-zero, five-one, five-two, and five-three."

The Nav ET announced, "I've got a good sat fix."

Seth glanced at me. As Navigator, he knew our track took us close to the shallow water of Burdwood Bank. He wanted specific guidance from me.

"Take her to one-ten feet and ten knots. The waters around here are not well charted yet. We don't want to discover a seamount the hard way."

I returned to my cabin and called the XO to join me. A few minutes later, he arrived with two cups of joe.

"Thanks," I said, taking a steaming cup from him. "Roger, we have about twenty hours before we surface off Mare Harbour. We've gained five hours since departing Mare Island. On Saturday, drop an hour from each watch section and one from four on Sunday. That way we'll synch with daylight in the Falklands."

"We could just shift to Zulu time," Roger said, "and let the COW keep track of rig-for-red."

"I thought about it," I said. "That's what the Boomers do, but they hang out in an area, so the crew gets used to the setup. We're transiting, and we'll cross another six time zones by the time we reach the Prince Edward Islands. The crew is more comfortable when rig-for-red conforms to the clock on the wall."

"You've got a point there. The Prince Edwards are plus three, right?"

"Right," I answered.

"So, we got another six hours to deal with. How do you want to handle it?"

"I don't anticipate near surface ops between here and there," I said. "Let's spread it out across the first six watches."

✳

On the 1MC: "This is the Executive Officer. The ship will be moving the clock ahead five hours, one hour each watch commencing with Section Four on Saturday morning. Be sure to set your watches forward each watch so you don't arrive late for watch or miss a meal. Check with the COB for any questions."

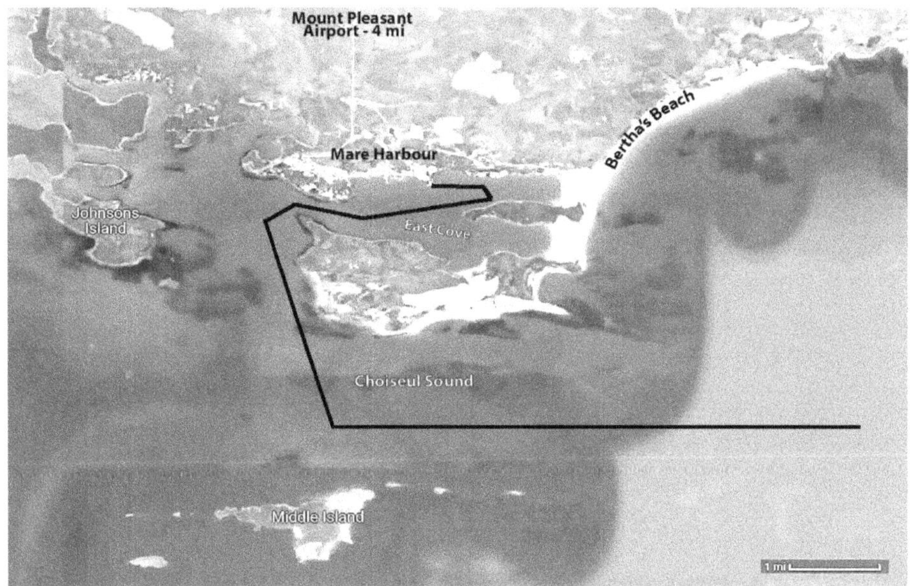

Track into and out of Mare Harbour, the Falkland Islands.

CHAPTER TWELVE—The Falklands

0000, SUNDAY, JULY 16, 1989—*USS TEUTHIS*, SURFACED, THREE NAUTICAL MILES EAST OF MARE HARBOUR, THE FALKLAND ISLANDS

Senior Chief Radioman Garth Walkman, Sparks to one and all, was Chief of the Watch when Jerry, as Roger's JOOD, gave the order to Senior Chief Electronics Tech Rusty Jackson, "Diving Officer, surface the ship!"

This was a big deal for everybody. We had been submerged for thirty-four days, which meant we had blown sanitaries at least once, venting the tanks inboard, of course. The charcoal filters and CO-H2 burner worked hard, but you could not really get rid of the stench. You just got used to it—got nose blind to that particular "wavelength" of stink. The crew definitely was ready for some fresh air.

We had already spent several minutes at periscope depth cataloging nearby fishing vessels—five of them, none closer than two miles. Jeff Davis already had them positioned on his chart. Frank Sportsman's

Seaman Pope George (Popeye) remained at the helm, while Seamen Pete Gustaffson and Herbert Hammer (whom the other seamen called Dick after the Mike Hammer TV detective program) donned heavy jackets and grabbed binoculars, squawk box, and compass repeater, and climbed to the bridge. Jerry followed them.

I grinned at the XO and said, "I'll take over from here, Roger." Then I announced to the Control Room, "The captain has the Deck, Mr. Plummer has the Conn." Shortly thereafter, I joined the bridge crew.

Almost immediately after I arrived on the bridge, Borysko leaped into the air, whistling loudly, his entire six-ton body clearing the water.

On my instructions, Jerry increased our speed to ten knots and headed due west for the entrance to Choiseul Sound.

Jerry maintained ten knots until Middle Island was directly south of us. Then he turned right and, after a mile, slowed to five knots. Borysko kept pace with us, although we could only see him in the darkness when we put a spotlight on him. At 0300, as we approached the turn into East Cove, on my order, Sparks set the maneuvering watch. It was an ungodly hour to get the crew up and moor the sub, but things were what they were. Borysko cavorted around us as we reversed course in East Cove and sidled up to *HMS Talent*, the newly commissioned British sub under the command of Cmdr. Johnny Harris, that had moored the previous afternoon.

Tied to the dock in front of *Talent*, *HMS Tireless*, commanded by Cmdr. Timothy Pentreath McClement, had moored several hours ahead of us.

Cmdr. Harris was on *Talent's* bridge with a salute and welcoming wave. To my surprise, Col. Harry Brisbane was on the fully lighted dock to greet us, prim and proper, with his swagger stick tucked under his left arm, barking orders to the line handlers, who had, themselves, turned out in full work dungarees, and were working from *Talent's* deck. From the dock across *Talent's* deck, the colonel saluted me smartly in proper British fashion with palm facing out. I returned his salute, thanked him for his docking assistance, and asked, "Colonel, can you join me in my Wardroom for breakfast at oh six hundred?"

"Delighted, Captain," he said, saluted again, did an about face, and left the dock for the open Land Rover waiting for him.

While we were talking, Cmdr. McClement showed up on the *Tireless* bridge. He saluted and waved a welcome. I returned his salute.

I turned to Cmdr. Harris on *Talent*. "Would you join us as well, Captain?"

"See you at 0600, Sir," Harris answered with a snappy British salute.

I turned to Cmdr. McClement on *Tireless*. "Would you also join us, Captain?"

"Be delighted. See you at oh six hundred."

King's deck gang tied us up securely, accepted the brow the British sailors pushed across the gap, and helped bring a small wood guard shack for our topside watchstander, to keep the chilly Antarctic breeze away. King and his men went below. We secured the bridge and went below ourselves. King set the in-port watch, Section Four. And the ship settled down, waiting for the morning meal to be served at 0600.

0700, SUNDAY, JULY 16, 1989—*USS TEUTHIS*, MOORED AT MARE HARBOUR, THE FALKLAND ISLANDS

Col. Brisbane leaned back in his chair with a satisfied sigh. "Now that is what I call a proper way to break one's fast." He took a sip of tea. "These popovers are remarkable. Wherever did you find a chef who could make them?"

I signaled Rivera, who slipped out to get the Senior Chief.

When he arrived, I said, "Gentlemen, let me introduce Senior Chief Cedric Hurst, the very best cook in America's Navy. Cedric has been with us since *Teuthis* was commissioned."

"Bravo!" the colonel said.

"Well done!" Cmdr. Harris added. "*Talent* should be so fortunate."

"I couldn't agree more," Cmdr. McClement said.

I sipped my second cup of coffee while my officers chatted with Harris, McClement, and Brisbane about British submarines, Mare Harbour and the Falklands, and about the recently concluded war with Argentina.

Brisbane turned to me. "Your provisions will arrive this morning. I'll have workers standing by to assist in the load out."

"Thanks."

"I understand both British subs and *Teuthis* will get underway Monday at oh nine hundred for DSRV training ops."

I acknowledged.

"You are tentatively scheduled to return on Tuesday at seventeen hundred hours."

Harris, McClement, and I nodded.

"We'll have to schedule a celebration at the pub on your return," Brisbane said with a chuckle. "Our opportunities to celebrate are few and far between down here."

"Would you like to join us on our little operation?" I asked Brisbane.

"I thought you would never ask."

"You can go out on *Teuthis*," I said and glanced at Harris, who nodded slightly, "and return on *Talent*."

I turned to Harris and McClement. "*Mystic* can accommodate twenty-four passengers. You are welcome to let your crew members experience the DSRV firsthand. We'll make two round trips to each sub, so we can handle several groups."

Harris shook his head. "I can't afford to have twenty-four personnel absent, but we could handle three groups of ten."

"I agree," McClement said. "More than that would be a problem."

"So," I said, "ten from each sub could ride out on *Teuthis*. Ten from *Talent* would transfer with the first DSRV docking, ten more could return to *Teuthis* on *Mystic* and then return on the next docking, and finally, ten could return on *Mystic* to *Teuthis*, to remain for the ride to Mare Harbour. We would do the same sequence with *Tireless*. This would give one group from each sub two trips, but will accommodate thirty people per submarine."

"We might be able to accommodate fifteen people for the round trip," Harris said, "perhaps even an officer or two."

"I agree," McClement said. "That works for me, too."

"My COB will work with whomever you designate to work out the details," I told both skippers.

✳

While the crew was getting ready to load stores when they arrived, I called Brisbane. "Can we meet in your office in thirty minutes?" I asked.

When I entered his office, Brisbane said, "Mac, I know we just had breakfast, and I have no coffee, but can I offer you a cup of Earl Grey?"

"Thanks. I would enjoy your tea."

"It's your nickel, Mac, as you say in your idiom."

"I have two confidential matters, Harry. First, I have two ChiCom divers aboard *Teuthis*. They are still decompressing with my divers. They'll surface early Tuesday morning while we are on DSRV ops. I have notified ComSubLant, but they may not get someone here before I depart again. Can you hold them from eighteen hundred on the eighteenth? They don't speak English, but they will cooperate. I have a crew member who can give them final instructions in Chinese before we leave. No one but you and your immediate security team should know of their presence." I sipped my tea while looking him in the eye.

"Of course, I'll accommodate you, Mac," Brisbane said. "By the way, how are your shoulder and leg?"[17]

"I still have some shoulder pain from time to time," I said, "but generally, I'm fully healed."

"Good to hear. You had us all worried, you know." He refreshed my cup. "You mentioned a second matter…"

"Yes…A four-man Israeli Shayetet Thirteen commando unit will arrive at Mount Pleasant Airport in an unmarked aircraft today along with their Shayetet Thirteen secretive commander, Rav-Seren Yisha-yahu Brosh—known as Shaikeh by all his commandos. Can you meet them personally—no driver—and escort them to *Teuthis*? They will be dressed as civilians, and they should pass virtually unnoticed if nobody calls attention to them." I knew I was asking a lot of this traditional British officer. I waited patiently.

Brisbane carefully refilled his cup, checked its temperature, and took a cautious sip. He arranged two pens on his desktop, straightened a photo, and then placed his hands flat on the desk in front of him.

"I will do this thing, Mac, and I will not ask what their presence means. I will look forward to some future moment when you can explain this all to me."

---

17 Referring to gunshot injuries I received on my visit to Mare Harbour during *Operation White Out*.

1400, SUNDAY, JULY 16, 1989—*USS TEUTHIS*, MOORED AT MARE HARBOUR, THE FALKLAND ISLANDS

The stores arrived, and Brisbane's men worked with King's deck gang to get everything below decks and properly secured. They loaded a lot of cartons and boxes with sufficient provisions to keep the crew fed through the end of August. Under Cedric's watchful eye and careful note taking, King's people stowed everything throughout the sub, ensuring that nothing would cause a sound short to the hull. They were still doing this when Brisbane drove up in an enclosed Land Rover with darkened windows.

The first man out was medium tall, muscled, with short-cropped, curly dark hair, deep-set eyes, and a prominent nose—Shaikeh, commander of the feared Shayetet 13. Brisbane joined him and spoke briefly, pointing to the *HMS Talent* brow. Four other men exited the Land Rover, each carrying an oversize duffle bag. They crossed the brow to *Talent*, crossed the second brow to *Teuthis*, where King met them and brought them below through the forward hatch. King brought Shaikeh to my cabin and then dropped the four commandos off at the top deck of the DOC, above the DDC. Four bunks had been installed back at Mare Island to accommodate them.

I motioned the Shayetet 13 commander to the easy chair and turned my desk chair around to face him. "Welcome aboard, Sir," I said.

"Thank you, Captain. Please call me Shaikeh."

"Okay, Shaikeh it is. Your men have been shown their quarters, such as they are. I presume all four speak English."

"They do. It was a requirement for this mission."

"How long before you depart?" I asked.

"We have some equipment to load, equipment that should not be exposed to prying eyes. Do you have a suggestion?"

"After dark, you can borrow a pickup from Colonel Brisbane, pick up your equipment, and drive it to the waterfront a hundred yards or so to the west. Your guys can swim it underwater to a lock on our dive complex directly beneath where your people are berthed. Their compartment has room to stow the equipment out of sight."

"That works. Can one of your divers accompany us?"

"All the divers are currently decompressing. Their schedule has a couple more days. Chief Warrant Officer Hamilton Comstock is their boss. I'll make him available." I picked up my phone and called Ham.

"Ham, can you join me in my cabin, please?"

When Ham arrived, I introduced him to Shaikeh, explained briefly what he needed, and told them to work out the details in the Wardroom.

✳

In the Wardroom, Shaikeh asked, "Can we bring my team leader into this discussion?"

"Of course," Ham said. "What is his name?"

"Rav Nagad Hadriel Davidov—Chief Warrant Officer in English. The men call him Ranag." He grinned. "How can I reach him?"

"That handset," Ham said, pointing, and gave him the number to dial.

"Ranag," Shaikeh said into the handset, and then rattled off in Hebrew.

"You all speak English, right?" Ham asked.

Shaikeh nodded.

"It would be helpful if you and your people would use English when around anyone aboard *Teuthis*," Ham said with a gentle smile. "On a sub, we get nervous when we cannot understand what someone is saying."

"You're right, of course," Shaikeh said. "I'll make sure my people comply."

A knock on the door brought in a man in civies, taller and younger than his commander and less muscled. His eyes were dark as coals, and his close-cropped black hair matched his closely clipped full beard.

"Chief Warrant Officer Hamilton Comstock, meet Rav Nagad, uh…Chief Warrant Officer Hadriel Davidov."

They shook hands.

"Good to meet you," Ranag said in perfectly enunciated American English. At Ham's startled reaction, he said, "Born and raised in America, Oklahoma. Emigrated to Israel when I reached twenty-one."

After some small talk and a discussion of what the Israelis needed, Ham said, "Let's take a short walk. I'll show you where to bring the pickup, and where your guys will meet you. I'll be suited up and with your team, Ranag, when we do the deed."

Ham and the two Israelis left *Teuthis* and walked a short distance up the road leading to the wharf. They turned left, passing behind the Special Ops Bunker, and left again to the water. At the shore, the water was shallow, but dropped away quickly, "To about fifty feet," Ham told them. "You can back up here, move everything quickly into the water, and then take your time getting it into *Teuthis*."

While they stood at the shore discussing the matter, the water rippled, and a large black and white snout lifted out of the water a few feet from the shoreline.

The two Israelis jumped back, startled.

"Hey, Borysko!" Ham said.

The cetacean whistled back and slapped his tail. Then he pushed his head up against the gravel beach and opened his six-foot mouth. Ham reached in and scratched his tongue.

"Go ahead," Ham said. "He won't bite. It's how you make friends with him."

Davidov reached out to scratch. "Fuckin' amazing!" he said. "Try it, Shaikeh."

"He'll be with us tonight in the water," Ham said. "You can count on it."

✻

The sun set in the winter sky behind a veil of gray clouds. It got dark quickly. Shaikeh walked to the motor pool up the road and took possession of a well-used Toyota pickup. He used only the parking lights until he was well on the way to Mount Pleasant. Once Mare Harbour dropped behind him, he turned on his lights and increased his speed to complete the trip as soon as possible.

At the completely unguarded airport, he found the warehouse where they had earlier stowed their equipment—a collapsed rubber boat and some other things they would need at Prince Edward Island. He loaded everything into the pickup, tossed a tarp over it, and headed back to Mare Harbour. As he approached, he extinguished his headlights. He passed the motor pool, turned right past the Special Ops Bunker, and swung around to back up against the narrow gravel beach. When he shut down the engine and turned off the lights, he was virtually invisible.

A dark head poked up through the black water, followed by four more. The divers left the water and deposited their SCUBA equipment on the narrow gravel strip. They all pitched in to unload the pickup, completing the job in five minutes.

Shaikeh returned to the motor pool using only parking lights and walked back to the wharf. He crossed *Talent's* deck and entered *Teuthis*, flashing his temporary credentials to both topside watches.

In Dive Control, Bill had moved the still saturated divers into the DDC and sealed the door to the Port Lock. He pressurized the lock to the ambient pressure at the keel. Shaikeh entered Dive Control just as Ham pushed open the hatch for the Port Lock. He climbed into the lock and pulled up another diver—Rav Samal Rishon Chaim Meiyr. Then, together, they hauled the collapsed boat and several other pieces of equipment into the lock.

Davidov stuck his head through the hatch.

Ham told him, "You three go back for the next load. Meiyr and I will move this load into storage." Ham grabbed the handset. "Surface the lock, Bill."

Surfacing took five minutes. Ham and Meiyr moved the collapsed boat and other equipment through the upper hatch into the space above where the team was berthed. They dropped back into the lock, and Ham told Bill to pressurize it to ambient again. Shortly after they opened the hatch, Davidov and the other divers appeared with the next equipment load.

"One more load," Davidov said with a thumbs up.

Another half hour found the Shayetet 13 team back aboard *Teuthis* with all their equipment stowed. They took a long, hot shower, dressed, ate a hot meal Cedric prepared for them, and crashed in their temporary bunks that seemed far better than sleeping on the ground, as they had to do so many times before.

I stopped in to Dive Control to congratulate the divers on their successful mission. I spoke briefly with Shaikeh and accompanied him to the Torpedo Room hatch, where I shook his hand and bid him godspeed.

Col. Brisbane brought his Land Rover with its blackened windows onto the wharf and drove Shaikeh to Mount Pleasant Airport, where he entered his unmarked aircraft for the long journey back to Israel.

I never saw him again.

2000, SUNDAY, JULY 16, 1989—THE PUB, MARE HARBOUR, THE FALKLAND ISLANDS

Mare Harbour sports a small pub across the road from the Special Ops Bunker. It's where I first got involved with Lt. Heather Wells and nearly destroyed my Navy career.[18] The pub carries beers and ales and has a surprisingly wide selection of hard liquors. And most importantly, it accepts Yankee dollars.

That evening, Roger and I visited the pub. Several of the crew were already there, behaving themselves, fortunately. The divers were still decompressing, so that was one worry off my mind. Roger and I joined two British officers standing at the end of the bar.

I greeted the tall, lanky lieutenant, Brisbane's adjutant, "Lieutenant Akins, nice to see you again."

Akins popped to attention. "Captain McDowell."

The other shorter, stouter officer, Lt. Ainsley Geoffery, was the Mare Harbour Supply Officer.

"Lieutenant Ainsley," I said, nodding to him. Like his partner, he came to formal attention.

"Relax," I told the pale-skinned, light-haired officers. "This is your down time. Enjoy it." I grinned at them both. "May I introduce my Executive Officer, Commander Roger Barnes?"

They started to come to attention a second time, but Roger forestalled them by reaching out and shaking their hands. "Gentlemen," he said with a smile.

The pub door opened, and in walked a woman, medium height, stocky, not wearing makeup, with brown hair pulled into a bun. She approached the bar and greeted the British officers with a curt nod. Then she turned to me and offered her hand.

---

18 See *Operation White Out*, vol 4 in *The Mac McDowell Missions*.

"Lieutenant Margaret Goss—she pronounced it leftenant—SO-SUS Group Commander," she said with a firm handshake. "I know what happened during your last visit.16 I very much regret that. We run a tight ship now. You're welcome to drop by before you leave."

I thanked her and introduced Roger. "May I buy you a drink?" I asked.

She smiled. "I appreciate it, Captain, but I owe you one, to make up in small part for my predecessor's behavior."

Obviously, I would not win this one, so I ordered a Lagavulin.

"You know your scotches," she said and placed an order for two.

When the drinks arrived, she lifted hers and said, "To two peoples separated by a common language!"

I chuckled and touched her glass with mine. Then we tossed our drinks back. "Thank you, Lieutenant."

"Maggi," she corrected with a hearty laugh. "Gotta go. I've got a new section chief coming on line. I need to check her out before I let her loose in the bunker."

✳

Some of my crew had found female companionship—probably members of Maggi's group. I silently wished them well. Back against the wall, I saw something that reminded me of my previous visit to this pub. A lone civilian sat nursing a beer. To all appearances, he was just relaxing for a few minutes before turning in. The fellow last time had turned out to be a Soviet informant who played a role in my taking two bullets. When King arrived with a couple of other chiefs a few minutes later, I waved him over.

"Don't look now," I said, "but when you turn around, you'll see a guy by himself nursing a beer. Last time, a similar guy turned out to be a spy. Do what you can to keep the troops from revealing anything he might use."

King wandered over to the sailors and their companions. He spoke to a couple and slapped one on his back. Then he stumbled into the lone drinker's table, spilling his beer.

"I am so sorry," King exclaimed as he grabbed napkins to soak up the beer, "Please let me get you another."

The man stood, cursed King in Spanish, and stomped out of the pub. King turned and winked at me before sitting at a table with some of his guys.

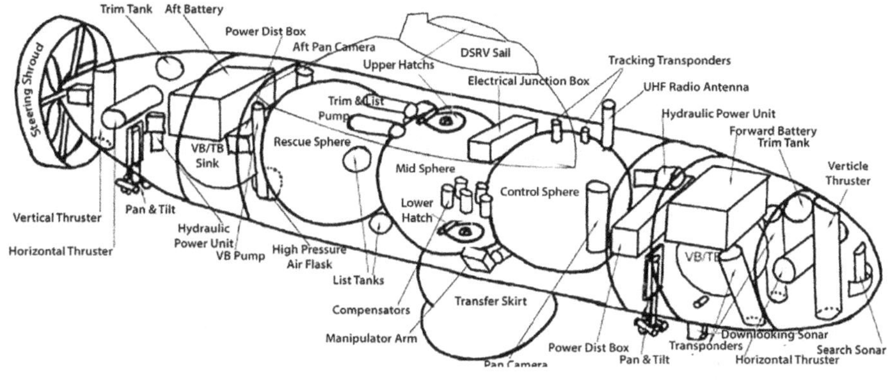

DSRV cutaway.

CHAPTER THIRTEEN—DSRV Ops

0900, MONDAY, JULY 17, 1989—*USS TEUTHIS*, UNDERWAY ON SURFACE, TRANSITING TO DSRV OPS AREA, 100 NAUTICAL MILES EAST OF MARE HARBOUR, THE FALKLAND ISLANDS

We carried twenty-one extra people as we headed for the DSRV ops area, ten from each British sub, including an officer each, and Col. Brisbane. The sub officers and Brisbane lounged in the Wardroom, while the rest nearly filled the Crew's Mess.

The moment we got underway, the COB commenced rigging for dive. Since we knew we would return to sea not long after we docked in Mare Harbour, most of the ship had been left rigged for dive. The exceptions were what we needed for shoreside operation. We did not connect shore power, so we remained on ship's power, which meant the engineering department had to remain in ship's power mode. All this meant that we were ready to dive the moment we crossed the fifty-fathom curve, and the Falkland Islands' coastline dropped off remarkably fast.

I asked our visitors to remain in the Crew's Mess during operations, because there simply isn't enough room for twenty extra people to be wandering around the sub while we were doing things. An hour after we left Mare Harbour, Ham, as Waverly's JOOD, informed me we were ready to dive. I had spent that hour on the bridge with Waverly, Ham, and their lookouts.

Borysko led us out of Mare Harbour and then rode our bow wave as we headed toward the DSRV ops area. He seemed to sense we were ready to dive. He stood off our starboard side, pushing his great body up out of the water, whistling the entire time.

I left the bridge first, followed by Waverly and the lookouts. Ham remained topside to secure the bridge.

"Status?" Ham asked as he dropped into Control.

"Green board," the COW said, indicating that all openings to sea were securely closed.

Since modern nuclear submarines do not dive very often, unlike the old diesels, Ham took advantage of this opportunity, going through all the motions. He placed himself on the Attack Scope while I took the Nav.

"Diving Officer," Ham said to Tubes, "Dive the ship. Make your depth six-five feet, periscope depth. Flood Main Ballast and sound the diving alarm."

Dokey sounded the klaxon twice and announced on the 1MC, "Dive! Dive!"

I had trained the Nav Scope forward and watched spray shoot above the sub as Dokey opened the large vent. I whipped around to the stern, looking past the DSRV to see the spout from the after tank. Ham did the same, and within a minute, Tubes announced, "At six-five feet."

"Conn, Sonar," King announced from Sonar, "I have two submerged submarines off our starboard bow bearing zero-nine-five and zero-nine-seven at a range of five and six miles respectively, designate Sierra-five-four and five-five. These are *HMS Talent* and *Tireless*. I also have five surface contacts in our starboard quarter bearing two-five-five through two-six-five, designate Sierra-five-six through Sierra-six-zero. These are fishing vessels probably headed for Burdwood Bank. We should lose them in an hour or so. They might be a factor when we return."

1800, MONDAY, JULY 17, 1989—*USS TEUTHIS*, SUBMERGED AT 500 FT, 100 NAUTICAL MILES EAST OF MARE HARBOUR, THE FALKLAND ISLANDS

Following the script we received from our respective commands, Harris and I worked out a protocol for our exercise that would involve his and my Control Room and Sonar people, and give *Mystic's* pilots experience docking to a non-U.S. sub.

The initial exercise had *Talent* in a tactical situation when she suffered a personnel casualty—a seriously injured crewmember who required evacuation. Because of the tactical situation, *Talent* could not surface to offload the injured crew member. *Talent* sent a burst message distress call that was picked up by the British Admiralty and forwarded to ComSubLant.

The exercise commenced with *Talent* sending the burst message. This was an excellent test of the combined Command and Control Systems of the British and American Atlantic fleets. Nearly an hour passed before *Teuthis* received emergency orders to come to *Talent's* aid. This slow response was going to require corrective action well above my paygrade, and Johnny's, too.

The emergency message from ComSubLant identified itself as an exercise message just to cover everyone's butts. It gave *Talent's* coordinates and specified a silent approach—no active sonar.

Seth had just completed his watch as we started the exercise, so he could concentrate on finding *Talent*. Rob Borka and Chop had the watch in Control. Rob let Chop run the op.

"Sonar, Conn, where is the layer?" Chop asked.

"At four hundred feet, Conn."

"*Talent* is supposed to be at five hundred feet," Chop said. "Frenchy, how much water under my keel?" he asked Quartermaster Theron.

"Fifteen hundred feet, Sir," Theron answered.

Chop turned to Chief Oberst, who had the Dive. "Diving Officer, make your depth seven-zero-zero feet, fifteen degree down-bubble."

"Frenchy, heading to *Talent*?"

"One-seven-five, Sir. Five miles distant."

"All stop. Left full rudder. Make your course zero-nine-zero." He picked up the mike to Sonar. "Sonar, Conn, try to find *Talent*. She should be five miles off our starboard beam. I suspect she's in silent mode."

"We got her, Conn, four and a half miles. Do you know her depth?"

"She's supposed to be at five hundred feet, Sonar."

"She's above us, but we're both beneath the layer."

I was hanging out at Plot, watching Chop do his thing. He turned to me. "How do you want to handle this, Captain?"

"Check with Deckhart," I answered. "See how close he wants *Teuthis* to be."

Chop used the handset and then turned to me again. "Deckhart wants to be within a mile."

"That works," I said. "Now you know what to do."

Chop moved us closer to *Talent* by about three miles and change. He turned broadside to the British sub again. "Sonar, Conn, get me good range information on *Talent*."

"A mile directly off our starboard beam. Two hundred feet above us."

Chop turned to his OOD. "They can determine depth like that?" he asked.

Borka grinned. "Not really. You already told them she is at five hundred feet. They know we are at seven hundred. Voila."

Chop blushed and picked up the 1MC mike. "Now, prepare for DSRV ops. Now prepare for DSRV ops."

✳

King, as COB, organized the guys waiting in the Crew's Mess and got the appropriate officer from the Wardroom. Within a few minutes, they assembled near the after escape trunk. Chief Gamble got them into *Mystic*, and distributed them in the Rescue and Mid Spheres. Elton sealed the DSRV, and the engineers closed the escape trunk hatches.

On Chop's order, Derrick launched the Basketball and drove it over to watch *Mystic* unlatch and depart.

"Request permission to unlatch and get underway," Deckhart said over the circuit.

"Permission granted," Chop responded.

On the monitors, we watched *Mystic* lift off her cradle, turn right, and head into the darkness with a slight up angle.

Deckhart picked up *Talent* on his high-frequency forward sonar after several minutes. Ten minutes later, his forward-looking camera picked up *Talent* in the DSRV's floodlights.

On the Gertrude, Deckhart said, "*Talent*, this is *Mystic*. I am ten yards off your starboard bow. I will approach and settle on your forward escape hatch ring. Over."

The echoey, haunting sound of *Talent's* response sounded throughout *Mystic*. "This is *Talent*. Roger. We are standing by. Over."

Deckhart brought the little sub up and over *Talent's* forward deck and settled down on the ring around the hatch. Using his thrusters, he pressed down hard, while Chief Gamble began pumping water from the skirt. When the skirt was dry, external water pressure kept *Mystic* firmly sealed to the ring. Gamble opened the mini sub's bottom hatch, releasing some pressurized air into the Center Sphere. He pounded on the submarine hatch with a hammer, and shortly the hatch locking mechanism began to turn. Moments later, the hatch swung up into the skirt, with a British sailor standing on a steel ladder rung just below.

"Hey up!" the sailor said with a wide grin.

Gamble drew back slightly as the sub smell hit him. He pasted a grin on his face and said, "Hey, British. We got ten passengers for ya."

"Send 'em down, Yank," the sailor said and dropped to the deck below.

Once all the passengers had debarked, the sailor stuck his head into the skirt again and said, "Now, we got ten fer ya."

He dropped back, and ten obviously excited sailors climbed into *Mystic*. Elton pointed them to the Rescue Sphere. When everyone was seated, Gamble pushed the submarine hatch down, and someone dogged it from below. He closed *Mystic's* lower hatch and commenced flooding the skirt. In less than a minute, *Mystic* started rocking gently as it lifted free from *Talent*.

"*Talent*, this is *Mystic*. I am clear of your deck and heading back to *Teuthis*. Over."

"This is *Talent*. Roger, out."

✳

As *Mystic* approached her cradle on *Teuthis*, a black and white image filled the forward-looking monitor. When the beast turned away, Deckhart caught a glimpse of a dorsal fin missing a chunk from its after edge.

"We have a visitor, people, an old friend. It's Borysko, an Orca that has accompanied *Teuthis* on all her excursions from the Arctic to the Antarctic. You may have seen him cavorting in Mare Harbour before you got underway. He poses no danger, even though he's thirty feet long and weighs six tons. He just wants to be part of what is happening. Since we are at seven hundred feet, he cannot remain with us for very long. With any luck, he'll return, and you can watch him on one of the internal monitors on *Teuthis*."

Fifteen minutes later, thirteen British sailors found themselves enjoying a snack in the Crew's Mess, while the two officers sipped Black Oolong tea in the Wardroom, chatting with Deckhart and XO Roger Barnes. The XO referred to a protocol sheet.

"*Talent* will reposition herself on the bottom at a thousand feet and send off another emergency burst message. Hopefully, the system will be more responsive this time. She's scheduled to send the signal in about twenty minutes." He looked at the two guests. "Hang loose until we get the signal."

I stepped into Control at the time *Talent* was to have sent the emergency burst message. I glanced at my watch, wondering how it would work out this time. To my pleasant surprise, thirty minutes later, we received a SUBMISS/SUBSUNK notification from ComSubLant. This was half the previous reaction time. The message contained the last known location of the missing submarine.

Frenchy marked the location on the chart. "It's five miles distant at one thousand feet," he announced.

Chop got a heading from Frenchy and headed us that way at twenty knots. After twelve minutes, he ordered, "All stop, back one-third."

Within a minute, *Teuthis* was coasting slowly forward. "Helmsman, left full rudder." When *Teuthis* had swung ninety degrees left, Chop ordered, "Rudder amidships." He called Sonar, "Sonar, Conn. The distressed sub should be broad off our starboard beam. Find her and report."

"Conn, Sonar. Located the distressed sub broad off the starboard beam at one mile. She appears to be on the bottom at one thousand feet."

"Bottom depth," Chop asked Plot.

"One-zero-zero-zero feet, Sir," Frenchy answered.

"Diving Officer, lower the skids to full extension and put *Teuthis* on the bottom at one-zero-zero-zero feet."

Chop put *Teuthis* on the bottom like he had been doing it all his life. Wally was on the Basketball, so everyone got to watch *Mystic* lift off her cradle and disappear into the blackness.

While *Mystic* was away, the watch changed, with the XO and Jerry in Control. Roger let Jerry run the whole op. As he got started, Ham called Control on the dial phone. The XO answered and handed the phone to me.

"For you, Captain. It's Ham."

"The divers just surfaced, Captain. I thought you would want to know," Ham said.

"What about the captives?" I asked.

"I'm keeping them in Dive Control. They're pretty mellow, but I'm keeping my divers close, just in case. I'm also keeping Billy here so we can communicate. Don't worry, Sir, things are going well."

I didn't disagree with Ham, but my job was to worry. I definitely would be happy to offload them.

The bottom operation went without a hitch, and a half hour later, *Mystic* returned with a fresh load of fifteen visitors. I reported the "rescue" to ComSubLant, and we got ready for the next exercise, this time with *Tireless*.

I would like to tell you that our DSRV training with *HMS Tireless* went as well. Unfortunately, I cannot. Initially, things went well. *Tireless* sent her burst message, and we received orders to respond just fifteen minutes later. That was a dramatic improvement over the hour it took the first time. Borysko played a role throughout, to the delight of our visitors.

Matters took a strange turn, however, when *Mystic* lifted off the foredeck of a bottomed *Tireless*, simulating her need for complete evacuation.

One of the fifteen crew members designated to return on *Mystic* apparently was nervous about boarding *Mystic* in the first place. When he expressed his reservations, several of his shipmates shamed him into going, anyway. In order to make the exercise more realistic aboard *Tireless*, Captain McClement had his OOD make appropriate announcements, as if *Tireless* were in actual trouble. By the time this 19-year-old sailor, who had just graduated from Submarine School, found his seat in *Mystic*'s Rescue Sphere, he had concluded that the exercise was real, that *Tireless* was actually lost.

Chief Gamble reported later that as *Mystic* got underway, the lad was sweating profusely and appeared to be terrified. When *Mystic* tilted up, he began to scream in terror, got to his feet, stumbled into the Mid Sphere, and tried to open the lower hatch. Petty Officer Elton grabbed the terrified lad's shoulder, spun him around, and clipped him soundly on his chin.

Deckhart called me on the Secure Gertrude, which prevented either *Tireless* or *Talent* from overhearing the conversation. "Captain, we got a problem."

He quickly explained the situation and requested permission to return to *Tireless*.

"Make it so," I told him, "and contact me again when you depart *Tireless*."

Deckhart called *Tireless* on the standard Gertrude. "*Tireless*, thus is *Mystic*, over."

"This is *Tireless*, over."

"*Tireless*, we have a situation onboard and need to return to *Tireless*. I will be delivering an injured crewmember. Please stand by to receive him."

"This is *Tireless*. Roger. What is your ETA?"

"This is *Mystic*. Twelve minutes. Out."

Mystic docked, cleared the skirt, opened the hatch, and pounded on *Tireless*' hatch. When the hatch opened, Gamble lowered the still unconscious sailor. He turned to the Rescue Sphere hatch opening.

"The exercise is terminated. You people need to return to *Tireless*." He motioned the senior lieutenant in the group to wait. When they were alone, Gamble said, "Lieutenant, please ask your Executive Officer to join me. I need to debrief him."

When the XO climbed into the Mid Sphere a few minutes later, Gamble shook his hand and said, "Commander, I am Chief Petty Officer Warren Gamble. Please allow me to brief you on what happened."

Gamble then related the sequence of events that lead to the sailor losing it. "We've had nervous people before, but they always pulled themselves together and usually ended up enjoying the trip. Sorry about knocking him out. He was trying to open the lower hatch." Gamble pointed at the open hatch sticking up into the Mid Sphere. "It's possible to open the hatch while underway. That would have flooded *Mystic* and killed us all." Gamble presented a rueful smile. "Sorry Petty Officer Elton had to get physical, but we had no choice."

"You did the right thing," the XO said. "We'll handle him from here." He shook Gamble's hand and dropped down into *Tireless*.

✳

"*Teuthis*, this is *Mystic*," Deckhart transmitted on the Secure Gertrude. "*Mystic* is coming home with no passengers."

0900, TUESDAY, JULY 18, 1989—*USS TEUTHIS*, SUBMERGED AT 200 FT, TRANSITING TO MARE HARBOUR, THE FALKLAND ISLANDS

Since carrying passengers was not an official part of the combined exercises, I left the incident with the British sailor out of my report. I didn't know, of course, whether Cmdr. McClement would include it in his report to the Admiralty, but I figured that if he did, the report would remain with the Admiralty. The chances of it reaching ComSubLant, V. Adm. Bacon, were slim to none.

We had seven hours before us as Waverly and Ham settled *Teuthis* at 200 feet and twenty knots, heading west for Mare Harbour. *Talent* left for Mare Harbour when we completed our exercise with her, so she would arrive a couple of hours before us. Sonar had noted that *Tireless* quickly departed after *Mystic* uncoupled, so she would arrive ahead of us as well. That was fine by me. We had a brief, fifteen-hour layover before getting underway for Prince Edward. I had my cabin door open so I could hear what was going on in Control.

"Conn, Sonar, we have what looks like a fishing fleet off our starboard bow. They're about twenty-five miles distant. Seem to be fishing the shallower water to the northeast of the Falklands. We won't designate any of these unless one breaks away from the fleet and approaches our track."

"Roger that," Ham said. "Keep an eye on them."

By the time Seth assumed the watch at noon, the fishing fleet had slowly passed down our starboard side as we passed their fishing grounds at twenty knots, a speed none of them could reach on their best day.

Two hours into Seth's watch, we slowed to ten knots and then to five as we prepared to surface. Sonar had a couple of contacts at ten miles to starboard, freighters heading north toward Stanley. Sonar designated them S-61 and S-62, but they did not appear to be a problem for us.

Seth brought us to periscope depth, where both he and I scanned our surroundings, making sure we were alone.

"Diving Officer," Seth said to Master Chief Morris Jones, "surface the ship."

Jones turned to Chief Winder. "Oggy, announce our surface, sound the klaxon, and blow all main ballast."

"Surface! Surface! Surface!" on the 1MC, followed by three klaxon blasts sounded throughout the sub before the sound of rushing high pressure air drowned out everything.

Ten seconds later, under an overcast, rainy sky, *Teuthis* burst through the surface, water cascading down her sail from the bridge. Seaman Ezra Ben-Gurion remained at his fairwater-helm station. Dressed in foul-weather gear, Seamen Mike Overreach and Ivan Tuxin—Mikey and Tux to everyone—clambered to the bridge, carrying binocs, the squawk box, and compass repeater. Ham followed them, and I followed Ham.

We had wind off the port bow at about twenty knots, driving the rain into our faces. It was wet, cold, and uncomfortable. The sea presented us with long fifteen-foot rollers moving with the wind. As each passed us, first the bow and then the stern lifted, giving *Teuthis* a slow teeter-toter-like ride.

"Heading for Mare Harbour?' Ham asked over the squawk box.

"Two-seven-three, Sir."

"What's your head?" Ham asked Ben.

"Two-seven-zero, Sir."

"Ahead standard, turns for ten knots. Come right to course two-seven-three."

As we picked up speed, a whistle off our port side announced Borysko's presence as he assumed his favorite place riding our bow wave. Our increased speed amplified the roller action. I was definitely looking forward to entering Choiseul Sound, where land refracted the rollers around the inner waters.

"Land ahead," Mikey called out, "just off the starboard bow."

"I see Middle Island," Tux said, "low on the horizon just off the port bow."

Ham called to Control on the sound-powered handset. "As soon as Middle Island is broad off our port beam and we have come right to our new leg, set the maneuvering watch."

✳

It was a relief to slip into the shadow provided by the island as we moved into Choiseul Sound. Wave motion ceased entirely, and the wind dropped to less than ten knots. The rain did not let up, however, but at least it wasn't driving into our faces.

Ham showed up as the maneuvering watch JOOD. Waverly remained in Control as OOD. Ham lowered the outboards. King and his deck gang clambered through the forward hatch. I watched him clip each sailor into the safety line track. The sailors raised both capstans and opened four hawser lockers. A couple guys practiced throwing monkey fists, and they all shouted and whistled at Borysko.

Ham slowed to bare steerageway, and we rounded the spit just a stone's throw off our starboard bow, eased along the south side of East Cove, reversed our head, and slid gently against the bumpers the *Talent* crew had placed over her port side.

King's crew had already tied the monkey fists to hawsers fore and aft. They tossed the balls across the narrow gap between the subs—no need to throw—and handed off the hawsers to the *Talent* deck gang. They tied off the bow and stern and added bow and stern spring lines. Then they doubled all the lines and laid out the excess in neat, flat coils on the deck.

Waverly set the in-port watch, Section Three. I looked across to *Talent's* bridge. Capt. Harris saluted me smartly and waved.

"Hey, Johnny!" I shouted, returning his salute.

I looked across his deck at the rain slicked dock. Brisbane's Land Rover had just pulled up. The doors opened, and the Commandant got out with what looked like four civilians. It took a moment to register that three of the people looked distinctly Chinese.

I called Control. "Find the Duty Officer, Lieutenant Goff, and have him meet some guests who are arriving topside."

As I was leaving the bridge, I saw Chop come up through the forward hatch. He greeted the five, offering Brisbane a salute. I went to my cabin.

A few minutes later, Chop knocked on my door. "Captain, Colonel Brisbane, a State Department Assistant Undersecretary, and a Taiwanese captain are waiting for you in the Wardroom."

✳

I opened the Wardroom door to see Col. Brisbane accompanied by a middle-aged civilian and a person with Chinese features dressed in civilian clothes. Brisbane came to his feet.

"May I introduce Assistant Undersecretary of State Marvin Ramsay and Siōng-hāu Hsieh Tsung-han."

I shook hands with both. "May I offer you tea or coffee?" I asked.

Brisbane and Hsieh Tsung-han chose tea. Ramsay and I chose coffee. I gestured to the steward standing in the doorway to the Galley.

"Please sit," I said, pointing to the red Naugahyde couch against the outer bulkhead. I took the couch opposite them, with the coffee table between us.

"I am here in my official capacity representing the U.S. State Department," Ramsay said. "Secretary Baker and President Bush both send their personal congratulations for pulling off this extraordinary event with no international repercussions. Colonel Brisbane tells me that the captives are amenable to being turned over to the Taiwan Navy."

"They don't speak English," I answered, "but one of my seamen speaks Mandarin. He tells me the two divers are grateful to be alive. He says they hate the Communist regime. I'm unsure if they understand the concept of political asylum, but Billy (my Mandarin-speaking seaman) says they are eager to become part of the Taiwanese Navy." I turned to the Taiwanese captain. "I imagine, Siōng-hāu, this is why you are here."

He nodded. "I brought two security people with me, should they be needed."

The dial phone on the bulkhead by the door rang. The steward answered and brought me the handset with its extended cord.

"Captain."

"It's Ham. The Chinese captives are ready for transport. I took the liberty of obtaining their parole—I did not shackle them."

"You know that not being commissioned, their parole has no legal meaning?" I asked.

"I do, Captain, but I am confident they will remain docile."

I turned to my guests. "Gentlemen, the captives are ready for transport. On their promise of good behavior, we have not shackled them. The final decision on this, of course," I looked directly at Hsieh Tsung-han, "is yours, Captain."

I stood, signaling the meeting was over. I shook hands with Hsieh Tsung-han and Ramsay.

As we shook, Ramsay said, "I need to speak with you privately before I leave." I led him across the passageway into my cabin.

✳

I closed the door and indicated the easy chair. I turned my desk chair around and straddled it.

"Call me Marvin, please," Ramsay said. "I meant what I said earlier. Do you have any idea how we all scrambled when Admiral Bacon received your report? We're talking two vast bureaucracies—the Pentagon and the State Department. Bacon assigned a commander to walk the report up the chain to Chaney. Chaney personally delivered it to Baker, who called me into his office the same day and ordered me to contact the Taiwanese delegation and get my butt down here to meet you. He gave me his private jet. It's all the more awkward because we cannot give you the public accolades you deserve."

"I appreciate your input, but in fairness, my divers, the TOG team, pulled this off." When Ramsay started to interrupt, I raised my hand.

"I know how things work—I started out as an E-One way back when. I even made some pretty significant personal contributions back in the day, but the current accolades belong to my divers."

Ramsay sat quietly for a bit and then spoke up. "Captain, I will personally convey your comments to Secretary Baker. I promise, we will not overlook your divers." He smiled broadly. "As for you, Captain McDowell, with your permission, I would like to address all your officers in the Wardroom. Can you arrange that?"

"Everyone except the Engineering Watch Officer," I told him. "The plant is hot, so we are required to have a qualified officer in Maneuvering."

I called Control. Chief Panner was COW. "Please announce Officer's Call," I told him.

Ten minutes later, all the officers except Chief Engineer Bert Cobb had assembled in the Wardroom.

"This is Assistant Undersecretary of State Marvin Ramsay. He asked to speak with all of us."

Ramsay stood and placed himself so each officer could see him. "You have all just completed an extraordinary voyage, one where you encountered unexpected danger whose outcome directly affected the safety and security of the United States and her ally, The Republic of China. You, Captain McDowell, and all of your officers and crew traversed a tightrope as taut and hazardous as anything we have encountered in recent times. President Bush, Secretary of Defense Chaney, and Secretary of State Baker are aware of your critical role and send their personal congratulations. At a later time, appropriate awards will be made. But in the meantime," Ramsay turned and addressed me directly, "you, Commander McDowell, are being promoted to full Captain, effective immediately." He reached into his satchel and handed me a package. "These are your new rank devises." He turned back to the other officers. "It has been my honor to meet you all. That is not an empty statement. It is not often one gets to meet genuine heroes. You men fit that role to a Tee."

Ramsay looked at me and nodded. We left the Wardroom together. "If you are still around at eighteen hundred," I said to him as we descended to the Crew's Mess so he could exit through the Torpedo Room, "you are welcome to join me and my officers for dinner."

"I'll let you know," he said.

1800, TUESDAY, JULY 18, 1989—*USS TEUTHIS*, MOORED AT MARE HARBOUR, THE FALKLAND ISLANDS

We had a full Wardroom for dinner on the evening of our thirty-seventh day out of Mare Island. Instead of their blue jumpsuits, my officers wore khaki uniforms with collar rank insignia and black ties. Those who were qualified wore gold dolphins over their left breast pocket. I was hosting both British sub commanders, and Brisbane and Ramsay. The two British officers wore dress whites, Brisbane wore his dinner dress with kilts, and Ramsay wore a dark business suit.

The Wardroom table wouldn't seat everybody, so four junior officers took their meal on the coffee table. The meal was steaks to order, bakers, fresh salad brought aboard just this morning, Cedric's popovers, and fresh apple pie—all washed down with vintage bug juice, since consumption of alcoholic beverages, even beer and wine, is not allowed on U.S. Navy ships.

After dinner, I invited everyone to join me at the Mare Harbour pub, where I promised to uphold an old Navy tradition of buying the first round as a newly promoted officer.

✳

Lt. Morgan Atley was the Engineering Watch Officer. Rob Borka had the Deck. Chop should have been his JOOD, but he let him join the rest of us at the pub. Brisbane's three officers were present, and most of the two British wardrooms showed up. Siōng-hāu Hsieh Tsung-han arrived with Ramsay. We more than filled every place at the bar. For most of the bar length, we were two deep.

Every table in the room was occupied. My divers showed up with the two Taiwanese security guys, and, to my surprise, the two captured Chinese divers. They were all drinking beer and having a good time.

I looked at Hsieh Tsung-han. "I looks like you made an executive decision," I said with a grin.

"One does what one can," he responded in his perfectly enunciated English.

Despite his commissioned status, Ham sat with his divers. I walked over to their table. Billy was there to translate between the Americans and the Chinese captives. The entire TOG group lifted their glasses, speaking as one. "Congratulations, Diver Boy!" I noticed that the Chinese captives joined in the toast. Ham looked at me with a rueful shrug. Then he stood and said quietly, "No one deserves it more, Mac." He lifted his mug. "*Hooyah!*"

All the divers chimed in: "*Hooyah! Hooyah!*" Even the captives lifted their mugs in salute.

Then one captive stood and approached me. In halting English, he said, "Thank you, Captain Mac, thank you!"

The divers broke out in another round of, "*Hooyah! Hooyah!*"

I lifted my glass. "*Hooyah!*" I said, turning and heading back to the bar.

Johnny Harris grabbed my elbow and said, "Your crew seems to think a lot of you."

"We go back a long way and we've been through a lot together. They've had my back and I've had theirs. They're the best men I have worked with in my entire service."

Harris looked at me and raised his glass. "I wish I could do that."

I turned to look back into the room. That's when I spotted the same guy I had seen the day before, sitting at a small round table in the corner. I looked around for King and found him sitting at a table with several other chiefs. I caught his eye. He excused himself from his table and approached me at the bar.

"Congrats, Captain! You definitely deserve it. What's up?"

Without being obvious, I pointed out the guy in the corner.

"That's the same guy as last time, right?" King asked.

I nodded.

"Don't worry. I'll take care of him."

I'm unsure what the loner thought about the big black American approaching his table for the second time. He seemed to brace himself. A couple of King's deck gang saw him standing at the stranger's table, and they rose to join him.

The loner stood, pushed his table toward King and his men, and shouted, "*Me cago en vos!* (I shit on you!)" as he left the pub.

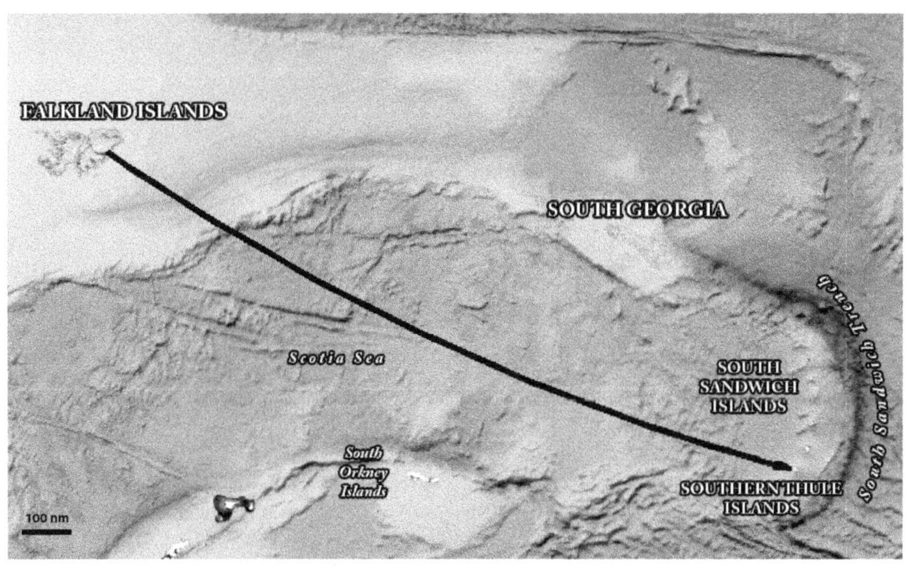

USS Teuthis *transit from Falkland Islands to Southern Thule Island.*

CHAPTER FOURTEEN—Transit to the Southern Thule Islands

0900, WEDNESDAY, JULY 19, 1989—*USS TEUTHIS*, UNDERWAY ON SURFACE, DEPARTING MARE HARBOUR, THE FALKLAND ISLANDS

Light rain still fell as we set the maneuvering watch on the morning of July 19. Borysko was particularly active, racing the length of East Cove, slapping his tail against the calm surface, and whistling loudly every time he passed the moored subs.

By the time I arrived on the bridge, Ham had singled up the lines and was waiting for my signal to get underway. Seth had laid out our track to Prince Edward Island that took us south of Southern Thule—the twin islands Thule and Cook, the southernmost of the South Sandwich Islands—nine days and change. That would get us to the Prince Edward Islands with a couple of days to spare, if the Israeli intelligence estimate was accurate.

My eyes lingered on Borysko for several seconds. What an interesting relationship the *Teuthis* divers and I had developed with this wild cetacean. He had tracked us all the way through the Arctic ice pack, finding his own way except for the long stretch of ice in Foxe Basin, where we broke the surface at intervals that allowed him to breathe.[19] He followed us to Antarctica during Operation White Out[20] and once again here, now.

One of the things I missed as captain was taking the sub in and out of port—I mean, giving the orders personally, feeling like the ship and I were one entity. Legally, I was *Teuthis* and *Teuthis* was me, but the people I trained actually drove the sub except for the most urgent situations where I thought only I had the experience and ability to get us out, or where I did not want to expose one of my officers to the liability that accompanies some extreme situations. I chuckled to myself. As a young officer, I wanted to drive the ship. Then I became one of the drivers, and I loved it. Then the ship was mine, and while I "owned" the ship, my officers did most of the driving—I really missed it.

I watched Ham put *Teuthis* through her paces, easing away from *HMS Talent*, rounding the spit of land marking the south end of East Cove, setting course for, and transiting, to Choiseul Sound, and finally setting the course for the first leg of our great circle passage to the Prince Edward Islands, 126 degrees. There was no point where I thought Ham needed correction or supervision.

It was nearly 1100 when I told Ham to secure the bridge and dive the ship. I dropped down to Control and informed Waverly. Ham ordered the bridge watch below and then dropped into Control, securing the bridge hatches. Waverly took the Attack Scope, I took the Nav.

"Green board," the COW told him.

"Depth beneath the keel?" Ham asked Juby.

"Twelve hundred feet, Sir," Juby answered.

"Diving Officer, dive the ship. Make your depth three-zero-zero feet."

On the 1MC, Tubes announced, "Dive! Dive!" followed by two klaxon blasts.

---

19 See *Operation Arctic Sting*, vol 3 in *The Mac McDowell Missions*.
20 See *Operation White Out*, vol 4 in *The Mac McDowell Missions*.

Waverly relinquished the Attack Scope to Ham who focused on the forward main vent. I focused on the after. Both vents spewed spray as the sub slipped beneath the surface.

"Ten degree down-bubble," Tubes ordered as Diving Officer.

"Ahead full, turns for twenty knots," Ham ordered. "Mark your head."

"One-two-four degrees," Beverton answered.

"Very well. Come right to new course one-two-seven degrees."

And, just like that, we slipped into our element and started punching a watery tunnel toward the Prince Edward Islands, some nine days and change away.

✳

On the 1MC: "This is the Executive Officer. The ship will be moving the clock ahead six hours, one hour each watch commencing with Section two on Wednesday at noon. Be sure to set your watches forward each watch so you don't arrive late for watch or miss a meal. Check with the COB for any questions."

1100, WEDNESDAY, JULY 19, 1989—*USS TEUTHIS*, SUBMERGED AT 300 FT, TRANSITING TO THULE ISLAND

Shortly after we submerged, we shifted to the underway watch, Section two. I asked Ham to join me in my cabin. He showed up with two cups of joe.

"You seemed quite comfortable on the bridge today," I told him. "Do you think you're ready for a qualification walkthrough?"

"Do you think I'm ready?" he asked.

I remained silent.

"I know the sub as well as anyone," he said. "As JOOD, I've gone through every drill on the list several times—many times, actually. If you're comfortable with my performance, I'm ready to do a walkthrough."

I liked his answer. "I'll tell the XO to set it up."

✳

Roger was, himself, still learning about *Teuthis*. Because of his extensive experience on other subs, he was on the watchbill. Having him walk Ham through the sub was a way for Roger to test himself. I'm sure he appreciated that. For the engineering spaces, Bert joined them. This gave Roger an opportunity to test himself further as Bert put Ham through the ringer.

Afterward, both Roger and Bert told me they were impressed with Ham's knowledge and his poise. Bert told me, "I would have no qualms with Ham on watch in a real emergency. He's cool, collected, and he makes decisions right the first time. That's a quality you can't buy."

✻

Chop and Jerry were also ready to qualify. Chop interested me specially because he did not have to qualify, he wanted to. He was young—this was his first shipboard assignment. He had to learn how submarine supply matters differ from everything he had learned in Supply Officers School. He attacked his job with a determination I had never seen before. And on top of that, he dove right into officer quals.

Roger took Chop through his quals walkthrough. Bert joined them in the engineering spaces as he had for Ham. Nobody expected Chop to do as well as Ham. He had neither the experience nor the seniority. But Chop surprised us all. He answered every question, he handled every emergency thrown at him, and while he appeared a bit nervous from time to time, he remained in charge and retained the confidence of Bert, the XO, and me.

Jerry Plummer, as Radio and Sonar Officer, had much to do besides qualifying, not so much as Chop, but he kept busy. His walkthrough with Roger and Bert was entirely satisfactory, but it fell short of Ham's and Chop's. He seemed less certain of himself, more hesitant with his emergency responses. I was comfortable qualifying him, but I wanted his OOD watches to be when I was awake until he had some experience under his belt.

We had a brief ceremony in the Wardroom, where I pinned their gold dolphins to their jumpers. The ship's photographer memorialized the occasion. After that, we took up our new routine.

Seth had the midwatch, Chop, the morning watch, Jerry, the afternoon watch, and Ham, the evening watch. I took Roger off the watchbill since we didn't need him and he had way too much to do, anyway. I took Waverly off the watchbill so he could concentrate on his duties as Senior Watch Officer (SWO) and Weaps. Since Robert Borka would be more than busy in the coming days, I took him off the watchbill as well.

I could sleep comfortably with Ham and Seth on watch. Chop and Jerry could cut their teeth during the day with me available.

✳

Jerry assumed his watch by late afternoon on Wednesday, July 19, our thirty-eighth day since departure. *Teuthis* was at 300 feet doing twenty knots. Sonar had no contacts and wasn't likely to get any. This was the beginning of the endlessly boring routine that is part of every submarine patrol. It was a good time for Jerry to stand his first unassisted watch.

Jerry turned over the watch to Ham and joined us in the Wardroom for dinner. I thought he carried himself with greater pride than before his qualification.

"How did it go?" I asked.

"Piece of cake," he answered. "We had nothing to do, so we worked through some watch section drills."

I had noticed that through the open door of my cabin, but I refrained from telling him. He would do fine.

✳

We had been underway for two and a half days following our great circle track to the Prince Edwards. We were near the southern extension of the South Sandwich Islands that stretched in an eastward arc from South Georgia Island. Sixty miles east of the island arc lies the South Sandwich Trench, which reaches a depth of nearly 27,000 feet. Our projected track took us over the southern end of this trench.

Toward the end of Jerry's watch, Sonar called. "Conn, Sonar, we have a suppressed cavitation contact off our port bow, designate Sierra-six-three."

"Sonar, Conn, I will slow and clear baffles and then give you a beam aspect to Sierra-six-three so you can get more information," Jerry told the Sonar watch supervisor, Godfry Mason.

Once S-63 was broad on the beam, Sonar got to work. Within a few minutes, Mason reported, "Conn, Sonar, Sierra-six-three is the Argentine sub *ARA San Juan* (S-42). She's a two hundred twenty foot long, thousand-foot capable, single-hull, diesel sub. She's doing twenty-five knots, her top speed, and seems to be headed toward Thule Island."

Jerry reported S-63 to me. "Keep an eye on her," I told him and went to Plot to check things out.

While the watch changed and Ham came on as OOD, Seth and I examined the chart and *San Juan*'s path. It definitely looked like she was heading for the triple-island group. They consisted of tiny Bellingshausen Island, hardly more than a volcanic mountain top, Thule Island to the west with an active caldera on its eastern side, and the largest, Cook Island, with two active volcano peaks. Between Thule and Cook was a submerged caldera, now called Douglas Strait, that long ago might have been a land bridge between the islands.

From 1913 through the Falkland War, the Argentines had claimed sovereignty over the South Sandwich Islands despite Great Britain's long-standing recognized jurisdiction over the entire chain of islands from the Falklands through the South Thule Islands. They had even established a military base on the north side of the spit of land projecting southeast from Thule. The British had forcibly removed the garrison following the war and destroyed the buildings. It was possible that *San Juan* was attempting to reestablish a presence on the island. She carried thirty-seven crew, but could handle four or five more that could be left on Thule Island to establish a presence.

At 0500 toward the end of Seth's watch, Sonar reported, "Conn, Sonar, we have a volcanic eruption on one of the South Thule Islands, most likely Thule Island, since it is blocking the other two. It's a pretty big event. Definitely would not want to be nearby."

I went into Sonar to listen. I heard a deep, rumbling sound with occasional pops, like cannon shots. King joined us. After the next set of pops, King said, "Those are large rocks being shot out of the caldera. It must be like a Fourth of July display up there."

Three hours later, in the middle of Chop's watch, *Teuthis* was forty nautical miles south of Thule Island. The volcano was still rumbling, but the shots had ceased. The rumbling was at a much lower level, even though we were closer. I told Chop to slow to five knots so we could hear the volcano better. As soon as we slowed, through the rumble, Sonar picked up a faint Gertrude signal. It was warbly and washed out. King taped it and did his magic. Then he called me to Sonar.

"You gotta hear this, Captain," King said. "You just gotta."

The signal still sounded like a warbly echo, but the words were understandable. "Mayday! Mayday! This is *ARA San Juan* in distress at three hundred thirty meters just east of Thule Island in Douglas Strait. Mayday! Mayday!"

Then the message repeated in Spanish. English and Spanish versions cycled continuously.

"Captain, that's below her test depth."

I stepped out to Plot where Chief Henshaw had the watch. I pulled out a large-scale chart of the South Thule Islands.

"Lay a track at twenty-five knots from our present position through the gap between Thule and Cook Islands," I told him. "Watch out for shallow water. When we are one-point-two miles from the spit," I pointed with a pencil, "we'll come to periscope depth and five knots."

I motioned Chop to Plot. "Follow the chief's course directions. When the bottom is fifteen hundred feet, slow to five knots and come to periscope depth. Call me if I'm not in Control."

✳

An hour and a half later, I strolled into Control just as Chop slowed to five knots and ordered periscope depth.

"Hold a minute," I said. "Have you checked the overhead image for ice?"

"No, Sir. I'll do it right now." He sounded a bit sheepish. "There's a lot of brash, and there are occasional pieces of ice. Some seem pretty large."

"Come to all stop and hold your position and depth," I told him. "We need to think this through." I picked up the 1MC mike. "Lieutenant Deckhart to Control. Lieutenant Deckhart to Control."

When he showed up, I told him about the Mayday we received from *San Juan* and let him listen to a couple of cycles.

I said, "Jim, we need to pass through this gap into Douglas Strait, and we have to do it at periscope depth. It's just too shallow. The problem is, there's a lot of brash overhead and even some larger chunks. They can damage *Mystic*. I want you and Don to launch *Mystic* and drive her through the gap. You will meet up with us here, and we can decide what to do."

"Finally, something to do," Deckhart said with a grin. "Give us twenty minutes."

1000, SATURDAY, JULY 22, 1989—*USS TEUTHIS*, SUBMERGED AT 200 FT, DOUGLAS STRAIT, BETWEEN THULE AND COOK ISLANDS

Fifteen minutes later, Deckhart called Control. "We're ready to go, Roland."

On the 1MC, Chop announced, "Commence DSRV ops, commence DSRV ops."

On the circuit, Deckhart said, "*Teuthis*, this is *Mystic*. Request permission to unlatch and launch. Over."

"This is *Teuthis*. You've got your bearings and know your heading? Over."

I chuckled to myself. Chop obviously wasn't going to lose a DSRV on his watch.

"This is *Mystic*. Roger that. Over."

Chop picked up the dial handset and called Dive Control."Launch the Basketball," he said. "Keep an eye on *Mystic*."

He turned to me for final permission. I nodded.

"Permission granted," Chop said on the circuit. "Keep in touch! Out."

Mystic unlatched and pulled away from *Teuthis*, followed by the entire crew on monitors throughout the sub. Suddenly, a grinning black and white snout replaced *Mystic* on the monitors. A cheer rose throughout the sub, a sound that Borysko probably could hear through the hull.

"When's the next bird?" I asked the quartermaster.

"Twenty minutes, but it's only one."

"Better than nothing," I said. I turned to Chop. "In ten minutes, come to periscope depth, get a SatNav fix, and set course through the gap. Follow Juby's directions exactly. We're dealing with some shallow water here."

When my Nav Scope broke the surface, the wash from the sail pushed away a city block size piece of ice. Juby ran up the radar, so we had real-world confirmation of our position between the two islands—assuming, of course, that the islands were properly positioned on our charts. Both *Mystic* and Borysko kept pace with us, although the cetacean darted off from time to time to grab a tasty bite the abundant Antarctic waters offered him. I had to remind myself that Borysko required 600 pounds of seafood daily to remain in peak condition. The waters we were transiting were probably the world's richest for nourishing a creature like Borysko.

At five knots, it took us fifteen minutes to negotiate the gap. Once we were inside Douglas Strait, *San Juan*'s Mayday drowned out nearly every other sound except for the deep rumble of the volcano. Its smoke plume was the most prominent thing through my scope.

On the Secure Gertrude I said, "*Mystic*, stand by while we determine the status of *San Juan*. Over."

✳

On the Gertrude, I transmitted slowly, "*ARA San Juan*, this is U.S. Nuclear Submarine responding to your Mayday call. Over." I did not want to reveal our identity to her.

The warbling, echoing response arrived through the water. "This is *San Juan*. Thank you for responding. When Mount Larsen erupted, we were on the surface a kilometer east of Mount Larsen's steep slope. We were struck by two heavy objects, one striking our sail and the other ripping a hole in our forward ballast tank. We dropped to the bottom and are upright on the bottom at three hundred thirty meters. Our battery banks are three-quarter charged. We have forty-one people onboard. Our air is breathable, and we have no leaks. Over."

"This is U.S. Submarine. Have you any personnel casualties? Over."

"This is *San Juan*. We do not. Over."

"This is U.S. Submarine. We are carrying saturation divers. We have the ability to examine *San Juan* closely to determine if your snorkel mast can be freed and if your ballast tank can be patched. If we can make repairs that allow you to surface, we will do so. If we cannot, we will notify ComSubLant, who will transport a Deep Submergence Rescue Vehicle (DSRV) by air to the Falklands where it will deploy on a British sub for transport to your location. Over."

"This is *San Juan*. Roger. Thank you. Over."

"This is U.S. Submarine. How long can you last in your present condition? Over."

"This is *San Juan*. Five days—we can last five days. Over."

"This is U.S. Submarine. Roger. Standby. Out."

✳

If they were repairable, I was reasonably certain my divers could do the job. The problem was our primary mission. Under no circumstances could I allow the timeline to be compromised, nor could I bring their crew aboard. Our mission had to remain invisible to the world.

I checked our schedule carefully. I could remain here for two days—no more. I called for the XO.

When Roger arrived in my cabin, I explained the matter to him. "In two days, we should be able to determine the extent of their damage and deliver several oxygen bottles through their escape hatches. Have Jerry draft a detailed message to ComSubLant. I'll brief Ham so he can press a couple divers down for the oxygen bottle transfer."

On the Secure Gertrude, I briefed Deckhart. "Find *San Juan* and assess her damage as best you can. Don't reveal your presence to her."

An hour later, Deckhart called on the Secure Gertrude. "This is *Mystic*. The top and right side of *San Juan*'s sail are crushed. I don't think she can raise any masts. Her forward ballast tank has a round hole about one foot in diameter. It probably could be patched from inside the ballast tank."

"This is *Teuthis*. Roger. Return home."

1400, SATURDAY, JULY 22, 1989—*USS TEUTHIS*, PERISCOPE DEPTH, DOUGLAS STRAIT, BETWEEN THULE AND COOK ISLANDS

The idea of leaving forty-one men stranded in a small sub 1,100 feet below the surface in one of the remotest locations on the planet did not sit well with me. The only reason I did not simply do what was right and rescue them was my total confidence in the one hundred percent working cover story for our cable tapping activities,[21] the flyaway submarine rescue system maintained by Capt. Lonie Franken-Ester, Commander of Submarine Development Group One in San Diego, my former skipper.[22]

Jerry brought me his message draft. "It still needs some work," he told me. "I didn't have the latest info from Jim, and I'm sure you will want to add your personal comments."

"Take a seat, Jerry. I'll go through it quickly, and then you can put the final product together."

I changed a few things and added several comments. Jerry took it to Radio for a rewrite and brought it back a bit later. Here is the message we put together.

FLASH...FLASH...FLASH...FLASH

TOP SECRET

DATE: 22 JULY 1989 1300Z

TO: COMSUBLANT

FROM: USS TEUTHIS SSNR 2

SUBJECT: SUBSUNK NOTIFICATIONI HAVE

1. RESPONDED TO A MAYDAY DISTRESS CALL FROM ARA SAN JUAN (S-42), STRANDED ON THE BOTTOM AT 1,100 FT, ONE-QUARTER MILE OFF THE STEEP EASTERN COAST OF

---

21 See *Operation Ivy Bells*, vol 1 in *The Mac McDowell Missions*.
22 See *Operation White Out*, vol 4 in *The Mac McDowell Missions*.

THULE ISLAND AT THE WESTERN EXTENT OF DOUGLAS STRAIT, 59.4500 DEG S, 27.3333 DEG W.

2. I IDENTIFIED TEUTHIS AS "US NUCLEAR SUBMARINE." I HAVE INSPECTED THE EXTERIOR OF SAN JUAN. THE TOP AND RIGHT SIDE OF HER SAIL ARE CRUSHED AND THERE IS A ONE FT BY ONE FT HOLE IN HER FORWARD BALLAST TANK. SHE CANNOT SURFACE WITHOUT FIRST REPAIRING THE BALLAST TANK HOLE AND SHE WILL NOT BE ABLE TO USE ANY MASTS. THE DAMAGE WAS CAUSED BY LARGE BOULDERS SPEWED FROM THE ERUPTING LARSEN VOLCANO CALDERA STRIKING SAN JUAN WHILE SURFACED.

3. SAN JUAN HAS A CREW OF 41. NONE ARE INJURED. THEY HAVE SUFFICIENT AIR FOR FIVE DAYS. USING DIVERS, I WILL TRANSFER THREE FLASKS OF HP OXYGEN THROUGH *SAN JUAN*'S ESCAPE HATCH. THIS WILL GIVE HER AN EXTRA FEW DAYS. SAN JUAN IS UNAWARE OF MYSTIC'S PRESENCE, AND OF MY MISSION.

4. TEUTHIS WILL DEPART THIS AREA AT 1400 UTC PLUS 3. (TEUTHIS IS RUNNING ON UTC PLUS 3 TIME SINCE DEPARTING THE FALKLANDS.) I WILL MONITOR FOR YOUR RESPONSE UNTIL I DEPART. THEREAFTER, I WILL COME TO PERISCOPE DEPTH FOR FIFTEEN MINUTES DAILY AT NOON, UTC PLUS 3.

TOP SECRET

FLASH...FLASH...FLASH...FLASH

✳

Jerry sent the message as a burst transmission. I remained at periscope depth with antennas extended while Ham pressed two divers to a thousand feet. I really didn't know what to expect from ComSubLant. The military bureaucracy ended up surprising me. In just over an hour, we received a response.

FLASH…FLASH…FLASH…FLASH

TOP SECRET/SENSITIVE COMPARTMENTED INFORMATION

DATE: 22 JULY 1989 1415Z

TO: *USS Teuthis* SSNR 2

FROM: COMSUBLANT

SUBJECT: RESPONSE TO SUBSUNK NOTIFICATION

1. THE U.S. STATE DEPARTMENT HAS NOTIFIED COMSUBLANT THAT SOUTH AFRICA POSTPONED BY THREE (3) DAYS ITS PLANNED NUCLEAR EVENT AT PRINCE EDWARD ISLAND. CONSEQUENTLY, USS TEUTHIS CAN REMAIN AT SUBSUNK SITE FOR THREE (3) DAYS, IF NECESSARY.

2. HMS TALENT HAS BEEN DISPATCHED FROM MARE HARBOUR, SHE WILL ARRIVE YOUR LOCATION IN TWO (2) DAYS. TRANSFER PERSONNEL FROM SAN JUAN TO TALENT AS REQUIRED BY CO TALENT AND CO SAN JUAN.

3. UNDERTAKE REPAIR OF SAN JUAN FORWARD BALLAST TANK IF POSSIBLE, USING DIVERS. IF REPAIR SUCCESSFUL, COORDINATE WITH CO TALENT AND CO SAN JUAN TRANSFER OF PERSONNEL BACK TO SAN JUAN.

4. IF REPAIR NOT POSSIBLE, INFORM
    COMSUBLANT. MARK SAN JUAN LOCATION
    WITH A PINGER AND TRANSFER ALL
    PERSONNEL TO TALENT. COMSUBLANT WILL
    DISPATCH USS ORTOLAN TO SUBSUNK SITE
    TO EFFECT REPAIRS. TRANSIT TIME FOR OR-
    TOLAN IS TWENTY (20) DAYS.

5. AT NO TIME REVEAL NAME OF TEUTHIS OR
    MYSTIC TO SAN JUAN.

TOP SECRET/SENSITIVE COMPARTMENTED
INFORMATION

FLASH…FLASH…FLASH…FLASH

✳

Jerry was still on watch. I told him to lower the skids and put *Teuthis* on the bottom at a hundred yards east of *San Juan.*

Ham approached me in my cabin. "Captain, I want to make sure you understand our diving situation with *San Juan.*"

"First," I interrupted, "we will not give them oxygen tanks. Com-SubLant and the British Admiralty are sending *HMS Talent* to transfer the crew with *Mystic* to *Talent.* We have some time to try and repair the ballast tank hole." I grinned at him. "Okay, you came to see me."

"You know, of course, that our system is rated for one thousand feet. *San Juan* is at eleven hundred feet. You need to make a command decision authorizing me to overpressurize the system to eleven hundred FSW."[23]

"If everything goes well," I responded, "the authorization will be a forgotten footnote in my mission report. If something goes wrong, they'll try to hang both of us." I looked at him earnestly.

"If you don't authorize it, we can't do the repair—but you know that at least as well as I do." Ham locked eyes with me. "The system has between fifty and a hundred percent safety factor. You know that, right?"

---

23 Feet Sea Water

"Of course." I sighed. "How long will you take to drop to eleven hundred from one thousand?"

"Thirty seconds."

"Okay…here's what we'll do. Press them to a thousand feet. Just before they exit, press down another hundred feet. Once they are out and on the job, come back to a thousand feet. When they need to return, press down just sufficiently long to get them inside, and then bring them to a thousand feet as rapidly as you can safely do it." I grinned at him. "I realize you will be making up decompression tables as you proceed, so keep careful notes. What you do will become part of a future protocol."

"Yah, right."

"I want to make sure we are on the same page, Ham. Would you please give me a short brief of what your guys will be doing for the next couple of days?"

"I've pressed down Jimmy, Ski, and José. They've got an eighteen-inch round steel plate, shoring lumber, welding and cutting equipment, cans of foam…"

"Foam…what's that for?" I asked.

"This will be a difficult weld. I'm thinking we might be able to fill the gap between the patch and outer hull with foam. Won't hurt to try."

I lifted an eyebrow.

Ham continued. "Besides that, they have a high-pressure water nozzle to blast away silt and open up space under the grill so they can enter the tank."

"That's fed from inside the DDC, right?"

"Yah…so we'll have to keep it at eleven hundred feet for that part of the operation."

"Nothin' ain't easy," I commented. "I presume Jimmy will be tending?"

"Right. You know, the Israelis are very interested in how we will do this. They even volunteered to press down and help us until I pointed out how long the decompression would be." Ham grinned. "These guys are something else, you know. Never saw anything like them."

"What depth are the divers?"

"Five hundred feet. Got a couple more hours."

"When they hit a thousand, give them several hours of sleep. There won't be much time for that in the next couple of days."

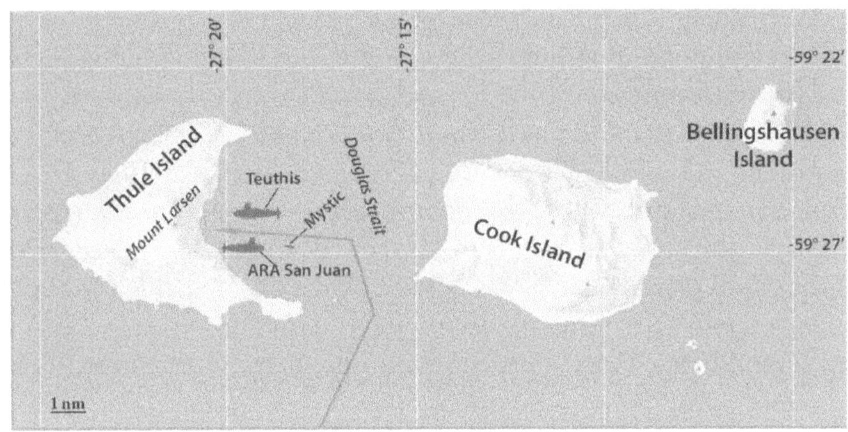

Douglas Strait—USS Teuthis, Mystic, *and* ARA San Juan.

CHAPTER FIFTEEN—ARA San Juan Repairs

2000, SATURDAY, JULY 22, 1989—*USS TEUTHIS*, BOTTOMED AT 1,100 FT, DOUGLAS STRAIT, 1.5 NM EAST OF MOUNT LARSEN.

Teuthis was bottomed at 1,100 feet just east of *San Juan*. We were ready to attempt a repair to the Argentine sub that would bring her to the surface. It was time to bring her up to date.

"*San Juan*, this is U.S. Submarine," I transmitted on Gertrude. "*HMS Talent* has departed Mare Harbour and will arrive here in forty-five hours. She is carrying a DSRV and will rescue your crew. In the meantime, my divers will attempt to patch your forward ballast tank. You may hear their activities as they clear the mud under the ballast tank grill, enter the tank, and set up scaffolding to effect their repair. Please send me the precise location, with respect to your forward hatch, of the bottom opening to the forward ballast tank. We will monitor our Gertrude to receive any questions you may have during this process. Over."

"This is *San Juan*. Thank you. Stand by for the opening location. Over."

Ten minutes later, *San Juan* called back. "The opening is on the centerline, one-decimal-three meters ahead of the forward hatch center. Out."

✳

I called Waverly on the dial handset. "Waverly, we are running a dive for the next four days. I want you to cover for Ham so he can keep his guys out of trouble."

"No problem, Captain, I was expecting your call. I'll take the rest of Ham's watch."

"The divers are pressing down and will take some sleep before they commence underwater ops in the morning. When you get to Control, send the messenger with the Night Order Book."

The Night Order Book contained my standard set of OOD instructions when I was asleep, plus any time-specific additions.

I wrote: 1. Waken me at 0545. 2. On the outboards, move *Teuthis* to within 100 feet of *San Juan*. 3. Commence dive ops at 0600.

I handed the book back to the messenger, took a quick shower, and settled down for a few hours of sleep. Because of our present circumstances, odds were I could sleep through the night.

0700, SUNDAY, JULY 23, 1989—*USS TEUTHIS*, BOTTOMED AT 1,100 FT, DOUGLAS STRAIT, 1.5 NM EAST OF MOUNT LARSEN.

Chop had assumed the watch just before the messenger awakened me with a steaming cup of joe. I hurried through my necessaries and arrived in Control as the COW announced, "Commence dive ops, commence dive ops."

Chop brought me up to date, sketching *San Juan* and our position relative to her—100 feet off our port beam.

"Nicely done," I told him, and then I went aft on the starboard side of the compartment and dropped down into Dive Control.

Ski and José had just entered the water wearing bright orange Unisuits and rebreathers. "The bottom is firm silt," Ski said, his voice warbly and squeaky as it passed through the water and then descrambler.

They wrestled the round eighteen-inch patch with an eyebolt protruding from the middle of one side through the hatch. Wally placed the Basketball for the best view until Borysko bumped it as he closed in on the divers to see what they were doing.

"Leave the shoring inside the DDC," Ski said. "Otherwise Borysko will think they are his."

They moved the round plate to *San Juan* with a lift bag.

Jimmy passed them high-pressure water and air hoses, and they dragged them across the bottom to *San Juan*'s bow as Jimmy fed them from the DDC. Except for the circle of light beneath the DDC hatch and the Basketball's floodlight, their surroundings were pitch black. Ski swam to the forward hatch, measured the 1.5 meter offset, and dropped a weighted line over the side to the bottom.

"That's where it's supposed to be," he squeaked and dropped to the bottom himself. Picking up the water nozzle, he said, "Let's do it, Buddy!"

When they opened the valve, immediately a cloud of silt engulfed their entire surrounds. There wasn't much current, so the cloud did not clear quickly as it would otherwise. In nearly zero visibility, they blasted a trench five feet deep and three feet wide to accommodate themselves and their equipment.

Three hours later, Ski shut the HP water valve and squeaked, "Looks like we got it!"

"Do you guys need a break?" Bill asked over the waterborne circuit.

"You shittin' me?" Ski responded, and then, "Get out of the way, Borysko. Move over!"

The Basketball showed the cetacean trying to push his snout into the trench. When he didn't fit, he backed off and opened his mouth. Both Ski and José took a minute to scratch his tongue.

"We're coming to get the shoring and a couple of wrenches, Jimmy," Ski said, as they returned to the DDC hatch.

First, Jimmy pushed a three-foot length of 4x4 through the hatch that José presented to Borysko. He took it in his massive jaws, and then promptly let it go and chased it to the surface. While he was gone, Ski and José moved four lengths of 4x4 into the trench, standing on them to keep them from floating up. They loosened the six flush bolts holding the open grill until it dropped slightly. Then they removed the bolts until only two remained. Ski grabbed a small lift bag, tied it off to the grill, and stuffed it between the bars until it was inside. He fed air through the grill, so it filled the bag. When the bag had the weight, the divers removed the last two bolts and lowered the grill into the trench. One by one, they pushed the 4x4s through the opening into the ballast tank.

"I'll get the jack," José said and headed back to *Teuthis*.

When he returned a few minutes later, he had suspended the jack from a small lift bag, pushing it ahead of him. Borysko closed in to investigate, but José waved him away. He also brought a reflectorless lamp that would brightly illuminate the ballast tank interior. As they reentered the trench, Borysko nudged each of them. He clearly wanted to join them. José squeezed through the opening, pulled the lamp into the tank, and turned it on. Immediately, the interior was bright as day, the water utterly transparent. Ski adjusted the jack lift bag so it and the jack glided through the opening into the tank as well. Then he followed.

They found the hole near the top both visually and by sound as Borysko stuck his snout through the hole and whistled loudly.

When the rock pierced the ballast tank, it made a jagged hole with sharp, triangular pieces penetrating into the tank.

The eighteen-inch round plate they had brought would do the job, but first, they would have to cut off the sharp edges with a torch to create as smooth an underside of the hole as possible. They conferred about the scaffolding they would build and decided to fetch another jack when they got a cutting torch and oxygen flask.

"I'll get it," José squeaked and headed down through the bottom opening.

He returned a few minutes later with the second jack suspended from a lift bag like the first, along with a torch and oxygen flask. He floated them up through the bottom opening and followed.

Ski grabbed the cutting torch, hooked it up to the oxygen flask, and brought it to bear on one of the downward pointing curved steel triangles. He struck the arc, focused it on the metal, and triggered the oxygen. The water filled with smoke and grit, but he kept cutting. Fifteen minutes later, the hole in the ballast tank was reasonably round with a smooth edge.

Ski attached a lift bag from one of the jacks to the eyebolt atop the disk. José exited the tank, retrieved the air hose, and filled the bag until the disk floated. They guided the lift bag up through the hole. As it rose, the air expanded, creating more lift, so that it held the disk against the hull. Ski tested it. The disk wasn't very firm, sliding back and forth as he manipulated it, but when he let go, it remained in place.

"Go topside and put more air into the bag," Ski told José. "Let's see how tight we can make this. Maybe we don't need the shoring."

"I'll return to *Teuthis* to get a large bag," José said. "I think that'll work."

Jimmy pushed a five-foot bag through the hatch. José grabbed it by its upper end and towed it back to San Jose. He pulled the air hose from the tank, swam the hose and bag to the topside hole, and securely attached the bag to the eyebolt. He filled it until air started bubbling around the bottom edge. Then he filled the smaller bag to capacity.

When he returned inside the tank, Ski said, "Let's do some welding!"

✳

Jimmy pulled Ski into the DDC, and they both pulled up José. Ski removed his helmet and said, "I need to take a leak and I'm hungry."

"Me, too," José added.

They took care of business and then relaxed as much as possible in their Unisuits, munching on tasteless sandwiches soaked with hot sauce to keep them from tasting totally like cardboard.

While they munched, Bill told them, "Batty wants to tell you something."

"Hey, guys, this is Batty. I was thinking, if *San Juan* were to release some HP air into the forward ballast tank, you should be able to accomplish the welding in air instead of water. Just saying."

"Won't work," Ski answered. "In the first place, the seal leaks too much. *San Juan* would have to add air almost continuously to keep it dry, and water would splash the weld, anyway. Second, I ain't gettin' inside a ballast tank saturated to eleven hundred feet when they release a bubble into the tank. If the weld holds, how they gonna keep the sub on the bottom? You tell me that!"

"You got a point, Ski," Batton said. "I guess I wouldn't do that either."

1330, SUNDAY, JULY 23, 1989—*USS TEUTHIS*, BOTTOMED AT 1,100 FT, DOUGLAS STRAIT, 100 FT FROM SAN JUAN.

Lunch was done, and Ski was eager to undertake the welding. Ham called and asked to see me. As usual, he arrived with two cups of steaming joe.

"You know how gung-ho Ski is," Ham said without preliminaries. "He and José just had lunch and took care of personal needs. Ski wants to drag the welding gear over and weld the patch before they quit for the day."

I nodded, waiting for the rest.

"They will have put in eleven hours with a one-hour break by the time they finish. They can handle it, but I want your concurrence before going forward." Ham put the onus on me.

I tossed the ball back to him. "If I were you and you were Bill, what would you advise me?"

Ham grinned. "Foul! But, okay…I would say it's doable, but we're taking a risk—not a large one, but a risk, nevertheless."

"You're monitoring them, and you've got Jimmy in standby. It's a modest risk that we can tolerate," I conceded. "Just make sure Bill keeps atop their vitals."

With that admonition, Ham returned to Dive Control, and shortly thereafter, Ski and José were moving the welding equipment over the bottom by lift bag, dragging the power cable behind.

As always at a thousand feet, it was pitch black. Derrick had the Basketball, which supplied the only illumination other than the divers' headlamps. The water had fully cleared from their blasting activities the previous session, so light beams were invisible. The only evidence of light were the bright circles on the bottom from headlamps and the Basketball.

Borysko showed up carrying his 4x4, shoving it at Ski and José. Ski took it and tossed it upward. Both 4x4 and Borysko disappeared into the darkness above them. He must have gone all the way to the surface for some air, because he took five minutes to return with his precious toy. By then, Ski was inside the ballast tank and José was in the trench guiding welding stuff up through the opening. In frustration, Borysko actually bumped his 4x4 against the hull several times to tell the divers he was ready to play.

When his friends didn't reappear, Borysko began going to the bottom, letting the 4x4 go, watching it disappear into the darkness, probably keeping track of it by sonar, and then darting up to catch it before it reached the surface. Derrick caught all this with the Basketball, much to the delight of crew members inside *Teuthis*.

Inside the ballast tank, Ski inflated his Unisuit slightly to lift him to the top. José aligned himself so his headlamp illuminated the spot where Ski wanted to weld. Ski placed the rod-electrode tip on the spot, started nitrogen flow, and struck an arc. He worked his way one-quarter around the patch and pulled the rod, what remained of it, back. José handed him a new rod, which he placed in the unit. As before, he started the nitrogen, struck his arc, and continued the weld.

His progress was slow and tedious. Several times he had to break off, and start again when the rod welded itself to his work. The water at the tank top got so dirty that Ski finally had to stop to clear it up. That turned out to be easier said than done. The ballast tank was without circulation. All it had was the bottom opening. The welding had warmed water at the tank top, so it remained there, lighter than the heavier, colder water at the bottom.

Comms with *Teuthis* from inside the take were sketchy, so Ski dropped through the bottom opening into open water. "Dive, I need you to have *San Juan* open the forward starboard main ballast tank vent valve. Welding has put so much shit in the water that I cannot see. Keep the valve open until I say to shut it."

Jerry had the deck watch. He got on the Gertrude. "*San Juan*, this is U.S. Submarine. Please open your forward main ballast tank vent valve."

The divers could hear the Gertrude sound in the water, but could not understand the words.

"This is *San Juan*, Roger. Opening the vent valve. It is open. Over."

"This is U.S. Submarine, thank you. Keep the valve open until I tell you otherwise. Out."

Ski rejoined José at the tank bottom, waiting for the valve to open. When it opened, the divers returned to the patch and removed their fins, waving them at the suspended silt, driving it toward the main valve. It took an entire hour to clear things up sufficiently to continue.

As they reached the end of the fourth hour on this session, Ski had completed all but an inch, which he kept open so they could try to fill the space with foam.

"Okay, divers, it's time to come home," Bill transmitted into the frigid water. "Leave everything as is. It's not going anywhere."

"Roger," Ski said, "we're coming back now."

They paused for a minute to scratch Borysko's tongue and throw his 4x4, and then they wearily climbed up through the DDC hatch, where Jimmy assisted in removing their suits and gear.

"A sandwich and a bowl of soup…then I'm going to crash," José said.

They both crashed before the food arrived.

*

Ham let the divers sleep eight hours, He gave them an hour to eat and suit up. Borysko must have heard their movements inside the DDC, because as soon as Ski exited, the cetacean was there for a tongue scratch. Ski and José spent several minutes with their aquatic friend and then moved to San Joan and worked their way into the ballast tank. They brought with them two pressurized cans of construction foam they intended to dispense between the plate and hull through the weld gap Ski had left.

José attached a six-inch tube to the nozzle of one can and handed it to Ski. Ski pushed the tube into the gap and squeezed the trigger. A small amount of foam moved through the tube and then stopped. Ski pulled the tube from the gap and tried to squeeze some foam directly into the water. Nothing happened.

"Well, Shit!" Ski said. "I thought this might happen. The pressure inside the can cannot overcome the external pressure."

José grabbed the welding grip and handed it to Ski. Ski struck an arc and finished the last inch of weld.

Bill called them. "Okay, guys. Leave everything in place except the welding equipment. Then start the topside weld."

"That was a wasted two hours," Ski said. "Whose lame-brained idea was the foam?"

"I think it was yours," Bill answered.

They floated the hose and other equipment to the topside deck.

"I'm gonna collapse the lift bags," Ski said.

"Hold that!" Bill said. "I know you are a super underwater welder, but make four tack welds from above before collapsing the bags—just to make sure."

"Probably not necessary," Ski said, "but caution never hurts."

José handed him the grip with a rod inserted. "You got nitrogen to the trigger," José said.

Ski struck an arc and tacked, struck one opposite the hole and tacked, and then placed two more at right angles. Borysko hovered several feet overhead, watching intently.

"That should do it," Ski said. "Let's collapse the bags."

As he collapsed the large one, Borysko grabbed it and swam between the subs where he dropped it. When it fell to the sea floor, he retrieved it, swam it up twenty feet, and dropped it again. When he picked it up this time, he shook it fiercely and brought it to Ski. Using the welding grip, Ski released some nitrogen into the bag so it just floated, and shoved it toward Borysko.

Once again, Borysko swam the bag between the subs and let go. Slowly, it began to rise. Borysko watched closely. As it rose, the nitrogen expanded, so it rose faster. Borysko still watched. It rose even faster, and Borysko began rising with it, watching. Wally on the Basketball followed all the action. When the expanding nitrogen filled about half the bag volume, and its upward rise accelerated even faster, Borysko lunged at the bag, closing his jaws around it, dumping the nitrogen. He let it go, and it dropped to the bottom.

Borysko retrieved the bag, brought it to Ski, and waited patiently for him to fill it with nitrogen again. Ski added extra gas, so the bag rose more quickly than before. Borysko followed it up until they both disappeared into the gloom. Three minutes later, he returned with the collapsed lift bag in his jaws.

"Okay, boys and girls," Bill said over the circuit, "recess is over. Let's get that patch welded."

Reluctantly, Ski and José returned to the job. José collapsed the small lift bag but did not offer it to Borysko.

Four hours later, Ski said, "It's as done as it's gonna get."

José attached the small lift bag to the welding equipment. "Okay, Bill, haul it back." He accompanied it back to the DDC.

Ski descended and entered the ballast tank. When José joined him, he passed the 4x4s through the bottom opening. José placed them on the trench floor under his feet to keep them from taking off on their own.

"Let's get these suckers back to *Teuthis* before we reinstall the grill," Ski said.

An hour later, they scraped away silt that had covered the grill, attached a lift bag, and guided the bag through the opening, manipulating the grill until it settled in place beneath the bolt holes. They screwed in the bolts just enough to take the weight of the grill. Then they removed the lift bag and tightened the bolts until they were flush with the hull.

"That's it, Dive Control," Ski announced. "We're done here!"

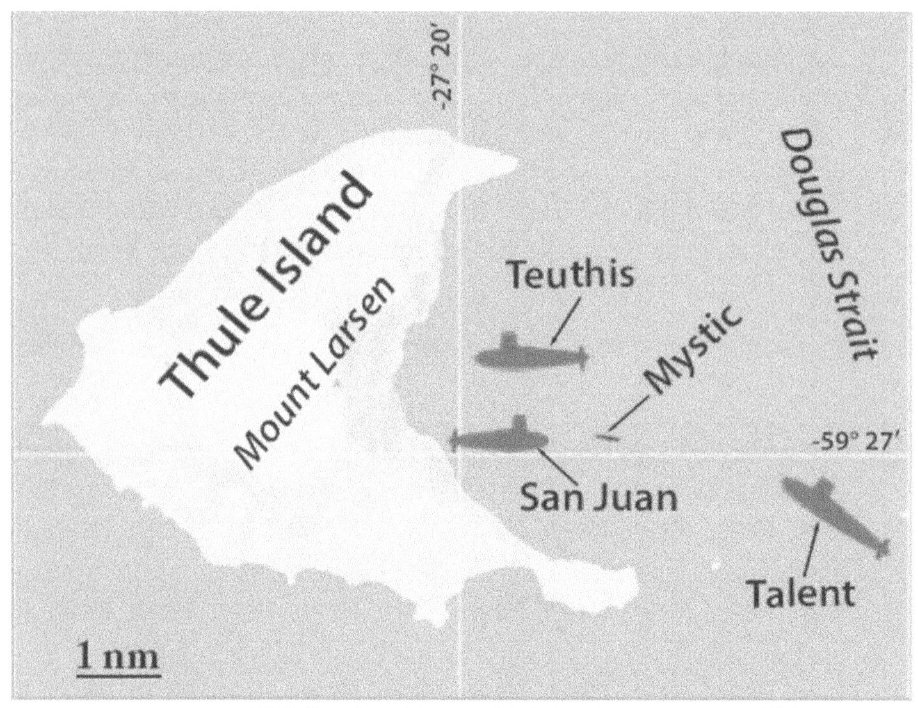

Douglas Strait—USS Teuthis, Mystic, ARA San Juan, *and* HMS Talent.

CHAPTER SIXTEEN—*ARA San Juan* Rescue

2000, MONDAY, JULY 24, 1989—*USS TEUTHIS*, BOTTOMED AT 1,100 FT, DOUGLAS STRAIT, 1.5 NM EAST OF MOUNT LARSEN CLIFFS.

After ten solid hours of in-water work, Ski and José crashed for six hours. Jimmy had not been in the water, but he was awake and alert for the entire time as well. He crashed right with them.

Waverly had been on watch for an hour in Ham's place when the Secure Gertrude sounded.

"*USS Teuthis*, this is *HMS Talent*, over."

Waverly answered right after he notified me. "*HMS Talent*, this is *Teuthis*, Roger."

"This is *Talent*. We are entering Douglas Strait from the north. Over."

"*Talent*, this is *Teuthis*. The north end of Douglas Strait is treacherously shallow with submerged rocky outcrops. Recommend you transit west of Thule Island and approach Douglas Strait from the south at periscope depth, monitoring bottom depth continuously. Over."

"This is *Talent*. Thank you. We will transit west of Thule and call you as we enter the strait. Over."

"This is *Teuthis*. Roger, out."

✳

I figured *Talent* would take two hours to work herself to the south end of Douglas Strait. I dropped down to Dive Control to see how the divers were doing.

I called them in the DDC. "Nice job, guys. We'll know in about five hours if your repair holds. In the meantime, we'll start bringing you up so you will be surfaced when we hit our OPAREA.[24] If we need you outside here, we'll just press you down again."

I called Deckhart. "In about two hours, we'll be doing DSRV ops."

"Yes, Sir. Waverly just told me."

✳

On the Secure Gertrude, "*USS Teuthis*, this is *HMS Talent*, over."

"This *Teuthis*, Roger."

"This is *Talent*. We're at periscope depth entering Douglas Strait from the south. Over."

I was in Control with Waverly. "Have her follow the coast for a couple of miles and then bottom at a comfortable depth, or if she doesn't want to bottom, hover at five hundred feet."

Waverly got on the Secure Gertrude again. "This is *Teuthis*. Recommend you follow coastline off your port side for one and a half nautical miles, and then either bottom at a depth of your choice, or hover at five hundred feet. *Teuthis* has identified herself to *San Juan* as U.S. Submarine. Do not reveal our name or *Mystic*'s name to *San Juan*. Over."

---

24 Military Operational Area.

"This is *Talent*. We will follow your recommendation and bottom in six hundred feet. We will maintain your confidentiality. Out."

✳

An hour later, *Talent* called. "This is *Talent*. We are bottomed one-third nautical mile from shore at five-hundred-fifty feet, one-point-five nautical miles along the shore from the midpoint of the gap between Thule and Cook Islands. Over."

"This is *Teuthis*. Roger. I will launch *Mystic*, who will locate you and dock to the hatch you choose. Coordinate directly with *Mystic* on this circuit. As a reminder, when communicating with *San Juan* on normal Gertrude, do not mention either the names *Mystic* or *Teuthis*. Out."

2300, MONDAY, JULY 24, 1989—*HMS TALENT* BOTTOMED AT 550 FT, DOUGLAS STRAIT, 0.3 NM NORTH OF THULE ISLAND PENINSULA.

Shortly after *HMS Talent* gave us her location on the bottom, I launched *Mystic*. I gave Deckhart a simple set of instructions.

"Using Secure Gertrude, coordinate with *Talent* to dock to her hatch of choice. Take on two *Talent* crew members. Return to *Teuthis* and drop off Gamble and Elton. Using normal Gertrude and as directed by CO *Talent*, proceed to *San Juan* and transport CO *San Juan* to *Talent*. When ordered by CO *Talent*, return CO *San Juan* and evacuate all but crew members needed to surface the sub, as determined by CO *San Juan*."

Talent signaled *San Juan* on standard Gertrude, which we monitored, as both sides of the conversation warbled through the icy water. "*San Juan*, this is *HMS Talent*. We are standing by with DSRV. DSRV will come to *San Juan* to transfer *San Juan* Commanding Officer to *Talent* to discuss crew transfer arrangements with CO *Talent*. Over."

"This is *San Juan*. Roger. CO *San Juan* will be waiting for DSRV arrival. What is your estimated time of arrival? Over."

"This is *Talent*. Approximately one hour. We will notify you this circuit when DSRV is approaching. Out."

A few minutes later, *Mystic* got underway after thoroughly sweeping the Mid and Rescue Spheres for anything that might identify *Mystic* or

Teuthis. Deckhart located *Talent* a nautical mile east and a half mile closer to shore than we were. In ten minutes, he embarked two *Talent* crew and headed for home. During the short transit, Gamble briefed the two British submariners on the *Mystic* procedures they would need to know.

Deckhart called me on the Secure Gertrude, "What about arming the British crew, Captain?"

"Are you armed?" I asked.

"Don and I are both armed."

"Are the British crew armed?"

"No, Sir."

"Are they trained in sidearms?"

"One moment, Sir."

About a minute later, "This is *Mystic*. Both have expert sidearms ratings."

"Roger. Return to *Teuthis*. As soon as you dock, we will pass two sidearms through the hatch."

✳

The Falklands war was over. Nevertheless, there was still much resentment. I wanted to effect the rescue of the Argentine sub crew, but was unwilling to put *Teuthis* or *Talent* in danger because of misplaced trust. As the former president said, "Trust, but verify!"

Mystic returned, and we passed two holstered .45s with extra mags to the *Talent* crew members. The DSRV undocked and moved toward *San Juan*.

Deckhart called *San Juan* on the standard Gertrude, which Waverly monitored.

"*San Juan, San Juan*, this is DSRV, over."

"This is *San Juan*, over."

"This is DSRV. Which hatch should I use? Over."

"This is *San Juan*. Use forward hatch. Commanding Officer is standing by. Over."

"This is DSRV. I will dock in ten minutes. After docking, I will pump down the skirt. Then I will pound on your hatch, signaling you to open your hatch. This is a peaceful rescue mission. If I see any weapons or sense something is wrong, I will close the hatch and depart."

"This is *San Juan*. We acknowledge your peaceful mission and are grateful for your rescue attempt. Out."

In Control ten minutes later, we monitored the interaction between *Mystic* and *San Juan*.

"*San Juan*, *San Juan*, this is DSRV, over."

"This is *San Juan*, over."

"This is DSRV. I am docked to your forward hatch. When you hear pounding on your hatch, open the hatch. Over."

"This is *San Juan*. Roger."

✷

Thirty-five minutes later, *Mystic* docked with *Talent*, and an Argentine skipper, Capitán de Fragata Liam Lautaro Romero, boarded a British nuclear submarine for the first time in history. I learned later that out of respect for his rank and position, the British sailors did not search him. He was piped aboard, as was standard for any visiting commanding officer.

In their discussion, Cmdr. Harris pointedly did not ask Capitán Romero what he was doing at Thule Island when Mount Larsen blew. It was apparent they both knew, but chose not to discuss it. By international salvage law, Cmdr. Harris could have claimed salvage rights to *San Juan*, and Romero knew it. Harris asked if Romero had landed any personnel on Thule, to which Romero responded that Mount Larsen blew before he had a chance to do so. That was the extent of their discussion about why the Argentine sub was at Thule.

Romero explained he had a 37-man crew and a 4-man geological survey team. To ensure safe surfacing, he wanted a maximum of ten crew members and himself on the stricken sub. They decided to move two groups of sailors, fifteen in each group. Both skippers went to the Control Room where Harris handed Romero the Gertrude mike.

In Spanish, Romero instructed his XO on the rescue procedure. He would return to *San Juan* with the DSRV. The XO and fourteen crew members would load into the DSRV. The XO would ensure that nobody carried weapons of any kind, not even pocketknives. The fifteen would be brought to *Talent*, and then the DSRV would return for the remaining fifteen. The Operations Officer would ensure that this group did not carry any weapons.

"Remember," Romero told his XO, "*HMS Talent* and the US Submarine will have rescued all of us from certain death. I have given my parole, and you and all the crew must comply."

My Spanish is marginal, but I understood Romero's order as we received it on the open-circuit Gertrude. We had experienced problems with parole given by ChiCom officers in the past,25 but I was confident that this proud Argentinian would honor his word.

✳

Deckhart took a full two hours to drive *Mystic* to *San Juan*, offload the skipper, onload the fifteen crew members while his British crew searched each one except the officers, and return to *Talent*. Once all fifteen were aboard *Talent*, Deckhart returned to *San Juan* to pick up the remaining fifteen. That left nine crew, the Engineer, and the skipper.

It was time to rock and roll.

I called Cmdr. Harris on the Secure Gertrude.

"*Talent*, this is *Teuthis*. You know about our Basketball. I will place the ROV near the patched hole as Romero tries to break free from the bottom. Have him put a bubble in his forward ballast, so I can check for large leaks. Please let him know there is a lot of brash above him, including some large ice chunks that could cause further damage. He will need to break free, and then vent his ballast tanks so he can surface under full control. I've got to believe he's drilled this scenario, so he knows what to do. Over."

"This is *Talent*. We walked through the procedure during our meeting. He has practiced it, but never from this deep. His drills were at fifty and a hundred meters. Over."

I did a quick mental calculation. That was 164 and 328 feet, give or take.

"This is *Teuthis*. I presume he knows the added depth gives him more time to gain control of his ascent. Over."

"This is *Talent*. He mentioned that. His big concern—and I agree with him—is doing more damage should he hit surface ice."

"This is *Teuthis*. Good. I've got the Basketball on station. I'll monitor the standard Gertrude comms between you both. I'll call you this channel should I see anything amiss. Out."

---

25 See *Operation White Out*, vol 4 in *The Mac McDowell Missions*.

0700, TUESDAY, JULY 25, 1989—*ARA SAN JUAN* BOTTOMED AT 1,100 FT, DOUGLAS STRAIT, 0.25 NM EAST OF CLIFFS BELOW MOUNT LARSEN ON THULE ISLAND.

Derrick hovered the Basketball a hundred feet off *San Juan*'s starboard bow. He widened the floodlight to its broadest extent. *San Juan*'s bow was sharply visible in the crystal-clear water.

I monitored Harris' warbled standard Gertrude transmission. "*San Juan*, this is *Talent*. We are observing you with a tethered ROV. If we see anything amiss, we will inform you immediately. Over."

"This is *San Juan*. Roger. We will commence the operation within five minutes. Out."

The first thing I saw or heard was air being let into *San Juan*'s forward ballast tank. Derrick moved the Basketball close to observe any bubbles from the weld. It appeared to be holding. *San Juan* let air into her after ballast tank. The Basketball picked up no movement.

At this point, I would have moved water from side to side, and that's just what Romero did. The Basketball saw nothing. Another burst of air into forward ballast…nothing …and then the after ballast…still nothing. Attempting to rock side to side…no motion. Another slug of air forward…nothing…a slug aft…movement…the stern lifted slightly off the bottom, raising billowing clouds of silt, blinding the Basketball.

"Stern has lifted," I announced on the Secure Gertrude.

Derrick ran the Basketball rapidly to the bow just in time to see the bow pull out of the muck before blinding the ROV with suspended silt. *San Juan* moved upward in slow motion, but building momentum, slightly down by the bow. Derrick pulled back to give a larger view. His floodlight was not really designed to illuminate an entire sub at once, but I could still make out the sub's slightly illuminated silhouette against the black background.

Romero opened his after ballast tank vent just sufficiently long to release a large bubble. *San Juan* still rose, but with a slight up-bubble now. A burble from the forward vent brought her to neutral, but accelerating upward.

San Juan was pointed east. Romero started her electric drive to get some forward momentum and move away from the overhead brash, and then released air from both ballast tanks. The sub was 200 off the bottom and near the extent of the Basketball cable. From what I could tell, Romero gained full control of *San Juan* and drove her to the surface, where he filled both ballast tanks with air.

I waited for what I knew would happen next. Five minutes later—just enough time to line up the diesels to operate without the snorkel, open the bridge hatch, and ensure a path through the sub for air to reach the diesels—Sonar called.

"Conn, Sonar, *San Juan* just lighted off her diesels."

✳

For the next hour, *San Juan* cruised slowly back and forth, charging her depleted batteries and flushing out her stale air. This was both good and not so good. The good part was obvious, but the air filling the sub was frigid, well below freezing. *San Juan* had an 1,140 nautical mile trip ahead of her, three-quarters on the surface with an open bridge hatch, sucking cold air into the sub. She could run surfaced on batteries for several hours every day while warming things up, but then it was time to recharge on diesels with the hatch open.

That lay ahead for *San Juan* and *Talent* and was not my problem. I called *Talent* on the Secure Gertrude.

"This is *Teuthis*. It looks like you are ready to return the crew to *San Juan*. Over."

"This is *Talent*. As soon as her batteries are fully charged—perhaps twenty more minutes or so. Over."

"This is *Teuthis*. Roger. I'll remain bottomed until transfer is complete, and you turn over operational control of *Mystic* to me. Over."

"This is *Talent*. Roger. Out."

A half hour later, *Mystic* got underway from *Talent* with her first load of *San Juan* crew. The Argentine sub waited for her at 100 meters—330 feet. The entire process was faster, because Deckhart's crew didn't have to search each passenger. By noon on the twenty-fifth, the Argentine crew was back aboard Jan Juan, the sub was surfaced on her diesels, and *Talent* was ready to escort her to Mare Harbour, 1,140 stormy miles to the northwest.

1230, TUESDAY, JULY 25, 1989—HMS TALENT AND ARA SAN JUAN SURFACED IN DOUGLAS STRAIT, HEADING SOUTH.

Before *San Juan* surfaced, I had one last Secure Gertrude conversation with *Talent*.

"*Teuthis*, this is *Talent*, over."

Jerry had just assumed the watch. He handed me the mike. "This is *Teuthis*, over."

"This is *Talent*. Since *San Juan* believes I am carrying the DSRV, and since we do not want Romero to think otherwise, I have adopted the following protocol. *San Juan* will proceed south out of Douglas Strait on the surface. I will follow at periscope depth. When we reach our turn point toward the northwest, she will switch to batteries and submerge to fifty meters. I will keep her on course as necessary, using Gertrude. When she needs to charge, she will surface, and I will come to periscope depth. We will continue this until we approach Choiseul Sound. The Admiralty will have a frigate standing by to take over the escort task. It's been jolly fun working with you. God speed on your task ahead. Out."

Did Cmdr. Harris know our destination and task? It sounded like he might.

✳

While thinking about what the commander might know, my eyes wandered across the large-scale chart of Douglas Strait. The chart notes said the strait was an old caldera left over from an ancient volcano that had blown away a land bridge between Thule and Cook Islands. That's not what the chart and my eyes told me. I saw a nearly circular hole in the ocean, 2,400 feet deep at the center and less than a hundred feet all around the edge except right at the foot of Mount Larsen, where it dropped to 1,100 feet.

In my youth, I had seen a formation just like this, although smaller scale and not underwater—the meteor crater in Arizona. I decided, with no more evidence than how Douglas Strait looked and the evidence of my eyes and memory, that this, too, was the remains of a small asteroid that hit here long ago.

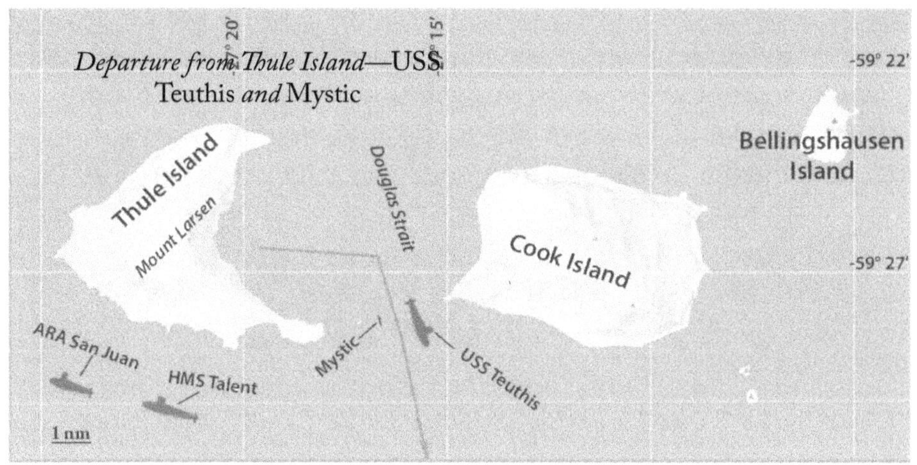

Departure from Thule Island—USS Teuthis and Mystic.

CHAPTER SEVENTEEN—Thule Island Departure

1400, TUESDAY, JULY 25, 1989—*USS TEUTHIS*, PERISCOPE DEPTH, EXITING DOUGLAS STRAIT.

*H*MS *Talent* and *AMA San Juan* had preceded *Teuthis* through the gap between Thule and Cook Islands. They were headed northwest toward the Falklands; we were headed in virtually the other direction, and traveling twice as far. We had over six days ahead of us traveling through little known waters, with uncertain charts. The good news was that the bottom was considerably deeper than average, down to 18,000 feet or more. So far as I could tell from the available charts between us and our destination, nothing approached the surface closer than 5,000 feet.

I had Jerry drop to 100 feet and call *Mystic* home. An hour later, the DSRV was firmly latched in her cradle, and Jerry dropped *Teuthis* to 500 feet and set course for the Prince Edward Islands—Initial course, 101 degrees.

As we transited the gap between Thule and Cook, the wind had picked up. That would be normal, since Thule Island protected Douglas Strait from the prevailing westerly blast. What we experienced, however, was a lot more than we expected. As we finished up DSRV ops and dropped to 500 feet, our ice scanning sonar that looked at the surface gave us a sense of what was coming. Already, waves averaged fifteen feet, with occasional fifty footers passing stern to bow. The Diving Officer was Master Chief Ocean Tech Morris Jones—Spook, as we called him.

"I can feel those guys," he reported to me. "They're sucking us up as they pass."

I walked over to Plot to check the chart. The bottom was approaching 8,000 feet with no rises in our path for several hours to the end of the chart.

"Take her down to eight hundred feet," I told Jerry.

As we passed 600 feet, the current layer, according to Mason, Sonar watch supervisor, Jerry cleared the baffles. As we came back to base course, but before we came up to speed, Sonar called.

"Conn, Sonar, we have a suppressed cavitation contact off our port quarter, designate Sierra-six-six. She's distant. We'll get you more info as soon as we can."

1600, TUESDAY, JULY 25, 1989—*USS TEUTHIS*, SUBMERGED AT 800 FT, ON TRACK FROM THULE ISLAND TO PRINCE EDWARD ISLAND.

I asked myself, Why would another submarine be out here? I know why we are here. Are we being tracked? Have we somehow been compromised? Knowing more about S-66 would help.

Jerry kept us at five knots while Sonar checked out S-66. I saw King enter Sonar, so I figured the problem was somewhat knotty. Then King came out to Plot and laid one of his oversize reference books on the table.

"You're not going to believe this, Captain. Sierra-six-six is the Soviet *Sierra I Class* sub, *Yaroslavl* (B-277)."

During Operation Ice Breaker, our divers had actually forced *Yaroslavl's* class lead ship, *Carp*, to the surface under the ice off Point Barrow by clogging her reactor intake lines with paraffin.[26] She was

---

26 See *Operation Ice Breaker*, vol 2 in *The Mac McDowell Missions*.

the best the Soviets had—all titanium, lots of automation, fairly quiet (but not nearly so quiet as we), and blazingly fast with an estimated top speed of forty knots.

"Her distance, course, and speed?" I asked.

"Two hundred ten nautical miles, course zero-seven-five, speed thirty-five knots. She's blind as a bat. When she slows for a Crazy Ivan, if we are at twenty knots, she might pick us up as an intermittent contact—if we're in the same layer." King grinned at me, his black face split, displaying even white teeth. "I'm gonna keep a Sonar Tech focused on her so we detect her Crazy Ivans as soon as they start," he said.

I got on the 1MC. "This is the captain. We have a Soviet submarine off our port beam. She is not aware of us. I want to keep it that way. Set your stations up so you can go to ultra-quiet at a moment's notice. When you hear an ultra-quiet announcement, help us make like a hole in the water."

At that moment, a loud whistle sounded through Sonar's speakers, clearly audible in Control, probably through the hull as well.

I keyed the mike again. "That was Borysko, helping us out." And he was, indeed. When *Yaroslavl* looked south and picked up something, Borysko's whistle would tell her that sonar had only picked up some whales.

0700, WEDNESDAY, JULY 26, 1989—*USS TEUTHIS*, SUBMERGED AT 800 FT, CROSSING SOUTHERN END OF SOUTH SANDWICH TRENCH.

Chop had the watch. I enjoyed observing how he handled new situations. Because of his lack of at-sea experience, virtually everything that happened to him was new, unless he had encountered it during his qualifications.

This time, the new was particularly spectacular. We crossed the southern end of the South Sandwich Trench. One moment, the bottom was about 6,000 feet, the next it was nearly 27,000 feet. This trench is the deepest with the steepest sides anywhere in the Atlantic. Chop watched the fathometer display on the periscope stand with wide eyes.

"I never saw anything like it, Captain!" he said, excitement filling his voice.

"Doesn't get deeper anywhere on this side of the world," I quipped. "The Aleutian trench gives it a good run, but misses by about three hundred feet."

"This will be something I can tell my grandkids," Chop said.

"Not in context," I cautioned. "Remember, we're not here."

"Oh, yah…well…crap!" Chop's eyes rolled up and to the left as he did a mental calculation. "That's almost five miles down." He grinned. "It's hard to believe."

"Conn, Sonar, Crazy Ivan!"

Chop grabbed the 1MC mike. "Set condition ultra-quiet!"

Within seconds, the ubiquitous submarine background noise disappeared. Anyone listening to *Teuthis* from the outside would have lost all contact. We moved forward on momentum, the screw making turns for five knows, driven electrically. We were virtually invisible.

I glanced at the overhead sonar. Wave height had reached an average of fifty feet, with occasional peaks approaching a hundred. Anywhere else, this would be the mother of all storms, but here it was just another weather event.

✳

The winter storm continued to rage overhead as we pushed toward our destination. This was one of the least traveled parts of planet Earth. We were 800 feet beneath the storm-tossed surface, with nothing ahead to impede our passage. Other than clearing baffles at random intervals once an hour, the OODs really had nothing to do—other than be ready to handle any emergency that might overtake us.

I didn't conduct any ship-wide drills, but each watch section worked through emergency procedures, keeping their watchstanders alert and practiced on what to do should something bad happen.

The storm lasted well into Chop's watch the next day. By the end of his watch, wave activity had dropped to a twenty-foot average.

"Conn, Sonar, Sierra-six-six is now just abaft our beam at three hundred sixty-six miles. it looks like she is pointed at Bouvet Island."

Now that was a mystery. Why, in the winter, would a state-of-the-art Soviet sub visit Norwegian owned Bouvet Island—perhaps the most remote island on the planet?

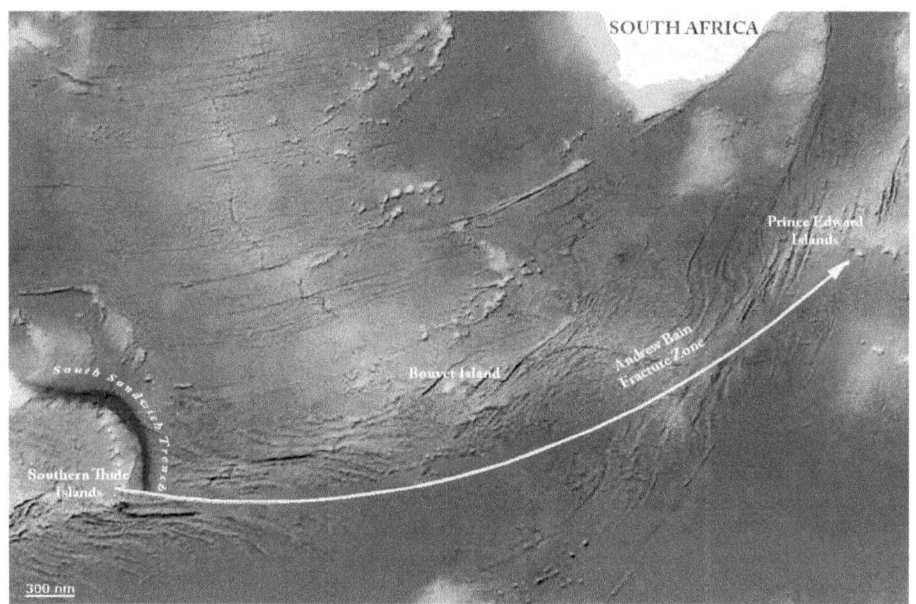

Transit to Prince Edward Islands—USS Teuthis *and* Mystic.

CHAPTER EIGHTEEN—Transit to Prince Edward Islands

0000, FRIDAY, JULY 28, 1989—*USS TEUTHIS*, SUBMERGED AT 800 FT, 510 NM SOUTH OF BOUVET ISLAND.

We were fifteen hours from the halfway point of our transit to the Prince Edward Islands. That placed us 510 nautical miles due south of Bouvet Island, the apparent destination of *Yaroslavl*. I knew a little about Bouvet, but not enough to guess *Yaroslavl's* motivation. I asked Roger to set up Officer's Call right after breakfast.

After breakfast, all my officers remained in the Wardroom except for Chop in Control and Zeb in Maneuvering. I wanted input from everyone on Bouvet. I would check with Chop and Zeb later.

"Here's the situation," I started out. "The Soviet state-of-the-art *Sierra I Class* sub *Yaroslavl* is making a run toward Bouvet Island."

"Bouvet Island," Robert Borka commented, "that's crazy. There's nothing there."

"Before we departed Mare Harbour," Waverly said, "I did a bit of research in their library, looking at things we might meet along the way. Bouvet Island is only nineteen square miles with virtually no decent landing points until between nineteen fifty-five and fifty-seven, when a major rockslide created a mile-wide terrace on the north-west coast called Nyrøysa."

"I'm impressed," I told Waverly.

"That's not all," he added. "The island is almost completely glaciated, except for Nyrøysa, but if you dig down twelve inches, the temperature is seventy-two degrees Fahrenheit."

"Anything else?" I asked.

The other officers were staring at Waverly. I decided any further praise would be counter effective.

"So why," I continued, "would a *Sierra I Class* sub visit this island in mid-winter?"

"We don't know she's actually visiting," Jerry said.

Seth scowled at him. "There's nothing else for more than a thousand miles. Where else would she be going?"

"I meant," Jerry said, perhaps a bit defensively, "maybe there's something going on nearby."

"That's a possibility," I conceded, "but what and why?"

Bert spoke up, "Only one thing anybody mentioned that carries any real interest. I'm talking about the warm temperature just under the surface."

"But why a state-of-the-are nuke…in winter?" I asked.

Ham had been quiet up till now. "*Yaroslavl* isn't doing anything there. She's picking up a team dropped off earlier by someone else, perhaps a summer research team."

"That makes more sense," I said. "A team investigating the subterranean temperature thing."

"The last time Bouvet blew," Waverly said, "was two thousand BC."

"So, is this about a remote volcano getting ready to blow?" Seth asked.

"Doesn't seem likely," Robert said. "There's got to be more to it."

"Thank you for your input," I said, rising to my feet. "Whatever is going on at Bouvet doesn't seem to impact our mission."

✳

Yaroslavl's presence had me concerned. Her home port was Petropavlovsk-Kamchatskiy on the Kamchatka peninsula. To get here, she would have had to cross the Arctic or round the Horn. Either was a big deal. So why *Yaroslavl?* The sub had some remarkable capabilities, including locking out divers. What was her mission? She was here, because the Soviets needed her capabilities here...now.

I was letting this get to me. I ran through every possible scenario. None made sense.

We passed the halfway point on Jerry's watch, 450 nautical miles southeast of Bouvet Island. I still hadn't come up with a satisfactory explanation, but the question was on my mind as we pushed on toward Prince Edward.

✳

The question was never far from my mind throughout the day. In the late afternoon, I asked Roger to join me for coffee and discussion. He joined me, carrying two cups of steaming joe.

"What's on your mind, Captain?"

"I'm still thinking about the *Yaroslavl*," I said. "I don't believe in coincidences, so tell me, what's she doing down here?" I sipped my coffee. "If this were summer, I might think she was involved in some kind of research. But this is winter. The Bouvet surf will be twenty feet or more. Even Nyrøysa would be impassable." Another sip. "Why now? What's going on in this part of the world?"

Roger's eyes got big. "The South African nuclear project." He straightened in his chair, "*Yaroslavl's* not going to Bouvet Island, she's investigating the South African project."

"ComSubLant knows she's here. The SOSUS array we install off South Georgia ensures they know."

"They're not stupid," Roger said. "They will have arrived at the same conclusion we just reached."

"Our mission was launched under such secrecy that I think it unlikely the Soviets know about us," I said. "They have their own mission, and it will most likely impact ours." I set my cup down and look straight at Roger.

"Prepare a burst message," I told him, "informing ComSubLant of the situation. Remind them of my previous involvement with *Carp*; have them check with ComSubPac for details."

0200, SUNDAY, JULY 30, 1989—*USS TEUTHIS*, SUBMERGED AT 500 FT, ENTERING ANDREW BAIN FRACTURE ZONE.

Andrew Bain was a South African geologist who influenced the science world far beyond his own boundaries. The area we had just entered was named after him.

Geologists consider this area of the Southwest Indian Ridge as a connector between the Somali Tectonic Plate to the north and the Antarctic Plate to the south. Normal ocean depth is 6,000 to 8,000 feet, but what they call graben, or trenches, drop rather spectacularly to 14,000 feet.

None of this concerned us directly, of course. I had Seth bring *Teuthis* above the layer to 500 feet. Sonar had lost contact with *Yaroslavl* more than a day earlier, so moving above the layer did not affect that. We were truly alone in this merging of the South Atlantic and Indian Oceans. We were nicely on schedule, with one and a half days to go.

Ham's divers were at 300 feet. By the time we got our bearings in the Prince Edward Island group, they would have surfaced and would be ready to work with the Shayetet 13 unit as they carried out the point of this entire operation.

*

The Shayetet 13 unit had pretty much kept to itself for the entire time since departing Mare Harbor. The two enlisted divers, Rasar Chaim Meiyr and Rasar Abdiel Mizrahi, spent part of their time with Ham's divers swapping sea stories. Rasam Bezai Azulay, the Israeli equivalent of a chief petty officer, spent time in the goat locker getting to know my chiefs. Their commander, Ranag Hadriel Davidov, their equivalent of a chief warrant officer, spent most of his time with Bert and Ham.

I had several private conversations with Davidov, where he outlined how he intended to proceed, subject to what we found upon arrival, of course. He was serious, focused, and entirely professional. In his mind, he and his team were preventing World War III. Personally, I went through the Navy's entire diver training program, including saturation diving.

I worked with SEALS and knew their capabilities. I can honestly say that I have met no team more focused and professional than these guys.

Davidov requested I install a spread-spectrum transceiver in the Control Room and connect it to one of my whip antennas. "This will give you two-way comms with my team," he said. "It's line of sight, but better than nothing."

1100, SUNDAY, JULY 30, 1989—*USS TEUTHIS,* PERISCOPE DEPTH, ANDREW BAIN FRACTURE ZONE.

The big storm had passed us, and the choppy waters in its wake were subsiding. Daylight was short, but when Chop and I raised the scopes just before noon on Sunday, July 30, the sky was blue with white clouds scudding from west to east across the blue dome.

We timed our upward excursion to get a good SatNav fix while we sent the burst message about *Yaroslavl.* Chop and I saw nothing. We got a good fix and reset the SINS. I informed ComSubLant I would listen next on the hour, then seventy-five minutes after that and seventy-five minutes after that for their response.

To Chop I said, "Take us down slowly so Sonar can get a complete three hundred sixty take above and below the layer."

At 500 feet, we were still above the layer. At 590 feet, Sonar announced, "Conn, Sonar, passing through the layer."

Shortly thereafter, Sonar said, "Conn, Sonar, we reacquired Sierra-six-six, the *Yaroslavl.* Estimate she is at two hundred meters or six hundred sixty feet. She's doing turns for thirty-five knots, so she' blind as a bat."

"Give me her course ASAP," Chop said.

Five minutes later, Sonar called. "Con, Sonar, *Yaroslavl* bears three-two-zero on a course of zero-eight-six."

Chief Henshaw had the Nav Watch. "That puts her on a direct course for Prince Edward Island," he said.

"Stay in the same layer as *Yaroslavl,*" I told Chop. "Inform me when you change layers."

Jerry assumed the watch at noon. He brought us to periscope depth to receive any transmission ComSubLant might send.

And they did.

FLASH…FLASH…FLASH…FLASH

TOP SECRET/SENSITIVE COMPARTMENTED INFORMATION

DATE: 30 JULY 1989 1000Z

TO: USS TEUTHIS SSNR 2

INFO: USS PASADENA SSN 752

FROM: COMSUBLANT

SUBJ: OPERATION VELA REDUX

1. THIS MSG ACKNOWLEDGES YOUR MSG DTD 30 JULY 1989 0900Z

2. CONFIRMING SOSUS DETECTION OF SOVIET SIERRA I CLASS YAROSLAVL (B-276) YOUR VICINITY, ON APPARENT COURSE TO PRINCE EDWARD ISLAND.

3. INTEL INDICATES YAROSLAVL IS UNAWARE OF TEUTHIS PRESENCE. SOVIETS RECEIVED INDEPENDENT INTEL RE SOUTH AFRICA NUCLEAR PROJECT. YAROSLAVL WAS VEC-TORED SOUTH THROUGH THE ATLANTIC FROM AN ARCTIC MISSION.

4. INTEL INDICATES YAROSLAVL IS CARRYING A MORSKOY SPETSNAZ UNIT. COMSUBLANT UNAWARE OF YAROSLAVL'S PURPOSE. ASSUME HOSTILE INTENT INVOLVING MORSKOY SPETSNAZ DIVERS.

5. UPON CONFIRMATION PARAGRAPH THREE ABOVE, COMSUBLANT DEPLOYED USS PASADENA (SSN 752) COMMANDED BY CMDR WILSON FRITCHMAN. ETA PRINCE EDWARD ISLAND 01 AUGUST 1989 1400Z.

6. PASADENA WILL ATTEMPT TO DIVERT
    YAROSLAVL, ENABLING TEUTHIS TO CARRY
    OUT YOUR MISSION. FAILING THAT,
    PASADENA WILL MAKE HERSELF AVAILABLE
    FOR ANY TASK TEUTHIS REQUIRES.

7. TEUTHIS HAS OPERATIONAL CONTROL.

TOP SECRET/SENSITIVE COMPARTMENTED
INFORMATION

FLASH…FLASH…FLASH…FLASH

PART THREE

Vela Redux

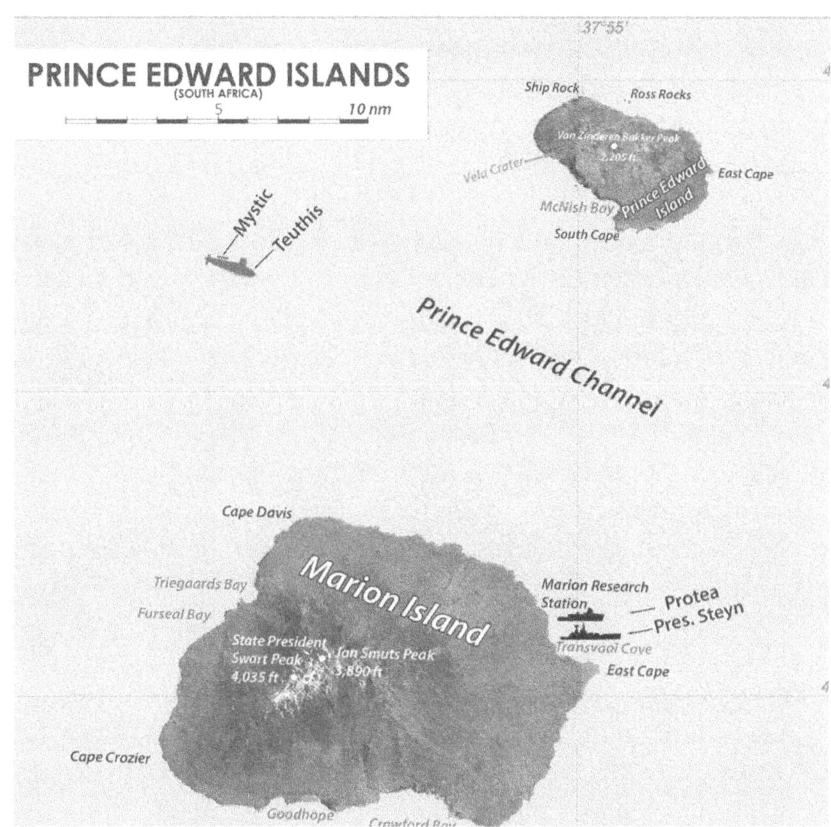

Prince Edward Islands showing Teuthis *and* Mystic,
SAS Protea *and* SAS President Steyn.

CHAPTER NINETEEN—Prince Edward Islands

1800, MONDAY, JULY 31, 1989—*USS TEUTHIS*, PERISCOPE DEPTH, APPROACHING PRINCE EDWARD CHANNEL

We started Jerry's watch at 500 feet—100 feet above the layer. About an hour earlier, *Yaroslavl* had slowed and moved above the layer. She was still a hundred miles behind us, and she was now moving cautiously. The *Teuthis* crew was on notice to go to ultra-quiet on a moment's notice. According to ComSubLant, *Yaroslavl* was unaware of our presence. I was determined to keep it that way.

Pasadena was out there, somewhere to the northwest, running deep and fast. Unlike *Teuthis*, she was unconcerned about being detected. In fact, *Pasadena* wanted *Yaroslavl* to detect her. That was the idea—distract the Soviet intruder while we accomplished our mission.

Pasadena was the fleet's newest *Los Angeles Class* fast-attack. She had been commissioned in February, and Cmdr. Wilson Fritchman was eager to make his first command noteworthy. In that sense, both he and I were in the same boat—we were on our first commands doing something quite beyond the ordinary.

Sonar was looking for *Pasadena*, but she was still 700 nautical miles out. We would not detect her for another few hours.

It was time to find out what we were up against in the Prince Edward Islands. I asked Davidov to join me in Control so he could see things firsthand.

✳

We had very little reliable sounding information for the waters around the Prince Edward Islands. I decided to pass down the middle of Prince Edward Channel at periscope depth, while Seth and his quarter-masters mapped the bottom. I started at the northwest end. Both islands were the volcanic peaks of a large shield volcano thrusting up from 6,000 feet. The bottom dropped off around the perimeter of the island group, but I suspected the twelve-nautical-mile-wide channel to be much shallower.

Ham had the Deck when we started our run. The bottom was 6,000 feet. By the time we were well between the islands, the bottom was only 300 feet. The night was moonless but bright with starlight. With the periscope at six feet above the surface, our horizon was 4.5 nautical miles. Since the channel was twelve nautical miles wide, all I saw through the periscope was water in all directions.

"Ham," I said, "bring us two miles closer to Prince Edwards."

He did. That let me see the shoreline. Our chart showed an indentation on the southeast end of the island, McNish Bay. The bay was a bit over a mile wide and three-quarters of a mile deep. It looked like a suitable spot for our operations base.

"Ranag," I said to Davidov, "examine this chart and then look at the bay through the periscope."

He pointed at a spot near the west end of the island. "This crater is where we and the South Africans set off the nuclear device a decade ago. There should be no residual radiation now, and we think that's where the South Africans will detonate their current device." He peered through the scope. "The bay looks good." He swung the scope left. "Can't see the Vela Crater from here."

"It's sixty-two-hundred feet along the coast from McNish," Quartermaster Theron said, pointing to the chart.

"That's about an hour on the DPUs," Davidov said.

"DPUs...?" Theron asked.

"Diver propulsion units," Davidov answered.

"Take us into McNish Bay," I told Ham.

The channel shallowed to 150 feet as we moved east. I thought it might be an old land bridge between the two islands. When we turned north toward McNish, the water deepened again to 300 feet, and then gradually shallowed to 150 feet in the bay, sloping down to the south.

"Are you okay exiting at one hundred fifty feet?" I asked Davidov.

"That's about forty-five meters. Sure, that's fine."

2300, MONDAY, JULY 31, 1989—*USS TEUTHIS*, PERISCOPE DEPTH, APPROACHING MARION RESEARCH STATION

Ham was still OOD when we turned toward Marion Research Station, twelve nautical miles across the channel. Marion Island was just becoming visible in the scopes when Seth assumed the watch. Because nighttime reigned topside, I had little worry that anyone would see our periscopes. We didn't use radar, because I was certain that the South Africans had some kind of support vessel tied up at Marion. Furthermore, since they were dealing with a nuclear detonation, they would most certainly evacuate the Marion Research Station personnel for several days.

When we were four miles from the station, I began to see lights, and as we drew closer, the outlines of two vessels. I recognized one profile, the *SAS Protea* that I had studied before we got underway. She was South Africa's premier research vessel. The other was a warship, a third longer than *Protea*, a frigate, I thought.

For eight hours, we cruised back and forth, three nautical miles from the Marion Research Station piers. Finally, about 1100 hours under an overcast sky, I saw movement on the pier, and then, as it got brighter, I saw a Wasp chopper parked ahead of the bridge on the frigate. The bow sported the hull number F147.

Chief Henshaw was the watch quartermaster. He looked up the designator and said, "That's the frigate *SAS President Steyn*. She's got a decent sonar, a good radar, guns, and torpedoes. She's three hundred seventy feet long. That's a hundred feet longer than the *Protea*."

I watched people walk down the pier with suitcases and board *Protea*. Clearly, I was watching an evacuation. *What are they wondering?* I thought. *They probably are not aware of the 1979 detonation, and there is no way the secretive South African government would tell a bunch of scientists they were about to detonate a nuclear device on this pristine nature preserve.* I grinned to myself. *Those poor bastards don't have a clue what's going on.*

I moved the scope focus to the frigate. Something was happening. Sailors scurried about the deck in what appeared to be random movements. As I watched, I identified the pattern. They were singling up lines. *President Steyn* was about to get underway.

0400, WEDNESDAY, AUGUST 2, 1989—*USS TEUTHIS*, BOTTOMED AT 150 FT, MCNISH BAY, PRINCE EDWARD ISLAND

Seth was OOD when I detected *President Steyn* preparing to get underway.

"Seth," I said, "Steyn is getting underway. Drop to fifty feet over bottom and take us to McNish Bay at fifteen knots. The Steyn has singled lines, so she should move from the pier in a few minutes. In fifteen minutes, slow to ten knots. The Steyn has no reason to suspect our presence, and may not light off her active sonar, but her sonar techs will be listening in any case. If they get even a hint of us, she'll go active."

As things developed, the South African crew of the Steyn took their time getting underway. They cast off a full thirty minutes after singling up.

"Conn, Sonar, Steyn has gotten underway and is heading due north at fifteen knots. Designate the Steyn Sierra-six-seven. Her active sonar is quiet. She cannot detect us on passive sonar at her present speed."

Quartermaster Jeff Davis had Plot. "She's headed straight for the Vela Crater," he said. "She cannot land there—it's surf against rocks. There's a small area where a launch could land, but not that big frigate."

"That's why she has the Wasp," I said, referring to her small chopper. "These frigates, and their British equivalents, can detect targets with sonar beyond their gun and torpedo ranges. They carry the Wasp to deliver munitions out to their detection range." I paused. "It looks like they will deliver personnel and equipment this time."

As the sky brightened an hour later, we settled into McNish Bay. We were getting ready to change the watch. Chop was up.

"Conn, Sonar, we just picked up old contact Sierra-six-six, the *Yaroslavl*. She's entering Prince Edward Channel. There's no way she cannot detect the Steyn."

"Set ultra-quiet before you pass the watch to Chop," I told Seth.

I stepped into Sonar. Sportsman was turning over the watch to King. I told them, "I need to know if *Yaroslavl* is passing through or looking to settle along the south coast of Prince Edward. The logical place is McNish Bay—where we are. Watch her closely!"

Back in Control, I told Chop, "Ease up to periscope depth. Be prepared to move out of McNish to the right if *Yaroslavl* turns toward the bay."

"Conn, Sonar, Steyn just let an anchor go. It looks like she will remain where she is for a while."

When we hit periscope depth, I focused on the Steyn. She definitely had an anchor out. Her bow was a hundred yards from the rocks, and she seemed to be swinging left and right on her anchor chain.

On the sound-powered phone, Sonar reported, "*Yaroslavl* has passed McNish Bay and is turning left. Looks like she is rounding the island."

"Probably wants to get away from Steyn's sonar," Chop commented.

"You may be right," I said, swinging my scope around to see the dim cape in the morning twilight. Before the rocky prominence filled my view, I thought I might have seen a periscope protruding through the surface. I swung back to check, but it was gone. I played the scene back in my mind. The scope was real and appeared to be looking at the Steyn, not in my direction. From the wake, I estimated a five-knot speed.

On the sound-powered phone, "Conn, Sonar, *Yaroslavl* has rounded South Cape. We've lost contact."

"Can you tell where the Wasp is going?" I asked Chop.

"Hard to tell," he answered. "It drops below the rocks as soon as it crosses the surf."

"How many trips have you counted?"

"They're returning from the fourth now," Chop answered. "That chopper is pretty small. They can't carry very much per trip. Looks like they dropped off four people and carried equipment on two trips."

Movement on Steyn's side caught my eye. "They are lowering a Zodiac-type boat into the water," I said.

As I watched, a group of camo-clad men, replete with backpacks and rifles, climbed down a cargo net into the inflated boat. The boat headed toward the shore, but its landing spot was out of my view.

"Chop, ease us out a hundred yards," I said. "No noise."

As we moved away from the bay mouth, I saw the boat beached on a small, rocky finger a few feet east of Vela Crater. The South African Marines, for I was certain that's who they were, would have a bit of a climb to reach the crater rim, but it appeared quite doable.

I stepped over to Plot and marked Chief Henshaw's chart. "They landed here," I said.

I continued to watch as the boat returned for another load of marines. It made a third trip with equipment—tents, perhaps. After that, it did not return to the Steyn.

As Jerry assumed the watch, I turned the scope over to him and let out a deep sigh.

"Jerry, remain at periscope depth and ease around the east end of the island. Stay at ultra-quiet, and keep a keen ear for *Yaroslavl*."

I called Roger. "I want you to take Ham's watches for the time being. He will be busy with dive ops."

I called Ham. "You told me we still had a drum of paraffin, right?"

"We do."

"Configure it like we did for the *Carp* off Point Barrow."

"Sir?"

"I think we will be doing a repeat on *Yaroslavl* in the next several hours."

I turned to Jerry. "Wake me when you locate *Yaroslavl*."

I went to my cabin and crashed on my bunk without undressing.

1800, WEDNESDAY, AUGUST 2 1989—*USS TEUTHIS*, SUBMERGED AT PERISCOPE DEPTH, NORTHEAST END, PRINCE EDWARD ISLAND

While I slept, Ham assembled the divers and asked the Shayetet guys to join them.

"A while back," he said to the group, "we were bottomed under the ice off Point Barrow, Alaska, in a five-hundred-foot-deep hole." He grinned at the Israelis. "That's about one hundred fifty meters."

They nodded, and Davidov said with a smile, "we speak inches and feet."

"I can't tell you everything," Ham continued, "because it's classified, but I see no harm in giving you the highlights—especially since you will be working with us this time.

"We were in a situation when a Soviet *Sierra I Class* boat—the *Carp*—showed up and bottomed nearby. She was unaware of us. For reasons that are immaterial to this story, we had several fifty-gallon drums of paraffin onboard and a Soviet submarine-reactor expert from the NSA—National Security Agency.

"We moved a heated drum of paraffin to the *Carp*'s reactor cooling water intake, and pumped liquid paraffin into the line. Our intent was to freeze up the line and scram the reactor—shut it down. The *Carp* was carrying a Morskoy Spetsnaz unit that she launched through her torpedo tubes, coincidentally as we were pumping paraffin. Remember, *Carp* was unaware of our presence.

"In the ensuing underwater fight—remember, we were at five hundred feet—we sustained some injuries, but were able to eliminate all the Soviet divers. When *Carp*'s reactor scrammed, her crew panicked and emergency-surfaced, right through the ice cover. We had no further contact with her."[27]

Ham answered several questions from the Israelis and our new guys. Then he continued.

"*Yaroslavl* is the same *Sierra I Class* sub as *Carp*. Instead of five hundred feet, she's at one hundred feet, maybe. We have no real idea why she's here, but a *Sierra-I* does not normally carry Morskoy Spetsnaz. These guys are like you guys. They're here for a purpose. The fact that *Yaroslavl* is close in, bottomed in shallow water tells me that the Morskoy Spetsnaz guys are going ashore. I'm not going to speculate why."

✳

Roger had the messenger wake me at 2300 with a hot cup of joe. I got to my feet, splashed cold water on my face, and carried my coffee to Control.

"We're still at ultra-quiet," Roger told me, "and a bit over a mile offshore, three miles along the north coast from East Cape. We're at periscope depth, but there's nothing to see out there. Pitch black, no lights. We've located *Yaroslavl*. She's just inside Ross Rocks, bottomed with her turbine idling. She's making too much noise to be at ultra-quiet.

"Ham and I decided to have *Mystic* tow the divers and paraffin drum to just outside Ross Rocks."

"Good thinking," I interrupted.

"By the way," Roger said, "Borysko is back with us. He supervised unlatching *Mystic* and getting her ready to go. The drum is ballasted and ready to go in the water. The divers are standing by, including the Israelis. All we need is your okay."

"Thanks, Roger. I needed that shut-eye time. Okay, let's do it."

---

27 See *Operation Ice Breaker*, vol 2 in *The Mac McDowell Missions*.

Prince Edward Island showing Teuthis, Mystic, Yaroslavl, *and* Pasadena.

CHAPTER TWENTY—Prince Edward Island

0100, THURSDAY, AUGUST 3 1989—MYSTIC, SUBMERGED AT 100 FT, ONE NM OFFSHORE, 3 NM NORTHWEST OF EAST CAPE

Mystic had left her cradle and was standing by ten yards from the DDC lock. The Basketball under Wally's firm hand gave us a clear view in Control and wherever else monitors were set up.

The engineers had heated the paraffin drum, so the contents were fully liquid, wrapped it with a heating coil, and insulated it with a thick blanket. A waterproof high-capacity battery powered the heating coil and the pump the divers would use at the reactor intake.

Without all the added stuff, the drum and contents were twenty pounds buoyant. With everything added plus a five-pound diver's weight, the drum floated neutrally.

Ham assigned Jimmy, Ski, and José as his active divers. Earlier, Davidov's people had adjusted their underwater comm frequency so

223

both groups could talk to each other underwater. This would be their first active dive with Ham's divers.

The three *Teuthis* divers carried on their backs a fully loaded Russian APS Underwater Assault Rifle and three extra twenty-six-round magazines. To everyone's surprise, the four Shayetet divers also carried APSs—made in Israel. They were modified with a smaller horizontal cross-section and a shorter dart, making them easier to handle tactically underwater.

Russian APS Underwater Assault Rifle

Israeli APS Underwater Assault Rifle

"Listen up, guys," Ham said before they dropped through the DDC hatch. "*Yaroslavl* can pick up your transmissions. If their sonar techs are any kind of sophisticated, they will not only know you are out there, but will be able to understand you. So…don't use underwater comms except in an emergency. Everybody got that?"

"What if one diver needs to alert the others quietly?" Ski asked.

"Trigger your transmitter twice," Ham answered. "The double-click should be audible to everyone but likely will be missed by the *Yaroslavl* sonar techs. Should you hear a double-click, stop what you are doing, freeze in place, and carefully check your surroundings." Ham grinned at the divers. "Remember, you will be dealing with Morskoy Spetsnaz divers—possibly the best spec ops guys in the world."

"Right…give me a break," Davidov snickered. "Shayetet eats Morskoy Spetsnaz for breakfast!"

"One more thing," Ham added. "When he's done with the paraffin, Ski will trigger three clicks, instructing you to form up and return to Ross Rocks."

✳

The seven divers in drysuits and rebreathers with their drum were about a nautical mile from Ross Rocks. Each diver found a location on *Mystic* for a handhold. They tied the drum to the manipulator arm.

As the divers settled themselves around the outside of *Mystic*, Borysko made an appearance. The Shayetet divers had seen how the *Teuthis* divers interacted with Borysko and were eager to try it out themselves. Ski took them one by one to the cetacean and introduced them by placing their hands inside Borysko's huge mouth on his tongue.

Mystic got underway, moving less than three knots so the divers could comfortably maintain their holds. It was approaching 0330. The sky over their position was darkly overcast. When they started, the bottom was 200 feet below them, but within several minutes it had shallowed to fifty feet as they approached Ross Rocks.

Deckhart flashed a downward pointed light momentarily, a prearranged signal telling the divers they needed to continue on their own. Ski and Jimmy took point, pulling the neutrally buoyant drum with them. José followed them closely. The four Shayetet divers spread out behind the *Teuthis* divers, forming a shield. Behind them, a curious Borysko followed, not interfering, just keeping track of them with ultrasonic sound bursts.

They skirted the northern surf zone at the rocks and dropped into deeper water toward the island. The bottom flattened out. Ski turned on his light and cautiously examined the water in front of them.

Nothing.

They swam another hundred yards, and this time when Ski turned his light on, it reflected dully from the black-painted starboard side of *Yaroslavl*. Ski used his light to beckon the divers to him. He pulled his white message slate from a leg pocket and wrote on it with a black grease pencil. Before they left the DDC, each diver received a numbered skullcap. They were, in order, Ski—1, Jimmy—2, José—3, Davidov—4, Azulay—5, Meiyr—6, and Mizrahi—7. Ski sketched *Yaroslavl* with an arrow pointing at the coolant intake, and positioned the divers' numbers, 1 and 2 at the intake, 3 standing off from 1 and 2, 4 and 5 above the upper torpedo tube outer doors, and 6 and 7 at the lower torpedo tube outer doors near the seafloor. Borysko hovered over them, intensely curious, but still not interfering.

Ski and Jimmy moved the drum down and aft toward the coolant intake. José guarded their perimeter. As they moved in the darkness, Ski caught a flicker of light. Without hesitation, he triggered his transmitter, "Click…click."

✳

All seven divers froze. Other than the momentary flash toward the bow, Ski and his group saw nothing. Davidov and Azulay had swum toward the upper torpedo tube doors with Borysko close behind. Four doors were open—the two upper and middle doors. As they floated silently, Davidov scanned the dark seafloor twenty feet below. He knew Meiyr and Mizrahi were hugging the seafloor beneath the turn of the bow as they approached the lower tube doors, invisible in the darkness.

There…a moving spot of light…twenty meters or so toward the island! His thoughts tumbled over each other. *One light, four open doors…did they leave a rearguard? They are unaware of us, so why do that?*

While he watched, Borysko darted toward the Soviet divers, placing himself near the seafloor directly in front of them. The lead diver's light focused on the cetacean, followed by three other beams. Borysko opened his mouth, expecting these new humans to scratch his tongue. Instead, the four divers fired APS darts, one into Borysko's massive tongue, and three into his head, missing his eyes. The reverberating sounds of the shots filled the water, nearly masking a transmission the divers made back to *Yaroslavl*.

Borysko squealed and clamped his six-foot jaws around the lead diver, crushing the life out of him. The remaining divers backed off, keeping their APSs between them and the Orca. One of them transmitted something, using a frequency the *Teuthis* divers' equipment could detect but not decipher.

On their underwater circuit, Davidov said, "Now!"

His divers dropped from above, ripped off the comm gear from the three remaining divers and plunged knives into two necks. They expertly disabled the third diver, trussing his arms and legs while allowing him continued use of his rebreather.

Ski showed up with Jimmy and José. Davidov pointed to Borysko and his bleeding tongue. Jimmy reached into the Orca's mouth and extracted the steel dart. Davidov indicated three more darts in the cetacean's head. Jimmy and José searched by feel, finding and removing them.

Borysko shook his massive head, and with his mouth picked up a dead Morskoy Spetsnaz diver, crushing and dropping the body. Then he picked up the second one, giving him the same treatment.

While they watched the cetacean's terrible retribution, the water around them resounded with a transmission from *Yaroslavl*. It happened twice more in short order.

During the third transmission, Ski said on their circuit, "Quickly, back off into the darkness!"

✳

Ski heard rather than saw the four torpedo tube outer doors close. After several minutes, the two middle doors opened again, and bright light beamed from the openings. Two divers cautiously exited the tubes and dropped to the seafloor, each holding an APS at the ready.

From above and behind, Ski watched the Morskoy Spetsnaz divers cautiously examined the floor and the surrounding water, moving their light beams up and down, back and forth. He knew Borysko was nearby, but didn't know if the cetacean could recognize the divers' intent.

As the *Teuthis* divers watched, Borysko swam up above and behind the Soviet divers and emitted a loud whistle. It is very difficult to determine the direction of a sound underwater. The two divers could not have missed the whistle, but did not know its direction. One turned, flashed his light upward, and spotted Borysko. He immediately loosed two darts, one striking Borysko's dorsal fin, the other flying wide. The sound was deafening.

Borysko dropped his six-ton mass to the seafloor and grabbed the diver in his jaws. The second diver, seeing an opportunity, darted past

Borysko's flank and plunged into the nearest open torpedo tube. A few seconds later, both outer doors closed.

Ski gathered the divers around him and wrote on his slate, 4 5 6 7 remain here on guard. 1 2 3 pump wax.

0400, THURSDAY, AUGUST 3, 1989—*USS TEUTHIS* AND SHAYETET DIVERS, NEAR YAROSLAVL, BETWEEN ROSS ROCKS AND PRINCE EDWARD ISLAND

Ski, Jimmy, and José returned to *Yaroslavl's* after starboard side—the reactor coolant intake port. The drum was where they had left it. Ski attached the hose while Jimmy held the open end against the screen protecting the coolant inlet. José pulled a roll of duct tape off the drum top and wrapped several lengths around the hose and the scoop just abaft the screen. Ski inspected the setup. This had to work the first time.

The lineup looked good. Ski started the pump. Within seconds, gallons of liquid paraffin flowed into the reactor coolant intake. It moved with the flow of seawater, cooling and solidifying as it worked its way into the reactor secondary cooling system. In two minutes, the fifty-five-gallon drum was empty of paraffin and filled with seawater. José attached a lift bag to the now heavy drum. and the three divers moved it toward Ross Rocks.

As they left, they heard a shrill alarm from inside the sub as *Yaroslavl's* reactor scrammed. While this is a normal part of routine reactor operation, for a sub reactor to scram under a light load was way out of the ordinary. It terrified the Russian crew, who were already hypersensitive about Russian submarine reactor systems.

In less time than Ski would have imagined, *Yaroslavl* lifted off the bottom, turned over her screw, slowly at first, then ramping up to speed, rapidly disappearing in the nighttime underwater gloom.

As the divers assembled, the sound of rushing air drowned out every other noise around them. *Yaroslavl* had emergency-surfaced as soon as she was clear of the Ross Rocks.

✳

Davidov had his divers unbind their captive's legs so he could swim. They kept him tethered between two divers. Using his underwater compass, Ski led the group around and beyond Ross Rocks, where the bottom was several hundred feet below them. José released the lift bag and dumped its air as the drum dropped to the bottom, where it probably never would be seen by human eyes again. Borysko, who had accompanied the divers, followed the drum to the bottom and carried it back in his jaws. He opened his mouth, trying to give it to Ski, but it immediately dropped to the bottom again. Back down he went, bringing it to Ski a second time. When Ski refused it, the cetacean carried it off toward deeper water. When he returned, the drum was gone.

Their captive watched this interplay with fear-filled eyes, doing his best to keep at least one other diver between him and the Orca.

That was the moment a loud, low-frequency sonar pulse hit the eight divers and their cetacean escort. *USS Pasadena* had arrived and announced her presence.

0900, THURSDAY, AUGUST 3 1989—MYSTIC, TRANSITING AT 100 FT FROM ROSS ROCKS TO EAST CAPE

The divers had established no rendezvous time with *Mystic*. The plan was the DSRV would hang out near the drop-off point until the divers returned. But it was nighttime dark, the divers had no accurate position data, and they needed to remain at 100 feet because of their long bottom time near *Yaroslavl*. They would decompress when they returned to *Teuthis*. Furthermore, they had no ocean current information, and the bottom was too far below to use as a reference.

Ski assembled the divers around him where they linked together. Ski transmitted, "*Mystic*, seven divers plus one hanging out at or near drop-off point. Come fetch!"

Minutes later, *Mystic* floodlights brought each of them into sharp visual focus. The beams were invisible in the clear water. They waved, and Ski transmitted, "We need to remain at one hundred feet."

Deckhart blinked his lights.

The divers unlinked and grabbed handholds on *Mystic*. Meiyr and Mizrahi made sure their captive was securely fastened to the DSRV. They had a four-mile trip ahead, so where possible, the divers placed themselves out of the water flow.

※

Inside *Mystic*, Deckhart and Fortune manned the Control Sphere, while Gamble and Elton remained in the Mid Sphere. The hatch between the spheres was open. Deckhart kept his speed at two knots to make the divers' trip less stressful.

"Ski did say 'seven plus one,' right?" Deckhart asked Fortune.

"That's what I heard, too."

"You think they got themselves a prisoner?" Gamble asked.

On the Secure Gertrude, Deckhart transmitted, "*Teuthis*, this is *Mystic*. I am inbound with seven divers and one captive. Per Ski, set pickup depth at one hundred feet."

When *Mystic* arrived at *Teuthis*, Deckhart dropped to the level of the brightly illuminated Egress Hatch. Derrick manned the Basketball, getting a wide-angle view of the divers clinging to the outside of the DSRV. Borysko pushed his snout to the Basketball lens, much to the delight of everyone inside *Teuthis*.

José and Jimmy entered the hatch first, stripped their equipment, and prepared to receive their prisoner. Ski and Meiyr took charge of the prisoner, but Ski held up a hand and waved at Borysko. Curious, the Orca joined them. The prisoner's eyes widened with fear, but Ski undid the Russian's right hand and waved it at Borysko. Borysko approached with open mouth. The prisoner pulled back, struggling with all his strength. Ski turned and looked directly into his helmet mask, placing his own hand on Borysko's tongue and scratching. Then he took the Russian's hand and pointed at the Orca's tongue. The Russian shook his head and tried again to get loose. Ski grabbed his hand and forcefully placed it on Borysko's tongue, rubbing it back and forth in a scratching motion.

At first, the Russian resisted. Then, when nothing seemed to happen, he started scratching on his own. When he pulled his hand out of the huge mouth, Borysko closed it and gently nuzzled his chest. Ski pointed to the hatch, and the Russian allowed himself to be pulled inside by José and Jimmy. The four Shayetets followed, and then Jimmy pulled Ski inside while José shut the hatch.

The DDC hatch was open. As the divers removed their equipment in the Port Lock, they stepped into the larger DDC.

"Do you speak English?" Ski asked the Russian.

"A little," he answered with a heavy Russian accent.

"I speak Russian," Azulay volunteered, "and Ukrainian and Polish," he finished with a grin.

"What is your nationality?" Azulay asked the prisoner in Russian.

"I Ukrainian, not Russian peasant," he answered emphatically in English.

Ski looked at Jimmy. "Did you hear that? Just like Sergyi Andreev?"

The prisoner looked up. "You say Sergyi Andreev, Ukrainian diver lost in Sea of Okhotsk?"

"Yeah," Ski answered, "that one."

"He my older brother," the prisoner said, overcome with excitement. "Sergyi still alive?"

"Very much so," Ski answered. "He got married a while back. He's close friends with Captain McDowell, commander of this submarine." Ski looked at him. "What is your name?"

"Danilo Andreev."

The Ukrainian diver sat in a chair, put his face in his hands, and wept with joy. In Ukrainian, he muttered, translated by Azulay, "Sergyi, Sergyi, you were my hero. I became Morskoy Spetsnaz because of you. You are alive, my Hero! You are alive!"

✳

To ensure their safety, Ham gave the divers an hour of gradual decompression. There were no official tables for this kind of thing. He simply used his best judgment in surfacing them. He called me while they were decompressing.

"Captain, the captured Morskoy Spetsnaz diver is Ukrainian. His name is Danilo Andreev, and he appears to be Sergyi's little brother. I know it sounds crazy, but it's not impossible. The Morskoy Spetsnaz is a small, elite group, smaller than our SEALS. Everyone knows everyone. Sergyi wasn't Morskoy Spetsnaz, but the Soviet saturation diving community is small. Every diver in their system, including Morskoy Spetsnaz, would have heard about the Okhotsk disaster with loss of all the divers. Danilo says he joined Morskoy Spetsnaz because of Sergyi."

"Does he speak English?" I asked.

"Some."

"Russian."

"Seems to."

"Get him something to eat, and then bring him to me," I said. "Keep him hooded with hands behind his back outside of Dive Control."

✳

On its face, it seemed improbable—Sergyi's little brother, captured as a Morskoy Spetsnaz diver from *Yaroslavl*, down here, at the bottom of the world? A knock at my door announced Ham and Danilo.

Ham and Danilo entered, the Ukrainian's head covered with a black hood, hands zip-tied behind his back.

"Thank you, Ham," I said. "I'll be alright."

Ham closed the door, but I think he remained close by, just in case.

"Turn around," I said in Russian, drawing a knife. He turned, and I cut his zip-ties. "Please, remove your hood."

He did, and I could see the resemblance. Any doubts I might have had disappeared. Danilo definitely was Sergyi's little brother. He looked like a younger version of my friend.

"I know Sergyi very well," I said. "I saved his life in the Sea of Okhotsk, and later, he directly saved mine."[28] I smiled. "We are like brothers. That makes you my little brother, and that presents a problem." I sighed. "You are a captured enemy diver from a Soviet submarine operating illegally in South African waters."

"That is no problem," Danilo answered. "For Ukrainians, family comes first. I will cooperate in every possible way to be reunited with my brother. For all these years, I thought he was dead."

"What about your sub and fellow Morskoy Spetsnaz teammates?" I asked.

---

28 See *Operation Ivy Bells*, vol 1 in *The Mac McDowell Missions*.

"The Russians are pigs! They abandoned me and my teammates to that killer whale, not knowing if we were alive or dead. I hate them. I respect my Morskoy Spetsnaz teammates, but they all think I was killed by that Orca. I died with them in honorable service. I have no loyalty to the Russians who usurped my homeland and abandoned us. My only loyalty is to my brother, Sergyi, and to you, his friend, if you allow."

It was an impassioned speech, typical of Russians and Ukrainians. I believed him, but he still was a problem.

"I need you to tell me why *Yaroslavl* was putting Morskoy Spetsnaz ashore."

Danilo looked at me with wide eyes. "You don't know?" he asked.

I shook my head.

"The South Africans are detonating a nuclear device on the island shortly. Our job was to stop it without anyone knowing."

"Why?"

"I don't know for sure," Danilo answered, "but I believe it is part of a plan to coerce South Africa into becoming part of the Soviet Block."

"Ham," I said, raising my voice, "I know you are still out there. Please join us."

Ham opened the door and joined us with a sheepish grin.

"How is your English?" I asked Danilo.

"It pretty good," he said, sounding much like Sergyi when I first met him.

"Ham," I said, "my little brother, Danilo, will be our guest until we can offload him. He must remain in Dive Control. Fix him up with a cot and arrange for him to take his meals there. Remind your people not to discuss our operations with him or within his hearing."

I turned to Danilo. "Danilo, give me your solemn word that you will remain in Dive Control and follow all of Chief Warrant Officer Hamilton's instructions."

Danilo stood and saluted. "I give you my word, on my brother's life, Captain McDowell."

1200, THURSDAY, AUGUST 3 1989—*USS TEUTHIS*, BOTTOMED AT 150 FT, MCNISH BAY, PRINCE EDWARD ISLAND

When we surfaced *Carp* through the ice off Point Barrow, her skipper was seriously concerned about the reactor. This was the first Soviet *Sierra I Class* sub. The Soviets had been plagued with reactor problems, which may account for their installing two reactors on their subs. *Carp* had only one reactor. I think her skipper was seriously spooked.

Yaroslavl was the Soviet's third *Sierra I Class* sub. They had gained a tremendous amount of operational experience with these subs since *Carp*. When *Yaroslavl's* reactor scrammed, her skipper took her out of where she was and emergency-surfaced. His next step would have been to look for radiation. Since there was no damage, there would have been no radiation. He probably communicated with Petropavlovsk-Kamchatskiy, and then his engineers would have gone through everything. When they found nothing (because, of course, we had temporarily stopped their secondary coolant flow, but not otherwise damaged anything), he would have started up the reactor and returned to what they were doing before the scram. All this would take at least a day, perhaps two.

This meant *Yaroslavl* was out of my hair, at least for the time being. I turned my attention to the Shayetet operation. For the next couple of days, this was Rav Nagad Hadriel Davidov's operation.

After Roger moved us back to McNish Bay, the Shayetet team assembled in the Port Lock. Beside their air-rebreather units and drysuits, Davidov's people assembled four each small spread-spectrum comm units (for use in air, not water), a regular comm receiver, insulated sleeping bags, diver propulsion units (DPUs), APSs and twelve spare magazines, a waterproof Geiger counter, a collapsed inflatable boat, and—to my surprise—a set of rock climbing equipment.

By the time the Shayetet divers were ready to go, darkness had descended over Prince Edward Island, enhanced by a heavy overcast and freezing rain and sleet. The four Israelis entered the DDC, and Bill pressed them to 150 feet. Without conversation, they opened the

Port Lock hatch. Two dropped into the water to accept the equipment the other two passed through the hatch. They were joined by Borysko, who nosed about, checking things out, but leaving them undisturbed.

They loaded everything into cargo nets they attached to the DPUs. With Davidov in the lead, they set off three feet over the bottom, Davidov focusing a narrow beam down on their path. Each cargo net carried a bright, blinking red light at the net end that the trailing diver could follow.

Davidov set a three-knot speed, which would get them to Vela Crater in sixty minutes. The bottom shallowed until they reached sixty feet, and then Davidov brought them up to thirty-two feet. Borysko tagged along, occasionally darting to the surface for air.

Halfway there, a group of rocks jutted up from the seafloor. Davidov spotted them with his focused spot and steered to the left around them. Mizrahi was the last man in the string. He kept his eye on the blinking red light ahead of him, but drifted to the right, smacking into the outermost rock. He signaled a halt on their comm circuit.

The divers gathered around him. He indicated he was unhurt, but his DPU was damaged. The divers quickly distributed his load among the other two cargo nets, and dropped the DPU to the bottom. Mizrahi doubled up with Davidov, whose cargo load had not changed. They lost twenty-two minutes taking care of the problem. They finally reached their destination at 1730 hours. The water was thirty-two feet deep, so they could remain submerged indefinitely without risking the bends. Brash ice covered the surface, and they felt no surf surge. This would make things easier as they left the water to inspect Vela Crater, just beyond the rocks above them.

They did not spot Steyn's anchor chain, but they clearly heard activity from inside the large frigate arriving at their location from deeper water beyond their location. Meiyr found a five-foot depression at the base of the rock slope leading to the surface. They stashed their equipment in the natural cave and gathered around Davidov. Borysko joined them, paying close attention to their activities. Davidov asked a question with his hands, and everyone answered with thumbs up. He pointed to Azulay and Meiyr, and then to the cave; he pointed to himself and Mizrahi, and then up.

Azulay and Meiyr pushed into the small cave. Davidov and Mizrahi doffed their fins and rebreathers, including their helmets, donned facemasks with attached snorkels, and commenced working their way up the rock slope toward the surface, expelling puffs of air as they ascended to avoid embolizing. Davidov trailed two strong cords that would enable them to send equipment to the rim and allow the others to climb the rocks faster. As they climbed, he tucked the cords into crevasses so they would not appear as straight lines up the rocks.

Prince Edward Island showing Teuthis, Mystic, President Steyn, Yaroslavl, Pasadena, *and Shayetet 13.*

CHAPTER TWENTY-ONE—Shayetet 13

1800, THURSDAY, AUGUST 3, 1989—SHAYETET 13, ON THE BOTTOM AT 30 FT, AT THE BASE OF VELA CRATER

When Davidov and Mizrahi reached the brash ice surging against the rocky slope, Davidov cautiously pushed the brash aside and lifted his head high enough to expose his eyes behind his faceplate. Wind-driven sleet struck his face and the rocks behind him. They were slippery with ice. Even though he knew *President Steyn* was illuminated, anchored a hundred yards away, he couldn't see it. That was good—they couldn't see him either.

The Steyn *must be shielding us from the surf,* he thought, wiping the sleet off his facemask.

He tapped Mizrahi's head, and the Rasar poked his head up beside him, bumping into something. They dropped their facemasks around their necks, and Davidov focused a narrow, dim light beam on the object Mizrahi had bumped. It was the Zodiac-like inflatable boat that brought the marines ashore. It was tied off to a rock. Davidov shined his light toward the rocks to their right.

"That's the way up," he said in Hebrew.

Their boots had sand-embedded soles that bit into the ice covering the rocks as they ascended to their right. They moved slowly and carefully, taking a full fifteen minutes to reach the crater rim. What they could see of the crater was dark, but they were blinded by driving sleet.

"I think we can presume," Davidov said, "that the technicians are huddled in tents somewhere down there." He pointed into the crater. "Twelve marines, too," he added. "The other marines are probably on the mesa atop the cliffs behind us." He looked up but could see nothing through the sleet. "We need to get Meiyr up there as soon as possible."

Davidov followed the cords back to the rocky slope into the water. He tugged one several times to extract it from the crevasses. When it was free, he pulled it hard and received an answering pull. Two minutes later, he received another pull. He and Mizrahi hauled the cord hand over hand until a cargo net appeared at the surface. They hauled it up the slippery rocks to the top.

Davidov untied the cargo net, and while Misrahi hid it behind a rock outcrop, he tossed the weighted end into the water. He loosened the other cord from the rock crevasses and tugged it. He received an answering tug, and three minutes later, the hauling cord tugged sharply.

Once again, Davidov and Mizrahi hauled a cargo net to the surface and then up the rocks. That was all they needed. The rest would remain on the bottom in the small cave.

Five minutes later, both Azulay and Meiyr appeared through the brash, and a few minutes later, joined Davidov and Mizrahi at the crater edge. Davidov showed them the layout.

Meiyr spoke up. "I think we should cover the cargo nets with camouflaging grass so the chopper can't detect them when it flies over next."

"Do it!" Davidov said. *I must be slipping,* he thought.

0200, FRIDAY, AUGUST 4, 1989—SHAYETET 13, AT THE RIM OF VELA CRATER, PRINCE EDWARD ISLAND

The sky was darkly overcast, and the sleet-filled wind bitter cold, but it was dying down.

"By daylight," Davidov said, "the wind and sleet should be gone. We might even have some sunlight." He grinned at Meiyr. "You, my sticky-fingered friend, have to be up there by then." He pointed to the unseen cliff behind them. "Take your weapons, comm unit, and bedroll. Start whenever you wish. Watch yourself, Kid. Those twelve marines probably used the canyon a click that way," he pointed to the north. "They are unlikely to patrol the cliff edge, but assume nothing. Use all the tricks I taught you. Call me when you reach the top."

Meiyr shrugged and grinned crookedly. "You chose me, Ranag, because I'm the best. You boys get a good night's sleep." He trudged off toward the unseen 200-foot-high talus rampart facing the 1,600-foot-high rock wall a quarter mile to the east.

＊

Fifteen minutes later, Meiyr reached the foot of the talus rampart. It consisted of flattened rock chunks hand to dinner plate size, slippery with an ice veneer. They slid over each other, making a traverse difficult and dangerous. The cliff blocked the wind and sleet, so in his light beam Meiyr could see where the talus rampart intersected the cliff. The rampart sloped at about forty-five degrees and was 300 feet or so up the slope from base to cliff.

Meiyr placed his left foot sideways on the rampart, pushing his sole into the loose talus. It held. He stepped out with his right foot, doing the same. It slipped a bit and then held. Left foot again, but higher. It held, but then a fat rock under his foot slipped out, and Meiyr found himself sitting on the ground at the rampart face. He unstrapped steel-pointed hiking sticks from his back and started over, this time pressing the sticks into the talus before putting weight on each foothold.

Meiyr traversed several yards, gaining height with each step, and then reversed direction, continuing to work his way up. It was slow going, but the little Israeli knew what he was doing—even in the dark.

He timed himself at an hour and twelve minutes from the base to the cliff face. That left a 1,400 feet vertical climb, in the dark.

Meiyr anchored a piton at chest height and tied off his safety rope. If he fell, he didn't want to redo the rampart. No matter what happened, he could pull himself up to the anchor piton—if it held. The cliff face was volcanic and well weathered. Meiyr placed a piton every few yards for safety, but found the climb to be nearly effortless. He reached the top an hour later. As he poked his head above the edge, a stiff wind but no sleet lashed his face. He left rope and pitons in place. The odds of anyone spotting them were minimal at best. They would enable a rapid descent.

Meiyr unsnapped the comm unit from his belt. "One, this is Four. I made it. Over."

A sleepy voice responded, "This is One, Roger. Get some sleep. Out."

Before bedding down, Meiyr transmitted, "*Teuthis*, this is Four. I am on top of the cliffs overlooking the crater. I have line of sight to the team and you. Over."

"This is *Teuthis*. Roger, out."

0530, FRIDAY, AUGUST 4, 1989—SHAYETET 13-4, ATOP THE CLIFFS, THE BASE OF VAN ZINDEREN BAKKER PEAK, PRINCE EDWARD ISLAND

Rav Samal Rishon Chaim Meiyr hunkered down against a rock cropping that blocked the wind and wrapped himself in his insulated sleeping bag. He was at least two clicks from the bivouacked marines. On a night like this, there was no way they would patrol where he was. He dropped into a deep sleep.

He awakened when the sun peaking around the south slope of Van Zinderen Bakker hit him full in the face. He glanced at his watch—0830 hours. He grabbed a protein bar and washed it down with a caffeine-boosted energy drink from his canteen. He checked his surroundings and then took care of his bodily needs behind a convenient boulder. After stuffing his sleeping bag into his backpack, he crept on his stomach to the cliff edge and cautiously peaked over, careful not to present a silhouette against the clearing sky.

He knew the rest of the team was on this side of the crater rim, but he could not pick them out. They were well hidden. Down in the crater's bowl, seven tents lined up, north to south, six two-man pup tents and a larger one. He watched several marines crawl from their tents and relieve themselves off to the side. He detected no sense of urgency or serious security concerns. After all, they were on a remote subantarctic island with nothing threatening inside of 1,500 miles.

Time to check out the soldier boys hanging out to his north. Ever mindful that a silhouette against a bright sky is more visible at a distance than almost anything else, Meiyr stayed away from the edge and moved quickly and easily from cover to cover. He kept his ears tuned for sounds that didn't fit and his eyes peeled for unnatural sights.

He passed a gulch-like canyon that formed the end of the high cliffs to the west—the ones he had climbed. He was pretty certain the marines had come up through the canyon. Obviously, the marines had turned north, possibly to overlook the easy-to-land-on northwest shore. He rounded the canyon head and ducked behind a thick bush. Fifty yards beyond, six tents, identical to those in the crater, lined up north to south. The marines lounged around in typical fashion for deployed military with nothing to do.

Meiyr backed off to the canyon head, dropped down into some heavy foliage and reached for his comm unit.

"One, this is Four, over."

"This is One. Go ahead."

Meiyr described what he found and his present location.

"The Steyn is still anchored," Davidov said. "When she evacuates everyone, we will need to leave immediately. We do not want to be anywhere near if they trigger the detonation. We intend to stop the process. We either can do this under the eye of Steyn, or we can hope Steyn leaves temporarily to investigate *Yaroslavl*. That will enable us to clear out the technicians, the marines, and the bomb materials."

✳

Davidov crawled cautiously to the crater rim. Using small binoculars that fit in the palm of his hand, he focused in on the larger tent. The flap opened, and a technician stepped out. He waved at the marines who were performing calisthenics in the grassy stretch in front of their tents. Their sergeant called cadence. He beckoned the technician to join them. The slightly heavyset technician declined with a wry smile.

The other three techs joined the first outside their tent. They munched on what looked like some kind of breakfast bars. Two marines brought them cups of hot coffee. Because of the bowl shape of the crater, the voices of those on its floor could be easily heard on the rim where Davidov and his men were concealed.

"Today is a good weather day," one said.

"I think we can set up the device," another added.

0900, FRIDAY, AUGUST 4, 1989—*USS TEUTHIS*, PERISCOPE DEPTH, MCNISH BAY, PRINCE EDWARD ISLAND

Chop had the watch hovering at periscope depth at the mouth of McNish Bay when Meiyr's transmission arrived. Chop called me; I was up and about doing paperwork in my cabin.

"Captain, we've established comms with the Shayetet team. They're relaying through Meiyr, who is on the high ridge."

I went to Control and picked up the Secure Gertrude mike. "*Pasadena*, this is *Teuthis*, over."

"This is *Pasadena*, Roger."

"This is *Teuthis*. Nice job luring *Yaroslavl* away from the island. We scrammed her reactor. She will take at least a day to figure out what happened.

"I need you to lure *SAS President Steyn* away from her anchorage near the southwest end of Prince Edward Island. Try to force an engagement between Steyn and *Yaroslavl*. That will keep them both busy. Be aware Steyn carries type one-seventy and one-seventy-seven-M active sonars—range about four nautical miles. She is armed with depth charges and modern active-search torpedoes launched over the side, or carried by a Wasp chopper to the target's general location. She's near the end of her useful life but will vigorously defend the current South African operation. Over."

"This is *Pasadena. Yaroslavl* is twenty miles northwest of Prince Edward Island. I am northeast of Prince Edward Island. I will pass through mid-channel heading northwest and ping Steyn. That should lure her out to where I can lead her to *Yaroslavl*. Expect me to pass within the hour. Over."

"This is *Teuthis*. Good hunting! Out."

※

I called the Shayetet team. "One this is *Teuthis*. Over."

"*Teuthis*, this is Four. I will establish a live relay to One and call back. Out."

Two minutes later, I heard, "*Teuthis*, this is Four. You can speak directly with One. I will keep this relay open. Over."

"This is *Teuthis*, Roger. One this is *Teuthis*, comm check, over."

"This is One, Roger."

"This *Teuthis*. A U.S. submarine will pass through the channel and draw Steyn out to sea. As soon as she leaves, you can commence your operation. Godspeed! Over."

"This is One. Roger. Out."

※

Forty-seven minutes later, Sonar called Control. "Conn, Sonar, I have a new contact, emerging from my port quarter, designate Sierra-six-eight. Sierra-six-eight is the *Pasadena*."

Sonar tracked *Pasadena* doing ten knots at 100 feet, driving up the middle of the channel. She was five nautical miles from Steyn when she transmitted two pings.

"Conn, Sonar, *Pasadena* pinged twice and has increased her speed to fifteen knots."

"Conn, Radio, we received a transmission from Steyn to the Prince Edward Island shore party. It reads: 'Urgent. Marine detachment, return to *President Steyn* immediately. Leave everything except weapons. A sergeant and two men remain on the island with the science party.'"

"Conn, Sonar, Steyn is hauling in her anchor and bringing up her boilers. She's preparing to get underway."

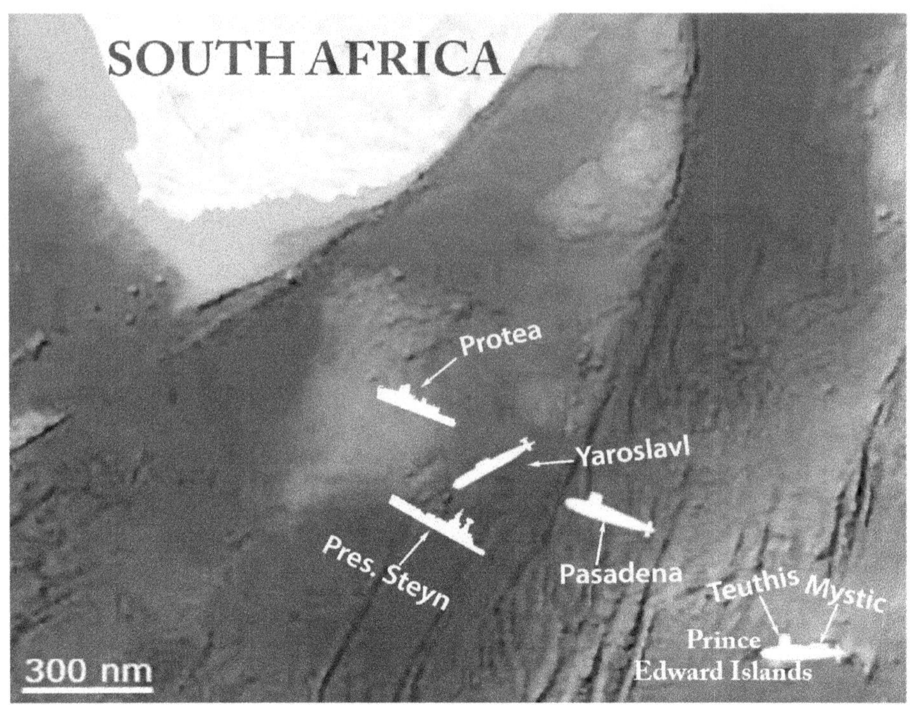

Open ocean between South Africa and Prince Edward Island:
President Steyn, Yaroslavl, Pasadena, *and* Protea. Teuthis *and*
Mystic *at Prince Edward Island.*

CHAPTER TWENTY-TWO—Sea Battle

1200, FRIDAY, AUGUST 4, 1989—VELA CRATER, PRINCE EDWARD ISLAND

I trained the periscope on Steyn when *Pasadena* hit her with two pings. Within seconds, I saw sailors running along the main deck—in response to a general alarm, I guessed. I couldn't see the Marine activity on the island, but Steyn started raising her anchor. Within less than a half hour, I watched marines slide down the rocky incline into the beached rubber-sided boat. Several ended up in the water before they got into the boat. They managed to squeeze twenty-one marines into the craft before they pushed off the rocks and headed for the frigate.

Within forty-five minutes of *Pasadena's* pings, Steyn was backing away from her anchorage. Shortly thereafter, she steamed out of the channel at her maximum speed of thirty knots.

*

Davidos glanced at his watch. "About three more hours of daylight," he told his immediate companions. He checked in with Meiyr. "Four, what is your status?" Typically, Shayetet 13 dispensed with formal radio protocol when on ops.

"I'm taking it easy, acting as a relay. Nobody is left up here."

"We got about three hours till darkness. Let's all get some rest between now and then." Before he dropped into sleep, he called *Teuthis*. "We're taking a three-hour rest break. I'll call when we're active again."

0000, SATURDAY, AUGUST 5, 1989—OPEN OCEAN, 300 NM TOWARD SOUTH AFRICA FROM PRINCE EDWARD ISLAND

Pasadena had a much higher top speed than Steyn, but Cmdr. Fritchman slowed down to let Steyn catch up with and acquire him. Then he bounced in and out of Steyn's sonar detection range on her Type 177M search sonar. It had a 360 degree ping with a range of 3.2 nautical miles. He led the frigate straight toward the still stricken *Yaroslavl*.

As a precaution, he loaded his torpedo tubes with Mk 48s and put his Fire Control group on hot standby.

*

After *Pasadena* had driven *Yaroslavl* away from the island, the Soviet sub had emergency-surfaced and contacted her Petropavlovsk-Kamchatskiy headquarters. When an initial check revealed no radioactivity, she submerged to periscope depth, running on batteries and diesel while her engineers double-checked everything. *Yaroslavl* headed in a northwesterly direction while this was going on.

Because Soviet nuclear submarines had a troubled reactor history, sub crews were understandably nervous about reactor safety.

When *Yaroslavl's* reactor scrammed unexpectedly for no apparent reason, if the skipper had not taken immediate, obvious corrective measures, he might have faced a mutiny. He had a task to accomplish on Prince Edward Island, but he needed a submarine and crew to accomplish it.

By the time *Pasadena* had lured Steyn to *Yaroslavl's* neighborhood, the Soviet skipper had decided there was nothing wrong with his reactor, and that his nuclear system had undergone one of those mysterious happenings that plagued Soviet subs since they first got into the nuclear submarine business. He dropped to a hundred meters, ready to return to Prince Edward Island to finish what he came for.

0100, SATURDAY, AUGUST 5, 1989—OPEN OCEAN, 300 NM TOWARD SOUTH AFRICA FROM PRINCE EDWARD ISLAND

When *Yaroslavl* dropped to 100 meters, Steyn's active-search sonar acquired *Yaroslavl* virtually close aboard, mistaking the acquisition for the sub she had been tracking. Two things happened immediately. Steyn received a solid bearing and range on *Yaroslavl*, and *Yaroslavl* went to battle stations.

Steyn immediately turned toward her unknown submarine contact, closing range as fast as possible while continuing to ping her search sonar. She activated her Type 170 attack sonar, and two minutes later, acquired *Yaroslavl* in its beam at 1.5 nautical miles. She manually pointed her bead at the unknown contact and increased the ping rate.

Upon hearing the increase ping rate, *Yaroslavl's* skipper ordered the outer doors of tubes one and two opened.

Not knowing with what he was dealing, Steyn's skipper prepared to launch a Mk 37 anti-submarine torpedo over the side.

Yaroslavl's sonar picked up the launch preparation sounds, and *Yaroslavl* came to ahead slow and pointed at Steyn.

Steyn misinterpreted the unknown sub's actions as an attack and launched the Mk 37 in a spiraling search mode that was very effective in killing nearby submarines at unknown depth.

Upon hearing the launch, *Yaroslavl* launched two 53-65 wake homing torpedoes, launched a bubble-cloud-generating countermeasure, and then went to flank and headed deep.

Steyn's Mk 37 detected the bubble cloud, chased it down, and exploded harmlessly.

When Steyn detected the launch of two torpedoes from the unknown sub, the skipper went to flank at thirty knots, trying to keep ahead of the 45-knot torpedoes until they spent their fuel. The torpedoes were designed with a thirteen-minute run. They commenced their run 1.5 nautical miles behind Steyn. The torpedoes were closing the frigate at fifteen knots. When they struck Steyn's stern, they still had six minutes runtime left.

As the chase got underway, Steyn launched the Wasp. When the outcome became certain, the skipper sent a distress call, and the crew tossed inflatable lifeboats over the side. The torpedoes blew off the entire stern. The frigate sank quickly, but most of the crew found lifeboats, except those on or near the stern when the torpedoes hit.

0200, SATURDAY, AUGUST 5, 1989—*USS PASADENA*, SUBMERGED AT 500 FT, 3 NM SOUTHEAST FROM BATTLE LOCATION

After leading Steyn to *Yaroslavl*, *Pasadena* set condition ultra-quiet, opened tubes one and two outer doors, and hung out at 500 feet, five nautical miles to the southeast. Her tubes carried Mk 48 torpedoes set for wire guide mode. They could be actively controlled by the sub until released to complete the task using internal active and passive sonar. Fire Control maintained an active firing solution on *Yaroslavl* through the battle. When it became clear to Cmdr. Fritchman that *Yaroslavl* had actually sunk Steyn, he felt he was left with no choice. He readied his Mk 48s. When they were, he ordered, "In swim-out mode, shoot one!"

Making virtually no sound, the torpedo swam out the tube, laying a thin wire in the water as it moved forward. Within seconds, it headed toward *Yaroslavl* at fifty-five knots—at least fifteen knots faster than the Soviet sub. It was so quiet that *Yaroslavl* could not have heard it had she been moving ahead dead slow.

The *Sierra I Class* Soviet sub dove at maximum speed to her test depth of nearly 3,000 feet, blissfully unaware of the deadly Mk 48 on an intercept course, still guided by wire as it approached the one nautical mile range. The torpedo shifted to internal sonar, acquired *Yaroslavl*, adjusted course, and shifted to a high ping rate. Even through the noise generated by her flank speed, *Yaroslavl's* sonar detected the incoming torpedo. The skipper ordered a crashback—changing from flank to back full in order to stop the sub's forward motion.

The crashback took fifteen seconds to implement. The titanium-hulled sub shuddered mightily from stem to stern, but before it came to a full stop, the Mk 48's proximity fuse backed up by its internal electronics, triggered an explosion of 647 pounds of high explosive five feet from the titanium hull directly beneath the Control Compartment.

The Control Compartment crew died instantly as the sub broke in half. The bow and stern sections tilted and dropped, tumbling crew members forward in the bow and aft in the engineering compartments. The crew members who survived the initial explosion had about fifty seconds to contemplate their fate before the titanium bulkheads imploded, carrying their bodies to the seafloor some 16,000 feet below.

✳

Protea was a hundred miles distant when the battle took place. Her crew did not know about either *Yaroslavl* or *Pasadena*. They would learn later that Steyn had engaged an unknown submarine, and that sub had sunk her. It took *Protea* six and a quarter hours to reach the wreck site. The Wasp met her halfway, nearly bingo fuel. She rescued all the crew who survived the sinking.

Eleven hours later, *Protea* tied up to the dock at the Marion Research Station.

Shayetet 13, Teuthis, *and* Mystic *at Prince Edward Island.*

CHAPTER TWENTY-THREE—Exfiltration

2000, FRIDAY, AUGUST 4, 1989—SHAYETET 13, VELA CRATER, PRINCE EDWARD ISLAND

Davidov was deeply worried about an early return of Steyn. They had much to do before light returned—a clean sweep with minimum loss of life, his orders read. It was a big order.

"First, we take out the guards," he said to Azulay and Mizrahi. "You take the north one." He pointed at Azulay. "You," he pointed at Mizrahi, "take the middle one. I'll take the south one. No noise. We don't want to alarm the techs. We can't let them broadcast anything."

They crept around the north side of the crater and eased down the inside slope. The air was crisply cold. The star-filled sky gave sufficient light, so they did not use their flashlights. Azulay stopped at the first tent and waited at the entrance flap. Mizrahi stood by the second. Davidov, the third. When Davidov dropped his arm, they entered the tents simultaneously, flashlights turned to maximum intensity.

With eyes blinded by the lights, the three unsuspecting marines had no chance. Three quick jabs down through the left side of the neck, and all three were dead before their circumstance had a chance to register. The three commandos backed out of the tents and gathered at the larger tent flap. They sheathed their knives and carried zip tie restraints. On Davidov's mark, they entered the tent together, quickly restrained the techs' arms, and then pulled them out onto the grass, where they zip-tied their legs together.

The leader yelled at them in Afrikaans. "What the fuck is this? Marines…help…help!"

"Shut up!" Davidov said. "No one can hear you, and nobody will help you. If you give us trouble, we'll kill you here and now."

The lead tech snapped his mouth shut, and the other two whimpered.

In the star-illuminated darkness, the three commandos dragged the three bodies to the crater wall and then up over the rim. Using Minox cameras and low-light film, they photographed everything in sight. When they finished photographing, they tore down the tents and piled the material near the south end of the crater. They pulled together the test and other equipment, handling the aluminum case containing the bomb with care. Using a shovel and rake, they disbursed the evidence of human presence, until the crater bowl looked much like it had before the South Africans arrived.

Using their cargo nets, they dragged everything up the crater slope and over the edge, piling it above the ice-covered rocks leading into the water.

Azulay and Mizrahi donned their drysuits, slipped masks around their necks, and grabbed their fins. With wide grins, they slid down the ice-covered rocks and plunged into the icy water. They adjusted their masks, donned their fins, and rolled over, diving to the bottom. Together, they retrieved the small, collapsed Zodiac, filled it with the DPUs and other stuff from the cave, and inflated it from a bottle on their way to the surface.

Davidov tossed them a line that they attached to the boat and tied it off on a rock. Then he slid three of the collapsed tents and other trash down the rocks. Azulay and Mizrahi caught it and loaded it onto the small boat.

Using a DPU, they drove the boat about a mile out, dumped the material in 300 feet of water, including the two remaining DPUs, and returned to shore. One more load completed what they had to dump, except for the three bodies.

Davidov collected the Marine's dog tags. He had no idea what he would do with them, but he felt compelled to collect them. Azulay and Davidov wrapped each body in tent material and added several large rocks. They secured each with line, making certain the bodies would remain wrapped with the rocks until the bottom critters had done their work.

"Okay, guys," Davidov said, "load the bodies."

As they slid down the icy rocks, Davidov said, "Sorry fellows, it was your bad luck your sergeant chose you to remain behind." He saluted and said quietly, "*Zichronam livracha* (May their memory be for a blessing)."

Azulay and Mizrahi drove the boat out and dumped the bodies. As they sank, both commandos whispered quietly, "*Vayanuach b'shalom* (Rest in peace)." No one would ever know what had happened to them.

0200, SATURDAY, AUGUST 5, 1989—SHAYETET 13, RIM OF VELA CRATER, PRINCE EDWARD ISLAND

Meiyr joined them when the Zodiac returned from its body-dumping trip. He brought with him what he could carry from the cliff base—a coil of line, a bag of pitons, and his comm equipment.

The four commandos returned to the cliff base with cargo bags and loaded as much as possible. The bags were heavy and awkward, but between them, with two on each bag, they dragged them the quarter mile to the crater rim. Davidov and Meiyr returned to the cliff base for the last load, while Azulay and Mizrahi loaded the Zodiac.

When they reached the base, Davidov asked, "Tell me how you took down the camp."

"I collapsed the six tents and dragged them to the cliff top. I used a tent pole to scatter their shit leavings. One good rain will make them undetectable. I erased my drag marks right up to the cliff edge with a branch. As I descended, I pulled the pitons and retrieved the line. There's nothing left."

"Well done, Meiyr. I'm glad I selected you for the team." He put his arm around the shorter commando's shoulders. "Let's drag this shit out of here."

Azulay and Mizrahi were waiting for them when they dragged their cargo net to the rim.

"Let's unload the net and get this crap out of here," Davidov said, glancing at his watch. "It's going on 0400. We're running out of time."

Azulay pulled a tent pole from the net. "Damn, this stinks! What did you do, stir their shit dump?"

"Pretty much," Meiyr answered. "They had no shovel, so I improvised."

"Wonder what those fuckers ate?" Mizrahi snickered as he tossed the messy tent pole into the Zodiac.

Davidov got on his comm unit. "*Teuthis*, this is One. I need a *Mystic* pickup one-half mile off Vela Crater in sixty minutes—three captives, my team of four, and miscellaneous equipment. Over."

"This is *Teuthis*, Roger. *Mystic* will display a light from her upper hatch. Over."

"This is One. What about the Steyn? When do you anticipate her return? Over."

"She's not coming back. The Russian sub sunk her. Over."

"No shit! Roger. Meet you in an hour. Out."

0600, SATURDAY, AUGUST 5, 1989—MYSTIC, ONE NM OFF VELA CRATER, PRINCE EDWARD ISLAND

Seth got *Teuthis* underway in the last hour of his watch on day fifty-three since we left Mare Island. The previous day had been nearly cloud-free, which eased Shayetet 13's job of evacuating Prince Edard Island. As we got underway, however, clouds obscured the stars, and sleet pelted the periscope lens.

Radar would have given us a good fix, but I was reluctant to use anything that might reveal our presence, even though *Protea* was probably well on her way to Cape Town, and *President Steyn* no longer existed. We crept away from McNish Bay, trusting SINS to keep us out of trouble. Seth had the fathometer going at low power as a backup.

Mindful of the time, when Chop assumed the watch, I had him speed up. We arrived at the rendezvous spot with fifteen minutes to spare. Chop launched *Mystic*, and Deckhart transmitted on his Secure Gertrude that he had the Zodiac on his sonar scope.

✳

Davidov and his team moved slowly away from Vela Crater. Driving sleet slowed the boat's progress to about a knot. Their cargo consisted of three bound, cold, and miserable nuclear techs, the nuclear device in an elongated aluminum case, and some items they had brought with them and didn't want to discard. Among these were several cassettes of exposed Minox film securely wrapped in double plastic to keep them dry. These were destined to be the only evidence of the failed South African attempt to detonate a nuke on Prince Edward Island and indirectly of Israel's role in preventing the detonation.

At their slow rate, it took the better part of an hour to reach the rendezvous spot, as best as Davidov could figure with only a compass and watch.

"We're here. Try to pick out *Mystic*," Davidov said before he realized he had just given the captives the submersible name. "Cancel that," he said. "I meant to say Myrtle. There are so many submersibles in use now, I get them mixed up."

A few minutes later, Azulay shouted, "There she is. I see her." He pointed to a dim light about fifty yards ahead of them.

Davidov steered the Zodiac toward the light, and shortly they could distinguish *Mystic*'s side through the sleet.

Myrtle, not *Mystic*, Davidov reminded himself.

The hatch opened, and Elton stuck out his head. Davidov was right there. "Our captives think you are the Myrtle," he told Elton. "You guys better play it that way."

"First things first," Davidov said back in the Zodiac as he man-hauled the aluminum case to the hatch.

Elton received it and passed it gingerly down to Gamble, who stowed it in the Central Sphere. The rest of the gear followed. Only the Shayetet 13 team and their three captives remained.

Elton handed three hoods to Davidov. "Not sure we can cover every instance of our name. These should help."

Davidov sent Meiyr and Mizrahi to *Mystic* to handle the captives as they entered. He slipped a hood over each captive's head and untied their feet. He told them in Afrikaans, "I will untie you now. When I tell you, climb into the minisub—we'll help you since you cannot see— and sit where my people tell you. Leave your hoods on and no talking. If you don't follow my directions, we will truss you up like pigs and handle you like slabs of meat."

"We're cold and hungry," the lead tech said.

"You will be warmed and fed soon enough," Davidov snapped. "Now shut up!"

As soon as he spoke, he regretted it. *So far as I can tell*, he thought, *these guys are just doing their jobs. They aren't high enough in the nuclear hierarchy to have any meaningful say. Just their bad luck that we interfered with their assignment.*

He softened his voice. "Nobody will hurt you. Just cooperate and everything will be fine." He grabbed one tech's shoulder and put a smile in his voice. "Let's get you inside the minisub before you freeze to death."

✳

It took another twenty minutes to get the technicians inside *Mystic*. Then Davidov and Azulay punctured the Zodiac pontoons with their knives, and let the combined mass of the DPU and Zodiac pull it to the bottom.

Azulay headed up the ladder followed by Davidov, and they dropped into the Central Sphere. The relative warmth of the air was a welcome change from the frigid water. Davidov went aft into the Rescue Sphere, where their captives sat, shivering quietly. He handed each a blanket and then picked up a handset.

"We're ready back here, Jim. You've got the ball."

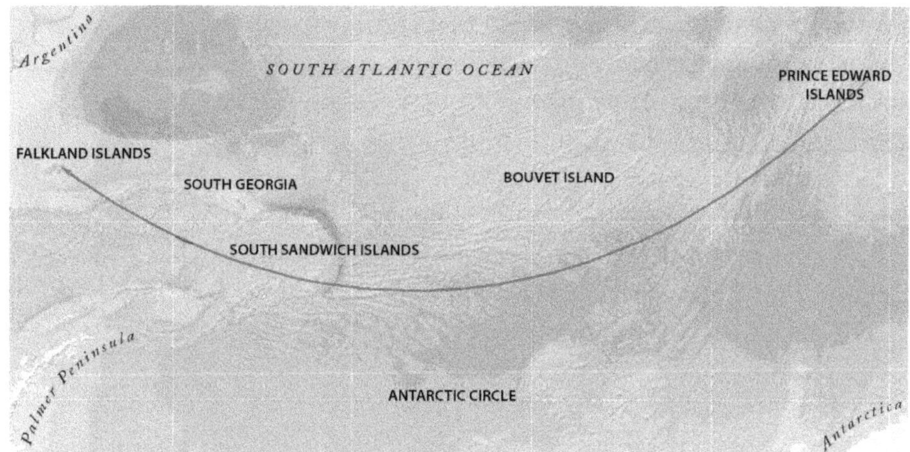

*Transit from the Prince Edward Islands to
the Falkland Islands.*

CHAPTER TWENTY-FOUR—Departure

1300, SATURDAY, AUGUST 5, 1989—*USS TEUTHIS*, PRINCE EDWARD CHANNEL, PRINCE EDWARD ISLANDS

In a very real sense, one could say that Operation Vela Redux was over. We had prevented the nuclear detonation, interdicted Soviet interference, and were departing the theater—all without once being detected by anyone. In the real world in which I live, however, we carried three South African techs who could not be allowed to know about *Teuthis*, an unknown factor who seemed to be Sergyi's little brother, an undetonated nuclear device, and four Shayetet 13 commandos who needed to get home as surreptitiously as possible, and with the fewest *Teuthis* crew members knowing who they were.

I called Roger and Ham to my cabin. Ham arrived before the XO, who told me he had to complete a vital piece of paperwork first.

When the two had settled in with cups of joe, Roger commented, "I had to add six hours during our transit to get us to Falkland time."

I took a sip from my cup and shared my thoughts. "The South African techs are a problem. I understand why the Shayetet 13 guys let them live, but we need to decide how to deal with them. I'm inclined to toss the ball to ComSubLant. Your thoughts?"

"We've got them for nine plus days in any case," Ham said. "I can make them reasonably comfortable in the DDC pressurized sufficiently to prevent their leaving."

"That solves the immediate problem," I said, "but that still leaves what to do when we reach Mare Harbour." I looked at Roger. "XO…?"

"I think I agree with notifying ComSubLant," Roger said. "Ultimately, this falls to the State Department. That's way beyond our paygrades."

"That brings up Danilo. Your thoughts?"

"He's been keeping with the divers," Ham said. "He sleeps on a cot in Dive Control, and hangs out there all the time. He plays a lot of chess."

"But what do we do with him in Mare Harbour?" I asked, suspecting I already knew the answer.

"I think the answer once again is ComSubLant," Roger said.

"So far, we're amind," I said with a smile. "It makes things easy when I don't have to fight my XO."

"Now for the last thing. We have a live nuclear device on our sub. I know you are aware of this, but I'm just saying."

"That's above even ComSubLant," Roger said.

"The Israelis may want to retain it," I said. "They certainly have a vested interest."

"Not a decision you can make, Mac," Roger said.

"Yeah, I know." I grimaced. "It's time to brief the boss."

✳

I composed the message to ComSubLant, info ComSubPac, and gave it to Roger to add his input. He thought the message needed to contain additional detail. After we talked it over, I agreed with him. The final message included nothing about the sinking of Steyn or *Yaroslavl*, because *Teuthis* was not directly involved with those incidents. It was a concise narrative of what happened from the time *Teuthis* entered Prince Edward Channel until *Mystic* picked up the Shayetet 13 team and their captives.

Since we had nine days to get our ducks in line, I told ComSubLant we would come to periscope depth for twenty minutes every five hours. Until we received their response.

Frankly, I figured that when ComSubLant got this message, he would burn up the lines to State, and soon, all the players would be involved. I didn't expect a response for two or three days.

*

We sent the message by burst transmission as we exited Prince Edward Channel. At 2100 hours, Ham had the watch, dropped us to 500 feet, and set our initial great circle course of 226 degrees.

0900, MONDAY, AUGUST 7, 1989—*USS TEUTHIS*, PERISCOPE DEPTH, ON GREAT CIRCLE ROUTE TO FALKLAND ISLANDS

In this narration and earlier accounts, I have said that submarining consists of endless hours of tedious boredom interrupted by moments of sheer panic. Ahead of us lay 3,500 nautical miles of potentially tedious boredom—over nine days.

We were traveling in circum-Antarctic waters that generate the stormiest waters on the planet. I anticipated at least one major storm during our transit. When Ham dropped us to 500 feet, however, the skies were mostly clear, although a crisp west wind was already ripping the wave tops. At 200 feet, *Teuthis* was stable, and at 500 feet, you couldn't even detect the sub's motion.

We came to periscope depth six times without receiving ComSubLant's response, but finally, thirty-five hours after our burst transmission, we received this message.

FLASH...FLASH...FLASH...FLASH

TOP SECRET/SENSITIVE COMPARTMENTED INFORMATION

DATE: 8 AUGUST 1989 0000Z

TO: USS TEUTHIS SSNR 2

INFO:　　　　　US DEPT OF STATE
ATTENTION: HON JAMES BAKER
FROM:　　　　COMSUBLANT
SUBJ:　　　　OPERATION VELA REDUX

1.　THIS MSG ACKNOWLEDGES USS Teuthis MSG DTD 5 AUGUST 1989 1800Z

2.　NEW INTEL FM ISRAEL VIA US STATE DEPARTMENT: SOUTH AFRICAN GOVT ISSUED ORDERS TO SOUTH AFRICAN MARINES ABOARD SAS PRESIDENT STEYN TO EXECUTE THE THREE NUCLEAR TECHNICIANS FOLLOWING DETONATION OF THE NUCLEAR DEVICE.

3.　A U S STATE DEPARTMENT REPRESENTATIVE WILL MEET TEUTHIS TO TAKE CUSTODY OF THE THREE SOUTH AFRICAN NUCLEAR TECHNICIANS.

4.　SHAYETET 13 HQ IS SENDING AN AIRCRAFT FOR SHAYETET-13 MEMBERS.

5.　A US ENERGY DEPT REPRESENTATIVE WILL EXAMINE THE NUCLEAR DEVICE YOU CAPTURED. WHEN HE HAS COMPLETED HIS EXAMINATION, HE WILL TURN OVER CUSTODY OF THE DEVICE TO SHAYETET-13.

6.　A SECOND US STATE DEPT REPRESENTATIVE WILL MEET TEUTHIS TO TAKE CUSTODY OF DANILO ANDREEV.

7.　A SOVIET VICTOR III CLASS SUBMARINE VOLGOGRAD HAS BEEN DISPATCHED TO WATERS AROUND THE FALKLAND ISLANDS.

8. A SOVIET SIERRA I CLASS SUBMARINE CARP IS INVESTIGATING DISAPPEARANCE OF YAROSLAVL.

TOP SECRET/SENSITIVE COMPARTMENTED INFORMATION

FLASH...FLASH...FLASH...FLASH

＊

I met in the Wardroom with the three South African nuclear technicians. Before they were escorted forward, Chief Rivera ensured that identifying markings in the Wardroom were covered. I had them sit around the coffee table, where Rivera removed their hoods.

"I presume you all speak English," I said.

They nodded, clearly frightened and feeling helpless.

"I am the captain of this submarine. We are not sharing names with you, because the less you know about us, the less likely your lives will be in further danger. We have discovered that the South African government issued orders to execute you three once the nuclear test was completed."

The three techs gasped, and their leader said, "Are you certain? Why would they do this?"

"Our intel is very reliable, gentlemen. As to why, your guess is as good as mine. The test was a secret to be kept from the world. Perhaps they considered your knowing the details too great of a risk. We can only speculate on that. Should you return to South Africa, however, you will not long survive."

I let them think about that for a minute.

"You will be turned over to a United States State Department representative when we arrive in port a few days from now. You will be respected and well treated. In the meantime, you will continue to be confined as you were before coming to see me." I smiled at them. "Do you have any questions?"

"Why are we being confined in that strange contraption?" the lead tech asked.

"We do not have meaningful confinement facilities aboard this sub. That is our best option. You can be comfortable, can sleep, and we can feed you. Ask for reading material, board and card games, and even movies we can project through a port. We still have about a week till we reach port."

✳

The tedium continued. Roger threw in several drills to keep the crew on its toes. At worst, they interrupted the boredom. Our routine had the Deck Officer clear baffles once an hour at random intervals, so this kept the Control Room crew occupied.

We were at 300 feet. At twenty knots, Sonar could not hear much, except when we slowed for baffle clears. Consequently, the sonar techs had a lot of idle time. King kept them busy listening to training tapes of different foreign and domestic vessels, so they could learn to identify them by sound alone.

Our track took us just thirty nautical miles from Thule Island. We slowed while passing so Sonar could get a good listen, but they heard nothing unusual. Finally, a day out of Mare Harbour, Sonar picked up something.

"Conn, Sonar, I have a new contact, actually several new contacts bunched together off our starboard bow at twenty nautical miles. This is a fishing fleet out of the Falklands. I will not designate these unless one breaks out and becomes a concern."

Somewhat later, Sonar called again. "Conn, Sonar, the fishing fleet is fading into our starboard baffles, but I have a new contact with suppressed cavitation, ten degrees off the starboard bow, drifting left. Designate Sierra-six-nine."

A few minutes later, "Conn, Sonar, Sierra-six-nine is fifty nautical miles distant on a course of one-eight-zero, doing ten knots. She will cross our bow at forty-seven nautical miles in ten minutes. If you give us a starboard aspect, we can determine who she is."

I followed the conversation from my cabin and walked out to Control. It was 2100 hours on Sunday, August 13. Jerry had the watch. He slowed and commenced a baffle clear to the left. When S-69 was fully broadside, he held his course so Sonar could do their thing.

Five minutes later, Sonar announced, "Conn, Sonar, Sierra-six-nine is the Soviet *Victor III Class* sub *Volgograd*. She is very capable when doing ten knots or less."

"Roger, Sonar," Jerry said, and turned back to base course, still about a day out of Mare Harbour. He looked at his COW, Oggy Winder. "Chief of the Watch, get the word out that we may have to go to condition ultra-quiet on a moment's notice."

Ten minutes later, "Conn, Sonar, Crazy Ivan! Crazy Ivan!"

Jerry signaled Oggy, and *Teuthis* became a silent hole in the water. I was very impressed with how well it went. Roger's training was paying off.

"Conn, Sonar," this time on the sound-powered phone, "Sierra-six-nine has turned to her left on our reciprocal course at forty nautical miles."

I stepped into Sonar. Godfry Mason was Supervisor. "Is *Volgograd* that good?" I asked. I had dealt with *Volgograd*, commanded by Captain First Rank Vladimir Ivanovich Vasnetsov, on two previous occasions. In Bellot Strait in the Arctic, another *Victor III* was stranded on the bottom. She deployed her escape module, and we assisted *Volgograd* in the rescue.[29] Then, *Volgograd* surfaced near our Crossing the Line Ceremony during Operation White Out.[30]

"If she's using her towed sonar array, yes, Sir, she's that good. That would explain how she picked us up."

"Where's the layer?" I asked.

"At six hundred feet, Captain."

"What's her estimated depth?"

"Towing the array, Sir, no more than a hundred meters, call it three hundred feet."

I went out to Control. "Jerry, drop to six hundred fifty feet and work closely with Sonar and Plot. I want to get close to Sierra-six-nine—*Volgograd*. We're both doing ten knots, so we'll be near each other in two hours. That's close to watch change. When we're close and Ham is with you, call me if I'm not already here."

---

29 See *Operation Arctic Sting*, vol 3 in *The Mac McDowell Missions*.
30 See *Operation White Out*, vol 4 in *The Mac McDowell Missions*.

I left to talk with Deckhart.

One hour later, I had Jerry ascend above the layer for two minutes and then drop below again. A half hour later, I did it again. I explained my thoughts to Jerry, Mason, and Henry Bass, the watch quartermaster.

"Conn, Sonar," on the sound-powered phone, "Sierra-six-nine has slowed to bare steerageway. I think she's trying to find us."

Jerry put *Teuthis* back in condition ultra-quiet.

I stuck my head into Sonar. "What's she doing?"

"I think she's trying to find us. She got us clearly when we popped above the layer twice. She knows we're close. She's trying to pinpoint our location."

"Announce on the sound-powered circuit, Commence DSRV ops," I told Ham, who had just assumed the watch. Jerry hung around, wanting to see what happened. We didn't launch the Basketball this time, so we were visually blind.

Following my instructions, Deckhart slipped through the layer, making virtually no noise at all. He located *Volgograd* on his high frequency search sonar. So far as I knew, the Russian sub had no way of detecting *Mystic*'s sonar. Then Deckhart came up a hundred yards behind *Volgograd*, located the slender towed sonar cable, and snipped it with his manipulator arm.

Deckhart dropped as quickly as possible down through the layer. *Volgograd* did nothing for several minutes—probably troubleshooting the towed array sonar system. Then, without warning, she went active. I anticipated this and had already ordered Ham to take *Teuthis* to the bottom rapidly, but quietly.

Volgograd's sonar blasted right through the layer and definitely received an echo from us. Because the layer was very distinct here, resulting from significantly different surface and depth temperatures, *Volgograd*'s sound beam was radically deflected on both the downward and return paths. The Russian sub's sonar tech detected us on his screen, but we were actually at an entirely different location because of the strong deflection of the sound beams.

Volgograd didn't detect *Mystic*, because her shroud was made of sound absorbing fiberglass. There may have been a small, intermittent blip, but the *Teuthis* blip occupied the sonar tech's entire attention.

Ham lowered the skids three feet and settled *Teuthis* on the bottom, which consisted of rolling low hills, some a hundred feet tall. *Teuthis* disappeared from *Volgograd*'s sonar scope.

Deckhart located us in a few minutes and returned to his cradle. *Volgograd* hung around above us for another hour, trying various combinations of active and passive sonar. He knew we were there, but could not find us. We remained at ultra-quiet on the bottom and waited.

Three hours after our first close encounter, *Volgograd* started her turbine and set a course that would take her down around the Cape and eventually home to Petropavlovsk-Kamchatskiy on the Kamchatka peninsula.

We waited around on the bottom at ultra-quiet until I was quite sure *Volgograd* was gone for good. Seth had just assumed the watch. He took us to 200 feet at twenty knots, clearing baffles according to my Night Orders. About twelve hours later, Sonar called.

"Conn, Sonar, we've picked up Sierra-six-nine again. She's coming around the north end of the Falklands."

That sneaky bastard, Captain First Rank Vladimir Ivanovich Vasnetsov, I thought. Feinting to the south, and then coming around the islands from the west and north.

"What's her range?" I asked.

"Fifty nautical miles. She's running balls to the wall—thirty knots or even faster."

"What's she heading?"

"Looks like she's heading for the waters around the harbor entrance leading to Choiseul Sound. Should arrive in ninety minutes."

"Keep a close eye on her. We will run at twenty knots until she slows down enough to detect us. Obviously, Captain First Rank Vladimir Ivanovich Vasnetsov does not understand our sonar capabilities. Tell Conn and let me know the moment she slows down."

I stepped to Plot. "Show me the large-scale plot of the entrance to Choiseul Sound."

Twenty miles out, the bottom was 300 feet. It shelved up to 100 feet four miles out. "When is the next double bird pass?" I asked Quartermaster Theron.

"Ten minutes, Sir."

"Get ready to take it, and then reset the SINS."

"Periscope depth, Ham," I said, "and afterward, get back over the bottom." I motioned him to Plot. "We're going to ride the bottom right up to here." I pointed to the entrance to Choiseul Sound, where the depth was sixty to seventy feet. "We'll surface here, and head into the Sound and Mare Harbour. As soon as we surface, set the maneuvering watch."

1500, MONDAY, AUGUST 14, 1989—*USS TEUTHIS*, SUBMERGED AT 100 FT, 4 NM FROM ENTRANCE TO CHOISEUL SOUND, FALKLAND ISLANDS

Teuthis crept along ten feet over the bottom, heading 270 degrees, four nautical miles east of the Sound entrance. *Volgograd* hovered eight nautical miles due north, as silent as I've ever heard her, with her bow pointed at the middle of Choiseul Sound entrance. We were at ultra-quiet with turbine idling, running on both outboards with the skids extended so we would not accidentally hit the bottom, which consisted mostly of rocks and sand. *Volgograd* could not have heard us a hundred yards distant, and she was eight miles to the north.

I was impressed by Capt. Vasnetsov's audacity, and thankful my sonar techs were well trained. The Russian skipper did not know with whom he was dealing, but it had to be British or American. The Argentines could not have carried off clipping his towed array, and besides, since the Falklands war, they were quasi-Soviet allies. Because of his encounter with *Teuthis* near the start of Operation White Out, he knew we operated in Antarctic waters, or at least we had. His intelligence service would have informed him of the presence of *Tireless* and *Talent*. He might logically have concluded that *Teuthis* was back for DSRV training with these British subs. Vasnetsov reminded me of the wily *Whiskey* sub skipper we encountered while I was on *Halibut* in the Sea of Okhotsk—stubborn and very smart.[31]

We progressed at a snail's pace until finally reaching seventy-feet-deep water at 2230 hours. Ham, who was coming on watch,

---

31 See *Operation Ivy Bells*, vol 1 in *The Mac McDowell Missions*.

was ready to take the bridge. He and his lookouts were bundled against the wind and rain. I suited up to join them. Marcel Theron was quartermaster.

"Use radar to keep us in the channel," I told him. "Be especially vigilant for something suddenly showing up behind us."

I turned to Ham. "Okay, surface, but without the klaxon and 1MC announcement. Have Pots set the maneuvering watch as soon as we turn north. Keep the navigation lights off until we turn north."

Pots passed the notice to surface over the sound-powered phone circuit, and moments later, the rush of air into the ballast tanks signaled our change of status. While Ham and his lookouts scrambled to the bridge, I raised the periscope and scanned around for anything unexpected. Pots set the maneuvering watch belowdecks, with the deck gang standing by for our turn north. King assembled them in the Crews Mess.

Once Ham had the squawk box working, I climbed to the bridge, wincing as the freezing rain hit my face. I slipped on a pair of goggles so I could see. Except there was nothing to see. *Teuthis* was completely isolated in an icy, water-logged cocoon, surrounded by wet blackness.

Jubal Henshaw had just assumed the Nav Watch and called on the squawk box, "Recommend coming right to course three-five-two."

Ham picked up the mike. "Now, set the maneuvering watch."

The only maneuvering watch stations not already manned were the bridge and the deck gang. Waverly, Walton, and Orfutt showed up promptly. I presumed Beverton had the helm in Control. The forward deck hatch opened, the projected light beam flickering off thousands of raindrops. King made sure each deck sailor was clipped to the safety rail.

Off the port bow, I heard a loud whistle, but only heard Borysko. It was difficult to see the bow in the driving rain, let alone my seagoing friend out in the water.

Waverly knew Mare Harbour like the palm of his hand by now. He brought us around the bend into East Cove, and then around the back end and forward so we could tie up starboard side to against *HMS Talent*.

It was an ungodly 2200 hours, but *Talent* deck personnel came topside in the driving rain to tie us up, waving and shouting good-naturedly.

"Set the in-port watch, section one," Sam Dokey announced on the 1MC.

I grinned to myself as I descended into Control and headed for my cabin, wondering if Capt. Vasnetsov was still out there, patiently waiting for us to appear on his sonar screens.

HMS Talent *and* Teuthis & Mystic *docked at Mare Harbour.*

CHAPTER TWENTY-FIVE—Mare Harbor

0800, TUESDAY, AUGUST 15, 1989—*USS TEUTHIS,* MOORED AT MARE HARBOUR, FALKLAND ISLANDS

I slept through the night, the first time in weeks. The messenger woke me at 0630 with a hot cup of joe, and I felt wonderful. I called Control and told Chop to send my compliments to Capt. Harris on the *Talent*, and invite him to join me for breakfast—0715. I showered and dressed and crossed the passageway to the Wardroom. Both the XO and Engineer, Roger and Bert, were breaking their fast when I joined them.

A few minutes later, the 1MC announced, "*Talent* arriving, *Talent* arriving," and shortly thereafter, Chop opened the Wardroom door for Cmdr. Harris.

"Johnny, glad you could join us," I said with a welcoming grin.

He grinned back. "The sun's out," he said, "crisp and cold," and sat to my left, where I indicated.

I wasn't sure he knew Roger and Bert, so I introduced them, "My XO, Roger Barnes and Engineer, Bert Cobb."

Johnny shook hands with both. "Nice to see you again, Roger," he said, settling that question. "Nice to meet you, Bert."

Breakfast was to order, with officers coming and going as their schedules demanded. I ordered eggs over easy atop hash browns, crisp bacon, and popovers.

Johnny said, "Same for me, with a cup of tea, please."

Chief Rivera set a glass of fresh orange juice in front of each of us.

"Where the hell did you get this?" I asked.

He grinned. "Compliments of Colonel Brisbane, Captain."

"Tell me about your return trip from Thule Island," I said to my guest.

"Slow and tedious for us, and damned uncomfortable for *San Juan*. We went through one storm with fifty-foot waves running west to east. The poor buggers on *San Juan* must all have been seasick.

"Apparently, they actually were trying to establish another outpost on the island. Mount Larsen really bollixed their plans. It's out of my hands now. The Admiralty is looking into it."

Rivera brought our breakfasts, and we dug in. We lingered over coffee and tea for a while, and then it was time for me to meet the first government VIP, Dr. C. Abernathy, from the Energy Department.

❋

I waited in my cabin for the Dr. to arrive. At 0840, Chop knocked on my door.

"Enter," I said.

Chop opened the door. "Captain McDowell, may I introduce Doctor Caileigh Abernathy, from the Department of Energy."

I came to my feet and shook the groomed hand of an absolutely stunning woman in her mid-thirties, dressed in a dark pants suit. In her flats, she was a bit shorter than me, her long blond hair pulled into a professional something at the back of her head. Her classical face carried minimal makeup, and her hand was cool as she firmly shook mine.

She smiled broadly, displaying white teeth, and said, "The legend in person…please call me Caileigh. May I call you Mac?"

I nodded, not trusting myself to speak at that moment. To say she was overwhelming would be an understatement. She was the last thing I had expected.

"Coffee?" I asked, working to bring my reaction under control.

"Please—black," she answered as she sat in my easy chair and crossed her legs.

Through it all, I remained the stoic submarine commander, but I suspected she saw through my charade.

Rivera brought us two coffees, and while we sipped them, I said, "I'm sure you know I wasn't expecting your kind of C. Abernathy."

She smiled. "I get that a lot."

I knew I had a short fuse when it came to beautiful women, but I found myself reacting to Caileigh like I had reacted to Kate when I first met her. I glanced at the ivory cylinder hanging over my desk. Then I turned my chair around and leaned on the back. "Tell me your plan of procedure," I said. I needed to get this meeting back on track.

She extracted a small notebook and pen from an inner pocket. She wasn't carrying a purse. "I want to meet with the South African techs. We know they were to be executed following the test, so they should be happy to tell me what I need to know. Then I want to see the device and run some tests. Since we will be releasing it to the Israelis, I want to learn as much as possible.

I looked at her. "How does a girl…, I mean woman, like you…"

She interrupted. "Girl is fine. I'm not one of those bra-burning types."

"Great!" I said, "So, how does a girl like you become a government nuclear weapons specialist?"

"I grew up in a family with three very smart brothers, a scientist mom, and an engineer dad. My brothers actually built a small atomic pile in our basement, but they didn't shield it enough. The authorities found out, and the EPA had to come and dispose of it." She laughed, a laugh that reminded me of Kate's rich laugh. I worked at keeping a neutral face. She continued. Their experiment got me interested in the other side of things nuclear, and I jumped into a personal study of how we developed nuclear weapons, and how we deal with them. I carried my interest through high school and then college—I took a degree from MIT in nuclear engineering and then a masters and doctorate in general applied nuclear science."

"I'm impressed," I said, meaning it. "And the government?"

"The Energy Department recruited me out of grad school."

You could have blown me away with a breath of air. What a story!

"What about you, Mac? How did you become a hero that even a nerd like me has heard of?"

I think I blushed.

"I wouldn't use that word," I said. "I was fortunate enough to lead a group of extraordinary men who accomplished something heroic. Their heroism washed over me, but they deserve the accolades." I grinned. "Several of them are still with me here on *Teuthis*. And they are still as heroic as the day I met them."

"You weren't always captain of this sub?" she asked.

"I worked my way up," I answered. "Started out as an E-1 recruit."

"And now, here you are. Now it's my turn to be impressed." Her smile nearly caused me to lose my composure.

I pulled the conversation back to topic. "So, you learn what you can from the South African device and then you turn it over to the Israelis. Then what?"

"Once the Israelis have the device, I'm free for the day." Her blue eyes twinkled. "Will you have any free time?"

"I have a meeting with a State Department rep, and I meet with the Garrison Commander. After that, I'm free. I would like to introduce you to a very special friend, and then we could have a bite of supper in the Wardroom and visit the local pub, which is quite good, considering."

"Why, Mac, are you asking me out on a date? But we just met!"

I think I blushed.

"We'll be with my officers and the wardrooms of the two British subs. It should be a lot of fun."

"Of course, I'll join you. How often does a girl get a chance to date a genuine legend?"

This time, I blushed for sure. "I told you, my guys are the heroes. I just went along for the ride."

"Whatever," she said with a tinkling laugh.

"I'll have the techs brought to the Wardroom," I said, "and we can meet them there."

I called Chop to have them brought up. Fifteen minutes later, Chop called. "They are waiting for you in the Wardroom, Captain."

I stood and offered a hand to Caileigh. She took it and stood, squeezing my fingers lightly.

"I like you, Mac," she said with a lilting laugh.

✻

We met with the three South African techs in the Wardroom. They registered surprise when Caileigh told them she had a doctorate in nuclear science with a specialty in fission and fusion devices. Actually, I was equally surprised about the specialty. Caileigh was one interesting girl.

Caileigh spent some forty-five minutes asking questions about South Africa's nuclear bomb program and their stockpile of nuclear weapons. The techs knew little about the overall nuclear program—it was way over their paygrades, they told her. On the other hand, they were very forthcoming about the on-hand nuclear weapons. South Africa had eight nuclear weapons. Five were being dismantled, as President de Klerk had publicly stated. One was slated to be dismantled, but they didn't know when. The eighth was what they brought with them for detonation on Prince Edward Island.

Caileigh impressed me with her ability to wring information out of the techs. At the end, there really was nothing more they could tell her.

I took Caileigh to the machinery space, to a spotlessly clean bench whereupon the aluminum weapon case sat. Earlier, she had some special equipment delivered. It was waiting for her. She asked everyone to leave except me. She opened the case, removed the device, and secured it to the bench. She carefully checked every part of the device with a radiation probe. She found nothing. Using a Minox camera—another surprise—she photographed every part of the device—top, bottom, and both sides. Then she disassembled it, documenting every step, sometimes using a magnifying glass for better detail.

She placed the lead-encased plutonium sphere inside a glass box that she explained was constructed of leaded glass doped with cerium to keep it transparent over time. Without the cerium, it would turn dark brown after a few exposures to gamma radiation.

Using lead-lined gloves that extended into the box, she removed the lead casing and examined and photographed the plutonium sphere. Using a probe, she checked the gamma flux around the sphere. Then she reassembled the sphere, removed it from the box, and reassembled the rest of the device. The entire task took her two hours of concentrated effort.

"I didn't check the tritium inside the sphere," she said, "but it has to be refreshed periodically, anyway."

She closed the weapons case and grinned at me. "I think it's time for your next meeting."

She was right. I left for my cabin.

1100, TUESDAY, AUGUST 15, 1989—*USS TEUTHIS,* MOORED AT MARE HARBOUR, FALKLAND ISLANDS

I was in my cabin writing notes about my meeting with Caileigh when Chop called to say the State Department rep was here. I asked Chop to bring him to my cabin.

"He is a him, right?" I asked.

"Yes, Sir. Sorry about the last time. I should have warned you."

Chop knocked, opened the door, and introduced me to Jordan Fortnight. Fortnight handed me his card. It read, Jordan E. Fortnight, Esq., Assistant Undersecretary of State for Ukraine. I didn't know there was an Assistant Undersecretary of State for Ukraine. That seemed to be way down in the weeds.

I pointed to the couch. Fortnight sat and opened his briefcase beside him. He was short, about five feet eight, with short-clipped brown hair, small round glasses, a narrow tie, button-down collar, and a tweed jacket. Harvard Law School bristled all over him.

"May I offer you some coffee?" I asked.

"No thank you," he said, clipping his words as he spoke. "I'll take a glass of water, if possible." He removed his glasses and polished them with a white cloth he pulled from inside his jacket.

I picked up the handset and called for water for him and a cola for me—all the stewards knew I preferred the diet variety. While we waited, Fortnight checked his glasses and cleaned them again. The drinks arrived, he accepted his, took a sip, and pulled a sheet from his briefcase.

He squinted at the sheet, cleared his throat, took another sip, and then spoke, still with oddly clipped words. "This is an odd coincidence, and generally, I do not believe in coincidences." He cleared his throat again and took another sip. "This water tastes somewhat odd—perhaps flat is a better word."

"It's distilled from seawater using heat from our reactor," I told him.

He held his glass against the room light and squinted at it. "Any chance of radiation?" he asked.

"Zero chance. It doesn't work that way. Depending on which tank is online right now, it could actually be local water. We topped off our freshwater tanks this morning." I changed the subject. "Are you suggesting that Danilo is a Soviet plant?"

Fortnight cleaned his glasses again. "Possibly. It's how the Soviets do things, you know."

"I take your point," I said, "but consider the circumstances. The Soviets did not know *Teuthis* would be at Prince Edward Island. Furthermore, they could not have known that an Orca friendly to my divers would try to prevent their divers from harming mine, and in the process, kill all their divers except Danilo. That would be entirely beyond their ability to orchestrate."

I looked at him and asked sharply, "Who came up with that harebrained idea?"

Still polishing his glasses, Fortnight said, "It was my idea."

"Is it still your idea?" I asked, trying hard to keep the scorn out of my voice.

"It's how the Soviets do things," he said again.

"Mr. Fortnight, in the greatest possible shroud of secrecy, *Teuthis* traveled from the San Francisco Bay to Antarctica, and then crossed over to the Atlantic, stopping briefly in the Falklands to conduct DSRV operations with the Brits, and then we continued to Prince Edward Island. The Soviets could not have known our destination before we arrived at Mare Harbour." I took a deep breath and continued before he could speak. "It is humanly possible for a Soviet agent in the Falklands to have discovered our destination. If that agent informed Moscow immediately, and if Moscow did everything as efficiently as possible, their submarine *Yaroslavl* still could not have gotten from where she was then to Prince Edward Island at the time she actually arrived." I leaned forward in my chair. "It's simply not physically possible, don't you understand that?"

I drank some cola. "You are an attorney. You guys throw shit against a wall to see what sticks. I get that." I smiled at him. "This one didn't stick, so let it go!"

He leaned back defensively, reaching for his glasses. "You make a good point, I guess," he said. "I was assigned to come down here because of my theory. A good attorney accepts facts at face value." He swallowed and gave me a glum smile. "Okay, I'm convinced. I was wrong."

The little guy was starting to impress me. Admitting you're wrong goes a long way toward gaining my respect.

"Would you like to meet him?" I asked.

He nodded, sipping his water.

"I'll have him brought up."

✳

Chop had the watch, but Ham brought Danilo to my cabin. When he saw me, his face brightened.

"Captain Mac, my brother. So good to see you!"

Fortnight looked somewhat taken aback and started polishing his glasses again.

"Danilo Andreev," I said, "meet U.S. State Department representative, the Honorable Jordan Fortnight."

Danilo came to attention and saluted in British fashion, palm pointed away from his face. "My pleasure, Sir."

I motioned for Danilo to sit in the easy chair and nodded to Fortnight.

"Mr. Andreev," he commenced.

"Please call me Danilo. Everyone does."

"Danilo, please tell me how you came to be on the Soviet submarine *Yaroslavl*." Fortnight sat upright, pen poised over his notebook.

Danilo launched into a story that started with his childhood in Ukraine with Sergyi, continued with Sergyi becoming a saturation diver with the Soviet navy, his believed death in the Sea of Okhotsk, Danilo joining the Morskoy Spetsnaz, and ultimately ending up on *Teuthis* following the disaster in the water outside *Yaroslavl*.

"I must admit," Fortnight said in his clipped words, "that is a very convincing story. You just do not make up something like that." He smiled broadly at Danilo—the first time I saw him smile. "I'm here to take you to your brother. He is a good friend of the U.S. State Department. You will be proud of him."

1300, TUESDAY, AUGUST 15, 1989—COL BRISBANE'S OFFICE, MARE HARBOUR, FALKLAND ISLANDS

I called Col. Brisbane on the landline. "Do you have a few minutes to meet with me, Colonel?"

"Always for you, Mac. I'm free now."

Jerry had just assumed the watch. I let him know where I would be. A few minutes later, I sat comfortably in the colonel's office. Nothing had changed. His desk faced the door, and a map of Mare Harbour adorned the wall behind. He had prepared a pot of tea, and I was enjoying a cup.

"I have a request similar to my last one, Harry," I said after we had exhausted small talk about the weather. "Remember the man you drove to Mount Pleasant surreptitiously the last time?"

He nodded. "Indeed. A mystery you have yet to explain."

"I need you to do it again tonight, but for four people with their equipment. As before, I cannot tell you what is going on, but I really need your help."

"Of course, and perhaps someday you can finally tell me," he said with a wink. "Will you be at the pub tonight?"

"For a while," I said. "See you there."

1500, TUESDAY, AUGUST 15, 1989—EAST COVE, MARE HARBOUR, FALKLAND ISLANDS

The day had been pleasant thus far, but a chilly wind built up across Choiseul Sound, sweeping into East Cove. I met with Caileigh, loaned her a foul-weather jumpsuit, and hustled her into the Zodiac I had checked out from the harbormaster. I started the outboard and headed out into East Cove.

"Okay, Mac, what's this all about?" Caileigh asked.

"You will know in just a few minutes," I said, winking at her. "You are about to meet a good friend of mine."

I couldn't have timed it better. At that moment, Borysko whistled loudly and leaped into the air a few yards from the Zodiac. Caileigh squealed with delight and looked around for the Orca's location. That's when he surfaced beside the rubber pontoon and whistled quietly. He backed off and turned so his six-foot mouth faced the pontoon. He opened his mouth and lolled his tongue onto the pontoon. I reached out and scratched it for several seconds. Then I took Caileigh's hand in mine.

"Do you trust me?" I asked.

She nodded, perhaps afraid to say anything. I pushed her hand against the giant tongue and rubbed it back and forth. She started moving her hand on her own, scratching.

"This is my friend Caileigh," I told Borysko. "Caileigh, this is my friend, Borysko. Now, lay your arm on his tongue, palm down, and leave it there for thirty seconds."

She did as I asked. That probably was the longest thirty seconds in Caileigh's life.

"You and Borysko are now bonded for life. He will give his life protecting you. He follows us everywhere we go. When we travel faster than he can swim, somehow he finds us anyway."

I slapped Borysko on his snout and backed away. "Let's take a circuit of the Cove so he can show off to the sailors watching us from the subs."

Caileigh turned to look, and waved at about fifteen sailors who watched their skipper driving a pretty girl around the Cove with Borysko as escort.

"You are a fascinating man, Mr. Legend," Caileigh said, grabbing and holding my hand. "When you invited me on a date, I simply had no idea."

*

Caileigh joined the Wardroom for a steak dinner. When the officers were seated, I stood and announced, "Please meet my guest, Doctor Caileigh Abernathy, the nuclear weapons specialist the Energy Department sent us. I introduced her to Borysko this afternoon. I think he likes her."

That got a hearty chuckle from around the table.

"Will you join us at the pub this evening, Doctor Abernathy?" someone asked; I missed who.

"Call me Caileigh, and yes, it would be my pleasure."

Caileigh absolutely enjoyed her shipboard dinner with a group of female-starved officers who had politeness ingrained into them—especially toward pretty women.

With dinner over, including fresh apple pie with ice cream, I escorted Caileigh out of the sub, across the brows for the short walk to the pub.

*

We walked through the pub door and the chatter quieted as every male eye in the place examined the lovely woman on my arm.

"Do you always have that effect when you walk into a place?" I asked Caileigh.

"I wish," she said a bit wistfully. "When I was a twenty-something I often had that effect, but I was too busy becoming what I am now to pay much attention to the sensual side of life. Now that I'm in my mid-thirties, the men who appeal to me are all taken."

As we stepped up to the bar, she turned my face to hers. "Are you taken?"

I caught my breath and fingered the ivory cylinder in my right pocket. "I was, but we were in a terrible accident. I made it but Kate didn't."

"Oh, you poor dear," she said, brushing my cheek with her fingers.

"Are you a scotch drinker?' I asked.

"Islay," she answered with a sly smile.

Maggie joined us. "Introduce me to your girl, Mac," she said, and turning to Caileigh, said, "Aren't you a lovely one?" She turned to the bartender. "Give them what they're drinking."

"Two Lagavulin, neat," I ordered. "Thank you, Maggie. Please remain with us. You rarely get to socialize with a woman." We walked together to an empty table, and the bartender brought our drinks.

It didn't take long for the two women to be deep into conversation, relating to each how they both came to be here, now.

"So, you just met Mac?" Maggie asked.

"Just this morning, in fact," Caileigh said.

In her straightforward way, Maggie said, "Well, it's obvious to a woodpecker that you two have something good going. What are your plans for the night?"

Caileigh blushed. Maggie said, "Honey, you're at the bottom of the world, and somehow you captured the best man in ten thousand miles. Don't blow this, Girl!" She grinned at me. "Tell you what—you both stay at my place. I'll crash with a friend." She got up. "Come on. I'll take you and get you settled."

✳

Maggi took us to her place, a bungalow with a bedroom, living room, kitchen, and bath.

"I changed the sheets this morning," she said, her eyes twinkling. "You can call your ship's landline to tell them where you are." She put her arms around us both. "Now you guys get to know each other really well."

She laughed and skipped out the door.

Now what? I thought.

"Wow!" Caileigh said a bit breathless, and sat in one of two chairs.

I picked the other, turning it to face her. I was feeling like a schoolboy. "So," I said hesitatingly, "what do you think about Borysko?" It was lame, but I couldn't think of anything else to say.

Her eyes twinkled and she let out a lilting laugh. "He and I bonded, didn't we." It was a statement, not a question.

Our awkward conversation limped along for another minute or so, and then we both stood and came to each other's arms.

I decided not to record a lot of details about that night in this account. I told Caileigh about Kate and showed her the ivory cylinder. She reacted the way Heather had reacted, except Caileigh was 100 percent real, 100 percent genuine. I knew without a shadow of a doubt that I was no longer footloose and fancy free.

✳

When Caileigh waved goodbye from the Mare Harbour dock the following morning, I knew we would be together again soon.

Teuthis got underway, and I relied on Waverly to get us through the gap and out of the Sound. I locked my eyes on Caileigh until the bluff at our turn cut her off. I went below with a song in my heart. I had finally found someone to fill the awful hole Kate left when we plunged off that New London bridge in my Corvette, forced by evil men who wanted me dead but took my love's life instead.

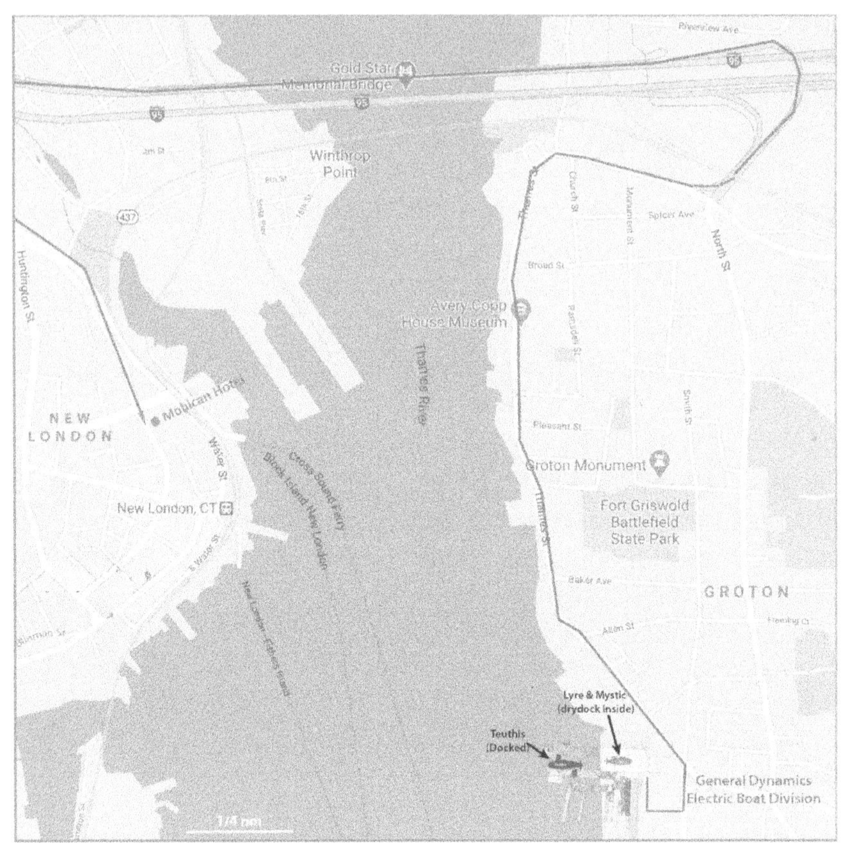

Path from General Dynamics Electric Boat
across the Gold Star Memorial Bridge to the Mohican Hotel.

CHAPTER TWENTY-SIX—New London

0600, THURSDAY, AUGUST 31, 1989—GENERAL DYNAMICS, ELECTRIC BOAT PIER, GROTON, CT

At 0600 hours, fifteen days and nineteen hours after our departure from Mare Harbour, the first monkey fist sailed over to the Electric Boat wharf at the General Dynamics complex on the Thames River in Groton, Connecticut. The day was summer-warm with a gentle breeze rippling the placid river surface. The cloudless sky was bright blue on this seventy-ninth day since our Mare Island departure on the other side of the continent.

From the bridge, I watched Borysko cavorting in the sun-warmed river water. Suddenly, he stopped, raised his massive head above the surface and headed to shore just south of the wharf. I could hear him whistling loudly. Out of the corner of my eye, I saw a taxi drive to the wharf. The back door on the passenger side opened, and a woman emerged, tall in heels, wide-skirted silk dress printed with large, colorful flowers billowing in the breeze, and her shoulder-length blond hair fanning out in the moving air. I turned my binocs on her and saw dangling earrings matching her dress pattern. It was Caileigh, and I couldn't take my eyes off her.

Caileigh looked at *Teuthis* and then turned toward Borysko's whistle and walked toward the quay where he had lifted his head, resting his chin on the creosote soaked 8 x 8 beams. Borysko's snout reached past the messy beams, mouth wide open, looking for Caileigh's ministrations. From the bridge, I saw her squat, bright skirt riding above her knees in her lap, and reach deep into his mouth and scratch. Then she went through the bonding ritual a second time. The Orca's joy was palpable, even from my distance.

Caileigh stood, shaded her eyes, and scanned the sub. When she saw me on the bridge, she waved and ran across the lot to the wharf. To see her in the breeze, silk dress and hair billowing, no one would have guessed she was a top-rated nuclear engineer. She was just a happy girl, flushed with joy at seeing her man after a long absence.

Seth was the duty officer. As soon as the brow went over, he brought Caileigh aboard and escorted her to my cabin—heels and all. She entered with a squeal of delight while Seth quietly shut the door behind her. We kissed like we hadn't seen each other for years.

When we came up for air, I stammered, "M…my gosh, you're beautiful!" I whirled her around and then held her close again. "Caileigh, I have some things to take care of before I can leave. May I ask you to make yourself comfortable in the Wardroom? There's plenty of reading material in the magazine rack. I'll hurry through the necessaries as quickly as possible."

"Of course, Mac." She paused and pursed her lips. "Did I tell you that I love you?"

"In so many words—sure you did!" I kissed her and opened my cabin door, pointing. "That's the Wardroom."

✳

The XO, Engineer, and Navigator met with me for a few minutes. We each had reports to submit and had worked on them during our transit north. I pulled them together and handed them to Roger.

"They're your baby now," I told him. I had gone through that routine myself during Operation White Out, so I knew only too well what it involved. Roger would be here for several more hours.

"Guys," I said, "Caileigh met us when we docked. She's in the Wardroom being very patient. Do you have any other urgent matters that cannot wait until Monday?"

They grinned at me.

Roger commented, "I don't think you would comprehend anything else we might say."

"You need to take your leave," Bert said with a grin. "We got it!"

Seth, as Navigator, was too junior to feel comfortable exchanging quips with me. He was working hard, however, to stifle his grin.

"Okay," I said with a sigh, "I'm outta here. I'll be back Monday morning. My pager works, if you need me."

I grabbed a duffel bag I had packed earlier, left my cabin, and entered the Wardroom. Caileigh stood, smoothed her skirt with her hands, and kissed me quickly.

"We're off to see the wizard," I said with a grin.

✳

The base Chief Petty Officer had arranged to park my Vette in the CO slot on the wharf. Holding Caileigh's hand, I walked her across the brow and to my Vette. The Chief had even arranged for it to be detailed. I made a mental note to thank him officially.

"This is a replacement for my Vette that went off the bridge. I'll show you when we pass the spot." I turned toward the river. "Hey, Borysko," I said and walked over to scratch his tongue.

"He knows the Vette sound. He'll follow us up the river and across the bridge until he loses us in New London Traffic."

We climbed into the low-slung sports car. Caileigh flashed me as much leg as she could with an impish grin. We fastened our seatbelts, and I started the engine. I honked the horn twice at Borysko and backed out of the parking spot. Borysko pushed up out of the river and watched as we drove through the gate. The Vette engine produced a distinct rumble that Borysko could hear easily. When he submerged, it reached him through the water. I'm certain he associated it with me and Caileigh.

We turned north along Thames Street. "Look!" Caileigh said, pointing to the river, her voice filled with excitement. "There's Borysko. Do you think he can see us?"

"I don't know," I answered, "but I suspect he can hear the Vette through the water. His hearing is incredible. Up in Victoria Sound under the ice pack, he tracked us a hundred miles away."

We passed Broad Street, heading for Interstate 95. I whipped around the curve, picked up the on ramp, and merged into the light morning traffic.

"The place Kate and I went off the bridge is just ahead," I said.

"You went off here?" Caileigh asked. "We're more than a hundred feet up."

"One hundred thirty-five to be exact," I said. "Two semis coordinated their efforts and pushed me off. We didn't have a chance."

"Oh, my sweet Love." Caileigh took my right hand in hers and brought it to her lips.

"Borysko saw the Vette tumble over the side. He followed us sixty feet down through the water and somehow picked up both Kate and me in his mouth. He brought us to the surface and swam the two miles back to the wharf. I was alive, barely, but the crash when we hit the water broke Kate's neck. She died instantly."

I glanced at Caileigh. Her eyes brimmed, and she wiped a tear from her cheek. I took her hand and said quietly, "You have finally made the hurt go away. I didn't think it was possible, but you made it happen."

She squeezed my hand, and we drove on in silence.

0800, THURSDAY, AUGUST 31, 1989—PENTHOUSE SUITE, MOHICAN HOTEL, NEW LONDON, CT

I pulled up in front of the Mohican Hotel, a magnificent turn-of-the-century brick-façade building.

"Back in 1896," I told Caileigh, "Frank Munsey, publisher of Munsey's Magazine, built this building to house his magazine production. The creator of New York's Carnegie Hall, architect William B. Tuthill, designed the tall building using a then new technique of steel-skeleton framing. Six months later, a workers' strike led Munsey to shut down his New London magazine production and convert the building into a grand hotel. The building reopened in 1898 as the Mohican Hotel, destined to become one of the finest hotels in Connecticut. In 1916, Munsey added two floors and a roof garden." I grinned at Caileigh with a wink. We have the penthouse suite for the weekend."

"Oh my!" Caileigh said with wonder in her voice. "I heard you don't do things in a small way." She leaned over and kissed my cheek. "There's more of that to come," she said huskily, "lots more!"

*

The following morning, I awakened to the bedside phone ringing. Caileigh's head was nestled against my shoulder, blond hair spread across the pillow and my chest. Her warm, unclothed body partly covered mine. A bit awkwardly, I reached for the phone.

"Captain McDowell, this is the front desk, Sir. You have three guests in the lobby. Mr. Andreev says to take your time. They will wait for you in the lounge."

I rolled over so I could look down at Caileigh's beautiful face. She opened her deep blue eyes and stuck out her tongue. I kissed the tip and wrapped my arms around her. It was a good thing Sergyi had said to take my time.

Finally, we showered together, and Caileigh dried her hair in front of the mirror, letting the water dry on the rest of her while I dressed—in civies I had stuffed in my duffel bag.

There was no doubt I had hit the jackpot with Caileigh—stunning beauty and genuine brains linked to nearly wanton sensuality. What more could a guy want?

We took longer than we should have. Caileigh slipped into the same silk dress she wore yesterday, and finally, we crossed the hall to the elevator. We exited on the mezzanine, seven floors below. I took Caileigh's hand in mine and led her to the top of a broad staircase winding down to the lounge.

As we descended the staircase, Sergyi saw us and shouted, "Mac!" When we reached the lounge, he gave me a bearhug. Then he stepped back, gripping each of our hands, and looked Caileigh up and down.

"Allow me to introduce Doctor Caileigh Abernathy," I said.

Sergyi wrapped his arms around Caileigh and kissed each cheek. "You make me happier than you can imagine," he said to her, looking her up and down once more. "Doctor of what?" he asked.

"Nuclear Engineering."

"Oh, my!" he said. "Good match for Mac."

A short woman with dimpled cheeks pushed her way into our little circle. "Don't you hog Mac," she told Sergyi. She reached up on tippy-toes and kissed me full on my mouth. She turned to Caileigh, threw her arms around her neck, and kissed her lips. "You love Mac— that makes me love you!"

I told Caileigh, "Meet Joey, former Navy Lieutenant Jolene Kaper, former Antarctic chopper pilot,[32] and more recently, Mrs. Sergyi Andreev." I put my arm around Joey's shoulders and squeezed. "I was their best man. Joey nursed me back to health when I was recovering from a gunshot wound. She thought she was in love with me until this big Ukrainian stole her heart."

Caileigh slipped her arm around the shorter woman and squeezed. "Then I will love you back, Joey."

I looked over at Danilo, smiling quietly three feet away. "Danilo, it's good to see you again. Obviously, you got things straightened out with State."

"Good to see you, Mac," he answered with a heavy accent. "I am free to do what I wish. I think I become American citizen. And,…oh, nice to meet you, Doctor Abernathy."

"Caileigh, please."

---

32 See *Operation White Out*, vol 4 in *The Mac McDowell Missions*.

"I bet you guys are starved after last night, and I know you need some coffee," Joey said, her purple-blue eyes twinkling. She took Caileigh's hand and led her into the dining room. The rest of us followed.

0900, FRIDAY, SEPTEMBER 1, 1989—DINING ROOM, MOHICAN HOTEL, NEW LONDON, CT

The Mohican Hotel prided itself on doing things right, which is how it became one of Connecticut's premier grand hotels. Off in one corner of the dining room by a picture window, our round table was covered with crisp linen and set for five. An attractive young woman who told us later she attended Connecticut College was our server.

Following our day and night in the penthouse suite, Caileigh and I had hearty appetites. The others ordered more conservatively. The food arrived promptly and was hot and absolutely delicious. I was on my third cup of coffee when Sergyi smiled around the table and cleared his throat.

"Mac and Caileigh," Sergyi started to speak, "I have something very important and special to tell you."

My first thought was that Joey was pregnant, but I was way off. Caileigh reached for my hand under the table and squeezed.

"I never told you about my uncle, Sasha Andreev. Despite the Soviet Union's restrictions, Uncle Sasha became very wealthy in oil, coal, and other raw materials. You could say he was a real billionaire oligarch. I was his favorite nephew. After you captured me and everyone back home thought I had died, I contacted Uncle Sasha surreptitiously, and helped him transfer his wealth outside the Soviet Union. We kept my being alive a secret from the rest of the family. Uncle Sasha met Joey right after we got married, and then he suddenly died." Sergyi bowed his head. "I think the KGB killed him, but I can't prove it." He looked deep in my eyes.

"You saved my life, and I saved yours. We are blood brothers until we die. Nothing can change that, nothing." He leaned forward, resting his arms on the table, and said earnestly, "I am the sole heir of Uncle Sasha's empire."

That came as a total shock. I looked at him in astonishment. "So you, Sergyi, my Ukrainian brother, are a multi-billionaire." I pounded the table with my free hand. "Holy shit!" I grinned at Joey. "You, Girl, got yourself one hell of a deal!"

She stuck out her tongue at me. "Sergyi lets me go shopping," she said with a giggle.

"I'll bet…"

I turned to my friend. "Sergyi, it couldn't have happened to a better man."

"Sure, I get that," he said quietly, "but that's not all." He turned to Caileigh. "Caileigh, do you have any idea what you got yourself into when you fell for this lunk?"

"I'm beginning to understand what you mean," Caileigh answered hesitatingly.

Sergyi gestured the four of us toward him and whispered, "I acquired the *Alfa* and installed a new Westinghouse plant, and I made some other modifications. She belongs to us, Mac, you and me!"

"You what?" I said in a shouted whisper. "You what?!"

"Like I said," Sergyi grinned at me, "I bought the *Alfa* on salvage and fixed her up."

Caileigh turned to me and whispered, "What's he talking about?"

"It's a long story, but I promise to fill you in; I promise."

❋

Somewhat later, we assembled in our penthouse suite. Sergyi paced back and forth in the center of the sitting room.

"Like I said, I installed a new Westinghouse plant. I modified the escape pod so it is also a six-thousand-foot-capable piloted submersible. I upgraded the internal computers and electronics, and I installed a lock-out saturation dive system similar to *Teuthis*."

He stopped pacing and looked directly at me. "Don't you understand, the Navy made you Captain. Sure, they'll make you admiral, but you never get another sub. You at the top. Quit while you ahead—retire with honor." He laughed. "Then you and I do what we do best!"

❋

The thought had never entered my mind before Sergyi uttered those fateful words. As the possibilities dawned on me, I voiced my thoughts to the group.

"Under a perfectly legal letter-of-marque issued by the U.S. Government, the *Alfa* could take on any hostile vessel anywhere on Earth, and we could profit from the takings where possible, and just make them disappear otherwise. Smuggling operations, terrorist activities, rogue nations, pirates, slave traders—the possibilities are endless."

I turned to Caileigh. "I can matter in a way that was never before possible," I told her, my voice filled with excitement.

"And grow the legend," she said, and kissed me deeply in front of everybody.

EPILOG

OCTOBER 1989, CAPE TOWN, SOUTH AFRICA

They called him Bafana. He was a man of mixed race, living in the Cape Town suburbs with his European wife and two children. He was a foreman in a factory that manufactured engine parts. It paid enough, but he supplemented his income as a surreptitious asset for Israeli intelligence—the Mossad.

On a chilly October morning, he received a plain envelope through the mail. He recognized that it was from Mossad. In it, he found three sets of dog tags and a brief note with instructions. The note read:

Locate the families of these three Marines and mail the tags to them in envelopes without return addresses.

***

Please post a review for
Operation Vela Redux

Authors rely on reviews, so I really appreciate your posting a review on Amazon and Goodreads. To post a review, scan the pertinent QR code below and follow the prompts. You will be prompted to log onto the platform. If you are not a member, you will need to sign up. It's free. Amazon will require a minimum $50 purchase volume during the past twelve months. Goodreads has no requirement. Thank you very much for going through this effort!

Scan to review on Amazon

Scan to review on Goodreads

A Note About Saturation Diving

The air you breathe is about 21 percent oxygen and 79 percent nitrogen. When you dive on scuba, your equipment supplies you with compressed air that matches the pressure of the surrounding water, which increases by about one atmosphere every thirty-three feet. So, at a thousand feet, air enters your lungs at about thirty atmospheres or 450 pounds per square inch (psi).

Normal air becomes toxic under too much pressure. When you inhale more oxygen than about twice the amount you would when breathing pure oxygen at the surface, the oxygen becomes toxic. This happens at about two hundred feet when breathing compressed air. Furthermore, nitrogen becomes narcotic at about the same depth. This is a lethal combination: You're breathing toxic gas and are so narked by nitrogen that you don't know what to do about it.

We solved this problem by reducing the total amount of oxygen in the breathing gas mix so that the actual amount in each breath is about the equivalent of the 21 percent we breathe on the surface. We replaced the nitrogen with helium that does not become narcotic. It made us talk funny, but we didn't get narked.

The formula for the resulting oxygen percentage at any depth is:

$$\%O_{2\,(at\,depth)} = \frac{.21}{\left(\dfrac{depth_{feet}}{33}\right) + 1}$$

Consequently, at 1,000 feet, oxygen in the gas mix is 0.7%. At 470 feet, oxygen in the gas mix is 1.4%.

Right now, your body is saturated with all the nitrogen it can hold. Your cells, bones, organs, everything, have absorbed all the nitrogen possible. If you dive to thirty-three feet (one atmosphere) and stay there long enough, you will become saturated at thirty-three feet. If you stay at a hundred feet, five-hundred feet, same thing—stay long enough, and you saturate; you can't take up any more nitrogen, or helium if you are breathing a mixed gas.

If you are saturated to thirty-three feet, you can come right to the surface without suffering any consequences. But if you saturate at forty feet, you cannot come shallower than about seven feet without suffering the bends when the dissolved nitrogen or helium in your body comes out of solution to form bubbles. The bends are very painful and can be fatal. A body can tolerate a one-atmosphere difference between its saturation level and the ambient pressure. That's the background information. In practice, we have discovered there is increasing leeway as the saturation depth is deeper.

An Upward Excursion Limits Table in the Navy Diving Manual lists the excursion limits for any saturation depth.

EXCERPT FROM
OPERATION IVY BELLS
(The first Mac McDowell Mission)
by
Robert G. Williscroft

At 1,000 feet depth off Point Loma

I hung motionless in the frigid water a few yards from the spherical Personnel Transfer Capsule a thousand feet below the surface. It was pitch black, except for two beams of light emanating from the PTC that terminated in white circles on the sandy bottom a hundred feet below. In the crystal clear water there was virtually no diffusion. I felt motion beside me and turned to see a flood of bubbles rising from Harry's plunge through the PTC hatch.

We each had a hundred feet of umbilical snaking back into the PTC, where Bill, the third member of our party, kept the slack out of our umbilicals and stood by to help in the event of an emergency. I put a finger in front of my mask indicating silence. Harry gave me a thumbs-up. We started drifting downward, not paying any attention to our depth. After all, we were saturated to a thousand feet; down was good.

"Red Diver, what are you doing?" Master Chief Ray Harmon was having a conniption topside. As the Sat Dive Unit's Master Saturation Diver, he was running the dive under Lieutenant George Franklin, the Officer-in-Charge.

"Checking something out, Control, just checking something out." I increased my descent and Harry followed suit. I could hear my distorted voice in my earphones.

"Red Diver!" It was the Master Chief again.

"Red Diver, aye." I needed to delay him for just another twenty seconds.

"Return to one-thousand feet NOW!" He was pissed.

"Say again, Control, say again." I needed just another ten seconds.

"Lieutenant McDowell, get your ass back to the PTC…NOW!" Oops, that was Franklin, and he was really pissed.

"Roger that." I scooped a handful of sand and stuffed it in my leg pocket and looked up at the PTC. It appeared as a lighted jewel against velvet black. Our activities near the bottom had stirred up some detritus, and the water around us sparkled with light flickering off tiny silt particles – an alien, fairytale world.

I gave Harry two thumbs-up, and we slowly ascended, our umbilicals snaking above us, live serpents in the frigid water. Inside the PTC, Bill recoiled the umbilicals to take up the slack. It took us less than two minutes to get back to a thousand feet; our total excursion had lasted no more than four minutes. I pointed to the expanded metal work bin attached to the outside of the PTC. Harry pulled out the make-work project for this training dive, and we started screwing screws and turning bolts.

And that's when it happened!

My first impression was a flashing shadow through one of the light beams, a flicker just below my threshold of awareness—something big and fast.

"What the fuck was that?" Harry squeaked, his voice distorted by helium and electronic descrambling.

"Green Diver, report!" That was the Master Chief.

"Jeezus…" Harry dropped down three feet and grabbed my left fin. I felt him trying to pull me toward him, toward the hatch. "Mac… the hatch!" Harry's desperation came right through his squeak. Then he jerked and let go. "Kee…rist!"

"Red Diver…what's going on down there?" That was Franklin.

Off to my right, a green phosphorescent shape flicked into and out of existence. A pink one materialized to my left. Suddenly, from right in front of me, something bright blue hit my faceplate with the force of a sledgehammer.

Everything went black. I don't mean I passed out…everything went black, literally. I reached up and discovered a really large thing covering my entire helmet. It was smooth and spongy, and it was undulating. I heard a scraping, grinding noise against my faceplate. Something wrapped itself around my left arm, jerking my hand away from the pulsing mass. I pulled my arm back and felt a rush of cold water enter my suit at the wrist. A tear…whatever it was had torn a goddamn hole in my suit! What the hell can tear a hole through compressed, nylon-reinforced neoprene? That shit'll stop a knife!

That's when I noticed that I still held a ten-pound steel wrench in my right hand. You don't move things fast underwater, but I put as much force into my haymaker as possible. The wrench sunk into the mass attached to my helmet, and in a flash, it was gone. I could see again. Several feet ahead of me I could make out two elongated hooded shapes arrayed vertically in the water, pulsing green to pink to blue. Large, almost human eyes as big as my hands gazed at me.

"Control, Red Diver…we got some kind of company… three or four giant squid, I think…" I looked down at Harry, backed up warily against the PTC just below me, dive knife glinting in his hand. I could see a big tear in the left shoulder of his hot-water suit. "Harry…you okay?"

"Yeah…what the fuck! Squid? You're shittin' me!" He waved his knife. "One of those fuckers took a chunk outa my suit!"

"You or just the suit?" I asked.

"Just the suit…I think. No blood in the water."

"Mac…" It was Franklin. "You guys get back into the PTC ASAP!"

"Working on it, Control…" One of the creatures hit the top of my helmet hard. Tentacles draped down the entire length of my body. I could distinctly feel razor-sharp sucker teeth dig into my suit. "Harry," I yelled, sounding like a compressed Donald Duck through the helium and electronics, "get this fucker off me!"

I felt Harry come up between me and the PTC and repeatedly stab the creature's carapace. With that, my personal squid apparently had second thoughts, as it unwrapped itself and disappeared. The other two with their changing color patterns, continued to hang about ten feet away, large unblinking eyes evaluating me. It seemed as if they were communicating by color and pattern. Suddenly, the right one went dark, dropped its tentacles straight down, and began to undulate. Two thin, suckerless tentacles danced around the creature in a meaningless pattern. I transferred the wrench to my left hand and pulled my knife from its sheath on my right leg. Then, in a blinding white flash, the eight-foot squid whipped to horizontal and propelled itself tentacles first directly at my chest. As it approached, its tentacles rolled back, forming an eight-legged basket filled with a thousand sucker teeth. In the center, I could see a mouth as large as my helmet surrounded by a ring of razor teeth reflecting the squid's phosphorescent pulses.

I jammed the wrench as hard as I could directly into the gaping maw and left it there. I grabbed an upper tentacle with my left hand and sliced. It was like cutting tough leather. I sawed frantically while the squid grabbed at my hand and knife with two other tentacles while keeping a grip on me with the rest. After what seemed like an hour, but actually was less than a minute, I held the detached, writhing tentacle in my left hand. I tossed it away, still squirming like a snake. With the tentacle out of the way, I could see the large, human-like eye, fully six inches across, staring at me malevolently. I plunged my knife into the orb—once, twice, a third time. That did it! The two thin tentacles whipped around frantically, and the giant disappeared into the darkness along with its pulsating companion.

"Harry, where are you?" I was concentrating on the water in front of me, preparing for another attack.

"Right below you, Mac. Let's get the fuck outa here!"

A very long minute later, I followed Harry through the hatch opening, and Bill pulled me all the way in.

"Everyone down there okay?" That was Franklin again.

"Control…PTC," Bill responded, "divers are back inside. Everyone seems to be okay."

Just then, the smooth water surface in the circular opening began to boil.

"Shee…it!" Bill shouted, as two thick tentacles darted through the surface and began whipping around the PTC interior. "Fucker's trying to get in the PTC!" Bill's distorted voice in my earphones matched his lip movements. His face registered not so much panic as total shock.

"Or pull us out," Harry added.

Bill and Harry grabbed their knives, slashing into the writhing appendages. I reached over the opening and grasped the hatch in both hands, pushing for all I was worth. I looked down into the six-inch eye of the invading monster as I swung the hatch down. I sensed intelligence, driven by pure malevolence. The last thing I saw before I dogged the hatch was a half-sliced-through tapered tentacle tip as it slipped back into the frigid water around us.

Harry removed his helmet and gave Bill a gloved high-five. From across the dogged hatch, I gave them both two thumbs-up and pulled off my own helmet and gloves. Then I grabbed a Ziploc baggie from my personal kit to fill it with my trophy sand, but when I felt my leg pocket for the sand, it was gone. Chalk up another one to the monsters.

"Control…this is Mac." I was sure they could hear the relief in my distorted voice. "To hell with the rest of this dive. Just bring us home!"

You have just been reading from Chapter One of Operation Ivy Bells, *the first book in Robert G. Williscroft's exciting submarine/tech-nothriller series,* The Mac McDowell Missions. *Download a copy of* Operation Ivy Bells *or order a hard or softbound copy or an audio version from your favorite online bookseller.*

About the Author

Dr. Robert G. Williscroft is a retired submarine officer, deep-sea and saturation diver, scientist, author, and a lifelong adventurer. He spent twenty-two months underwater, a year in the equatorial Pacific, three years in the Arctic ice pack, and a year at the Geographic South Pole. He holds degrees in Marine Physics and Meteorology and a doctorate for developing a system to protect scuba divers in contaminated water. A prolific author of both non-fiction, submarine technothrillers, and hard science fiction, he lives in Centennial, Colorado.

Dr. Williscroft is a member of Colorado Author's League, Independent Association of Science Fiction & Fantasy Authors, Science Fiction & Fantasy Writers Association, Libertarian Futurist Society, Los Angeles Adventurers' Club, Mensa, Military Officer's Association, U.S. Sub Vets, American Legion, and the NRA, and now spends most of his time writing his next book, speaking to various regional groups, and hanging out with the girl of his dreams, Jill, and her two cats.

Scan for more information: 

Other Works by this Author

Please visit RobertWilliscroft.com to discover other books by Robert Williscroft. Scan for more information.

Current Events:
 The Chicken Little Agenda: Debunking "Experts'" Lies
Children's Books:
 The Starman Jones Series:
  Starman Jones: A Relativity Birthday Present
  Starman Jones Goes to the Dogs (2026)
<u>Biographies</u>:
 Mission Possible (by Gladys L. Williscroft)
 Sŭbmarine-ër (by Jerry Pait; compiled by Robert G. Williscroft)
Short Stories:
 Reality Hack
 First Contact
 The Cold Spot
 The Virus
Novels:
 Mac McDowell Missions
  Operation Ivy Bells
  Operation Ice Breaker
  Operation Arctic Sting
  Operation White Out
  Operation Vela Redux
  Operation Alfa Rogue (2026)
 The Starchild Saga:
  Slingshot
  The Daedalus Files
  The Starchild Compact
  The Iapetus Federation
 The Oort Chronicles:
  Icicle: A Tensor Matrix
  The Oort Federation: To the Stars
  RAN: A Civilization in Hiding
  KEID: A Lost Civilization
  Beyond the Beyond (2025)

Connect with Robert G. Williscroft

I really appreciate you reading my book! Here are my social media coordinates:

Facebook: *https://www.facebook.com/robert.williscroft*
X/Twitter: *@RGWilliscroft*
Amazon author page: *https://buff.ly/2N5ZnlG*
Blog: *https://ThrawnRickle.com*
LinkedIn: *https://www.linkedin.com/in/argee/*
Book website: *https://RobertWilliscroft.com*
Newsletter: *https://eepurl.com/guZ5uv*

Glossary for *Operation Vela Redux*

1MC—Ship's announcing system.

AIP—Air Independent Propulsion. A much less expensive alternative to nuclear propulsion for submarines. Uses *Stirling engines* and HP air or oxygen and fuel, or uses fuel cells. Can typically remain submerged for two weeks or more.

APS—Underwater fully automatic assault weapon. Fires twenty-six darts in full automatic—lethal range forty feet. Magazine holds twenty-six darts. Was made in the Soviet Union for use *underwater* by Soviet frogmen as an *underwater* firearm. It was developed in the late 1960s and accepted for use in 1975. Underwater, ordinary-shaped bullets are inaccurate and very short-range.

ASR—Hull classification for submarine rescue ships.

Athwartships—Across the vessel sideways, i.e. in a direction at right angles to the fore-and-aft line of the vessel.

Attack Scope—The optical (non-electronic) periscope on a modern submarine.

Auxiliaryman—A U.S. Navy enlisted rating (job designator) for an engineer concerned with the various machinery on a ship other than the main propulsion gear.

Baffles—The area in the water directly behind a submarine or ship through which a hull-mounted sonar cannot hear. This blind spot is caused by the noise of the vessel's machinery, propulsion system, and propellers.

Ballast tank—A tank within a submarine that holds water used as ballast to provide hydrostatic stability and to reduce or control buoyancy, and correct trim or list. (See *Main ballast tanks*.)

Basketball—A slightly larger than basketball-sized, camera-carrying *ROV* on a tether.

BCP—*Ballast Control Panel*; the console from which water is pumped into and out of a sub, and distributed fore and aft in the sub. The *Chief of the Watch* occupies this position, under the control of the *Diving Officer* or the *OOD*.

Bedpan—A stainless sheet metal mattress pan. Fits atop a second locked pan attached with hinges at the back that holds a submarine sailor's personal effects.

Boat—Slang term for submarine. Officially, all modern nuclear subs are called ships, but in practice, most submariners call them *boats*.

Boomer—Ballistic Missile Submarine.

Bottom—Bottom of the ocean, the seafloor. As a verb as in to *bottom*, putting the submarine on the seafloor.

Bow—Front of a ship or sub.

Brash—Small, floating fragments of sea or river ice typically near the ice edge in the ocean and in narrow straits with high tidal currents.

Bridge—The place on a ship from which it is driven. On a sub, it is the conning station at the top of the sail. (See *Conn*.)

Brow—Gangway onto a vessel from the pier or another vessel.

Bunny Suit—An insulating inner garment worn by divers dressed in a *drysuit*.

Capstan—A revolving cylinder with a vertical axis used for hauling in a rope or cable.

Captain—The officer in command of the ship or sub. He is an absolute dictator, subject only to the Uniform Code of Military Justice and the orders of his superiors in the chain of command.

CDMA—Code division multiple access. (See *Secure underwater telephone*.)

Chief of the Boat—*COB*; the senior enlisted man on a submarine who serves as adviser to the *commanding officer* and *executive officer*. When a new enlisted sailor joins a *boat's* crew, the *COB* is usually one of the first people the new sailor will meet.

Chief of the Watch—*COW*; the enlisted watchstander (usually a chief petty officer) who sits at the *BCP* and controls the ship's load of ballast water and its distribution throughout the submarine. The *COW* is also the senior watchstander for all the non-engineering spaces.

Clear the baffles—A submarine tracking another submarine can take advantage of its quarry's *baffles* to follow at a close distance without being detected. Periodically, a submarine will perform a maneuver called clearing the *baffles*. The *boat* will turn left or right far enough to listen with the sonar for a few minutes in the area that was previously blocked by the *baffles*.

Cleat—A T-shaped piece of metal or wood, esp. on a *boat* or ship, to which ropes or lines are attached.

CO—Short for *Commanding Officer.*

CO-H2 Burner— An atmospheric auxiliary machine through which all ship's air passes. It burns carbon monoxide (CO) from smoking and cooking to carbon dioxide (CO2), hydrogen (H2) from oxygen production to water, and all other hydrocarbons to carbon dioxide (CO2) and water.

COB—See *Chief of the Boat.*

Commanding Officer—The officer assigned by the Navy to be in charge of a ship or submarine. He is an absolute dictator, subject only to the Uniform Code us Military Justice and the orders of his superiors in the chain of command.

Column—(Water column) All the water above and below a specific point.

ComSubLant—Commander, Submarine Force Atlantic; the commander of all submarine forces in the Atlantic.

ComSubPac—Commander, Submarine Force Pacific; the commander of all submarine forces in the Pacific.

Conn—(1) The location from which the sub is controlled by the *OOD*—also called Control. (2) The Conning Officer (*Conn*), the watch position for the person who controls the sub's direction, speed, and depth. The *OOD* usually has both the *Deck* and *Conn*, but can pass off the *Conn* to another qualified officer. Sometimes the *captain* will assume the *Deck*, leaving the Conn with the officer watchstander.

COW—See *Chief of the Watch*.

Crashback—A forward moving ship reversing the screw(s) to all back full—the highest reverse speed possible.

DCA—Damage Control Assistant; the engineering officer in charge of supervising ship's damage control.

DDC—Deck Decompression Chamber; a pressure chamber on a ship's deck or just below the deck, that contains a side lock for entrance and egress, a small lock for passing in food or medical supplies, emergency equipment, and depending on how it is being used, bunks, lavatory facilities, etc.

Deck—The watch position of *OOD* (*Officer of the Deck*); the person in charge of the sub when the *captain* is not in the Control Room or has not assumed the *Deck* while in the Control Room.

Dive Control Console—A console with gauges, valves, and indicators from where a saturation dive is controlled.

Diving Officer—The officer or specially qualified chief petty officer controlling the submarine depth. Works directly under the *OOD*. The *COW* works directly for the *Diving Officer*.

DIW—Dead in the water; a ship that is not moving through the water.

DOC—Diving Operations Compartment.

Dolphins—The insignia worn by qualified submariners, silver for enlisted, and gold for officers. It represents about a year of hard study to gain complete, detailed knowledge of the submarine. In addition, for officers, it requires qualification as underway *Officer of the Deck* (*OOD*).

Drysuit—A waterproof suit worn by divers that seals at the wrists and neck, and at the ankles if the suit does not have attached boots.

DRT—Dead Reckoning Trace. A mechanically generated ship's track based on input from the *SINS*.

DSRV—Deep Submergence Rescue Vehicle, a type of deep-submergence vehicle used for rescue of downed submarines and clandestine missions.

EB—Electric Boat Company, short for *General Dynamics Electric Boat Company*.

Emergency surface—Dumping high pressure into the *main ballast tanks* at a high rate, causing the submarine to surface very quickly.

Engineering Officer of the Watch—*EOOW*; the individual on watch who operates the powerplant.

EOOW—See *Engineering of the Watch*.

Executive Officer (XO)—Second in command of a ship or sub. Responsible for ship's administration and personnel.

Fake down—Loosely figure-eight a line so that it will feed from the top tangle-free.

Fast-attack—See *Nuke fast-attack*.

Fish—An *ROV* with high resolution, *sidescan sonar* that produces detailed images of the seafloor.

Fish—A torpedo.

FSW—Feet Sea Water

General Dynamics Electric Boat Company—A General Dynamics company that has designed, built, and maintained submarines for the U.S. Navy since 1899.

General Quarters—The ship's call that sends every crew member to his designated emergency station.

Gertrude—Underwater telephone. (See *Secure underwater telephone, Secure Gertrude.*)

Helm—Ship's wheel and steering mechanisms. The person manning the *helm*.

Highwayman's Hitch—A quick-release draw hitch used for temporarily securing a load that will need to be released easily and cleanly. The hitch can be untied with a tug of the working end, even when under tension.

Hot Water Suit—A class of diving suit that keeps a diver warm by pumping hot water into the suit down the spine and along the legs and arms, where it flows into the surrounding water or into gloves and boots before flowing into the water. A *hot water suit* requires an umbilical from the hot water source to the diver. This umbilical often also contains breathing gas and communications.

JOOD—*Junior Officer of the Deck*; the individual (usually an *OOD* in training) who works directly for the *OOD*. The *JOOD* is responsible only to the *OOD*.

Keepers—One-piece rubber straps that wrap around the ankle and under the arch. Keep the feet of a *Unisuit* from filling with air and blowing off a diver's feet when inverted.

Kirby-Morgan helmet—A hard helmeted full facemask specifically designed to work with both umbilical and *rebreather* saturation diving systems from the 1970s and 1980s.

Layer—(Also called *thermocline*) A distinct *layer* based on temperature in an ocean with a high gradient of distinct temperature differences associated with depth.

Line Officer—U.S. Navy or U.S. Marine Corps commissioned officer or warrant officer who exercises general command authority and is eligible for operational command positions.

Main ballast tanks—Saddle-shaped tanks that fit around a submarine's hull *port* and *starboard* near the *bow* and *stern*. They are open to the sea at the bottom and have large vent valves at the top. When the valves are opened, water quickly fills the *ballast tanks*, causing the submarine to submerge. Air entering the tanks forces water out through the bottom openings, bringing the submarine to the surface. Dumping high pressure into the *main ballast tanks* at a high rate causes the submarine to *emergency surface*.

Man-in-the-Sea Program—A program put in place by the U.S. Navy to develop saturation diving.

Maneuvering Room—That part of a sub where the engines, generators, and reactor are directly controlled.

Maneuvering Watch—(1) The special set of watch assignments for a sub or ship that is getting underway or returning to port. (maneuvering watch)(2) The watch assigned to the *Maneuvering Room* (*Maneuvering Watch*).

Mess Management Specialist (MS)—Operates and manages Navy messes and living quarters established to feed and accommodate Navy personnel.

Monkey fist—A type of knot, so named because it looks somewhat like a small, bunched fist or paw. It is tied at the end of a rope to serve as a weight, making it easier to throw from ship to shore.

Nav—Depending on context, the ship's/sub's Navigator; or the navigation stand—typically near the *Conn*. Also called *Plot*.

NavSea – Naval Sea Systems Command; U.S. Navy maintenance and construction.

Nav Scope—The electronic periscope on a modern submarine; typically used for navigation.

Negative tank—A variable *ballast tank* on a submarine that provides negative buoyancy and initial down-angle.

Nuke fast-attack—A nuclear *fast-attack* submarine; a hunter-killer submarine.

OIC—Officer in Charge; the Officer in Charge of a unit or operation. A lesser command responsibility than a *Commanding Officer*.

OOD—Officer of the Deck; the individual in charge of the ship or submarine at any given moment. The *OOD* is responsible only to the *captain*.

OPAREA—Military Operation Area

Operation Ivy Bells—A top secret Cold War plan to retrieve Soviet missile parts and tap into their underwater communication cables.

Ops—The Operations Officer.

Outboards—Maneuvering thrusters that are normally concealed in the sub, but can be lowered from the keel near the *bow* and *stern*. These can rotate to help steer the sub, or if pointed in the same direction, they can move the sub sideways.

Planesman—The enlisted submarine crew members who man the bow (or fairwater) and stern planes.

Plot—The watch station where the *quartermaster* keeps track of the ship's position. Also called *Nav*.

Polynya—A semipermanent area of open water in sea ice.

Port—Left.

Quartermaster—An enlisted navigation specialist.

Rebreather—A class of underwater breathing apparatus that recirculates the breathing gas exhaled by the diver after replacing the oxygen used and removing the carbon dioxide metabolic product.

ROV—Remotely Operated Vehicle, an unmanned underwater vehicle that is remotely piloted either by wire or untethered, using sound.

RTG—Radioisotope Thermoelectric Generator. An electricity-generating device that uses an array of thermocouples to convert the heat released by the decay of suitable radioactive material into electricity. This generator has no moving parts.

SatNav—A satellite-based navigation system developed by the U.S. Navy for obtaining accurate positions for its *Boomer* and *fast-attack* fleets.

Scott Air Pack—An open-circuit, self-contained breathing apparatus.

Secure—Stop or finish a process, such as "Secure from maneuvering watch;" or when used as a verb, to make something safe, as in "secure the lines in the locker."

Secure Gertrude—See *secure underwater telephone*.

Secure underwater telephone—A *CDMA* underwater telephone for secure underwater communications between submarines and between subs and surface ships. Without proper receiving equipment, it sounds like a faint, broad-spectrum hiss that blends completely into the background noise. Consequently, this type of underwater communication is undetectable. (See *Spread Spectrum*.)

Sidescan sonar—A towed *Fish* or *ROV* sonar that looks to both sides to produce a high resolution image of the ocean bottom.

***Sierra I* Submarine**—A Soviet nuclear submarine (Project 945 Barrakuda) with the NATO reporting name *Sierra I Class*. It features a titanium hull like the *Alfa*, enabling a test depth of 6,000 feet. It can launch diver vehicles through four bow torpedo tubes. It features a towed sonar array pod on the top of the rudder. It has an escape pod in the sail that can hold 110 people. The *Sierra I* is one of the quietest subs the Soviets built.

SINS—Submarine Inertial Navigation System, A system developed for nuclear submarines that senses the actual motion of the sub to produce a fairly accurate position that it sends to the *DRT*. Over time, the *SINS* position deteriorates and needs to be updated by a *SatNav* fix.

Snipe—A crew member from the engineering department.

SOSUS—Sound Surveillance System; a chain of underwater listening posts located worldwide in places such as the Atlantic Ocean near Greenland, Iceland, and the United Kingdom— the GIUK gap, and at various locations in the Pacific Ocean. The system is designed to track Soviet submarines.

Sound-powered phone—A shipboard communication system powered only by the sound of the speaker's voice.

Spread spectrum—A method for transmitting electronic or sonic signals that divides the signal into individual packets, each with lower intensity than the background, and spreading these packets across the entire electronic or sonic spectrum. This creates an intelligence carrying transmission that cannot be detected without specific knowledge of the spread pattern used in the transmission. (See also *CDMA*.)

Spring line—A forward *spring line* connects from a *stern cleat* on a vessel to a *cleat* on the dock at a minimum of half the vessel's length toward the *bow*. The aft *spring line* connects from a *bow cleat* to a *cleat* on the dock with a line minimum of half the vessel's length toward the stern. This prevents both aft and forward movement.

Squawk Box—A portable, water-proof box containing comm devices and navigation repeaters for use on a submarine *bridge*.

Starboard—Right.

Steerageway—The minimum speed a vessel requires for proper response to the *helm*.

Stern—Back of a ship or sub.

Stirling engine—A closed cycle engine that requires only a heat source to function.

Stokes stretcher—One of the oldest medical devices in continuous use by the U.S. military. A lightweight wire mesh molded stretcher created by navy physician and future Navy Surgeon General Charles Francis Stokes, it has been in widespread use throughout the military and civilian sectors for over 100 years.

SubLant—Short form of *ComSubLant*.

SubPac—Short form of *ComSubPac*.

Teuthis Squid—Also Colossal Squid, full name Mesonycho Teuthis hamiltoni. It is part of the family Cranchiidae. The only member of the Cranchiidae family to display hooks on its arms and tentacles. Inhabits the circum-Antarctic Southern Ocean. Adults are 39 to 46 ft long. Uses bioluminescence to attract prey. It is an ambush predator and is a major prey of the sperm whale.

Thermocline—See *Layer*.

TOG—Test Operations Group. The top secret saturation diving team created to tap into Soviet Communication cables.

Topside—The outside deck of a submarine. Can also refer to the watch station at the top of the sail when a sub is underway.

Transit bird—A *SatNav* satellite.

Under-ice sonar—A high frequency, upward-looking sonar for examining the undersurface and thickness of overhead ice.

Unisuit—The first commercial diving *drysuit* made by Poseidon.

***Victor III* Submarine**—A Soviet nuclear submarine (Project 671RTM/RTMK) with the NATO reporting name *Victor III Class*. It features a teardrop shape like the *Alfa*, but made of steel, allowing it to travel at high speed, but not so fast as the *Alfa*. It can launch diver vehicles through two *bow* torpedo tubes. It features a towed sonar array pod on the top of the rudder and two small propellers next to the hull on the *stern* planes. It has an escape pod in the sail that could hold 110 people. The *Victor III* is the quietest sub that the Soviets built.

VLF— Very low frequency radio receiver. Allows subs to receive signals while submerged.
Watchbill—A list of a ship's company divided into watches.
XO—Executive Officer (See *Executive Officer*).